MW00984528

PRAISE FOR *OPPOSITES ATTACK*
BY JO MAEDER

"Take three quirky characters who go to extremes to either pursue love or avoid love. Add a dash of dysfunction. A pinch of love. And a dollop of mystery. Marinate in a romantic setting. You've got the recipe for an amusing love story."

— News & Record

"Gobble up this rollicking romantic comedy, filled with scrumptious French food."

— O. Henry Magazine

"A fun tale and a nice testament to Maeder's versatility."

— Miami Herald

"Merci for taking me back to the deliciousness of Provence! I wish that my first stay in France had been this delightfully wicked."

— Teresa Engebretsen, The Sabbatical Chef

"This wonderfully entertaining novel will have you booking that trip to France you've been promising yourself for years."

— Charles Salzberg

What Readers Are Saying

"*Heartfelt adventure causing me to laugh, cry, and taste the beauty of a country I have yet to visit. A novel to savor!*"

"*Our book club books had gotten very serious and then we read* Opposites Attack. *So much fun, we even read bits out loud with the voices we imagined for each character. A delightful book and a good excuse to eat French food.*"

"*Jo Maeder has it spot on! I lived in France for 20 years and she captured the French exactly: charming, arrogant, romantic, and always obsessed with the perfect meal. She had me drooling over the recipes. Plot kept me engaged, curious, and in hysterics.*"

"*I was taken away to the French countryside and 'lived' the experience. I'm a sucker for fun locations, interesting characters and the push/pull of desire and sensibility. This book has all three and then some!*"

"*All-American Alyce generates one hilarious faux pas after another as she blunders her way through France. Jean-Luc is charming and annoying as he navigates his complicated life. Jo Maeder has created a splendid, spirited, delicious read.*"

"*Our book club read it and all 12 members gave it a thumbs up! I love a good book that I miss after I've finished it. This was one of those.*"

"*I truly enjoyed reading this book. The mixture of personalities and cultures was fun to watch. Also, the tragedies that humans must overcome to become whole again was sad but at the same time life-giving. I would recommend this book to anyone who likes a laugh, along with love and some awesome French food.*"

"*I loved the language of love, the learning, the clashes, the tension that builds between characters. I so wanted to be in Jean-Luc's kitchen.*"

Opposites Attack

A Novel
with Recipes Provençal

Jo Maeder

To Alanna,
Have fun in France!
J Maeder
9/5/2014

Author of the bestselling memoir *When I Married My Mother*

JO MAEDER

Opposites
Attack

*A Novel with
Recipes Provençal*

Copyright © Jo Maeder 2013, 2014. All rights reserved.
This is a work of fiction. The characters and what happens to them are
strictly the creation of the author's *imagination féconde*.

No part of this publication may be reproduced; stored in a retrieval
system; or transmitted in any form or by any means: electronic,
mechanical, photocopying, recording, or otherwise without the prior
written permission of the author.

Cover designed by Ploy Siripant. Interior design by Benjamin Carrancho.
Daubière watercolor by Jay Lindsay. All photos from author's private
collection. Scallop and fennel recipes courtesy of Mary-James Lawrence
from her book *Mary James Dishes It Out: Favorite Recipes and Personal
teaching Notes.* Wild boar daube recipe adapted from hers.

ISBN paperback: 978-0-9855482-2-3. ISBN ebook: 978-0-9855482-3-0

Published by Vivant Press
Special discounts available for bulk purchases in the U.S. by
corporations, institutions, and other organizations.
To reach the author for speaking engagements or interviews, or the
publisher: ContactVivantPress@gmail.com
P.O. Box 696, Oak Ridge, NC 27310 USA.

1. Learning to speak French — Fiction 2. Cultural differences — Fiction.
3. Francophile — Fiction. I. Title: Opposites Attack/A Novel with
Recipes Provençal/by Jo Maeder

Vivant Press

For Dennis and Eve,
and our irreplaceable Meg

Table of Contents

Then farewell, Horace; whom I hated so,

Not for thy faults, but mine.

— Lord Byron

My Nelson

My dear, darling Alyce,

Or shall I call you Sabrina? Soon you'll be breathlessly transformed and broadened like Audrey Hepburn in that wonderful movie—and back in Nelson's arms where you belong. Thank heavens that heartless conglomerate let you go. It freed you for this fantastic adventure! I admire your determination to pay your own way but please don't hesitate to ask for help. No one will think of you as a gold-digger. You-know-who already has that distinction.

I have so much faith in you, Alyce. Now you must believe in yourself. Trust me when I say you are different from all the other women who have tried to capture my Nelson's heart.

Placing an ocean between you is the true test! Nelson's father behaved exactly the same wishy-washy way when we were dating. I said "ta-ta" and took off for London. The moment my plane lifted off the tarmac at JFK he couldn't live without me. Work on you and have a fabulous time. Pretend Nelson barely exists. Just watch. Like father, like son!

Of course, Ronald didn't have a You-know-who and their son to distract him. It may not be that easy. Which is why I'll be coming over with my assistant Luther for a little visit. I'm overdue for a shopping spree in Paris. A side trip to the South of France to see you is just what I need after my recovery. I'll be looking for chic, sensible shoes in Paris, I can assure you. Ah, the French. They know a woman doesn't have to squeeze into pointy-toed shoes with heels that could double as a weapon to be sexy. I can't wait to see you covered in that special "je ne sais quoi."

Alyce, you are so young. But time flies. Before you know it, you'll be wishing you had settled down in your 20s the way people used to do. I can't believe my Nelson's 33 and I still have no grandchildren. (Legitimate ones, that is.) Curses, I must stop saying "my" Nelson, mustn't I?

Most truly yours,
Glorianna Hope Smythe Mansfield
Scarsdale, New York

2

A BETTER FIT

At last the *"liberté"* bell rang. Alyce hobbled to the classroom door, almost making her escape.

"Al-*ees!*" her instructor called out. "Madame Girard would like to see you in her office."

Claire never spoke to a student in English. This couldn't be good.

The French word for foreigner is *étranger*; close to "stranger." How perfect. Add to that her freshly scraped knee and elbow. At least "ibuprofen" needed no translation.

She nervously entered the *Marlaison Ecole Française* director's office and saw her battered luggage neatly stacked by the door. In an instant her throat shifted into the tight dryness she felt whenever a teacher asked her a question and she had no idea what she'd been asked, much less how to answer (which was every time).

"Madame Girard, please don't kick me out. I know I'm a terrible student but—"

"*Non, non,* Al-*ees,* it is much too soon to give up," the director said almost too sweetly as she motioned for Alyce to sit down. "It is only your first week."

She smiled as if nothing could possibly be wrong, even as Alyce tenderly lowered herself into the chair.

"We have another place for you to stay," she said. "A family emergency came up for the Lambournes. And you may call me Liliane."

The relaxed, sunny room that overlooked a lush courtyard felt like a cold, harsh interrogation chamber as Alyce considered what a disastrous choice her previous hosts had been. A 26-year-old city girl who spoke no French living on a farm with a couple in their 80s who spoke no English and served her the very rabbit she'd been cooing over? If only she hadn't stroked its soft fur, gazed into its big dewy eyes, and intently watched its nose that moved so rapidly it seemed motorized. It must have known what was coming.

Then she *accidentally* put a hole in the side of their barn that morning when she tried to ride a moped for the first time because she couldn't—surprise—understand their instructions on how to operate it.

Alyce leaned forward. "I promise I'll pay for the damage somehow. Can I work in the kitchen here?"

She couldn't tell if Liliane was on the verge of laughing or taking her over her knee and giving her a spanking.

"I am sure your moped mishap was unintentional," she answered. "The school has paid for the repair. You are fine, yes?"

It was Liliane's cautious look that made her realize she was as concerned about having a lawsuit on her hands as Alyce's well-being, perhaps more so.

Alyce let out a sigh and leaned back in her chair. "Yes, I'm fine. Just a few bruises. Mostly to my ego."

Alyce studied Liliane, who probably wasn't that much older than she and was already married with two children. With her exotic looks and long auburn hair pulled up sensually into a loose twist, she looked ready for a photo shoot. How did she do it all so effortlessly?

Aware she was staring at her too long, Alyce bent over to re-tie a loosened lace on one of her running shoes — not that she'd be jogging anytime soon.

Liliane practically purred, "I am sure you will do well with the Devreauxs. They have two young children, and Julien from the father's previous marriage. He and his father speak excellent English, though you should speak French as much as possible to get the most out of your stay."

Alyce forced a smile back. "I'd love to speak French, if I could *speak* French."

There was a playfulness in Liliane's delivery of "Julien Devreaux is 22. I think you will find our young men mature for their age."

Alyce's spirits perked up, especially with not one email from Nelson. But 22? *Non.*

"Monsieur Devreaux is coming to get you." She stood and shook Alyce's hand while uttering an "I wish you well" that she could have sworn had a dark tone.

A male staff member gathered up the luggage. He and Liliane rattled on in French.

Alyce's lost look prompted Liliane to say, "You will get bet-ter, Al-*ees*. We had a student from China who did not even read letters and was eventually able to converse."

Was it possible to feel any more stupid?

"Perhaps you would like to sign up for one-on-one tutoring in the afternoon."

She'd already considered that but the cost stopped her. Plus three hours every morning five days a week was enough agony, thank you.

Alyce waited in front of the school for her new host, break-ing into a dumb smile when people passed and spoke to her in

French as if she knew what they were saying. Her first insane year in Manhattan, straight out of a Minnesota community college, was a trip to the Mall of America in comparison to this total-immersion nonsense. At least in New York she knew when she was being insulted and could give it right back.

Within minutes of meeting Monsieur "Call me Yves" Devreaux, Alyce knew to stay on her guard. He may have been married, but it didn't seem to make a difference from the way he puffed on a cigarette, checking her out. He had thinning hair and nicotine-stained, slightly bucked teeth. He did have nice wheels, though.

Nelson, quite the car buff, had spoiled her in that regard (and many others).

As they cruised down a two-lane road, she ignored Yves' ogling as she focused on the creamy stucco villas with tile roofs and bougainvillea-covered walls; the wrought-iron terraces crammed with more flowering plants. On the wide sidewalks men and women moved along, casually elegant.

There was something so sexy and sophisticated about a French accent, so natural and carefree about the South of France. For years she had collected *Provence Living* magazine, neatly stacking them on the floor next to her bed in her tiny studio apartment, watching them grow steadily toward the top of her nightstand. As the number of issues increased, so did her longing. During countless subway rides to and from work, she'd flipped through glossy pages of rustic French homes, fields of lavender, luscious feasts resting on bright sunflower-patterned tablecloths, and yearned to step right into each photograph.

And now she had! Wanting to fit in somewhere, however, and actually doing it were two different things.

Yves Devreaux tapped her bare (good) knee. "You have never been to France before?"

He said it with a tone she noticed the French have that made it hard for her to tell if they were intrigued or appalled. She tried to answer in French that she'd never been outside America before. He quickly lost patience.

"Tell me in English why you are here for so long. You are trying to get over a man, *non?*"

She hardly wanted to bare her soul to this guy, but it was such a relief to speak her native tongue, he could have been a serial killer asking to eat her liver and she wouldn't have cared.

"Sort of. First, I lost my job. I was an assistant media buyer at a big advertising agency in New York called BOLD." She said harshly, "They fired a *third* of their employees and renamed themselves *BOLDER*. Can you believe it?"

"What is this job, media buyer?"

"When a company hires an ad agency to market a product, a budget is created to place the ads. Media buyers choose how it'll be divided among various media. They hold a lot of sway. But I was just an assistant. I should have been promoted since I practically did the job anyway."

"Where is the man in this story, eh?"

She took a sip of her bottled water, hoping to flush away the bitterness. "There I was with a job that I'd worked so hard to keep and, poof, it was gone. I felt, what's the point of having a career if it can be taken from you at any moment?"

She didn't tell Yves that she then drank too much French wine and told Nelson she was sick of working and wanted to be married and a mommy.

"We'd been dating six months. When he didn't propose or ask me to move in with him or offer to help me out, I said, 'Maybe I'll just go live in France.' He thought it was a great idea! I wanted to stuff a baguette down his throat."

Alyce still kicked herself for thinking she had a chance with a cute, rich guy like Nelson. Mind you, she'd had no idea he was loaded when she met him. She just saw those gold-flecked brown eyes under a shock of blond bangs and that sweet smile. Their eyes locked and that was it.

It only took a few *years* for him to ask her out. Once he did, it was like a fairytale. Rose petals all over their bed at the Delano hotel in South Beach. Hot-stone massages in the Hamptons. Long drives in the country in his sleek black Porsche Boxster. She should have known it wouldn't last.

Yves jarred her with another tap, this time on her thigh. "It is a drastic step, *non*? Why not just take a two-week vacation?"

She scrinched over to the right. "Because when he said we should see other people —"

"Ah! You wanted to stuff *two* baguettes down his throat."

She couldn't help but crack a smile. "No, I wanted to start over with someone new. *Moi*. How can I meet the right guy if I'm not happy with myself? Two weeks wouldn't be long enough to change that much."

"Other than your scrapes, you look fine to me, mademoiselle."

She made an attempt to pull her shorts down lower and felt a dull ache in her right elbow. He took another quick glance at Alyce's legs and athletic shoes.

"Are you a runner?"

"I jog."

"So do I! We will run on the beach."

"I won't be running anywhere with my injuries."

"They are not that serious."

The car was slowing down. Yves said, "I must stop here for a moment." He parked in front of an antique store. "Please come in."

Antique. Another French word commonly used in English. Her first class at MEF had covered French words she already knew: *à la carte, chic, cuisine, déjà vu, femme fatale, petite, rendez-vous, touché*. It had given her the false impression that learning this language would be easy.

There was a man behind an old carved wooden desk who had to be the owner, and another man in a denim shirt and faded blue jeans with wild white hair and an unkempt beard. She couldn't place his age. His face looked too young for the gray hair. And he was smoking—a habit Alyce could not fathom anyone developing. They both blatantly checked her out. The owner smiled. The old/young man? It was like he was studying her intently and pushing her away at the same time.

All she understood was *"étudiante"* when Yves explained who she was. The owner let out a French-sounding "hohn-hohn-hohn" and the white-haired guy made some remark that had "American" in it, causing everyone to crack up but her.

She noticed a dog at the strange guy's feet. Actually, she smelled the dog first. He—or she—looked like it slept in mud. And they let it in here? But she loved animals and put the back of her hand in front of the dog's mouth.

"Hi, there. How are you today?"

Instead of licking her hand, it farted.

The men howled. Her face flushed with embarrassment.

She wandered around the store. She heard Yves say "baguette" twice. The men had another good laugh.

Right, she thought. Real funny. Ha. Ha. Ha.

She lingered in front of a jewelry case, her eyes going straight to the diamond engagement rings, her mind straight to Nelson.

A necklace with an emerald pendant, her May birthstone, caught her eye. There was another big tug at her fragile soul as she thought about her birthday not far away and being all alone for it. She noticed a tag on the necklace that said: *Solde*. She held it up to her neck for fun and admired it in a mirror.

The owner called out to her in French. She thought he was reprimanding her for touching something that belonged to someone else. She quickly put it back and apologized. The men looked confused. Yves began to speak to her in English but the old/young guy stopped him. She understood he was telling Yves to speak in French, as he was supposed to, because she'd heard that 20 times a day for the last week.

They moved closer to her. The owner was saying numbers

that had to be prices. The nauseous dread that hit in class surged forth, but this was worse. She was in public.

The owner slowed down his speaking and increased his volume as though she were a baby with a hearing problem. She looked at Yves with pleading "Please tell him to stop" eyes.

"But it's sold! How can I buy something that's sold?"

The men's eyes widened. They spoke in French, then roared with laughter again.

Yves, his face crinkled up with glee, said, "Al-*ees*, s-o-l-d-e means it's on *sale*."

She dashed out and waited in the car. This trip wasn't transformational. It was *torture*-ational, with three more months to go. She'd sublet her place in Hoboken. She had to stick it out.

On their way again, Yves said, "That was Jean-Luc Broussard in André's store. He must still be having writer's block. He only comes into town when he can't write, and he's been seen around a lot the last couple of years."

"Who?"

"A famous novelist, though everyone would love to know his own story."

"Why?"

He turned on the stereo. Jazz filled the car. "Never mind. *I* am more interesting."

He began selling her on his wonderful house. View of the sea, swimming pool, *pétanque* court. *Pétanque* was like bocce, but with beautiful, metal, engraved balls, and one of the few things she showed any talent for.

"Here we are, Al-*ees*."

"Wow!"

A fantastic villa on the Mediterranean Sea sure beat a farm in the middle of nowhere. Maybe Liliane liked her, after all.

Her enthusiasm rose higher when she stepped inside. The foyer floor was made of cool, white marble. She could see straight through the living room to the blue water below that was glistening like a blanket of sequins. The décor was a mix of antiques, palms, and wicker furniture. Kind of tropical chic.

Yves called out to see if anyone was home. No response. *Uh-oh.*

Her room was downstairs, off from an area that led to a patio.

"You will have complete privacy," he said, with another leer. "Would you like a glass of wine?"

"Now? It's so early. No, thank you."

"La, Americans. So uptight."

He led her to the bathroom that had a bidet *(ooh la la)* and a special way of heating the water that made it instantly hot.

She stood outside the small room as he said, "There is not a big tank that controls the whole house like is common in the United States. Each bathroom has its own. You can burn your-self if you are not careful."

Alyce forced a smile and moved to the bedroom door. With her hand on the doorknob, she said, "I really need to study. When will your wife be home? I can't wait to meet her." He frowned. "I have no idea."

She closed the door in his pleading face and made sure it was locked. Then she flopped on the bed and picked up her main textbook, *French is Fun.*

The feeling took over of a thousand hot needles boring into her brain.

Where did she ever get the nerve to spend three months at a French language school and think, *voila*, she would be fluent? And she'd spent all of her severance pay on it, too! How had it slipped her mind that she was so bad at introductory Spanish in the seventh grade that the teacher urged her to pick another elective?

Her dream to live up to Glorianna's wild expectations (and her own) vanished as quickly as the smile on a Frenchie's face when she attempted to speak their magnificent language.

The only good thing about being thrown into Survival Mode was that it pushed Nelson way back in the things-to-obsess-about queue.

Sometimes.

3

Scorched Earth and the Baffling Bidet

Five kilometers away

The fragrant late afternoon turned cooler as Jean-Luc Broussard held court in his favorite spot: his kitchen. He shook local extra-virgin olive oil into a cast-iron skillet and gently turned it in several directions to coat the surface.

To his newly arrived houseguests, he said, "An American girl—a student, it turns out, at my sister's language school—walked into my friend André's store today. Her French was horrendous. She was wearing a New York Yankees baseball cap, big ugly sneakers, and hardly any clothes." He motioned to the top of his thigh. "Tiny shorts and"—he pulled his shirt back as he thrust out his chest—"a tight top."

Robbie cut him off. "Did she at least have a good body?"

He thought about that as he worked his long, prematurely white-gray hair into a rubber band. "It was toned, but there was no mystery. I prefer a woman to dress like a woman."

The achingly feminine Spanish beauty, Isabella, tossed her long black hair and smiled seductively. Robbie did not see it. Jean-Luc pretended he didn't either.

He continued with his story. When he reached the "But it's already sold!" punch line, he laughed almost as hard as when it happened. "You should have seen her face when she found out *solde* meant it was on sale!"

"Who are her hosts?" Robbie inquired.

"The lucky devils are the Devreauxs, after the farmers Fabien and Fabienne gave her the boot. According to Yves Devreaux, worse than driving a moped through their barn was that she couldn't distinguish the difference in the pronunciation of their names."

Robbie who spoke passable but not fluent French, replied, "It *is* subtle to the untrained ear."

"I wonder who will win her," Jean-Luc mused. "The father or the son? It has become a Marlaison pastime to place bets." Robbie laughed as Jean-Luc chopped the wild garlic he'd pulled out of the ground minutes before. "I would say the son, even though the father likes to jog and she looks like she has that dreadful athletic streak in her."

Isabella's sly contribution was, "Maybe she will sleep with both of them." Seeing Robbie's reaction, "Why not?"

He huffed and changed the subject. "That smells marvelous, Jean-Luc. Are you sure we can't help?"

"A Brit in my kitchen? That's almost as bad as an American."

"What about me?" The Castilian Isabella put a cigarette to her lips. Robbie immediately had a lighter underneath its tip.

Her ever-so-slight grimace at his gesture prompted Jean-Luc to say, "*Guests* are not allowed in my kitchen, either."

He hoped she would pick up on his true message. As ravishing as she was, she should not leave parental and pudgy Robbie and put down stakes with him. The Brit helped her as an artist, showed her paintings in his galleries, took care of her, gave her excellent advice even if she didn't want to hear it. Why did so many women want to snatch Jean-Luc's bachelorhood away?

"With your guest cottage," Robbie asked, "Do you ever host students?"

Jean-Luc's knife froze in midair. "Are you mad?" He stabbed the last slit into the leg of lamb and stuffed a sliver of garlic into it. The rest went into the skillet. "I need my privacy and I cannot stand to be around people for very long who do not speak French."

"I speak it," Isabella purred.

Robbie's antenna finally went up. He glared at Jean-Luc and took a swig of his brown ale.

The tension between them was interrupted by the phone ringing. He knew the caller would invariably be a creditor, past lover, lover-to-be, Raymond his editor, his sister (also a creditor), or a repugnant reporter.

He removed the skillet from the burner and answered the Australian journalist's rehearsed unctuous introduction with silence.

"I'm sorry. Do you not speak English?" the man asked with embarrassment.

"I speak it extremely well. I do not do interviews and you interrupted me while cooking dinner for guests. I said nothing because I have nothing to say." Affecting a perfect Down Under accent, he closed with, "G'day mate."

After his guests' eyes returned to their normal size, Robbie said with a haughty British clip, "Why don't I have the gall to be that way with customers? The next time one complains the painting doesn't match her sofa I'll just break it over her head."

"It better not be one of mine." Isabella lightly tossed her raven mane again.

"Jean-Luc, you are your own worst bloody enemy. You complain you are not appreciated and yet you drive off anyone who tries to help."

Jean-Luc rubbed the knot at the base of his neck as he returned to his glorious stove that had set him back 10,000 Euros.

How the money had flowed just a few years ago. How quickly it had stopped. He would never admit Robbie was right.

"They are not helping me. They are only feeding their egos and their bank accounts."

Isabella lightly pushed Robbie's shoulder. "If artists spent all their time doing interviews, they'd never get anything done. You need someone to field these things, Jean-Luc."

"And the e-mails! An electronic leash. At least I don't have a cell phone to bother me."

Robbie eyed him with disdain. "The world today quickly forgets those who keep a low profile. But enough about that depressing subject."

"Thank you." In a new jovial tone, he added, "All that matters is preparing us a delicious meal!"

He jammed a long two-prong fork into a leg of lamb and placed it in the garlic-seasoned skillet. The large yellow kitchen filled with sizzling sounds and heady aromas.

"You'll be having herb-stuffed leg of lamb, roasted rosemary potatoes and a fresh arugula salad. Now, what wine would work? A Greek Retsina would be a nice change, yes?"

They moaned their approval, yet Isabella didn't take the hint to change the subject. In her fairly good English that had an added zip from her Spanish accent, she said, "I suppose there is much to lament when you are a success. More to live up to, more questions about your work, more money to worry about."

She was 40, childless, and had that gaze he'd seen trap many a man. In addition, her toenails and fingernails were coated in deep red polish that reminded him of talons dripping with blood. Forty. He wasn't so far from that landmark birthday.

He focused on his cooking. He was particularly pleased this time with the mixture he sprinkled over the lamb: mint, parsley, basil, thyme, and chives. Transferring the chunk of meat to a plate then a pan for roasting, Didon rose from her place on the kitchen floor and followed him closely until he let his faithful canine companion lick clean the plate.

"What's this?" Isabella exclaimed a few minutes later as the rosebud he had surreptitiously taken from a vase on another counter magically appeared next to her wine glass.

"Put it in water before you go to bed," he said. "It will open tomorrow."

"Are you trying to steal my woman, Jean-Luc?" Robbie stood up and took off his jacket. "I'll punch your big nose in if you are."

"You have nothing to worry about now," Jean-Luc said, "but call my nose big again and you will."

He slid the roasting pan with the lamb into one of his expensive ovens and set the digital timer to remind him to check it in three hours. Slow roasting at a low temperature was the only way to cook lamb. He hated that digital timer. Nearly all ovens were made with one now.

Out with the old, in with the new.

Jean-Luc's company retired to the guest cottage not long after dinner. They were passing through Marlaison and catching a plane to Barcelona the next day. Isabella had picked at her dinner. Jean-Luc could see the wheels spinning in her lubricated brain.

He returned to his computer, fully intending to work on his latest novel, but the air was charged with excitement. Isabella mixed with an approaching spring shower was sure to unleash the whims of Aphrodite.

He played chess online with someone named KingTut and won in four moves.

It started to rain. A trancelike state settled over him.

His mind drifted to Colette.

He shook his head, went back to his computer.

He needed to escape the memories of Marlaison. But he had no money. He thought he'd learned his lesson as a teenager when he quickly went broke after his first bestseller. When money came pouring in again, what did he do? Throw it around as if he were an oil baron. His excuse, to himself, was that the inspiration for the wildly successful book caused him to feel he had exploited Colette and therefore did not deserve his good fortune.

Never mind that no one alive—save for Raymond—knew the real story.

He knew.

His many literary awards were now packed in a box and hidden at his sister's after he threatened to destroy them.

In *The Deer Park*, Norman Mailer wrote that life demands that one must grow or else pay more for remaining the same. Was it possible to change now? Would he ever get the chance to even try?

"Am I disturbing you?"

Isabella's sultry voice blocked out the sound of the soft rain caressing his office window.

Swiveling around, he took in her good looks as she leaned against the doorframe, arms crossed to accentuate her cleavage as she tried to warm herself up in the cool night air. She was still in her pink and red flowery dress; still woozy. Her hair and skin were damp.

"Do you need something?" he asked in what he hoped was a detached tone. "Forgive me for any oversights. This is a one-man operation."

"Are you a one-*woman* operation as well," she asked, "or are you still juggling several at once?"

"My tempestuous cruel Muse rules me now. If I do not spit out another book soon..." He swept his arms around the room. "I will lose everything."

"You are exaggerating."

"I am not. The grass here is not greener, Isabella. *It is scorched earth.*"

She responded with equal intensity. "I will take any kind of earth over the quicksand I am in." She did not break her intense gaze.

"Isabella, you are a beautiful, talented, smart woman. I thought you had more sense. Robbie may not be what you want, but he is what you need."

She shifted, pouted. "He was out the moment his head hit the pillow. If I hear him snore one more time I'll—"

"Wait until you hear me lose my temper."

"It is a sign of passion!" She paced his office; her sexy black sandals, click, click, clicked across the pine floor. "He is boring. And he wants to marry me! I cannot do it."

"Then don't. But do *not* drag me into this." He turned back to his work.

She walked behind his desk that was in the middle of the large room, faced him, and leaned over with a look of such longing he had to glance away. He silently asked his Muse to give him a sign. His answer was a warm sensation between his legs.

"Fine," he said, "if you decide not to make your plane tomorrow, you are welcome to stay. *But not for long*. I must write."

Alyce woke with a start, momentarily disoriented. Where was she? Oh, right. The villa of her new hosts. She glanced at *French is Fun*, face down on her chest. She'd read three words and fallen asleep. The window in her bedroom was open. She could feel it was cooler now, and much later. What time was it?

She checked her cell. Even though it didn't work here, not even for texting since she turned off her phone plan to save money (and not be tempted to call Nelson), she could use it as a camera and clock. Five o'clock. Wonderful. Now she wouldn't be able to go to sleep tonight. And she was just getting over her jet lag.

She eyed *French is Fun* again. She had nothing to worry about. She already had the printed version of Tylenol P.M.

She changed into jeans and a light fleece jacket and ambled onto the patio. A young man wearing sunglasses was stretched out on a lounger. On closer inspection, she found him to be quite cute in his baggy cargo pants and Bob Marley sweatshirt. As he listened to his iPod, he nodded to the beat, causing his long brown hair to fall into his face. It didn't take long for him to sense her presence.

"*Bonjour*, Al-*ees*!" He turned off his music, put his shades on top of his head, and stood to greet her with a handshake. "I am Julien."

Liliane was right about him being mature for his age. He had a totally different vibe from his dad—and amazing green eyes, even with the late afternoon sun behind him.

They sat for awhile drinking sparkling water ("water with gas," was what the French called it, he said) and talked about music, movies, her impressions of the French, his of Americans. The sky behind the house turned gorgeous shades of blue, violet, pink, and orange. She took a photo of it with her cell.

"Wait until you see the sun rise over the Mediterranean," he said.

Outside of the classroom, she thought, everything about Marlaison was pure magic.

She spoke too soon. Yves walked onto the balcony and seemed to be glaring down at them. Or was it that French bemused look again? Then his mother appeared. Alyce could have sworn she did the same. She stood up, waved, and was about to say hello but they disappeared. Maybe this wasn't going to be such a good fit after all. Or were they on their way down to meet them?

When they didn't show up, she turned to Julien. "What does your father do?"

"He is a heart surgeon."

"But he smokes!"

"He thinks his jogging will save him."

"And your mother? Does she work?"

"Yes, and she is not my mother," he said with little emotion. "*Maman* is dead."

"Oh." Alyce wanted to know more, but merely said, "I'm so sorry to hear that."

"Me, too."

She nervously rubbed her hands on her thighs. "I need to introduce myself to her. I'm being rude."

"Let me take you for a tour of Marlaison and dinner after you do that."

Her hands stopped moving. "Maybe later, Julien."

"Zhoo-lee-*ahn*," he corrected her. She repeated it several times.

"Where are your little sisters?" she asked, looking toward the house.

His shrug was followed by a look of keen interest.

To diffuse him, she said, "I can't wait to get married and have children."

He reached for his ear buds. "Why must you be married to do that?"

"You are way too young for this conversation."

He smirked. "You brought it up. And you are not the oldest woman I've asked out."

"Is that what your offer was? Well! In that case…"

"Yes?"

She turned and stood up before he could see her smile, but knew he heard it in her voice. "Now I'm *really* not interested."

Just then the sun dipped out of view.

Her ploy to play hard to get was short-lived. Julien's stepmother encouraged her to go out to dinner with him that night. Julien translated. "We did not expect you and they have made plans. She and my father have an actual date tonight. Dinner and a movie."

There was an exchange between Mrs. Devreaux and Julien. She gave him a withering look, said something, and walked off.

Soon Alyce was jumping on the back of his red Vespa motor scooter, making sure she didn't wrap her arms around him too tight.

After a delicious meal of chicken crêpes with a béchamel sauce, wine, and lots of sly gazes between selective soul-baring, she had a different view of him. So what if he was 22? She was in *France* to have a good time, grow!

And forget Nelson.

They hopped back on Julien's Vespa so he could show her Marlaison at night. This time she clung to him warmly.

Reaching their destination—the highest lookout point in Marlaison—Alyce removed her helmet. "Julien, you win. I know guys in their 40s who aren't as grown up as you."

He broke into a big, dimpled smile. She fought the urge to kiss him by turning to survey the lights of the boats dotting the sea and the houses built into the cliffs.

"The air smells so good here," she commented.

"Marlaison was a famous spa for the wealthy in the 1800s." His arm slipped around her waist. "It has magical, restorative powers."

She easily nuzzled closer. "You may be right."

Okay. There were only four years between them. No one could call her a cougar.

She soon discovered his lips were as soft as silk. Finally there was light at the end of this long dark tunnel she had moved into for three months with no escape.

"Let's go back home and listen to music, Al-*ees*. I have not enjoyed a woman's company so much in a long time."

"I find that hard to believe."

"It is true!"

When they returned home, his parents were still out. He

drew her close again. "You know we are going to make love. This could be our only chance."

Blame it on the wine, vacationitis, that sexy French accent, or his beautiful green eyes and seductive lips. Or just being angry at Nelson.

"Let's go to my room and cuddle," she said. *"That's all."*

It didn't take long before it was clear cuddling was not going to be enough.

Alyce stumbled into the bathroom (from being inebriated, not from her sore leg—what sore leg?), relieved herself, and spied the bidet. But of course, she had to try it.

One handle was marked "C." The other "F." She wondered if "C" came from cold and "F" from a form of "fire."

Her screams brought Julien to her door. "What is wrong? Are you okay?"

Again she had a hard time walking, but for another reason. Wincing as she slowly sat on the bed, she croaked, "I need some ice. Now!"

His frustration over their thwarted lovemaking dissolved into hilarity. "Al-*ees*, hot is *chaud*. Cold is *froid.*"

A few minutes later, still choking on his laughter, he left her staring at the ceiling with a towel full of ice cubes between her legs.

"It's not funny," she yelled out to him. "And don't you dare tell anyone!"

She knew he would.

Eventually, she hoped, she'd find it funny, too.

A light summer rain began to tickle the windows. She punched her pillow. She fought back tears. Would this loser leopard ever change her dumb spots?

Would she ever learn *any* French?

Would she ever stop missing Nelson? That seemed the most impossible of all.

And then Claire's voice drifted into her head with the very first French expression she learned.

"*Tout nouveau, tout beau, Al-ees. Tout nouveau, tout beau.*"

What is new, is good.

And she remembered it! It was a start.

4

Where's Wacko?

Alyce was convinced a genius created the teaching system at MEF. Straightforward conjugating verbs on a blackboard would be followed by passing out lyrics to a song. Some of the words would be left out. As the song played, the students had to fill them in. From there they'd do a lesson in the textbook, then watch a video of people talking and try to figure out what they were saying. After 45 minutes, there was a short break and a change of classroom.

The constant variety didn't make her a better student. It just broke up the misery.

There were letters you didn't pronounce. Every word was masculine or feminine, adding another complicated layer to short-circuit her brain. Even the numbers were cuckoo. Like, 90 was *quatre-vingt-dix*, or four times 20 plus 10. Huh? An older, unattractive married guy, whom Alyce befriended only because he was American, said the French did things like that to weed out spies during wars.

With few computers at the school, it was hard to check her email. Was she ever surprised when she finally did and there was one from Nelson! As she read his words, a prickly heat started at the base of her neck and moved up around her ears.

Subject: I MISS YOU

From Nelson Mansfield <nmansfield@musicworld.sales.com>

Alyce Donovan <mediagrrrl@gmail.com>

My dear, sweet, beautiful Ally,

First let me say I'm so proud of you for what you're doing. I'm sure it's not easy but you'll be parlay-vooing in no time and it'll drive me wild!

It's weird, honey. I can't stop thinking about you. Mother (who really likes you) said I should see a therapist, that there was nothing wrong with you. It had to be me. I'm making a lot of progress. I see how incredibly stupid I've been. And how I've let my mother control my life. I have to assert my independence. We even did a session together and she agreed to back off, though she claims she's just being supportive. Yes, supportive of what SHE wants.

I'd love to come over and see you. Would you mind? I'll understand if you never want to see me again. I hope that's not the case.

Junior says hi.

Hugs and kisses?? N.

Alyce clutched her chest, blinked several times. Coming here worked! Just like his mother said it would.

She also couldn't believe he was standing up to her.

Glorianna never called people by their nicknames (God forbid someone called her Glo or Glory). She never referred to the mother of Nelson's son by any name at all, other than You-know-who. After Alyce tried to be nice to Carmelita and received hostility in return, there was no love lost on her end, either. But Nelson loved his son, was a good father (even if he did spoil the kid rotten), and she reasoned everyone's going to have something unpleasant to put up with — after she thoroughly grilled him that he wasn't still sleeping with Carmelita.

"Why does every woman I go out with think that?" he asked, wounded. "Strap me to a lie detector. Junior is the result of *one night* of drunken sex when I was young and stupid."

Nelson was an account exec for *Music World* magazine and often called on Alyce's boss, Bernadette. For years, neither Alyce nor Bernie knew he had a son. One day, Alyce went into an ice cream shop in her Hoboken, New Jersey, neighborhood, and there he was—with an out of shape, well-endowed Latina woman in a tight zebra-print top, short skirt, and dangerously high heels. Between them was a young boy.

Who looked like the perfect blend of Nelson and this woman.

Alyce's heart pounded with joy over seeing him (as it always did) and fear that all was lost.

The boy said, "Dad, I want another scoop."

Yep, all was lost.

Nelson looked embarrassed for a moment. The woman smug.

"Uh, yes. This is my son. Nelson, Junior."

The woman said, proud as a peahen, "I'm his mother, Carmelita." Car-mah-*leeeee*-ta.

Alyce quickly shifted gears. "You know, the line is long and I'm in a hurry. Nice to meet you. Bye!"

The next day at work she consulted Bernadette. Bernie had fixed her up on countless horrible blind dates in an attempt to get her over Nelson.

"He comes from a lot of money," she'd counseled early on. "He only dates heiresses, preppie girls, and six-figures babes."

When she heard about Carmelita—after closing her gaping mouth—she said, "That explains why he's still single. Where's Wacko."

Bernie said that whenever she met a guy who seemed like

the perfect catch, she'd start looking for the nutcase lurking in the wings, like the way kids looked for Waldo in the *Where's Waldo* books. They usually had one because those kinds of women always went for nice guys with deep pockets.

Her cue to run was the words: "I can't seem to get rid of her." Or "She won't leave me alone."

"He doesn't want to be left alone! It's too gratifying to his ego."

As for Carmelita, Bernie shook her head a long time.

"She's got his kid. She's not going anywhere. And look at me. I'm 50, still single, and now wishing I'd put up with that skinny hemophiliac with the stutter who wanted to marry me. Go for it, kid."

Did she ever. As soon as Nelson was sure Alyce could look beyond Carmelita, he was Prince Charming. When she lost her job and was expecting a commitment, he turned into a royal toad.

Now in France, she waited a whole day before responding to his email.

Hi sweetie,

It's so great to hear from you. Of course I'd love to see you.

Now I'm in the home of the Devreauxs. Their Mediterranean villa is stunning—the complete opposite of the farm I was on. I've become good friends with the oldest son, Julien, who's 22 and seems much older. His mother died when he was a teenager and his father remarried and had two more kids. He feels pretty left out, I guess. He thinks I'm funny because I'm so un-French. He speaks English so who am I to complain?

Love to Junior.

Yours, Alyce

P.S. You would've had a big laugh over my using the bidet and burning myself because I thought "C" stood for cold. It was for chaud (hot).

Subject: LMAO

You can be a real hoot sometimes. Remember when we went to the MTV awards and you drank all that punch you didn't know was spiked and almost threw up on JustinTImberlake? And when you accidentally ate those doggie chocolates at my parents' house? Or what about the time...don't want to get into that in a company email. You know. In the Hamptons.

Anyway, I'd put you up in a hotel, but staying with a host family is key to learning the language. Just don't let Julien give you any "private" lessons. I'd write more but it's closing week for the magazine. I'll work on dates to come see you. Can't wait! Send me photos. Love, N.

Subject: LMAO—NOT!

Oh, Nelson, I do love your emails, even if they're short. I've been crazy busy, too, between school and ANOTHER switch in hosts. What happened at the Devreauxs? I went jogging with the father and he forced a kiss on me after staring at me while I did some stretching exercises. His lips were only on mine for a split second before I pushed him away so hard he fell, but it was long enough to catch that he tasted like an ashtray. And I told him.

Then I ACCIDENTALLY hit his wife in the mouth with a pétanque ball. They weigh about two pounds. I told her some women pay a lot of money to get their lips puffed up like that.

Then I ACCIDENTALLY pulled the showerhead out of the wall and that was the last straw. I'm not used to those wand thingies you hold. Especially while thinking about you ;-)

I'm now in the apartment of a widow named Solange. She must be in her 60s but still looks great and is very stylish (she talked me into cutting my hair to just below my ears). Well, have to run. Classes are starting. I'd send a photo if my cell worked here. You'll just have to use your imagination, darling. Alyce xxx

She did not mention that when she pulled the showerhead out of the wall she was really having naughty thoughts about Julien since he was standing right there. Another attempt to make love went, literally, down the drain.

With Nelson talking about coming over, it was just as well she was out of there.

The widow Solange was forever turning off lights Alyce wasn't using and reprimanding her for leaving them on. Still, she was sure she'd found the perfect host. Her English was good, too. The word she seemed to know best was *shit*. Alyce thought it hilarious to hear this well-preserved, chic woman say it with her French accent—until she used it to describe everything about Alyce. She was particularly harsh when she had a glass of wine in her, which she drank at every meal except breakfast.

"The way you dress is *sheet*."

"Your French is *sheet*."

"Your cooking is *sheet*."

Alyce found that drinking right along with her made her much easier to take. Also, she was right in her assessments. Perhaps Solange would be like the old count in *Sabrina* who took Audrey Hepburn under his wing?

Soon the widow was rummaging through her closet and insisting Alyce dump her "gym clothes" and wear her cast-offs. Most were summery dresses Alyce never would have bought for herself but she had to admit looked fabulous. Solange took her shopping for new shoes and showed her how to walk in them.

"One foot directly in front of the other, like you are on a tightrope. It *moooves* ze ass more."

When Alyce was drawn to an item that didn't meet with her approval, she uttered a curt, "As you wish." It was an oft-used phrase Alyce now knew meant "I think you're crazy, but go ahead and make an ass of yourself."

Alyce refused to part with the diamond stud Nelson had given her that pierced her bellybutton.

"It is vul-*gahr*," spat out Solange, catching the last syllable on the back of her throat.

"Maybe so, but it might be the closest I ever get to an engagement ring."

"As you wish."

When Solange deemed Alyce presentable, she dragged her out on the town—what little town there was—and gave her advice on how to get Nelson back.

"Keep making him jealous. If he does not respond it is a lost cause."

In one café they saw the writer she'd encountered with Yves at the antique shop. He sized Alyce up again with a look of interest and distance. Solange lit up when their eyes met. When she realized he was with a woman with amazing long black hair they were soon out the door.

Alyce blurted out, "Did you go out with him?"

"That is a very rude question!"

Alyce took that to mean yes.

"Do you know Jean-Luc?" Solange asked as her thin legs and high heels pumped so fast Alyce could barely keep up with her.

"I only know that he's some writer I've never heard of."

Solange stopped in her tracks. "He is not *some* writer. He is a great writer! He wrote *Taming the Black Sun* when he was 16. It is pure genius! And his last one was even more sublime. I hear the English translation is *sheet*."

"What's it about?"

"A tortured writer who cannot love a woman but falls for a horse. Then the horse... I will not tell you the rest. You must read it."

"That's okay. Doesn't sound like my cup of tea."

The renovated Alyce nearly skipped to school each weekday morning in her short dresses and chic sandals. On the day that she learned they were having a dance class and they weren't teaching the minuet, she was ecstatic. She loved to dance. Not only that, their instructor was gorgeous.

Philippe wore skintight jeans that showed off his firm ass and long, strong legs; a form-fitting top left no question that he was in excellent shape.

Had to be gay.

She and her fellow students followed him to the cafeteria where the tables had been moved to create space. Pop music thumped. Alyce learned how to say "bend," "spin," "lunge," "slide."

At one point, Philippe grabbed her and they danced together—no words at all—in front of an audience that now included the cafeteria staff. Their expressions ranged from delight to bafflement. More than once Solange's feminine dress flipped up to reveal Alyce's new pink lace panties.

It was the first time she paid no attention to the clock on the wall.

Could he be straight?

The class ended too soon. Philippe motioned toward the hall. "Come with me to my office, Al-*ees*. Oh, I am bad to speak to you in English. *Français, Français!*"

He took her to the side of the building. There was a door. He held it open.

She rolled her eyes after peeking inside. "It's a closet full of tools."

He grabbed her waist. "Your *fantastique* dancing has aroused me. I must kiss you."

Stunned, she acquiesced. For a moment.

She worked her way out of his grip and walked away that instant.

"We can dance anytime, but that's it. I have a boyfriend."

"You must come see me. I am a Super-Mec!"

She turned around. "A what?"

"Chippendale dancer. I am *Le Gentil Gendarme*."

"A cop?"

He leaned seductively against the wall. "You will be very happy to see what is under my uniform." He told her where he performed and added, "You have not seen the last of me."

She returned to Solange's and wasted no time flopping on the sofa and giddily telling her about Philippe.

"We have to check him out. What else is there to do here? Could he dance! And is there a ring on my finger? How do I know Nelson is being good?"

She had not noticed Solange had turned unusually quiet.

With narrowed eyes, her hostess said, "I already know his routine, Al-*ees*. He is my boyfriend."

"Wh-wh-huh?! Boyfriend or boy *toy*?"

Solange crossed her spindly legs in the other direction and sat up straighter. "We do not have the *boy toy* in France. A lover is a lover!" She continued to glower at Alyce. "He did not even notice that was *my* dress you were wearing? The little *sheet*."

Alyce had found Nelson's attraction to Carmelita hard to understand, but there was only a 15-year difference, and he was 23 (and drunk) when she seduced him. Solange had to have at least 30 years on Philippe.

"But he's so young and you're so ol—."

Alyce clamped her hand over her mouth. She could see by Solange's expression that it was too late. "Um, does this mean you want your clothes back?"

"*Non!* I never want to see them or you again!"

Get Thee to a Nunnery

Liliane pulled her chair closer to her desk, clasped her hands, and planted them before her with a thud.

"Here are your options, Al-*ees*. You may stay in a hotel at your expense; at a convent where you will be expected to attend all religious services, be up at dawn, do chores, and be asleep by 9:00, or in my brother's guest cottage. His property was once a vineyard so you'll be back in the country. It is a 20-minute bike ride."

For a millisecond she thought of taking Nelson up on his offer to foot the bill for a hotel, but if there's one thing she knew about him it was that he hated a woman who burned through his cash like You-know-who did. As did his mother.

Hotel = money I don't have.

Convent = NO WAY.

Cottage = free.

"Before you answer," Liliane said, "my brother is a well-known writer. Jean-Luc Broussard. He prizes his privacy and can be quite impossible. I am not sure he will agree to this."

Alyce drew in her breath as she recalled the face of the rude man with the wild gray hair laughing at her in the antique store.

"Not him! The convent's fine."

She cocked her head. "You have met my brother?"

"He's that old hippie who wrote the book about a guy who falls in love with a horse, right?"

"An old hippie," Liliane delicately touched her throat. "Amusing. Not to him, I am sure. He is only 38. His hair turned gray while he was writing that novel."

"He was with a woman with amazing long black hair."

"Jean-Luc has no shortage of female companions. That is Isabella. She is staying with him. For now."

While Alyce pondered how women could possibly find her brother attractive, Liliane picked up the phone and began to make a call.

"The convent it is. You can't get into trouble there." She broke into her sphinxlike smirk Alyce had come to know so well. "You will have no distractions and they will be very strict about not speaking to you in English. Think of how much your French will improve."

Alyce sunk back in her chair, shut her eyes and prayed right there. *Dear God, why are you punishing me? What did I do to deserve this?*

She heard her own inner voice reply: *Calling a convent punishment may not be the best approach with the Big Guy, Alyce.*

Liliane's final words were, "I suggest you change into something less revealing. And put on an extra layer or two. The abbey was built a thousand years ago and made of stone. Even on the hottest day it is cool there."

"Wonderful. Can't wait."

St. Pierre Abbey was covered in so much ivy Alyce could barely see the stones beneath the huge 11th-century structure. She shivered just looking at it. She hoped it had been updated with electrical outlets so she could plug in a heater.

Dream on.

A silent nun directed her to a room that was only big enough for a cot-sized bed and a small table next to it. On it was a Bible, a beeswax candle, and a pack of matches. At least she wouldn't have to rub two sticks together to light it. There was a tiny closet that her luggage barely fit into.

She asked in French where the *toilette* was.

The nun put her finger to her mouth and nodded for her to follow. Alyce considered the advantages of taking a vow of silence. She wouldn't have to speak French, would she?

By far the strangest part of her first day was when she was getting ready for bed. Part of her nightly routine was to pop a birth control pill. She stared at the tiny dot sitting innocently in her palm. How could she take this while staying in a convent?!

Maybe she shouldn't be taking them. Maybe there was a reason she was sent here.

She popped it anyway and crawled into the bed that was harder than her head that got her here in the first place. How could she have said that to Solange? One day *she'd* be that old.

She tried to see herself far into the future and drew a blank. In the pitch dark she drifted into Spiritual Mode. She shouldn't just ponder the meaning of her own life. How shallow. What about everlasting life?

She lit the candle and picked up the Bible next to her. It was in French. So much for that. She blew out the candle.

It was so damn quiet the *silence* kept her awake.

Fantasies about Nelson started. Mixed with a few with Julien. And one with Philippe. Oh, how she wanted to make herself feel good in that little marble slab of a bed. But here? Absolutely not.

She caught herself fiddling with the diamond stud in her bellybutton.

She let out a groan of frustration and pounded her thigh with her fist.

Soon someone knocked on her door and asked in French, "Are you okay?"

"*Oui, oui*. Uh, *mal…*" What was the word for dream? "*Mal* dream."

The woman's voice said softly, "*Mauvais rêve*."

Alyce repeated it. "*Merci*."

About 15 minutes later there was another knock. Alyce opened the door and a nun who quietly introduced herself as Sister Therese stood there with a cup of tea. She leaned in, whispered almost inaudibly, "An herbal tea to help you sleep. May I come in?"

Once the door was shut, Alyce said equally as low, "I didn't know you spoke English."

"There is a lot you don't know about me."

Alyce couldn't tell her age, somewhere between 30 and 50. She had the same serene smile all the nuns had. Then she told Alyce she was once a barmaid in New York City!

"I did not make enough to support myself and had to rely on boyfriends to survive. It was not a nice feeling to have such a loss of control. I became an alcoholic. Then I decided to devote my life to my Savior. I have no regrets."

Alyce's mind immediately went to Carmelita. She had been a barmaid when Nelson met her. She told Sister Therese about her.

"I want to feel compassion for her, but I can't," Alyce said. "She hasn't worked a day since she had their child."

"Perhaps she is jealous of you because she can't take care of herself."

Alyce's dry response was, "Seems like she can take care of herself just fine."

"When I was trying to be on my own," she said in the most soothing tone, "I envied women who did not need a man for money. They could walk away if he did not love her or she did not love him. I was not free until I came here and gave up all attachments."

Alyce gave her a serious look. "Don't you miss sex? Come on, be honest."

She lowered her eyes. "No." She looked at Alyce directly. "I really don't."

"Didn't you want to have a family?"

She shook her head. "There are many ways to feel fulfilled, Al-*ees*. Many. You will know in your heart which is the right one."

All Alyce knew right then was that becoming a nun was surely not one of them.

By the fourth day, Alyce was so sleep deprived from not being able to conk out in her uncomfortable cot and then, just as she did, being woken up by crowing roosters or church bells, she was ready to get in a cab and head to the freakin' airport.

She had just finished cleaning the breakfast dishes when Sister Therese came and whispered, "You have a visitor." The sparkle in her eyes made Alyce's heart pound a bit. Who could it be? Could Nelson have flown over to surprise her?

Julien Devreaux.

"I miss you, Al-*ees*."

"Do you see where I am? I should be wearing a chastity belt with no key."

"Let's go for a walk. The grounds are beautiful here. I must talk to you."

What could happen, she thought. We're at a convent.

Alyce clasped her hands behind her back as they strolled through the old gardens. He spied a bench and steered her to it, grabbing one of her hands as she sat down. He kissed it twice before she withdrew it.

"I think about you constantly, Al-*ees*."

She looked around to see if they were being watched. "How

much did it cost to fix the showerhead? I feel like I owe your parents—"

"Forget that. When can I see you again?"

"I'll never forget that."

He was so cute when his serious face broke into a smile.

A sister walked by and smiled politely. They smiled back. For the next hour they kept it on a mental level after Alyce made it clear he was too young and she had a boyfriend.

He replied, "But of course."

They talked about religion, how the universe began, and the power of prayer. It was pretty damn stimulating, and not just on her brain cells. Julien made her feel as though every word that came out of her mouth was fascinating to him.

"I love talking to you," she said.

"I love writing about you."

"What do you mean?"

"My greatest ambition is to become a novelist, and you have inspired me. It is about a young Frenchman who meets a mesmerizing American woman."

The intensity in his eyes as he spoke caused a powerful swoon to come over her she could not drive away. She would later blame it on vacationitis and her inflated ego. She pulled him behind the closest hydrangea bush. He gallantly took off his loose black T-shirt for her to recline on and in no time her breasts were freed from their pink Victoria's Secret Miracle Bra.

She moved her lips to his ear. "We really have to stop, Julien."

"No, it is beautiful, Al-*ees*. If it was wrong, why did God make it feel so good?"

"So women would be willing to endure childbirth."

"You do not wish me to use a condom?"

She set him straight on that one. "I'm on the pill. Condoms are for other reasons."

The sounds of the birds, the scent of spring flowers, the naturalness of it all, made her forget where she was until—

"OW!"

A sharp pain in her right thigh caused her to open her eyes and look straight into the fiery glare of the Mother Superior. She was holding up a long stick.

It was not an olive branch.

"Julien," she said, as they quickly put their clothes back on, "I think this is worse than the showerhead incident."

THE MUSE WHISPERS

Jean-Luc's affair with Isabella began, indeed, on a high note (after Robbie did, indeed, punch him in the nose). She was a wonderful lover, delightfully mischievous, and quite willing to foot the bill for their whimsies when he assured her a big check was coming and he would pay her back. They were soon frolicking in Corsica; exploring the cliffs and beaches by day, each other until dawn.

He took copious notes to convince himself he was doing work-related research. It also flattered Isabella to no end to think that he might write about her.

He should have stayed put in Marlaison, chained himself to his computer, and written anything, no matter how awful. The inevitable shift in Isabella's devotion came after they returned home and an exceptional dinner in town ended with her credit card being declined.

The owner politely waived the charge for his old friend, Jean-Luc. "I know you will repay me," he said.

"We spent 7,000 Euros in two weeks!" she screeched as she drove the Lexus SUV back to his place. She still didn't know the car wasn't his.

"Live, Isabella! Think of how much our trip to Corsica inspired your painting. You can write many of your expenses off your taxes. I will give you more than you spent. Be patient. You will come out ahead."

He delivered the smile and hand-squeeze that always calmed women down.

"You're right," she said with a sigh and a pout, also perfected over her years. "Perhaps I can work for you and you can make me one of your expenses?"

Merde. Someone to help with the dishes and grocery shopping would be nice, but it would put domestic ideas in her head.

"You should focus on your own work," he said gently.

She dropped the subject. He wondered for how long.

The problem of how to pay for the next night's meal was solved when his sister invited them to dinner. "Has Benoit forgiven me?" he asked.

"If you come with presents, he will," Liliane replied.

He was still ashamed of missing his nephew's birthday party. Benoit had bragged to all his friends that his uncle would be there to perform magic. Liliane was going to hire a clown, but Jean-Luc insisted it was the least he could do for her after all she had done for him. He truly meant it. The day came and he was felled by a crippling migraine. Instead of making up for it when he was better, he was too embarrassed to face the little boy.

Liliane, wisely, had hired the clown anyway as backup.

Before he and Isabella left for his sister's that evening, he went into his musty basement with tall ceilings where he used to produce wine. He briskly moved past the wine presses, thousands of empty bottles still in boxes and the long row of oak barrels crowned with glass taps to trap escaping gas.

He opened the cupboard that once held scores of jars of homemade lavender honey. There were three left. He reached for one to take to Liliane.

There would be one less reminder of Colette and the fun they had making it.

"Jean-Luc!" cried Stéphane as he came through the front door.

He lifted up his six-year-old nephew. "You are almost too old for me to do this."

"Then I don't want to get old."

"No one does."

Three year-old Benoit clung to his mother's leg while she sliced a shallot and warily regarded Jean-Luc. He made a caramel appear from under his chin and the precious boy grinned.

"A hug, please," he requested with open arms. "I can't bear to have you mad at me."

Soon they were in a tight embrace followed by Benoit ripping open the presents he and Isabella had brought.

The first was a charcoal sketch from Isabella that she had drawn from a photo of him. In it, he was in awe of a butterfly that had landed on his hand. He now melted, not only because it was of him, but that it had been drawn by a beautiful woman who looked at him so adoringly.

Jean-Luc gave Benoit a classic toy, the Slinky. Plus, a long yellow gourd they found in Corsica that had dried out and was an excellent maraca. He showed him how to get different sounds out of it by shaking it in various ways. To everyone's delight, Benoit ran to the top of the second floor of the house and let the Slinky make its way down the stairs while creating a musical accompaniment with the gourd.

Two hours later, after doing magic tricks for the boys, answering their ceaseless but adorable questions, flattering his sister, butting heads with Simon on politics (Liliane's lanky, duty-bound engineer husband), and making Isabella feel included, he was back in good graces.

But why had the calculating Liliane invited them over?

After dinner, she asked Isabella to read a bedtime story to

the boys. That was Simon's cue to clear the table and do the dishes.

"Let's take a little walk, Jean-Luc," She threw a shawl over her shoulders.

They strolled along the sidewalk of her neighborhood, arm in arm, as though whatever they had to talk about was nothing serious. Oh, but it was. First she broke the news that the royalty check he was expecting was just over 10,000 Euros—less than half what they expected.

"I must give Isabella 8,000 immediately."

"Jean-Luc, you cannot keep living hand-to-mouth. She is hardly the only expense you have." She took a few more steps before saying, "It is time for you to sell your property."

He halted, shut his eyes as if bracing for a terrible blow, and whispered, "I am a success *manqué*."

"You are a brilliant writer who could make a lot of money if you wrote your memoir. Everyone wants to know the real Jean-Luc. The man behind the myth."

"I am still in my 30s."

"Barely." She pulled him on.

"I would feel like my life was over." And spending months on end thinking about himself; churning up and dissecting the Colette catastrophe. He would rather drink hemlock.

He argued, "My property will be worth more when the new airport is built."

"I agree, but that's at least five years away. And nothing will improve its value without a lot of money to fix it up. If you want to keep your land, write your memoir."

He wanted to scream. He didn't have the energy after learning about the check.

"There's something else I would like to discuss with you, Jean-Luc."

He stopped again. Now what?

Liliane wanted him to consider having an American student, a young woman in her 20s, stay in his cottage.

"An American? How dare you ask me this!" Then it hit him. "Wait. Is she the girl who stayed with the Devreauxs? Fabien and Fabienne? Solange?"

"One of the worst students in the history of the school."

Liliane may have been the bane of his existence at times, but he respected her intelligence and instincts. When she coyly said, "I think your Muse will love her" he had to know more. She regaled him with a few stories he hadn't heard through the Marlaison grapevine. His body turned stiff as a guard dog that just heard a door creak open. She was a goldmine of material!

"She's been kicked out of every host home, Jean-Luc. Including the *convent*."

"What could she have possibly done there?"

"She was caught in their garden in a compromising position with Julien Devreaux."

He gleefully imagined the scene. "Was she moaning 'Oh, God' when she was found?"

His all-business sister let out a much-needed laugh. "Very funny, but there's nowhere left to put her." She got them walking again. "I am at my wits' end."

What was this American girl's story, he wondered. With the insecure Isabella here, drama was sure to ensue that would dislodge his writer's block—or one, or both, of the women.

"Would she help out around the house?" he asked. "*No cooking*."

"I'm sure it's negotiable."

"Let me think about it."

The ride home was uncommonly quiet. Isabella finally said, "Is there a reason why we left in such a hurry?"

"The check was half what we thought it would be. I will still repay you, don't worry, but she wants me to sell my property."

Isabella didn't waste time assessing the outcome. "How much is it worth?"

"I could net, maybe, a million Euros."

"That's *all*, for your house, a cottage, a swimming pool, a three-car garage, a vineyard and how many *hectares*?"

"Forty-eight, but I let the AOC lapse." *Appellation d'origine contrôlée.* "Too many regulations."

"But *Vins de pays* are all the rage now because they are often as good and cheaper. Can't you reinstate it?"

"It's not going to be sold to anyone! I am going to write another novel!"

"Even if you had it finished today you would not see that much, would you?"

He pulled back. "Thank you for that vote of confidence."

"I meant they don't pay the full amount up front, no?"

Nothing was said until the car turned on the dirt road that led to Jean-Luc's home. "I know it is a sensitive subject," she said, "but what is stopping you from writing your memoir?"

His answer never came. He was too preoccupied trying to figure out how to tell her goodbye so he could take a stab at writing it—and whether to tell her about his new tenant. He had a feeling it would make her want to stay even more.

He knew what he had to do. The Grand Gesture.

As she did her nightly ablutions, he dug into his bedroom closet and brought out his hidden 1929 Matisse lithograph. He kept it out of sight after what happened to the rest of his valuable art collection. He felt differently now. What was the point of owning something of such value if he didn't enjoy it?

It was waiting for Isabella on her side of the bed.

"Jean-Luc, is this what I think it is? Please turn on more lights."

He did. She held the image of the reclining nude as if it were made of spun gold. He wondered why that particular work of art was the one he chose to keep. It didn't seem that special now.

"It's worth a lot, Jean-Luc. Why haven't you sold it if you don't display it?"

"I will only pay off my debts with proceeds from *my* work, not someone else's."

"*Caramba,* I have never known anyone like you."

"I hope you enjoy it."

"This is a gift?"

It gave him immense pleasure to see her so touched. She put it aside and reached to pull him toward her. He stopped her.

"Isabella, I must write. I cannot do it with you here. Please leave tomorrow."

Her shock and hurt were hard to take in.

"Where am I to go?"

"You have friends all over the world. Sell the litho and go wherever you please."

"I can't sell it. It came from you!"

She sobbed as he wrapped his arms around her.

"Isabella, there is nothing wrong with you. You are a sensational woman. But I cannot give you what you want."

"I thought we were having a great time together."

"We were, but I liked my life as it was."

She dabbed at her nose and softly said, "It's been a long day. Let's not make any decisions right now. Tomorrow, eh?"

After making sure Isabella was sound asleep, he walked down the hallway to a locked room that looked out on the front entrance. Using a large old metal key, he opened the door. The smell of fresh paint had finally lost its battle against time. He stepped inside, closed the door, and flipped the light switch. It produced nothing. The bulb, too, had relinquished its power.

Slowly his eyes adjusted to the darkness, aided by the moonlight. He could make out the mural he'd been working on in the cozy room. His eyes moved downward to open cans on the floor. The paint in them had hardened so much that the brushes he'd been using jutted out like branches in a frozen pond.

He saw the photo next to one.

The tape on its back still had a little stick. He pressed it on the wall again. "So you can watch."

He would resume working on the mural at night. The daytime was too cheerful.

He needed to do this for himself.

Even more so, for Colette.

By morning his Muse had worked on him and decreed that Isabella should stay longer, at least until he saw how it went with his new tenant. He made a special breakfast for his awakening Spanish princess. She loved his *chevre* and fresh chive omelets.

When she saw what he had created for her, she showed her appreciation with an amorous hug and a promise of more to come.

Wearily he said, "Enjoy this first. The eggs are from my neighbor's hens, popped out an hour ago. The chives are from out back. The *chevre* is local. "

"What is wrong, Jean-Luc?"

After a long, soulful gaze, "I should not start your day with bad news."

"Are you asking me to leave again?" She gruffly reached for her cigarette pack on the nightstand, pulled one out, and brought it to her lips.

"I have changed my mind about that."

Her hands froze. "Oh?"

He gallantly lit her smoke then rested the tray on the dresser and climbed into bed with her. He joined her in her bad habit.

The red panels draped from the bed's canopy slowly undulated in the light breeze. The lovers puffed in silence. He watched a black ant crawl up the thick bamboo bedpost. What would be its fate? The males died shortly after mating. The queen lost her wings. He knew a lot of humans who had procreated and experienced the same, metaphorically speaking.

Didon barked outside, probably at a rabbit. The bedroom

window's cream-colored curtains fluttered open, allowing the morning sun to filter in. The spring air was charged with renewal, yet he felt gathering storm clouds moving in.

Isabella put her cigarette out, nestled next to him and slowly, deeply rubbed his neck that felt like petrified wood.

"That's enough, thank you."

She gradually pulled her hand away.

How he longed to be alone. The only problem with being alone was that it always led to feeling alone.

He sat up, looked at the clock by his bed. "She'll be here in two hours."

"Who? You have hired a maid?"

When he told her about Alyce Donovan, she fumed, "So this is why you wanted me to go! Jean-Luc, you are a beast!"

"No. I told you when Robbie was still here not to stay long. You wanted to break it off with him, I helped you do that. I lost a good friend, too. Now help *me*. Let me write!"

"How will you be able to do that when you're teaching this woman French?"

"I will do no such thing! With your help, I won't even notice that she's here."

"Ahhh. My help." She cuddled up to him, pretending she wasn't mad. Perhaps she wasn't now that she felt useful. "An American. How could Liliane do that to you?"

He shared with her some of the backstory on his new tenant in the hope that she might be intrigued as well. "She even tried to cook for Solange and burned everything to a crisp because she didn't realize the oven was calibrated to Celsius degrees."

"Who is Solange?"

"Then she drove her crazy looking for cheese you *squirt* out of a bottle."

"Dreadful. And Solange is...?"

"An old friend."

He stood up and slipped on the buttery soft Italian leather loafers Katrina had given him.

Isabella grabbed at one last straw. "Let's play a trick on the American girl. Let's act as though we don't speak English."

He mulled it over. "It seems cruel and could be more of an effort than speaking it."

"Isn't that the point of a total-immersion experience? We'll be helping her learn French."

He knew that she just wanted to keep him away from this girl. She did make a good argument, though.

"*D'accord.* I'll alert Liliane."

7

Dream Cottage. Nightmare Hosts.

Once again, it was Monday morning and Alyce was in Liliane's office. This time her forlorn bags were in a heap instead of neatly lined up.

"Al-*ees*, you have been a spectacular challenge."

Not even a French accent could make that sound nice.

"Am I going to your brother's?" Her apprehension was unmistakable.

"Yes. If it doesn't work out you are on your own." She eyed her the way she probably did with her boys when they misbehaved. "I suggest you exercise extreme caution in sharing with others where you are staying."

"No problem. I have no one to tell." Alyce turned optimistic. "I bet we'll get along fine. I read novels. James Patterson, Nora Roberts, John Grisham…"

Liliane said, "I suggest you keep that to yourself as well. It would be better you say you don't read at all than to mention those."

She was confused. "Don't all writers like each other?"

Liliane burst into laughter. "Oh, I wish I could watch this

unfold!" She looked down at the floor. "I almost forgot. This came for you."

It was a FedEx box from Nelson. Alyce ripped it open. "An international iPhone!" Inside was a note saying: *Text or email me. xoxox Nelson*

He had sent it precharged, too. "What a thoughtful guy."

Liliane was beaming. "Hang on to him, Al-*ees*. A man like that is hard to find."

Alyce picked up her new small shoulder bag that had replaced her knapsack. "Is there anything special I should know about your brother?"

"I would say he is a spectacular challenge as well."

With renewed trepidation, Alyce hopped in the waiting taxi.

The driver said, "You are to be with Jean-Luc Broussard?"

She studied his reflection in his rearview mirror. "Is that a good thing?"

"Eh... Jean-Luc... this is one time, no, *first* time he take in the student."

Was she about to step into a Stephen King novel? She made a mental note not to mention that writer's name either.

"I take you to Madame Solange."

Alyce was in such a distraught state over being kicked out of the Devreaux's she didn't recall how she got to Solange's. "Uh, yes, I remember."

His eyes danced. "Very beautiful lady."

French men did know how to appreciate a mature woman. She would definitely consider coming back here *in about three decades.*

"You are Al-*ees*." The French way sounded much better than the boring American *AL*-iss. He introduced himself as Maurice. They tried to chat, but his English was limited and after another morning of classes her mind was mush.

She admired her new gleaming phone. She was back with

Nelson, reconnected in cyberspace. She texted: *Got your gift. Love it! You're the best. xoxo*

No L-word. Too soon.

She couldn't stop smiling.

She played with the phone until she figured out how to get her email. She was surprised to see a message from her sister Chantilly, the model turned trophy wife.

Congratulations, Alyce! You're going to be an aunt! The due date is November 6th. Isn't it exciting? Hope you're having fun over there. It sounds like a lot of work. But I know you and you're probably enjoying every minute of it. xox Chantilly

Alyce dove into her bag for tissues. Her 21-year-old sister was going to be a mother. Before her. With her handsome investment banker husband.

A lifetime of envy oozed forth like a barely visible paper cut that wouldn't stop bleeding.

Chantilly the perfect baby.

Chantilly the child model.

Ooh. Aah. Isn't she beautiful!

She knew she should rise above this and be happy for her. She would. Eventually.

If everything worked out with Nelson.

Once her cry was over, she checked her face in her compact and decided to skip putting on any lipstick. Spending time with nuns glowing with an inner beauty that no makeup could re-create had her wearing less of it these days. She also didn't want to put any sexy ideas into this Jean-Luc's head. Thankfully she was covered up in her convent attire.

There were fewer and fewer houses as they headed up a dirt road into the higher part of Marlaison, population 60,000. Her time in the advertising world had taught her that was roughly the size of the readership of *Prosthetics and You* magazine—a highly profitable magazine, by the way.

Alyce's former life seemed so far away now. In truth, she was restless after the first year in that job. At least she was always learning something new here.

Seeing something new, too. An entire field of lavender appeared on her left! To the right looked like a field of sunflowers coming up. Oh, this placement had to work. It just had to.

Jean-Luc's *maison* was almost hidden by trees and overgrown vines. It wasn't huge, but wasn't small either. Definitely what a real-estate broker would call a handyman special. The beige exterior paint was peeling, curved orange tiles were missing from the roof, and a large, cracked ceramic pot had turned over, spilling dirt on the stone path. The grass hadn't been cut in some time. Off to the side was a rusted Mercedes two-door convertible with no wheels, and a new silver Lexus SUV. If it weren't for the birds cooing and chirping, flowers everywhere, and the bright sun hovering above in the deep blue sky, it would be a little creepy.

There was no door buzzer. Alyce lightly knocked on the old wooden door. It opened with a soft squeak into a foyer with a staircase. To the right was a living room with a terra cotta floor, creamy stucco walls, and African masks on vertical wooden beams. Shelves were crammed with books, mostly hardcover. There were many paintings but just as many empty spaces where she could see paintings had been. It looked like a museum exhibit in the midst of being changed.

"Downtown artsy-fartsy," as Nelson's mother would say.

Suddenly, the unmistakable sound of a woman about to climax came from somewhere above them, beyond the staircase. What the hell did women see in this guy?

To a grinning Maurice, she said in as blasé a tone as she could muster, "Please take me to a hotel."

"You will have much talk when you go to America." Carrying her bags, he headed toward the back of the house.

"Wait! I mean it. I'm not staying here!"

She followed him through a gorgeous modern kitchen and out a door.

"Maurice! Come back here!"

That dirty dog appeared, barking like crazy.

Then she saw it. About 200 feet from the main house, giving her plenty of privacy, was the most adorable cottage she'd ever seen. With turquoise wooden shutters and covered with vines, it was right out of *Provence Living*. She would have it all to herself!

In between was a swimming pool with a thick black plastic cover on it and a *pétanque* court that she wouldn't be using anytime soon after the image of Julien's mother's blown-up lips popped into her head. There was also a well-used fireplace made of rustic stones that almost matched the terra cotta roof.

As she came closer to the cottage, the scent of jasmine reminded her of expensive body lotion. The deep purplish-blue flowers covering the front were like a kind of morning glory she'd never seen before.

A black wrought-iron bistro table and two chairs were near the front door under a tree with salmon-pink, trumpet-shaped flowers that were so big they didn't look real. They looked like someone had strung them on like giant Christmas tree lights.

She tipped Maurice, bid him *adieu*. She took her first photo with her new cell: the tree with the amazing flowers. Just as she was bringing one of the large blossoms to her face to get a whiff of their scent, she felt someone standing behind her.

It was Jean-Luc's long-haired girlfriend (though it was quite tousled now) giving her a penetrating gaze.

She introduced herself to Alyce in French as Isabella.

"*Parlez-vous anglais?*" Alyce asked with optimism.

She shook her head and reeled off something so fast, all Alyce could understand was "*Non?*" at the end of it.

She replied, "*D'accord,*" figuring that had to be safe. "Jean-Luc *parlez anglais?*"

She shook her head no, then pantomimed that she was not

to go through the house to enter the cottage but to walk around the side of the main house.

She nodded in agreement. That out of the way, she returned to the big pink flower and took a sniff. It nearly covered her face.

"It smells like love," she said more to herself. She inhaled again. "I can't wait for Nelson to—" she turned to Isabella. "He's my boyfriend. He's coming to visit soon." Alyce wanted to make sure she knew she was no threat. "Oh, right, you don't speak English."

She tried to conjure up the correct French words but Isabella shook her head in disapproval and left. Some reception, Alyce thought. In a way, she was thankful. It was hard enough socializing at school. She would come home to people who expected nothing from her.

The cottage had one of those cute doors that split in two so you could open the top if you wanted, and a kitchen with a round pine dining table. There was no sofa, but two peacock wicker chairs and a coffee table, a double bed with an antique white metal headboard, and a bathroom with a showerhead built solidly into the wall (not a handheld thingie, thank God).

On another wall in the bathroom Alyce noticed a mural of Botticelli's *Birth of Venus*. The naked goddess, standing on her clamshell, had a cigar in her mouth. The signature in the corner was Jean-Luc Broussard. He was an artist, too? Alyce could barely paint her toenails.

She made sure the lock on the front door worked, walked back outside, and imagined waking up every morning with a steaming cup of coffee at her bistro table next to her Tree of Love with the enormous flowers. Considering she could be in a tiny dark apartment in Hoboken, or pounding the hot, stinking Manhattan pavement looking for a job, life wasn't so bad.

Her mind quickly went to how romantic it would be here with Nelson.

❧❧❧

Isabella took a sip of the espresso Jean-Luc had made for her.

"Her boyfriend in New York, Nelson, is arriving soon. Mmmm, this is good."

"Two Americans here? Impossible. They can move into a hotel."

"I'm glad to hear that."

"It's all in the bean, my dear. And the grind, the machine, the water, the tamp pressure, the temperature, the brew pressure, and timing. Easy as can be."

Their eyes twinkled in the same way at the same time. How long could they keep up this charade that they did not speak English?

Alyce had a naïveté about her that he had seen in many Americans traveling to France for the first time. He felt a modicum of pity for her.

Isabella leaned on the counter and bent over slightly so Jean-Luc could see she was not wearing a bra. She was wearing the same sexy dress she had on the night she convinced him to be her escape route from Robbie. He still regretted his compliance, though not entirely.

Jean-Luc eyed his cottage through the kitchen window and wondered how much longer he would stay here. He could feel it was time to move on. Or was that another excuse to avoid writing?

Isabella cautiously asked, "What are you thinking about, Jean-Luc?"

Using a small gold spoon, he stirred up the grounds in the white demitasse cup and searched for a response that would playfully tick her off. "I wonder which Devreaux will be sneaking in to see her. Or will she take another lover before her swain arrives."

Her cup came down with a clank. "It better not be you."

He turned to her. "You insult me. She is hardly my type."

"I thought every woman was your type."

He nonchalantly looked back at the cottage. "Now you insult yourself."

"Maybe *I* will seduce her."

She charged up the stairs to the guest room where she kept her suitcase. What come-hither outfit would she pull out next?

He took a suede shoulder bag off its hook by the kitchen door that opened to the back of his villa, checked that his clippers and pistol were in it, and headed to the woods to snip herbs and wild flowers.

Alyce darted out of the cottage. In French she tried to say, he deduced, "Do you have a housekeeper? This place is dirty." It came out as: "Have you a house that is gone? I need a bath."

He held in a laugh and played dumb. She mimed sweeping the floor and scrubbing counters. He mimed the same back, pointed at her, then the house.

"You want me to clean the cottage *and* your house? Yeesh."

As he walked off he heard her mutter, "Only 78 more days."

Out of her sight, he took a small notebook and pen from his back pocket and wrote down: *Yeesh*. He threw the pad in the suede bag so Isabella wouldn't find it, and went about his task.

He returned to find Alyce outside at the wrought-iron table, trying to do her homework. He came from behind and heard her making a common mistake—not connecting a word that ends with a "t" with a word that begins with a vowel so it sounded as though the second one began with the "t." And her accent wasn't just off, it was nonexistent. But it was one of the most oft-heard expressions: *comment allez-vous*. How are you?

It could be worse. She could be pronouncing the "z" and "s."

"*Co-mahn-tal-eh-voo*," he said.

She jumped. "You scared me!"

"*Excusez-moi*, mademoiselle." He handed her part of the

bouquet of wild flowers he had gathered for the dining table. *"Pour vous."*

She smiled and he observed that her teeth were typically American. Too straight and white. He would have to add that to his notebook.

"Merci boucoup, Jean-Luc. Uh... *très beau?"*

"Comme c'est beau." She nodded as if she understood. *"Répétez, s'il vous plaît."*

Haltingly she said, "Co-may-say-*bo."*

Over two months he would have to put up with this?

Nevertheless, he invited her, in French, to join them for dinner at 9:00. She couldn't answer in French, so she resorted to English while wildly bobbing her head back and forth.

"That's too late. But thank you, really!"

The eventual scent of pan-seared scallops and braised fennel changed her mind. She said almost nothing throughout the meal, but he could see her listening intently.

Like Colette used to do.

As his sister predicted, this student intrigued him. Not in a sexual way, though that was always a possibility. Was it paternal? Oh, please, not that! Well, maybe a bit. Or was it the assurance that Alyce was material for a story? There was more to this girl than he first imagined.

More than even she knew.

THE T-WORD

Alyce thought Jean-Luc's big dog with matted white-brown hair hanging in cords looked like a Rastafarian. She studied the female Didon who, after two weeks, no longer barked at the sight of her. She remembered something her mother once told her.

"The way a man treats his dog is the way he'll treat his kids. It's one of the reasons I married your father. He was so good with his little Pomeranian, Zuzu."

What about how he treated his girlfriend? Jean-Luc paid more attention to Didon than to Isabella. Either he was always a jerk or something was not right between them.

They had invited Alyce to dine with them the first night—much later than she was accustomed. They went through two bottles of wine. She sensed it was Jean-Luc's idea to have her there, not Isabella's, which made her feel even more of an intruder, especially when Isabella acted as though Jean-Luc were the only man alive and Alyce wasn't even there. Plus, they rattled on in French and quickly tired of teaching her anything. But the meal was so delicious she let their indecipherable conversation wash over her and hoped it would soak into her brain like sun into a plant.

The way Jean-Luc studied her also made her feel uncomfortable.

She was soon taking home leftover lunch at school to cover as her dinner in the cottage. Jean-Luc tried several times to get her to join them. She tried to say in French that she had to study; needed to eat earlier; wanted to be up at 6:00 to jog.

If she heard him say, *"Je ne comprends pas"* one more time she was going to scream. Was she that bad a French student? Really. Even taxi drivers here understood *some* English.

But oh, the wonderful aromas that wafted from his big kitchen painted a warm yellow. The wooden counters made it feel even cozier. It also had a professional eight-burner gas stove, *two* stainless-steel over-under subzero refrigerators, a wine cooler with a glass front, and every kind of pot and pan imaginable hanging above or on a wall. She often helped clean the dishes just so she could be in there and fantasize about her someday home with Nelson.

Alyce wondered about Jean-Luc's finances. That was an expensive kitchen to put together and he did have a Lexus, yet the house and grounds could look so much nicer. *So* much.

She was at her bistro table outside, finishing a ham and Brie baguette, when she heard Isabella screaming inside the house. She sure was a loud one when they made love.

Wait. Those were real screams.

"Ayúdeme! Ayúdeme!" Isabella appeared and motioned. "Come! Now! Help!"

Alyce ran inside. A red-faced, choking Jean-Luc was standing behind his dining chair, clutching the back of it with one hand while frantically pointing to his mouth with the other.

She grabbed him around the waist and did the Heimlich maneuver while Isabella prayed in Spanish. Didon joined the madness with her barking.

She couldn't help but notice he was in pretty good shape, but after two jerks terror set in.

Isabella ranted on.

Alyce yelled, "TELEPHONO AMBULANCE-O, YOU TWAT!" and gave one more mighty tug.

Jean-Luc staggered out of Alyce's arms gulping for air, reeled back into the table and laughed between gasps. In a high squeak, he managed, "*Twat!* I cannot believe you said that."

"You speak English?"

Isabella was furious, too. "You were not choking? It was a joke?"

"Yes, Al-*ees*," Jean-Luc confessed. "We speak it well. I was just having some fun." He stood up straight and threw back his shoulders. "I was getting bored!"

That did not go over well with Isabella.

"I mean I was getting bored with our *silly ruse*. I want you to join us for dinner from now on, Al-*ees*. We will make every effort to eat earlier. I need the discipline so I can write."

Isabella glared at him. Alyce marched out of the room.

She went back to her cottage and locked the door. What a couple of nuts.

A calmer Isabella stepped under the showerhead to rinse the shampoo out of her long hair. She saw the humor in his prank when he remarked, "You don't like predictable men. Remember Robbie?"

He was in his shower, seated on the stone seat built out of a chunk of Italian granite. He was at the perfect level at which to bury his face in her own *grotto d'amour*. He did not. One thing was certain. Alyce's arrival had brought out a different Isabella. She was doing everything in her power to keep him in her thrall.

She knelt before him. He pushed her away. "Not now."

"You better not be thinking about that girl."

He stroked her wet hair. "I suggest you stop mentioning her or the defiant boy in me will have to chase her."

"If you start a notebook on her, I will chase her. *Away*."

"That is too bad. I was going to write a five-volume set about her."

Soon they were back in bed. She draped her arm over his chest. He slowly began to stroke it. An owl in the woods screeched and his mind roamed to the day one of his noisy peacocks strutted by a delighted Colette, tossed his head and dropped a brilliant feather, as if presenting her with it. She became upset when she thought she lost it.

The peacocks were long gone. Not only was it pretentious to own them, he couldn't bear the sight of them anymore. He thought of swimming naked in his pool with Colette, feeling the arch of her back in his hands as she floated peacefully before him, eyes closed. Now the jars of lavender honey they made together came drifting to the surface; her long, curly brown hair pulled back into a ponytail so it wouldn't fall into it while she concentrated. She would often stop and inhale deeply.

Moments that seemed so small at the time were the ones that lasted the longest in his mind. If only there had been more. He never imagined there wouldn't be.

He gave Isabella a kiss and focused on her smoky, tarragon taste. Like a Ben Shan oolong tea, it made him crave a thin, light, orange-flavored cookie. She reached to undo the towel he was using as an absorbent sarong. His mind raced, yes/no/yes/no, until his body decided for him.

Her moans intensified until she was begging to have all of him. He reached for a condom from the supply he kept in an antique box on the nightstand.

"Where are they?"

Isabella slowly pulled out the ivory chopsticks holding up her silky mane, causing it to cascade over her bare shoulders like a river of ebony temptation. "We've been very busy, no?"

He had to be strong. "There were two left."

She looked like she wanted to poke one of the sticks in

his eye. "I am too old to get pregnant. And I never cheated on Robbie—until you, that is. I have no diseases."

She was a bad liar. "If you are too old, *then why are you taking Clomid?*"

She matched him in volume. "It's for making my periods regular, and I would appreciate it if you didn't look through my things!"

"I was looking for my razor that you borrowed!"

"Then why didn't you use it?"

"I was too angry after finding your *fertility drug*. It has nothing to do with your cycles. It is to produce more eggs!" In the past he would have physically thrown a woman right out of his home if he'd discovered such a deception. Hard times had taken the starch out of him.

He fell back on the bed, exhausted. "Isabella, if I can't take care of myself, how can I take care of a child?"

From now on, no more women. He'd had enough to last him five lifetimes.

In the most melancholy of tones, she said, "I understand now, Jean-Luc. I didn't know the extent of your troubles. But if you are losing interest in me, please be honest."

He reached for her long dark hair and gently stroked it. "Isabella, I simply cannot be what you want me to be. I cannot be what *I* want to be."

9

A Litter of Loirs. A Gaggle of Girlfriends.

Alyce's alarm went off far too early. Shuffling into her kitchen, she thought about all the homework she, again, didn't get done the night before and how poorly she was doing at school.

Bleary-eyed, she realized she was out of coffee and went in search of more. She reached for a cupboard door she hadn't opened yet.

"AAAAIIIIEEEE!"

A gray rodent resembling a shrunken squirrel jumped out and onto the counter. She stayed there, rigid with fury, on all four legs, screeching at Alyce. Behind her, in a pile of leaves, twigs, and torn up cardboard, was a glob of tiny, hairless writhing babies, eyes unopened.

"It's okay, Mama," Alyce backed away. "I'm not going to hurt you or your babies."

The mother's warning subsided into mean chirps. Her babies were so helpless and strangely beautiful that Alyce was still staring at them when Isabella—dressed only in panties and a man's unbuttoned shirt—arrived at the door with Jean-Luc's hyper dog. The mama *loir* jumped back in the cabinet, still screeching.

"What's going on?"

"Don't let Didon in here!"

She pulled Isabella inside, shut the door behind her, and tried to ignore her bare breasts. After a quick inspection, Isabella closed the cabinet door on the little animals.

"They are *loirs*. She got in through a hole in there. Kill them all or you will never sleep. Lucky she is the *glis glis*. A delicacy."

They could still hear the mother angrily chattering at them.

"Eat her?"

Isabella cocked her head. "I know just the recipe. A stuffing of pork, pignoli nuts, parsley, and anchovy paste tucked inside that little cavity, sew it all up—"

"Ewww."

Didon stopped barking when Jean-Luc appeared. He had on jeans, no shirt. Unlike the hair on his head, his chest hair was a rich dark brown.

"What the hell is the matter?" He rubbed his neck.

"*Loirs*," said Isabella.

He explained that the outdoor sonic detector that kept them away had broken and he never fixed it. Then he had the nerve to suggest, "You should have it fixed."

The pressure of being a stranger in a strange land, the humiliation of being a terrible student, the cruel we-don't-speak-English joke they'd played on her and their condescending attitude in general, opened something in Alyce akin to the mother *loir* defending her litter.

"Me fix it? Some host you are! First you pretend you don't speak English, then you—"

"Now that you know we can," his eyes narrowed, "do not irk us with questions like what does this mean, how do you say that, and what did the horse symbolize in my book."

"Don't worry, I'll be staying far away from both of you! And your damn book! I'll eat dinner alone from now on."

He punched the air with his right index finger like an

impatient person attacking an elevator button. "You will still help in the kitchen."

Her voice nearly cracked when she said, "I'm not your damn slave!"

They pulled back, more amused than insulted.

As they walked away, Isabella put her arm over the back of his low-slung jeans and curved her finger into one of the belt loops. The weight of her hand pulled down his pants a bit. He wasn't wearing underwear.

Alyce heard him mutter something, which caused Isabella to lean into him and laugh.

She hopped in the shower. Slowly her hands stopped shaking as the warm water calmed her. She finally stepped out, only to hear a commotion in the kitchen, the mother *loir* screeching again. She quickly put on her robe, heart pounding.

"What are you doing?" she asked Isabella, who was heading out the door with a pillowcase in hand, the mama *loir* fighting to escape.

"No!!" Alyce tried to wrest it from her. "How will her babies survive? I don't mind them!"

A tug-of-war ensued with Isabella repeatedly yelling "Yes!" to Alyce's "No!"

"We are eating her! *You* can be the babies' mother."

Alyce let go out of shock. The horror of what was about to happen left her gulping back tears. Couldn't they have waited until the babies were bigger?

It hit her that one man's adorable pet was another's pest. And food. Nelson once told her when he was in Machu Picchu, he was invited into the home of a native family. He saw furry animals that looked like guinea pigs roaming all over. He thought they were pets. Turned out they were their main source of protein.

She came to France to have an adventure. She was getting one.

She also recalled Nelson saying, "Machu Picchu is one of the most amazing places on earth. I'd love to go there with you one day. In fact, I'd love to see lots of places with you."

Her heart melted into a big gooey pool then. He saw a future with her. Not long after that he was singing a different song. What happened? And what made him suddenly want to be with her again? Was it as simple as seeing a therapist; putting an ocean between them?

On her iPhone she Googled *loirs* (after spelling it wrong many times).

Alyce learned they were also known as dormice. Photos showed them sleeping on their backs, curled into tiny balls, with little pink hands and feet dangling, cute as could be. They'd open their eyes in three weeks, eventually eating berries, leafy green vegetables, and nuts. They were particularly fond of apples. Dry dog food was also acceptable. Right now they needed milk.

She called Liliane and told her she had to miss school and why. She expected Liliane to scold her over the notion of caring for baby rodents.

"You are having strong maternal urges, Al-*ees*?"

Sounding almost guilty about it, she answered, "Yes."

"I understand, very much so. My husband found a litter of abandoned newborn kittens when we were dating. We took turns feeding them warm milk with an eyedropper. It was sad when we had to find them new homes. It was also what prompted us to start our own family."

She paused. "One day, our boys convinced us to get an aquarium. We filled it with fish and plants. They quickly lost interest and the fish died. We will not be doing that again. I can give you the aquarium for the babies to nest in. I have an eyedropper somewhere. I will pick them up at lunchtime and bring them to you. I need to see Jean-Luc about something anyway."

"That would be wonderful!"

Alyce spent the morning coaxing the babies to lick warm

milk off her finger. As they twisted, squeaked, and instinctively pulled in the direction of her hand, a wonderful feeling surged through her.

There was one thing she could do well.

Around 1:00 she was distracted by the sound of a horn honking and another woman's voice coming from Jean-Luc's kitchen as well as Liliane's. She thought about wandering over but was afraid she'd see a butchered mama *loir*.

Her curiosity and hunger pangs got the better of her.

A petite Asian woman was showing her diamond engagement ring to a mildly interested Jean-Luc, smiling Liliane, and envious Isabella.

"If it had not been for Jean-Luc I would not have known how wonderful Paul was."

Everyone's head turned toward Alyce.

"Am I interrupting? I just wanted something from the refrigerator."

"Hello." Mazuki eyed her with curiosity.

Liliane said, "Don't worry. I brought us lunch."

Jean-Luc explained Alyce was a student of Liliane's staying in his cottage.

Mazuki shook Alyce's hand. "*Enchanté.* Just remember, there's no one better than Jean-Luc for fun. If you keep it in the right perspective, it won't be so bad when it's over."

Before Alyce could correct her, Isabella did it for her. "*I am his lover, not her!*"

Jean-Luc sighed, held out his hand. His sister placed an envelope in it. He examined its contents, divided it in half between the two women. Oddly, they seemed reluctant to take it.

Liliane shook her finger. "That is more than you owe them. Why do you do that? And now that Mazuki has claimed her car, what will you drive?"

"I will make more money, it would have cost the same to rent a car, and Isabella needs cash for a plane ticket." Isabella looked like she had been punched in the stomach. "Isn't that what we decided last night?" he asked, sounding confused.

"I didn't think you meant it!"

An awkward silence followed. Alyce felt she should hightail it back to her cottage but was too transfixed to leave.

Mazuki interjected, "I am sorry, Isabella. I should have told *you* what I said to Al-*ees*."

Isabella, knowing she could not win, asked her, "Could you give me a ride to the train station? I will only be a few minutes."

She fled the room after taking the money from Jean-Luc.

Then it hit Alyce. "Did you eat the mother *loir* already?"

Jean-Luc said, "She is marinating in the refrigerator. Would you like it, Liliane? I don't care for it. I told Isabella not to bother."

"Thank you, I will," his sister answered.

Bile rose in Alyce's throat. She ran to her cottage in time to dry heave into the toilet.

When she came out, Jean-Luc was placing the aquarium on the dining table. Liliane had a shopping bag with her.

"I thought we could eat together, Al-*ees*," she said.

"*Merci*," Alyce said, "but I don't have an appetite now."

"I must work," said Jean-Luc. Before he left, he added, "I am very sorry for what Isabella did. She was just threatened by you."

"So she killed an animal? A *mother*?"

"I bring out the best and worst in women."

Once the aquarium was set up and the babies securely in it and asleep, Alyce was ravenous. They ate their baguette sandwiches with fresh local tomatoes, cheese, arugula, and mustard at her bistro table by the Tree of Love. They could hear the faint typing of Jean-Luc at his computer through his office window on the second floor. It was far enough away that they could speak without being heard.

Liliane squinted as though deep in thought. "I admire your

determination to learn French. I think you will get it in time. Often it is not a gradual incline but big leaps, then a plateau."

That was reassuring, but she still couldn't imagine speaking anything close to understandable French.

"You are welcome to babysit anytime," she said. "It would help you with your French, my boys with their English—" she gave Alyce a wink "—and give me time with my husband."

"I'd love that."

"Of course we will pay you."

"Oh, no," she protested. "Well, maybe if I have to move into a hotel."

"Let us hope that will not happen."

Alyce refilled their glasses of apricot-rosemary tea.

"How is everything going there?" Liliane asked.

Alyce wasn't sure where to begin. "Well, unpredictable, I'd say."

"A nice way of putting it." She pursed her lips. Oh, the stories Alyce knew she could tell.

She thought Liliane was through with the topic of her brother when she said, "Jean-Luc has had a difficult life, Al-*ees,* and he is an artist. Put the two together and you have a radio that does not tune into the frequency of real life. It can be tiring, but he is so intelligent and entertaining it is impossible not to love him—just like a little boy."

Alyce struggled with a question. "Do you and Jean-Luc have the same parents?"

It turned out they were half-siblings with the same mother who was no longer alive. Jean-Luc's father left when he was a child.

"It was easy for *Maman* to spoil him since she was so alone. He also had the energy of a hurricane. Most geniuses do. Later, when I was a child, she married my father, an Algerian. He took the much-needed upper hand. Jean-Luc was 16 and fled to Paris.

"He soon found success with his first novel. It proved to

be too much, too young. He lost his mind and spent time in a sanitarium. I did not know him well until he wrote *Renée*, which the publisher changed to *The Horse*. Did he hate that title! Until it was a hit." She shook her head. "He was so overwhelmed. I wanted a closer relationship with him. I helped him."

Alyce put down her baguette. "Could you go back to the lost-his-mind part?"

Her head tilted to the left as she considered how to answer. "He hit bottom. He needed to. Now he is much stronger. But he has a new demon. Growing old. He is 38 and thinks he has one foot in the grave."

Her candor prompted Alyce to say, "I can see why. He already looks dead."

Liliane burst out laughing. It made Alyce feel good to crack up a woman so poised at all times. She also felt bad for saying it.

"You should have seen him when he had a tan and dark hair," Liliane said. "Quite the lady-killer. What am I saying? Women swoon over him just as much now."

"Don't count me among them."

"That is good to hear."

Alyce sat back and inhaled the country air. She didn't want this lunch to end. She wanted to know more about Jean-Luc.

"Liliane, I get the impression he's not good with money. To me, that's a turnoff."

"I'm with you, Al-*ees*." She told Alyce that her brother had made a lot but would overspend on women, friends, the less fortunate. "Or he gives it to the fire department, my school, the police. He is greatly admired here for his generosity but does not know how to look out for himself. He needs a good, sensible woman. If only he would surrender. I fear he never will."

Liliane shook her head, sat back, and pushed her half-eaten sandwich away.

"Is something wrong?"

An expression came over her Alyce had never seen before: guardedly warm.

"Morning sickness is not confined to mornings."

"Oh!"

"I meant what I said about babysitting. Simon and I would like to have a little fun before we're tied down again."

Why was everyone getting pregnant around her? First her sister, now Liliane. "I'd love to help. You're happy about this, right?"

"It's unexpected, but good." She added wearily, "Jean-Luc is going to have to sell this property, though. I cannot keep helping him."

A vivid image of living here with Nelson and their children made Alyce smile.

The painful thought of Jean-Luc losing his home did not.

BESOTTED

Alyce was sitting at her cottage bistro table with her *French is Fun* book, trying to figure out when to use "le" and when to use "la" when her cell started playing the samba music she'd chosen as her ringtone.

"*Bonjour, mademoiselle. Ees thees ze sex-ziest womahn een ze world?*"

"Nelson!"

"I wanted to hear your voice, honey."

"Awwww. That's so sweet."

"What are you doing and what are you wearing?" After she told him, he said, "Sure you don't want to come home now?"

She dropped her pen. "I thought you were coming here."

Still sounding sweet as can be, "Come on, you made your point, sexy."

She wasn't sure how to respond.

He filled her silence with "You know what I mean. That you can live without me but I can't live without you."

A warm rush zapped her face. Her lips tingled. It intensified when he said, "I just want us to be the way we were."

He went on in his privileged voice about "all the places we'll see together in this big wide world, the sooner the better." Alyce barely heard him after that, though she came back to earth when he said, "I'm sending you a credit card that earns points toward almost any airline." Huh? No man had ever done that for her before. "I know you won't go crazy with it, one of the many things I like about you. Not that I don't enjoy spending money on someone I adore, but I don't want to feel used, either."

"I don't blame you."

She was absolutely certain God was listening to her when he said, "Ally, when you emailed me that your host's property was going to be sold and it used to be a winery and was now run down and needed a lot of work... well, I talked it over with my parents and if it's as good as it sounds, I might buy it. I'll have my own business *and* be far away from my mother. And how cool would that be, to own a vineyard in the South of France! What do you think?"

This time she nearly dropped her phone.

In the six months they dated, he'd talked about buying a foreign car dealership, starting a restaurant, launching a website, and other ideas so he could retire by 40 (seven years away).

"Nelson, you know I'll support you in whatever you want to do. If it doesn't work out, life goes on. Regretting not trying would be worse."

"I love you, Ally."

He said the L-word.

"I love you, too, Nelson."

"I'm so glad to hear that. I wish I were there right now. I need to *feel* you, baby."

She closed her eyes and moaned, "Mmmmm. I need to feel you, too."

His business voice jarred her. "Of course, my parents will be helping financially. Mother wants to see it and other properties, too. And you."

See how much she'd *transformed and broadened* herself was more like it.

His voice went sweet again. "Then it'll just be you and me, sweetheart. How about we take a quick trip to Paris?"

"*Très bien.*"

"Shall I get us a hotel while I'm in Marlaison? That writer probably wants to be alone with his girlfriend."

She thought she saw Jean-Luc in the kitchen eyeing her. "Actually, she just left."

"It's just the two of you?"

"I hardly see him. He's either holed up in his office or I'm studying."

"I don't like the idea of you being there alone with him."

"Oh, please. I'm not remotely interested in him and I'm hardly his type. It'll be so romantic if you come here compared to a hotel. And if you're thinking of buying this place, it'll be a test drive." She sat down and pouted. "All I do is think of you, sweetie. All this beauty and charm and you're not here to share it with me."

"Oh, honey. I'll be there before you know it. I'm sorry I'll just miss your birthday. But I'll make it up to you in Paris."

Before they hung up, she told him she was changing her email address. "It's just Alyce dot Donovan at gmail. I'm not a media grrrl anymore."

"Sure, honey, but you may not be a Donovan much longer either."

Her arms turned into one solid zingy goose bump.

But the best part of their conversation was that neither You-know-who nor their child was mentioned once.

My sexy amour,

Itinerary coming in a separate email. Can't wait to see you!

I Googled Jean-Luc. There were a lot of articles on him in French but you know how it is when you hit the Translate This Page button. It comes out pretty bizarre. I did learn he's never been married or had kids and has quite a reputation with the ladies. If you're a Francophile, he's an American-vile. Can't stand us. Sure you don't want to get a hotel? xoxo
N

He attached a photo of himself at a *Music World* magazine party with a famous actor. Damn, he was cute. Cuter than the actor, she thought. There was something about his face, his scent, that still made her stomach tighten.

She considered Nelson owning a vineyard. Here. With her. It was insane. But good insane. Bad insane: an email from Glorianna.

Re: Coming to visit

To: Alyce Donovan <Alyce.Donovan@gmail.com>

Fr: Glorianna.Mansfield <gmansfield@aol.com>

Darling Alyce,

Didn't I tell you your trip was the best thing you could do to reel in my little Nelson? He was absolutely besotted the moment you slipped away. I can't wait to see how France has changed you. I can see you now, all chic and sophisticated. (I highly approve of the new email address.)

Now, before I come I need you to...

The Password

"*Bonjour*, Jean-Luc."

"It is a delight to see you, Pauline."

They did the South of France customary three-cheek kiss, right/left/right. He invited her in. She immediately began taking notes.

Appointed by his sister to be their real estate broker, he had heard she just left her husband, or he left her. They had been miserable for years. Jean-Luc always enjoyed flirting with her when she was unattainable. Now?

"So much character!" she trilled.

Absent-mindedly he answered, "Yes, yes. So much character."

He watched her from behind as she headed toward the kitchen. There was nothing like a recently liberated woman: vulnerable, insatiable, and pumped up by friends and family with the conviction that she was wiser, stronger, and better off without her no-good husband. He could spot one instantly. Caution stiffened the knees, the desire to surrender swished around in her ass.

He had finished his mural and needed to write, dammit! Pauline would have to wait.

He needed a car, too. Fast. With those odious Americans coming to visit Alyce (she certainly wasted no time telling them about his misfortune), it would be thoroughly emasculating if he did not have his own chariot. It would also be obvious he was broke. They would swoop in like vultures.

"The kitchen is superb," Pauline cooed. "You were wise to update it. The rest of the house, hmm, it wouldn't take too much to make it presentable." As she scribbled away, she said, "How do you really feel about selling, Jean-Luc?"

He gave a Gallic shrug. "Do you mean how desperate am I?"

"I would use the word flexible."

He did feel, at times, a deep sadness from all the sentiment attached to his home, especially its connection to Colette. Or was imprisonment a more accurate description? A glorious elation put the wind in his sagging sails when he envisioned walking away for good and starting over somewhere else—as long as his new place was to his liking. That would take a good amount of money.

"Liliane tells me you have no mortgage," she said, to fill the silence.

"Yes, I will be flexible. But I want to buy another home, of course. It is in your best interest to sell this for as much as possible."

A pleased grin filled her 40ish face that still looked youthful.

He directed her outside. "Is there something wrong with the swimming pool?"

"No. I never use it."

She gave him an odd look. "It's a big selling point. I strongly recommend opening it up and showing it off."

A nasty edge came forth. "Let people use their imagination."

Pauline shook her head and jotted down a note. "Let's look at the cottage."

"I have a tenant in there. She should be here when you do that."

"She?" Pauline teased. She nevertheless walked over and peered in the window. "What's in that aquarium?"

"Pet *loirs*."

"They must go immediately!"

She wrote another note that Jean-Luc took a look at. *Poison*.

"That won't be necessary. I can fix the sonic detector that keeps them away."

"My way is cheaper."

He did not look forward to broaching the subject with Alyce. He found her attachment to them oddly comforting. Heartbreaking, too. She could not be their mother forever.

C'est la vie.

She looked around. "Where did you make the wine?"

He took her into the basement filled with the aromas of oak, earth, stone, and dust. As she looked around, he opened the cupboard that now held only two jars of lavender honey.

Pauline was delighted with his gift. She hesitated with an expectant look. For a moment he thought she might be the perfect woman for him. For a moment.

He cleared his throat, took her elbow, and led her out into the sun.

Her hope was still there when she asked, "Are you free for dinner tonight? I hate to cook for myself."

He did have to eat at some point. But at her place? Too cozy.

"If you treat me to dinner at a restaurant as you would any client, I won't say no."

That met, somewhat, with her approval.

As he finished signing the contract that would give her 5% of the selling price, the damn American girl arrived. Pauline sized her up while he explained to Alyce, in English, who she was and that she'd like to see the cottage.

"Sure. It's open. I only lock it at night."

Jean-Luc found that comical.

Pauline sighed, relieved to get that piece of information. "Do you wish to accompany me?" she asked Alyce.

Jean-Luc touched her arm. "I need to discuss something with you."

The broker arched an eyebrow as she tried to determine just what was going on here. "I won't be long," she said. "Then we'll be on our way."

Alyce saw the contract on the table, the pen still in Jean-Luc's hand. "Wait, Pauline. Did Jean-Luc tell you my boyfriend has an interest in buying this place? He's flying over in a week."

Pauline's chin went up a bit.

"In America," Alyce said, "the seller pays a commission to the broker. Is that how it works here?"

"Yes," she answered curtly. "I see where this is going."

Alyce turned to Jean-Luc. "Wouldn't you like to save tens of thousands of dollars?"

He stared at her, dumbfounded. Not giving Pauline a commission for a sale she had nothing to do with never entered his mind.

Alyce nodded at the contract. "Please put Nelson Mansfield down as a noncommissionable buyer."

Jean-Luc felt highly uncomfortable. Yet, she was right. He had to start being smart about his finances. "If Pauline makes no effort at all to sell it to him and has nothing to do with the negotiation, I agree with you."

Pauline did little to mask her disappointment. After she headed out the door to see the cottage, Alyce said, "Are you okay with what I just said? I'm trying to help you."

"I hate to be helped."

"Well, *excuuuse* me." She ran tap water into a glass and took a sip.

He walked to the screen door and watched Pauline go into

the cottage. "I do appreciate what you did, Al-*ees*. I am just having a hard time imagining anyone else living here."

"So what's the story with her? Another girlfriend? You don't waste time, do you?"

"I live my life and women appear. We will be going to dinner. Can you manage on your own?"

"Tonight?"

He detected delight in her voice. "Invite Julien Devreaux over?"

She loudly put down her glass. "Does everybody know everything about me here?"

"Have fun before your boyfriend arrives. Flings do not count when they take place in other countries."

"Says who. Wait, can I use your computer while you're out?"

She needed access to the Internet and explained the shortcomings of the school computers.

"No one is allowed on mine."

"*Please*, Jean-Luc. I haven't written my parents more than a couple of sentences."

"*No.*"

Her hands rested defiantly on her hips. "Everything's negotiable. What can I do for you to let me use your computer that doesn't involve sex?"

He forced himself not to laugh. "Don't flatter yourself." He gazed out the window and saw Pauline heading back already.

"I will let you use it if you can figure out how I can let go of the past."

His sudden openness surprised them both. They stood there, he with the pen in hand, clicking the point in and out as though a clock were ticking.

She leaned on the counter with one arm. "Focus on the future."

"Then I cannot write my memoir."

"It is quite charming," Pauline stated as she hastily came through the kitchen door. "You are a student of Liliane's?"

"*Oui*, Madame."

"How long are you planning to be here?'

"Until the middle of July. Unless Nelson buys this. Otherwise, it's back to America." She lifted her left hand and smiled. "Hopefully with a ring on my finger."

Her confidence restored, Pauline strode in front of Jean-Luc and toward the front door. He pulled Alyce close. "The password to get on the computer is Colette. *Do not share that with anyone and do not move a thing.* It may look a mess to you. It is an organized mess to me."

"Jean-Luc," Pauline called out. "I forgot to look upstairs."

Alyce sat in the kitchen as Jean-Luc and Pauline toured the upper level she had yet to see. Before long she heard a peal of laughter from Pauline and wondered what that was about. She crept to the hallway by the staircase. She picked up a few words.

Different. Good. Bad.

Finally they were off into the night.

Jean-Luc's office was at the top of the entryway stairs, to the left. To the right was his bedroom. Both were at the back of the house; their windows faced Alyce's cottage. Two other shut doors at the front of the house, she guessed, were more bedrooms or closets. The hallway, like the downstairs, looked like it once had lots of paintings hanging in it.

Alyce figured as long as this place was going on the market and Nelson might be the buyer, why not look around a bit? Really, that was all she intended to do.

She peeked in his bedroom. It was dark and tropical with a large bamboo four-poster bed that looked like it had been made for a jungle king. Crimson silk panels fell from rods that ran between the posters. The room smelled wonderfully spicy.

She checked out his bathroom. Almost every surface was covered in beautiful Italian tiles. She saw what must have amused Pauline. The shower had no door or curtain and looked like a cave that had been hollowed out of a rock. There was a stone seat Alyce was sure he used for more than just sitting on to clip his toenails.

My, my. How would Nelson feel about this, she wondered. He'd either love it or hate it. She rather liked it and sat on the stone seat to try it out. She closed her eyes and imagined having a little fun with Nelson right there. Oh, yeah.

One room in the front of the house was for guests. She could still feel Isabella's anger and heartbreak in it. The other across the hall was locked. What was behind it?

What ate at her far more was *Who was Colette?*

She settled in at his cluttered desk and started to research vineyards for sale in the South of France. One of the first things she learned was that land was measured in *hectares*, the equivalent of 2.471 acres. Some of the properties were enormous, much bigger than Jean-Luc's 48 *hectares*. Glorianna would love them. Alyce thought under 50 was just fine.

She'd never forget the first time Nelson took her to his parents' house. A black wrought-iron gate swung open and they floated up a long driveway that led to a Tudor mansion. She felt like she'd been shot in the head with Novocain, followed by a sick feeling that she was so not worthy of him. She smiled a lot, said little. His mother did most of the talking.

Wanting to jot down a few things now, Alyce opened the top drawer in Jean-Luc's desk hoping to find blank paper. She spotted a large, old key; the kind made of metal with a loop at one end and a few teeth at the other.

Maybe it opened the door in the hall? She'd see if it fit and if not, put it back.

No, that would be snooping.

As is often the case when she got on a computer with a

high-speed connection, the time flew by as she went off on all kinds of ridiculous and informative tangents. At one point she Googled Jean-Luc and was amazed at how much she found as well as how much she understood that was in French. It was speaking it that was impossible.

There were mainly glowing reviews of his books; interviews where he sounded intelligent and sensitive; bits on his outrageous life; and mentions of his mother, Stephanie, with photos of her at different ages. Nothing about a Colette.

She shut down his computer, lingered at his bedroom door. Pauline seemed like the "good, sensible woman" Liliane hoped he would find. Alyce hoped they would last.

She noticed the time. It was getting late. He probably wouldn't be home tonight. She gave that old metal key one last look.

It easily went in the lock to the door down the hall.

The room was dark. A photo fluttered down from somewhere and landed almost at her feet. She took a quick glance at it while she cursed. Where was it supposed to go? As her eyes began to adjust to the darkness, she saw a large white oval on one wall. She felt around for a light switch.

Too late. Through the window she could see a pair of headlights coming down Jean-Luc's long dirt road.

Dammit. Shit! The photo.

She left it on the floor, hoping it would look like it fell accidentally.

She slammed the door, fumbled with the lock, her heart racing.

She ran back to his office, put the key where she found it and flew down the stairs as quickly and quietly as she could, thanking God she didn't fall.

A car door closed outside the front door as she passed.

She sped up and really fell in the kitchen, knocking over a high stool.

SHIT!

Just as she got it upright again the front door opened.

She eased through the sliding kitchen door and ran to her cottage, never looking back.

Out of breath, she wiped the sweat from her neck and brow with a dishtowel. Her little *loirs* sensed her pacing, panting presence and began their chorus of chirps. When she calmed down, she fed them one by one while applying ice wrapped up in a towel to her left thigh.

She thought about the photo she had seen. It had been torn in half, leaving an image of a woman sitting at a bar, her eyes filled with happiness. Colette? She appeared to be middle-aged, had short blonde hair, and was a little chubby, from what she could see. She expected a stunning woman would have been the love of Jean-Luc's life, not one so ordinary.

She couldn't ask anyone about her. That would mean admitting she snooped.

She had to find out who she was. She had a feeling it would explain a lot.

The Bad Boy Nap

The next day, Alyce took a different route home after school and found herself riding her bicycle on the boutique and café-lined Avenue Gambetta. She had never seen sidewalks covered with dates. They'd fallen from the plentiful palm trees. It made her think of Nelson and how she would show them to him and he would smile, she was certain.

She rode by a café where Julien Devreaux and a friend were sitting outside. His long dark hair fell carelessly into a brooding face that lit up the moment he saw her. Somehow her bicycle turned around. He was just too ah-dor-*ah*-blah. (Didn't that sound better than a-*door*-ah-bul?).

He gallantly put her bicycle against the wall, pulled out a chair, and introduced his friend Fabrice, who gave her an appreciative glance.

"Al-*ees*, what luck to see you. Sit, sit!"

After they exchanged pleasantries, Fabrice asked, with a hint of a smirk, "How is your French coming along?"

"Slowly."

"Have they taught you the word *jouissance* yet?"

She could tell by Julien's raised eyebrows that Fabrice was having fun.

"No, what does it mean? Americans who act like idiots?"

He sat up straight and in a perfectly serious manner said, "It means orgasmic." He looked to Julien for agreement.

He was having a hard time keeping a straight face. "You are close. It is the moment *before* the orgasm!"

Even Alyce laughed along. She could well imagine what Fabrice already knew about her and was determined to not care, or at least not show it.

Fabrice politely excused himself and went inside the café.

"Al-*ees*, where are you staying now?" Julien wasted no time asking. When she told him, he clapped his head in disbelief. "Jean-Luc Broussard is your *host?*"

She remembered Liliane's warning to be discreet and regretted telling him.

"But he is so private and famous for disliking Amer—"

"I know. Please don't let anyone know I'm there."

"Certainly."

He said he had all of Jean-Luc's books, and his two bestsellers in English as well. "Would you like to read them?"

"Sure, I'm curious." Though she had a feeling she wouldn't like them.

Julien ordered her a glass of wine. While casually sipping his and trying to look older than 22, he told her Jean-Luc's vineyard had almost succeeded.

"He did not give it enough time. He plunged into writing *The Horse* and that was that."

"I could never live like he does," Alyce said. "It's too unpredictable."

"Most artists cannot live any other way. But what a character he is. He once drove a brand-new Lamborghini Countach into a lake. An Italian countess had given it to him. He was insulted she would give him such a gift, as though he were her plaything."

His next Jean-Luc story was about a critic who made disparaging remarks about one of his books.

"He wedged his car between two palm trees. The critic had to have a fender removed to get it out. He would have been run out of town if he'd cut down one of the trees. Oh, this is the best one. Jean-Luc lost a bet and had to ride a large pig down the street naked!" He clutched his side, laughing at the image. "How can you not love someone like that?"

"Considering how many women have," Alyce said, "I would say you can't love him for very long."

"Ah, this is so." He turned serious. He slid his chair in so he could be closer to Alyce. "I am going to stop talking about him this instant. He is my rival now."

She took a sip of wine as though it were perfectly natural to be drinking in the middle of the day. "Nelson is your rival. He's coming in six days."

Julien's face darkened. "Why do you torture me so, Al-*ees*?"

Fabrice returned but did not sit down as he and Julien chatted a mile a minute. Alyce was able to gather they were talking about skiing, but that didn't make sense in the month of May.

As the boys talked, she studied the perfect blue sky. It wasn't a light blue, but a deep one that easily lulled her into a state of tranquility; a state Jean-Luc did not seem to know. What a strange, fascinating, *hopeless* mix he was.

After Julien's friend left, he said, "We are planning a ski trip to Argentina. We go every summer, when it is winter there."

"I was right!"

Ulrike and Jutta, two German girls from the school, waved to her from across the street, causing her to tell herself to get over her insecurities and start hanging out with them more.

"Look," Julien nodded to an older, chic woman sitting several tables away. She was reading *The Horse*.

"Tell me," Alyce asked in almost a whisper, "was there someone who broke Jean-Luc's heart?"

He took out a pack of cigarettes and put it away when he saw her horrified expression. "Not that I'm aware of. It has been the other way around many times. Why?"

"I just wondered why he never settled down with someone. What's he afraid of? It doesn't seem normal to want to be alone."

"Jean-Luc Broussard is rarely alone."

"You know what I mean."

He studied his wine glass, hair in his face. Finally, he looked up. "I think it is admirable he has not fallen into the cliché of the artist who needs a family to get away from in order to create. He could easily have done that to be socially respectable and then live a double life—if not multiple ones—with other women and children. In those cases, everyone feels cheated, but the man. He just feels *very* tired."

They exchanged another flirtatious glance.

Alyce asked him to teach her insults in French that she could use on Jean-Luc.

"No, he will kick you out if you say these things."

She considered his reaction to her use of the word twat. "I doubt that."

"There is one term you must know, though it is not an insult. *Sieste crapuleuse.*"

She tried to figure out what he was saying. "*Sieste* sounds like siesta."

"Good, good."

"*Crapuleuse?*" She threw up her hands. "Loose crap?"

He shook his head. "No. It comes from *crapuleux,* which means crime. *Crapuleuse* is more, how would you say it? Villainous?"

"I think I'm getting it."

"The Bad Boy Nap. What do you think happens during the

midday break when the stores close? Everyone just goes home to eat lunch?"

She hated to admit it, but such a nap with Julien didn't sound like a bad idea. If she really was going to be Mrs. Mansfield for the rest of her life, shouldn't she have a *little* fun before sealing off all the exits?

Her birthday was tomorrow. She could ask the two German students to celebrate with her, but knew she'd end up going on about Nelson and missing him terribly. Or spend an evening with Liliane and her family and end up wishing she had what Liliane had with Simon but with Nelson. Perhaps she should consider Julien a present to herself. But that would lead to missing Nelson even more.

She threw her handbag over her shoulder. "I need to be going."

Julien didn't want her to leave. She stayed. Did she have anything better to do?

They shifted to the subject of his real mother, who drowned when he was 13. His stepmother-to-be zeroed in on his dad and never let go. She quickly became pregnant, they married, his cheating started.

"I feel more like a referee than a son."

Alyce wondered what she would do if she married Nelson and found out he was unfaithful. Carmelita's face popped into her head. Her only encounter with her was in the ladies' room at the Manhattan mega-toy store F.A.O. Schwarz. Nelson was meeting her there to do a "switch-up" with Junior (after he plunked down $500 on various stuff she was sure the boy would have no interest in the following month).

Alyce recognized her from photos she'd seen at Nelson's apartment. There was one of her and Junior done by a professional when his son was still a toddler. It was nicely framed and prominently displayed in his living room.

"I feel obligated to my son to keep it out," he'd said.

She wished he'd put it away in between visits but said nothing. Wanting to come off as unthreatened, she said, "She's pretty."

He showed her another where she was more natural. She was grinning so much you could see a prominent gold tooth.

Sometimes Alyce put herself in Carmelita's place. She wanted a better life and she took the only path she knew how to get it. Could Alyce blame her?

When Alyce saw her in the ladies' room at the toy store that day, she put on a smile and introduced herself. Carmelita had the nerve to say, "I know you must be havin' a good time with him because I taught him *everything*."

Alyce refused to be intimidated. "Thank you. You did a great job."

She kept coating her full lips with dark red lipstick. "That's right, Annie."

"Alyce."

"What-evah. I stopped rememberin' the names a long time ago."

She flashed her metallic smile and turned on a spike heel, leaving Alyce holding her leather purse so tightly it was permanently damaged from sinking her nails into it.

"Al-*ees*? Are you listening?"

"Sorry, Julien. Lot on my mind."

This time she got up to go for real.

"Julien, would you like to have dinner tomorrow night? It's my birthday."

"I would be honored to celebrate with you."

"How about at my cottage? We can cook." He brushed his hair out of his eyes to get a better look at his good fortune. "First, though, I have to see how Jean-Luc feels about it."

"I will not be upset or surprised if he does not agree. I will take you out."

"I'll text you." Flashing a smile, she said, "You're so cute."

"Dogs are cute. I am sexy."

When she arrived home, she walked through Jean-Luc's kitchen (no more walking all the way around the house through grass that hadn't been cut in ages now that Isabella was gone) and spied dirty dishes on the counter. Better to get them out of the way before more joined them. She plugged up one sink, filled it with soapy water, and pulled on long yellow plastic gloves.

He appeared a few moments later looking annoyed. What was his problem now?

"Al-*ees*, how am I supposed to work when women cannot stay away from me."

Good grief. What an ego. "Stay away from *them*."

"Precisely. Why do they take it so personally?"

She slid some leftovers into Didon's dish. "Once you sleep with someone, Jean-Luc, it's pretty hard not to take things personally. Stay away from women *before* you—"

"I did! I told Pauline I was not interested and she persists in inviting me out." He rested his index finger on his chin. "Where were you?"

Going back to the sink, she answered, "What are you, my father?"

In a low voice he snarled, "American she-devil."

She wheeled around. "Your insults are like the birds that fly into the windows here and bounce off the screens." She pretended she had just done the same and teetered with a stunned expression. "Boing! No harm done."

"A most beautiful simile, Al-*ees*!" She thought he was going to hug her until he said, "If you weren't from the United States, I might like you."

"A man intelligent as you hating an entire nationality seems pretty dumb to me."

"Mmmm," he responded, as if he relished her harsh words.

She remembered one insult Julien taught her, held her right yellow-gloved arm out straight, slapped the soapy left one on the bicep and brought her right hand back sharply toward her face, sending water and bubbles everywhere.

"*Va te faire foutre.*"

His eyebrows arched. "Most women don't tell me to fuck off until they know me better."

"You really are pathetic."

"That is true."

"Incidentally," she said, as she scrubbed coffee stains out of a cup, "I'd like to have a guest for dinner tomorrow. May we use your wonderful kitchen?"

"No."

"So then you'll cook for us?"

"Is it your lover Julien?"

"We're *friends.*"

Reaching over her and the sink, he turned off the water and pulled off her gloves.

"Come, let's have a glass of wine. And you will tell me why you are *friends* with Julien when you are supposed to be in love with Nelson."

He set out a baguette, room-temperature brie, and insisted she try them together. She inhaled a bite and washed it down with two gulps of a local rosé that hardly tasted alcoholic.

"I came here to improve myself and get over Nelson, if he didn't want me back."

She went to cut another slab of cheese across its bottom and was stopped by the firm grasp of Jean-Luc's hand.

"Please cut the cheese wedge from the side so it retains its shape."

She stared at him a moment. "Is that a French thing, a Jean-Luc thing, or are you gay?"

She didn't wait for an answer as she gulped down more of the cheese, baguette, and wine. Oh, that cheese. It had an earthy scent, and a taste that went from robust to almost burning her throat, and yet she could have eaten the whole wedge right there.

"Stop eating and drinking so fast! Savor it!"

"Okay, okay." She put her glass down. Between the wine with Julien and this, she was getting schnockered. "So I was sure it was over with Nelson but it isn't over, so nothing is happening with Julien."

"You are exhibiting remarkable restraint. I hope it works out with your Nelson." "So do I. How long were you and Isabella together?"

"Not long at all."

"What happened?" She brought the yummy snack to her mouth and took a delicate bite instead of shoving it in.

"I did not love her and never would. It is as simple as that."

Alyce wanted to ask him about the woman in the photo but couldn't let him know she'd found it. "Jean-Luc, how many times have you been in true love?"

"I am not sure. Either countless times or never. Why?"

"I was just wondering who Colette was."

He seemed to clench his teeth. "Why do you say that?"

"You know, your password on your computer."

He rubbed his stubbly chin, as though thinking about whether to tell her something. "She was a dog I loved very much that died. Now I must work."

"What kind of dog? Do you have a photo?"

"No! And never mention her again!"

She knew the French loved their dogs, but that seemed an extreme reaction.

"I will do the cooking tomorrow night as my birthday gift to you."

Nothing like changing the subject. "That's so sweet. Thank you." Another thought hit her as she turned to leave. "Are you sure it's not because you're afraid I'll screw up something in your kitchen?"

He didn't answer.

"And you need an excuse not to write?"

"That, too."

As she made her way back to her cottage, she gazed again at the pool and wished she could swim in it. Perhaps Pauline would see to it that it was fixed.

La Vie en *Rogues*

Alyce was surprised when Liliane poked her head in her class-room door and motioned for her to come out.

Once in the hallway, she said, "There is something you need to see."

"Your timing couldn't be better. We were about to do a con-versation exercise."

She thought they were going to her office but instead kept walking. When they reached the *pétanque* court, Liliane pointed in the air. Alyce leaned back. Written in white smoke against the pure blue sky:

HAPPY BIRTHDAY ALLY

SEE YOU SOON

XO NM

"Omigod! I can't believe he did that!"

Liliane smiled. "Ah, to be adored by a man whom you adore in return."

Alyce took out her phone and snapped photos. During the next break she couldn't resist sending one to her sister, Chantilly. Her husband had never done anything that over-the-top.

Liliane gave Alyce a handcrafted birthday card from her two sons that put her on the verge of tears. She easily translated: *To Alyce who is getting better with her French. We love you, Stéphane and Benoit.*

Back home, Jean-Luc said to her, when they passed in the kitchen, *"Bon anniversaire,* Al-*ees.* You have a palpable glow today."

She showed him photos of the skywriting.

He sniffed. "No imagination."

She sniffed even harder. "Well, I loved it."

Before she exited toward her cottage in a huff, he said, "I could use some help preparing dinner. You may consider absorbing my great culinary wisdom a birthday present, too."

She was in too good of a mood to let his self-importance get to her. "But of course. Thirty minutes, okay?"

"D'accord."

She returned to his kitchen showered, hair still damp, skin perfumed, but not, Jean-Luc noticed, sporting a seductive outfit. She had on jeans and a loose blouse.

"That is what you are wearing?"

"I told you, Julien and I are just friends." She reached for a bowl of black olives on the counter and popped one in her mouth. "What's for dinner?"

"An essential dish that even you could manage. A roasted chicken." He produced it, uncooked, from the refrigerator. "It is from a neighbor's farm. What is wrong?"

"It looks sick. A chicken is supposed to be yellow. This one is practically white."

Mon Dieu! She was the most culturally deprived woman he'd ever known. "This is what a real chicken looks like! Not some hormone-fed creature."

He could not wait to tell this story to Liliane.

It got better when he showed Alyce what to do to before trussing it. "First rub sea salt inside the cavity and over the skin. Then cut a piece of ginger root and do the same. Again with half of a lemon. Now slice a lemon and slide the pieces under the skin, covering the breast. It will be infused with a lovely lemon flavor."

He then showed her how to truss it with metal skewers and kitchen string.

"What's the point of trussing, anyway?"

"To make the legs stay close to the body so it will cook evenly. Also to make it more attractive when you serve it."

"Looks fine to me without all that bother. And what's with the rubbing stuff on the inside of the chicken?"

He mimicked her. "What's with the rubbing stuff?" Back to his normal tone, he said, "It makes it more flavorful."

"But you don't eat that part."

"We will now speak only in French for as long as I can stand it."

Taking out a bottle, he explained in his native tongue, "I am serving you something special for your birthday. Rosé champagne. It is made by blending a touch of red wine with a base of white before the secondary fermentation."

About all Alyce understood was "rosé champagne," but it was enough for her to say, "Bring it on!"

He'd have to remember to put that expression in his notebook on her.

His toast was "To the new and improved Al-*ees*." Hers was "To a birthday I'll always remember."

"I doubt that will be the case if you stay *friends* with Julien." He waited until she had finished half of her glass before saying, "May I give you a social pointer?"

"Sure."

He told her she should always say *"Bonjour"* to anyone behind the counter of an establishment she entered and *"Au revoir"* when she left. When she asked a stranger for help to use these magic words: *Excusez-moi de vous déranger, madame, monsieur. Mais j'ai un problème.*

"Excuse me for…"

"Disturbing you."

"… but I have a problem?"

"Very good!"

She repeated it several times. "If the French are so polite, how come they're stereotyped as being rude?"

He patiently explained that the French are discourteous only when given good reason. Foreigners, especially Americans, are astonishingly gifted at providing such instances. The only person allowed to criticize a French person was his or her mother. Yes, they insulted customers who complained. Who wants to have their reputation and integrity publicly questioned?

"In the words of Napoleon," he said, "the French can be killed but not intimidated. This is the opposite of America, where owning up to mistakes and bending over backward for a customer—even if he is at fault—is typical."

"Sorry, but that seems flat-out obnoxious. Especially if you're being so nice to them when you enter and leave their store."

He liked the soundness of her argument. "I will think about that."

He slid lemon slices under the skin of the chicken breast, laid five sprigs of fresh rosemary on top, then put the bird in the oven to roast.

"Other than all that nonsense with the cavity," she said, "that was pretty simple."

He hated to admit she had a point. So he didn't.

By the time Julien knocked on the front door she had almost finished her wine. He knew what a lightweight she was with alcohol and couldn't wait to see what this night would bring.

But it wasn't Julien. It was a florist delivering two-dozen red roses to Alyce.

"How can you squeal with delight over such an ordinary gesture? Let me see the card. *Hugs and kisses on your 27th birthday. Love, Nelson.* That is it?"

She looked around. "I don't see anything from you other than cooking a dinner you're going to enjoy as well."

Damn her impertinence. He opened a cupboard and handed her a small, beautifully gift-wrapped box. He hadn't used paper. He found a piece of amber Chinese silk, put that around the box, tied it with the leaf from a palm frond and stuck a twig of fresh lavender in it.

"Jean-Luc, it's so beautifully wrapped. Who did it?"

"I did!"

"Oh." She carefully removed the silk from his gift. "Cheez Whiz I can squirt!"

Her joyous laugh flew around the kitchen like swallows darting about a barn at dusk. She gave him a quick but warm embrace. "Thank you. How did you know I liked this?"

"Tragedy spreads quickly."

"Where did you find it? I've never seen it here."

"But of course, the Internet."

She popped the top off and squirted a big blob on her finger as though she hadn't eaten in two days and popped it in her mouth. Just as he expected a satisfied grin to spread across her face, she made a terrible grimace, ran to the sink, and spit it out.

"That's *disgusting.* How did I ever eat that shit?"

Again she had him laughing harder than he had in a very long time.

With all the attention Nelson was showing her in emails and texts, Alyce wasn't inclined to get too cozy with Julien. She hoped meeting Jean-Luc would be enough to satisfy him. But by the time he arrived she was more than a little tipsy. He was so cute and smitten that she thought, again, how not having some-one to at least *snuggle* with on her birthday was so un-French.

She led Julien to the kitchen. Jean-Luc was standing at the screen door looking out at the swimming pool. A light breeze made his long gray hair move a bit. He turned and warmly ac-knowledged his visitor, who was carrying a bag with several of his books.

Jean-Luc held up one. "Horrendous translation."

Julien offered, "I thought Al-*ees* might like to read some of your books in English and French to help her comprehension."

He kept rummaging through the bag. "Crap, crap, and more crap."

"Would you please, if you don't mind, sign them for me?"

"If you insist."

Alyce punched his bicep harder than she intended. "Why do you have a problem with someone liking your work?"

Julien inhaled sharply.

"Down, girl," said Jean-Luc.

Didon was giving Julien a good sniffing. Leaning down and giving her a good chest rub, he said, "Poodles are very smart."

"That's a *poodle*?"

She directed Julien to the *toilette* so he could wash his hands. Back in the kitchen, Jean-Luc chided her. "What did I say about being polite, my delicate flower?"

"You said it was okay to be rude if someone was rude first. And you were rude."

That shut him up.

Alyce and Julien sat on stools by the wooden counter as Jean-Luc entertained his captive audience with his cooking skills and stories—and more bubbly. At this rate, she was going to pass out on the floor before the food reached the table.

Jean-Luc raised his flute. "A toast to our birthday girl."

She was surprised to feel a lump in her throat. Why did 27 feel so old?

Julien touched her glass with his. "To a real woman."

Jean-Luc added, "To a woman beginning to blossom but who still has a few prickly thorns."

She produced a most unfeminine guffaw and could not care less. "Takes one to know one."

For a split second, she was glad they were settling into a friendship. Of sorts. Or was it the wine talking?

"Jean-Luc." Julien looked to Alyce for reassurance. She had no idea what he was trying to say. He took a deep breath and it all came out in a rush. "As someone who wants to become a writer and eventually support a wife and family, your well-known financial difficulties are giving me second thoughts."

He let out a long, weary sigh. "Most writers struggle to make a living for various reasons. For me, a lot of it goes back to when I was a child, when my father left. My mother quickly became poor and turned to prostitution."

There was a detail Liliane had left out.

"She would flash me a roll of cash and call it 'dirty money.' She couldn't spend it fast enough. As I got older, on my own, I had the same feeling about money that came my way. And the more I made, the filthier I felt and the faster I spent it until I was penniless. I was arrested for nudity and institutionalized after I gave away all my clothes. It caused such a sensation, my books sold like mad and I became even richer."

He tasted the tomato salad and added a pinch of salt.

"I was deemed cured when I accepted I could not handle money and turned mine over to a reputable financial adviser. Here's the good part. He embezzled every cent I gave him and disappeared."

Pieces of a giant jigsaw puzzle clicked into place for Alyce. How do you get over a betrayal like that?

He let Alyce try a bite of the tomato salad. The tang of the shallots and salt played off the sweetness of the local vine-ripened fruit. Jean-Luc had explained earlier that tomatoes were botanically a fruit, not a vegetable. These were so succulent there was no question he was right.

"It's perfect. This could be the entire meal for me."

"What about teaching?" Julien asked, after trying a sample for himself. "You would have a steady income."

He winced. "I would either create false hope in those without talent or destroy it in those with it. I would have no time for my own writing."

"Why not a grant? There are so—"

"A refined form of begging."

"Surely a woman of wealth would take care of you."

"Even more demeaning! In the words of St. Thomas Aquinas, of all of the seven deadly sins, pride is the deadliest."

Alyce felt more than a little irritated at Jean-Luc. He could have whatever he wanted if he just let go of his ego. She was also starting to understand how hard it must be to be an artist, how a God-given gift could also feel like an incurable illness.

"I see why everyone wants you to write a memoir," she commented. "Everything you just said is a lot more interesting to me than a guy falling in love with a horse."

"Al-*ees!*" Julien scolded. However, he agreed a memoir was an excellent idea.

Jean-Luc's eyes bore into her. She regretted what she'd said until he answered, "To write is to stand naked before the world. To write is to scavenge from every possible source, even from people you love, especially from people you love. No one is safe from a writer's laser beam vision. But once you start thinking about what your wife, your kids, their teachers, their friends, their friends' parents, your parents think about your writing, you lose integrity. And yet, what is the essence of true love? Caring about another person's feelings. How do the two reconcile?"

Jean-Luc would not discuss the topic further, but said he would be glad to look at anything Julien had written. Julien was ecstatic. Alyce was impressed as well.

"And now let us move to a subject I want to discuss before dinner is on the table. The *loirs*." Looking at Julien, "She is keeping several as pets."

"*Loirs?* I have heard everything now."

"Pauline insists they go, Al-*ees*. I am sorry."

She knew this was coming. "Don't worry. I purposely didn't name them so I wouldn't get too attached."

Jean-Luc found her comment funny. He then launched into a discourse on exotic foods. A polar bear's liver has such a high Vitamin A content it can kill a human, but its fat is perfect for pastries. Muskrat is a delicacy in Belgium—look for *waterkonijn* on the menu, which translates to water rabbit, but isn't a rabbit at all.

Alyce yelled "Enough!" in the middle of a sentence about sheep vulva.

Julien gently, discreetly, ran his fingers around her lower spine. It felt good.

Jean-Luc said the French were not as accepting of trysts outside of marriage as is commonly believed. "We like to think about it, yes. Attraction is up here." He tapped his head. "Where do you think the word *voyeur* comes from? Or *frottage*? The French."

"I know *voyeur*, but what's the other one?"

"*Frottage* is when you rub against someone, especially a stranger, and pretend it's an accident."

"Like what guys do in the subway? I thought that was called perverted."

Jean-Luc held up both hands. "Silence." He swayed to the song that was playing, a woman singing something about a rose. The life of a rose? It sounded familiar.

Julien took Alyce in his arms. As they slow danced around the large kitchen, she carefully guided them toward Jean-Luc, who was stirring dinner. She gave him a butt *frottage*.

"*Pardon*, monsieur."

"Shhh!" he said, though he didn't seem that upset.

When the song ended, he turned the stereo off. "I cannot listen to anything after Edith Piaf sings 'La Vie en Rose.'"

She asked him what the words were in English.

"It is about looking at life through rose-colored glasses."

No one said anything for awhile.

Two hours and two bottles of wine later, Julien and Alyce faced a mountain of dirty dishes in the kitchen. He took her hand and led her to the door toward her cottage. "I'll do them later. It's your birthday."

She croaked, "I don't feel so good."

She felt much better after she threw up and brushed her teeth. Much.

Julien was suitably good-humored when she came to bed in her un-sexy pajamas. "That wonderful meal. What a waste."

Wearing only his black briefs, he attempted to spoon behind her.

"I want to *sleep*, Julien." She pulled away, then scooted back into his body. "Just sleep."

"*D'accord*, Al-*ees*. *D'accord*."

The cicadas hummed. At first they drove her crazy. Now they were comforting. Her mind drifted to all that Jean-Luc had revealed over the evening. Again she wondered about Colette.

They both sat up at the sound of light knocking. Jean-Luc's knock was harder. She tiptoed to the door with Julien behind her.

"Who is it?"

"*Le Gentil Gendarme*."

"Philippe! How did you know where I lived?"

"Solange knows everything. Al-*ees*, I miss you so much."

She opened the door, glanced at the main house to see if Jean-Luc had heard him. The light in his office on the second floor was still on.

"You must go now."

"My ride dropped me off. I have no way home."

Now she was pissed. "You just assumed I would—"

"Oh, you have company." He took a closer look at Julien. "Are you a boy or a girl?"

"I'm Julien. Who the hell are you?"

"Philippe." He bowed gallantly. "How old are you?"

"Get out of here! Can't you see she is with me?"

"I cannot *walk* home from way out here."

"I'll take you home."

"No, Julien, you've been drinking. Please don't."

She succeeded in parking Philippe on the lounger by the pool with a blanket over him and briskly commanded, *"Stay there and be quiet."*

She climbed back into bed with Julien, eventually falling asleep.

She woke to the sound of chirping birds greeting the day. Still groggy, she snuggled up to Julien. He brought her hand to his hard-as-a-rock *zizi*.

She was wide awake now. Should she go on? She turned to look at him.

"Philippe!"

Julien sat bolt upright next to him. "Get out of our bed!"

Alyce jumped up. "GET OUT OF HERE!"

"The door was not locked. I was cold!" Philippe stood up in all his gorgeous aroused nakedness. "Let's have some fun. Your friend is cute."

With that, he grabbed himself with both hands and went to town.

Julien, who had mysteriously lost his briefs during the night and was also naked, dashed into the kitchen to grab the closest weapon: a metal spatula. "Get out of here you fucking—!"

Alyce couldn't translate his insult.

He smacked Philippe, who then knocked the spatula out of Julien's hand. Julien lunged. They hit the floor wrestling. Alyce was surprised at how well Julien fought, how passionately he defended her honor. She also wanted to laugh at the sight of them. But when he broke free, picked up a chair, and was about to break it over Philippe—

"*Stop!*" commanded a familiar voice.

The door swung open, freezing all of them in their respective positions like the dormice when they'd heard an odd sound.

"Are you all right, Al-*ees*?" Jean-Luc, still wearing last night's clothes, took in what was going on. "Ah, you *do* know how to have fun."

"I wasn't doing anything!"

He took in her pajamas. "In what you are wearing, I can see why."

Julien was mortified; Philippe was not.

Jean-Luc eyed the naked men and decreed, "For causing such a disturbance, you are to do the dishes *now* and fix me breakfast."

They quickly dressed and dutifully followed him.

She pulled Julien back. "I understood everything you two said! But what did you call him? A fucking what?"

"*Singe.* S-i-n-g-e. Monkey. Did you see how he was jerking off?"

One thing was certain. She would never forget her 27th birthday.

Or the word *singe.*

The Offer

That night Jean-Luc studied the mural in the upstairs room. He reached for the bottle of red wine sitting on the floor. It was empty.

He was not.

It felt good to finally finish this project, years after he started it, even if he was drunk and it wasn't his best work. He imagined how Colette would have enjoyed it.

Now he had to erase her and the past. He would beat this devil. He would.

He opened a fresh gallon of off-white paint, poured it into a metal tray, dipped a roller into it, and started applying it to the middle of the room. His stroke was tentative at first, then picked up speed.

Soon all traces of the mural were gone.

The Mansfield Express—Glorianna, her assistant Luther, and Nelson—was fast approaching, causing a nerve-wracked Alyce to toss and turn in her freshly washed sheets for a good hour before drifting off.

She was jolted awake by a pounding on her door and Jean-Luc bellowing, "We have important business to discuss!"

She grabbed her phone to see what time it was. Midnight!

While yanking on her robe, she bumped her thigh into the bedpost. "*Merde.*"

Jean-Luc and Didon had already made themselves at home at her dining table. Did she forget to lock her door again? Where was the New Yorker in her?

"I heard you swear in French." He slammed his hand on the table, weaved a bit, and broke into a dopey grin. "That is a good sign."

"Are you drunk?"

"I wrote a poem for you." In a theatrical way he delivered:

"There once was a pale little sow

Who had herself a grand three-way plow

But the man whom she loved

Was none of the above

O, what does the poor girl do now?"

He waited for her response.

"Little *sow*?"

"Yes, *little*. Which makes it a term of endearment."

"And what three-way plow? I didn't have sex with either one of them!"

He leaned in, almost falling over. "Are you sure?"

"Yes!"

Wait, did she? No, she was sure she hadn't.

"So?" he asked.

She looked at him, at Didon, and around the room. "So what?"

"What are you to do now?"

"Kick you the hell out, that's what."

"You need to rent a car," he said. "You have not seen a thing.

There is much beyond Marlaison. There is Avignon, Armagnac, the Pyrenees, Verdon Gorges, the Alps."

"Do you put that ridiculous face on every time you want something from a woman? I'm not spending money—"

"You are a cliché."

"You are an *ass*."

"I've been called worse." He took out a pack of cigarettes. She snatched them away. He snatched them back. "It was the best of times, it was the worst of times," he said as he lit up. A long exhalation followed as he waited for a response. "It is a far, far better thing that I do, than I have ever done. Have you no idea what I am quoting?"

"What is this, a quiz show? Like I don't get tested enough all day long."

The next shot of smoke was right in her face. "The first and last lines of *A Tale of Two Cities,* one of the greatest novels ever written! It is about London and Paris during the French revolution."

"Of course I've heard of it."

"Who wrote it?"

"Ummm." Damn. She knew it was somewhere in her fuzzy sleep-deprived brain.

"Charles Dickens!"

In his drunken gesturing, his cigarette fell from his fingers and onto the old wooden plank floor. She quickly picked it up and tossed it in the sink. He was more ornery than ever without Isabella.

"Just for the record, Mr. Elegance, I took a lot of math and business courses at college. Ask me anything about numbers."

"To hell with numbers. What do they teach in American schools? How to read the television guide?" His expression darkened further as another thought came to him. "You live in New York City. There is culture everywhere."

She made it clear she only worked in New York. She lived

in Hoboken, which was in another state, New Jersey, across the Hudson River. Try leaving your house at 7 a.m., returning at 7 p.m. or later, and see how much culture you get. Occasionally a client treated her to a Broadway show.

He looked like he had smelled rotten food. "That is an existence, not a life."

He was right about that.

"Here is what I will do for you. You procure a car and I will teach you culture. A small price to pay for learning how to be sophisticated." As usual when he was worked up, he poked the air with his finger like a woodpecker attacking a tree. "There are thousands of women who would jump at the chance to be my student!"

She woodpeckered right back. "Then go find one! And *you* teach me sophistication? You look like hell and your dog smells like rotting fish."

"And who called Isabella a twat?"

"You thought that was hilarious."

"Never mind." He switched to banging the table for emphasis. "I have the riches of the intellect, my little sow. I have dined with kings, made love to princesses, been quoted by the president of France!"

"Not that line about the five hundred cheeses. And stop calling me that."

He brightened. "You know that quote? What is it? All of it, please."

What had her dad said?

"It was de Gaulle who said it and the exact quote is, 'How can you be expected to govern a country that has 246 kinds of cheese.'"

"Right."

Warming to his new plan, "I will teach you to cook, to enjoy good food so you will never eat crap again." Glancing at her refrigerator, "You may as well be living in a toxic waste dump."

Wait a minute. Maybe this wasn't so crazy. Why was she here? To work on *her*. She had a lot further to go than cutting out Cheez Whiz.

"Would you teach me about wine?"

He gleefully held up his glass as if to toast her. "With pleasure!" She responded in kind as he said, "To Beaujolais, Pomerol, St. Emilion, Graves, Viognier, and many more. I will even teach you French." They took their respective sips. "Mornings at the school are not enough. You cheat. You find people who speak English."

"I try to speak French. They get impatient."

"They feel sorry for you. And please stop saying *get* or *got* so much. They *become* impatient is better. I detest when someone is recalling a conversation and says 'Then he goes' or 'Then she went.' It is wrong."

"But everyone does it."

"Everyone is wrong. You should strive to be right."

He mapped out what he called his Pygmalion Plan, after telling her what *that* meant. It was vaguely familiar and she guessed it was a disease. He said Pygmalion was a sculptor in a poem by Ovid. He had sworn off women, then fell in love with a statue of a woman he created.

"It is also a play by George Bernard Shaw that the movie *My Fair Lady* was based on."

There was Audrey Hepburn again. Sabrina, Eliza Doolittle. Was she any different?

She *was* getting stir crazy. With a car she wouldn't have to bike to school in the heat or occasional rain. It would also make it easier to shop for groceries. And yes, just go and explore. Why stay in this one little area after traveling so far?

"I'll see if Nelson will rent me a car after he leaves."

"No, now! I will pay you back. I paid back Isabella and Mazuki didn't I? Even more than what they spent."

"Jean-Luc, I don't have it. I lost my job, remember."

"You are receiving unemployment checks."

"No, I'm not. You have to be actively seeking employment to get those. I used all of my severance to do this!"

"You are renting your apartment."

At a *slight* profit. Still. What condition would it be in when she returned?

She gave in to him out of exhaustion and because, after witnessing it with her own eyes, she trusted him to reimburse her. And there was her bad case of vacationitis that made the reasonable part of her brain disappear.

"It will be our secret, Jean-Luc. Okay?"

"But of course."

She thought he would leave. Instead he jumped to another subject.

"Tell me about this mother of Nuisance. I mean, Nelson."

Alyce was glad to have someone to share this with, even if the recipient was toasted.

"Glorianna's father made a fortune in asbestos when she was a child," she said, "then another fortune in asbestos removal when it was found to cause lung cancer."

Revolted, he said, "Those are cold-hearted genes he inherited."

Even Nelson had a similar take on it. "He's completely different. You'll see."

"I'm fascinated. Tell me more about him."

He was raised in Scarsdale, a wealthy suburb of New York. His father was a corporate lawyer. He did well, but when Glorianna's father died she came into a fortune. Nelson's dad now spent most of his time playing golf. Glorianna was a socialite hell-bent on looking 40 forever and "extending the Mansfield brand" with suitable offspring.

"She used those words?" Jean-Luc asked.

"Not to my face. Nelson told me. He's an only child, so the pressure is really on him. His mother was furious when

Carmelita put Nelson Mansfield, Jr. on her son's birth certificate. She refuses to acknowledge him as her grandson. She pretends she's from noble British ancestry. Glorianna Hope Smythe Mansfield. Even puts on an upper-class accent."

He was sitting up straighter now. "Carmelita?"

That led to telling him all about her and Nelson's child.

His eyes became hostile slits. "Glorianna is quintessential *nouveau riche* and the entire family sounds horrifying, including Nelson."

"You know what?" Alyce said breezily. "You make me feel better about myself than I've felt in a long time."

"Why is that?"

The carefree tone was gone when she said, "Because you're in far worse shape."

"Montaigne was correct. We only experience through contrast."

"Sure." Whoever that was.

He finally left. She lay in bed steaming over how annoying he could be. True, he just broke up with Isabella. Maybe he really did love her. He was under a lot of pressure to write something that would sell. He was going to lose his home.

He pounded on the door again. She groaned. "Go away! I'm sleeping!"

"I must tell you something!"

Cursing in French and English, she got up and opened the top of the front door.

"*What?*"

He weaved a bit before clasping the ledge. "Colette was not a dog."

Stunned, she waited for more. "She was a woman?"

She could see his eyes shining with tears in the moonlight. "She was everything."

He stumbled off into the night.

Wide awake now, she stayed up feeding her poor mother-less baby *loirs* and thinking about how sad life could be. Was there anything that could mend Jean-Luc's broken heart?

Before making one last attempt to get some sleep, she checked her phone to see if Nelson had texted—her new ritual that she did every 20 minutes.

She re-read his last one of the evening: *Nite baby. CUsoon xoxo*

Her goodnight cyber kiss from thousands of miles away. It made her smile, feel calm, and be happy about the future. This time, she felt something different when she read it.

A little... bored.

GUNS AND GRUNKS

Jean-Luc roused Alyce with a tender offering of breakfast on a silver tray covered with a metal dome, like room service in a fine hotel. She rubbed her eyes as he set it on her dining table and whisked off the top with great flourish.

There were two eggs sunny-side up sprinkled with herbs and nestled on brioche. Fanned across the top of the plate were paper-thin slices of green apple and pear decorated with swirls of cinnamon. Next to his last jar of lavender honey was a slice of toasted lightly buttered baguette.

She pleased Jean-Luc by saying, "It looks too perfect to eat."

Pointing to a small white bowl that was filled with steaming brown liquid, he said, "That is the best Italian roast coffee you will ever drink."

She took her time sitting down, as if she wasn't sure how to respond to his gesture. "When I first saw you drinking coffee out of a bowl," she said, "I thought you were weird. I didn't know that's how a lot of people do it here."

"There is still far more to learn about France, my little sow."

She rolled her eyes and groaned. "Would you stop calling me names first thing in the morning?"

"It is permissible to call you names later?"

"Fine. I'll call you my wild boar."

"Superb!"

Even though a smile had crept onto her face, she remained cautious as he took the items off the tray and laid them on the table. When he was done, she didn't move.

"Is something wrong, Al-*ees?*"

"What do you want me to do *now?*"

"You think I have an ulterior motive?"

"Yes."

He motioned for her to try the *melon de Cavaillon* he had cut into bite-size pieces. "I want you to experience something truly divine."

After several slurpy chews, she said, "How will I ever eat the cantaloupes back in America?"

He loved to watch Alyce in these moments of simple delight. It was as though all the tension inside her vanished. But like a wrecking ball that had momentarily swung away from its object of destruction—

"Now what *is it* you want?"

"I would like to get the car today."

"You were so drunk last night I hoped you'd forgotten about that. After classes, okay?"

"With your wonderful Nelson coming today, how can you concentrate? And you will learn far more with me."

She studied him momentarily. "You know how to be a jerk better than anyone I know."

"Is that so?" He produced a piece of paper from his back pocket. "This was in my printer."

Subject: The future

From: Nelson Mansfield <nmansfield@musicworld.sales. com>

To: Alyce Donovan <Alyce.Donovan@gmail.com>

Dear Ally,

I've spent hours on the net researching properties over there. Jean-Luc's is a steal of a deal. I'm very excited about seeing it.

Can't wait to see you even more!

Yours forever.... N

"*Steal of a deal.* I may as well have bandits break in and ransack the place!"

At least she cringed. "How did that print out?"

"It is just the screen image. You must have hit the Print Screen button."

"Oh, right. I forgot. Well," she yawned, "he's a businessman. It *is* a steal of a deal or he wouldn't be interested. And I'm sure you've said unkind things about us. But can you please try to get along with him while he's here?" She turned her big brown eyes the color of pecans on him. "Please? It would really mean a lot to me."

"Only because I take pity on him." He reached the door and said, "Pay particular attention to the lavender honey. It is my last jar."

She examined the unlabeled glass container. "You made it?"

"No, the bees did. I put the hives where the lavender grows and simply gathered it. As soon as you are done we will forage for herbs and then get the car."

She saluted him. "Aye, aye, Captain."

Alyce finished Jean-Luc's delicious breakfast, put on shorts and a T-shirt and waited for him at her bistro table by the Tree of Love. Her now-ragged copy of *French is Fun* was as closed shut as her eyes as she turned her face to the morning sun.

The air was still crisp. The morning light bathed everything in gold. The birds sang in full force. She was particularly fond of the cooing doves. Their low "whoo-whoos" almost sounded like owls.

Just as she was feeling like nothing could possibly be wrong in the universe, Jean-Luc appeared and warned her in English only to go in the woods where he instructed.

"There are *real* wild boars. I am not joking."

He went on about how, even though related to a pig, the boar's meat is dark instead of light. It should be slow-cooked for at least seven hours and served with baked apples, *cèpe* mushrooms, and dauphin potatoes.

"In mythology, Adonis was mortally gored in the groin by a wild boar. My friend François was killed in the same way, though he was no Adonis."

He examined the blades of his clippers and handed them to Alyce. She pretended his words didn't concern her in the least until she saw Didon growl and back up at the edge of the path that led into the woods.

"Don't worry." He patted the canvas bag that was slung over his shoulder. "I have a gun." He then took it out.

"Put that away!"

He admired it. "This is one of the few American products I own. It is a Smith and Wesson .45. Don't be afraid. The safety lock is on."

Alyce had learned to shoot at summer camp when she was 12 and knew all too well how many accidents happen when people thought a gun was locked. She examined it herself.

"Please be careful, Jean-Luc."

"You will be glad I have this if we run into a boar."

Alyce tried to erase the gun and wild boars from her mind as she listened to his precise tutorial on what each herb looked like and how to cut it.

"Not exactly like snipping them out of a window box," she said.

"If you get any scratches or insect bites, I have an aloe plant that will fix them."

"That'll be *so* sexy when I see Nelson. I'll be itching all night."

"No, you won't." In a gentle voice he said, "Think about this instead. Soon you will be watching the phases of the moon. You will predict the weather by the color of the sky, the shapes of the clouds, the number of bees and butterflies."

They passed a dilapidated structure he said was a rabbit hutch. Her first night in France, when the old farm couple, Fabienne and Fabien, served her *lapin,* she gagged when she found out what it was. She loved rabbit now.

He pulled back branches and uncovered a cute stone house he said was a *pigeonnier,* where pigeons used to live.

"He swept his arm toward a field of thick growth. This was a thriving vineyard."

"What made you give it up? Writing your book?"

He stood for a moment taking in the landscape, arms crossed. "An unusually cruel winter." There was something tired in his voice when he said it.

They split up in silence. She gathered what she hoped was rosemary, thyme, savory, and lavender into a wicker basket. If only she could have stopped scratching long enough to enjoy the experience. Then she heard Jean-Luc singing in French in the distance. All negative thoughts vanished. She was utterly enchanted, easily daydreaming about what it would be like to live there. It was that peaceful.

Snip. Snip. La la la.

Grrrruuunnnk. Gruunnk.

A rustling in the bushes followed the scary sound.

Grunk, grunk, grunk.

Though Alyce had never heard a wild boar, every hair on

her body that was now standing at attention knew that's what it was.

She wanted to run but couldn't move. Her legs felt like toothpicks about to cave in. She managed to grab the closest branch. It snapped off. It wouldn't have supported a cat!

The noise was to her left, toward the house? Away? She was lost and afraid to call out to Jean-Luc for fear that the wild beast would come after her.

It was closer. Only a few feet.

Gruuuunk. Grunk, grunk, grunk, grunk.

Jean-Luc crashed through the bushes. "AAIIIIIIEEEEEEE! It's your wild boar!"

Her basket flew into the air and clumps of herbs landed on her head like clods of dirt.

"You shit!" Alyce yanked them off.

He bent over, convulsing with glee.

She stormed off. As soon as she was out of his sight, she covered her mouth with her hand to suppress a laugh.

16

FURY. FOOD. REPEAT.

They walked to rent the car for what seemed like forever with him yapping about art, writers, and politics. Alyce was more interested in thinking about the Mansfield Express.

In nine hours, Nelson would be driving Glorianna and her assistant Luther over to Jean-Luc's, they'd quickly scope out the property and head out to dinner. Nelson would stay with her in the cottage and, at long last, all would be right with the world. She'd decided she wasn't bored with Nelson. She was bored with texting. She wanted the real thing.

Jean-Luc gently pulled her elbow to get her walking again, as if he sensed she was putting down mental roots in another place.

The only thing she remembered him saying on their walk was that when two writers died—Hugo and Sartre—600,000 mourners turned out for their funerals. Just as she was realizing that being a writer was a big deal here, a car driven by one of his fans pulled over and offered them a lift. He declined, saying he was enjoying the walk. Alyce wondered if he didn't want people to know he had no car.

Shortly after they arrived in town, he was kissing the cheeks of a woman who was pushing a stroller with a little girl in it. She and Jean-Luc chatted while the man who was with her said nothing. Was Alyce supposed to talk to him? They were not introduced. She waited for him to speak first. He never did.

When they walked on, she said gruffly, "I felt like a nitwit standing there while you two gabbed."

He found the word nitwit amusing.

"That was not her husband. Here we do not make introductions in those instances because the person may be a lover. And that is the very last time we are to speak English today."

She was still pondering that take on life when they arrived at the car rental office. The woman who helped them was clearly flirting with him. He made Alyce do the entire transaction in French even though people were waiting behind them and she was unbearably slow. They seemed to enjoy watching Jean-Luc Broussard do anything.

She could understand a fair amount, but when she opened her mouth to speak, she froze trying to sort out if words were masculine or feminine, assuming she even knew the right ones. He prompted, explained, repeated, and praised her when she did well. She found herself thinking what a great father he'd be. That is, if he would stop being a child.

She didn't want to embarrass him by haggling, but when she heard what the cost would be her mouth dropped.

"Uh, is there a less expensive model?"

He had insisted on a Peugeot that wasn't the top of the line ("too ostentatious") but still showed class.

He gave her side a pinch and said to the rental lady, "We will take that one. I have misplaced my wallet and will pick up all charges as soon as I find it."

The lady politely acted like she believed him.

The real shock came when they reached the Peugeot she'd rented. He handed her the keys.

"I don't drive."

"What do you mean? That woman left her Lexus with you."

"Isabella drove it."

When she climbed behind the wheel, she said, "What about the Lamborghini you drove into a lake?"

He didn't seem surprised that she knew. "It was a kit car, a fake. I would never have done that to the real thing. Wait! You have not checked your side mirrors. Always do that every time you get in a car."

She complied, checked the rearview one, too. "You still *drove* it."

"And the woman who gave it to me loved me even more after that. She claimed I was the most passionate man she had ever known. Not the reaction I was hoping for."

Alyce couldn't understand how some women were capable of such enormous stupidity. "So why did you stop driving?"

"I just did."

There was something about the way he said it that told Alyce not to push it. She wasn't going to mention Colette again, either.

Within minutes she regretted renting the car. Jean-Luc yelled, "Faster!... Slow down!... Give it gas! You drive like an old lady!... Forget the lines in the road!"

"Dammit, Jean-Luc, I have no idea where I am and I have to translate what you're saying. If you don't like how I drive, drive yourself!"

"No, you are worse than an old lady," he said in English. "You drive like a Chinese doctor from New Jersey. They are the worst."

In the next instant she was giggling from what he said, plus his pronouncing Jersey "Joisey" like he was from there.

Something shifted. She saw his banging on the dashboard with his gray hair flying as side-splittingly funny; like a harmless cartoon. She planned to pull over until she calmed down but he would have none of that.

"Go, go, go!"

Funny or not, she couldn't wait for nice, calm Nelson to arrive and do the driving.

"Where are we going, Jean-Luc? Your place is the other way."

"To the *supermarché* to buy groceries for the delicious meal I will teach you to cook tonight for the Mansfield Mafia. It will knock their argyle socks off."

Alyce first had to adjust to the term Mansfield Mafia. She found it eerily accurate. Then she saw herself cooking for everyone in that gorgeous kitchen just as if it were her own, which it might very soon be. Okay, nothing wrong with that.

"Only one problem. The Mafia doesn't take kindly to changes in plans."

In frustration, he pulled at his long white hair. "This is your gift to them! *Mon Dieu.*"

"Gift? Let me guess. I'm paying for everything."

"Consider this part of your education. And when you marry Nelson you will get it back a million times over."

She thought over his idea. "You need to have a date for this. It won't look right if you're alone."

"I will ask Pauline."

"Are you seeing her?"

He didn't answer right away. "Perhaps."

"I know how much you're asking for your property. You could lose 50,000 Euros, maybe more, if she gets involved in the sale."

"I don't care about money!"

"How can you live like that?"

"I am a great artist and the universe always takes care of people like me."

"Oh, yeah?" She slowed down for a traffic light. "Didn't Van Gogh die penniless?"

He looked out the window and said nothing until they

started up again. "I will ask Liliane and her family to come over. We will dine *en famille.*"

"I'll send Nelson a text so they're not caught off guard. It's called manners."

Jean-Luc kept his mouth clamped shut after that retort. A little bickering was fun. Too much, no.

As Alyce steered the car into a space, she shared with him that the first time she came to this supermarket, she'd taken someone's shopping cart by mistake. She didn't realize you had to pay for your cart then receive a refund when you returned it to the area where they neatly waited to be used again.

Jean-Luc lit up in a way that he could see pleased her as well. "You are helping me view my own world in a new way."

As soon as they walked into the supermarket, heads turned, voices lowered. He was used to his celebrity by now. Alyce, though, was visibly agitated. When a young woman pretended to absentmindedly push her cart into theirs, then recognize him, Alyce grimaced and walked away.

"Don't walk off again," he hissed when he extracted himself from his admirer. "I need you to keep us moving. Be nice to someone like that but say we are running late."

She tossed a can of tuna into the cart with a bang. "Yeah, yeah. I know the drill."

"What do you mean?"

"Never mind."

He'd get it out of her.

He examined the can of tuna and deemed it acceptable.

They stopped at a display where the cheerful Marie-Laure was surrounded by large bowls of different olives. She delighted in his wanting to try each one. He placed a big green one in his student's eager mouth.

"I am switching to English for a while," he said. "My head is starting to hurt."

"Mine, too."

After choosing four kinds of olives, he declared, "We will buy as much as we can here, then move on to the specialty stores."

She stopped at a jar of truffles. "These are special, aren't they?"

"Ah, when fresh. Put them in a jar with brown eggs. Only use brown ones. They have better yolks. The eggs will become infused with the truffles."

"Then what?"

"Make pasta with those eggs and you will taste what I mean." He touched her shoulder. "You must come back after the first of the year and we will go truffle hunting. It's done with a muzzled female pig because the truffle smells like a male." He was struck with a ridiculous idea. "I will muzzle you, my little sow!"

She curled her lip at him like a tough street thug.

"Term of endearment, *chéri*, term of endearment."

Other fascinating information he imparted to her that day: After being transported, wine should rest for two days before being opened... Never buy butter that's too yellow. It shows that the cows it came from have grazed on too many butter-cups, which will affect the taste... Plant parsley after the full moon... The lighter the rainfall, the stronger the aroma of herbs. Provence herbs are the best since they get 300 days of sunlight a year. Most herbs are best fresh, except oregano. Buy it only as dried leaves, then crush them between your palms.

She gave him a strange look.

"What is going on in that interesting mind of yours, Al-*ees*?"

"I was thinking about old photos of you I saw on the Internet."

Ah, she was Googling him.

She cocked her head. "You looked good clean-shaven and with short hair."

"Al-*ees*," he said, discouraged, "once your hair turns gray, it makes no difference what you do to your appearance. You are *old*."

"Dye it. Be it a metrosexual."

"I will forget you said that."

She was already attempting a makeover and they had not even kissed!

After stopping at the bakery and fish market, they returned home. She began throwing things in the refrigerator.

"No, no!" He had a specific method of storage based on how often products were used and the variations of the zoned temperatures in the refrigerator.

"How can you keep this so neat and your office such a mess?"

"It is not a mess. I can always find anything I need."

He ran a fresh strawberry under cold water, plucked its green top off, and popped the fruit in her mouth before she could say another word. He watched her face as he imagined the flavors of the fruit exploding then, too quickly, melting away.

She scooted onto one of his tall stools, her summer dress lifting up just a bit to show her toned legs. Her next question steered his thoughts in a different direction.

"What's with you and money, Jean-Luc? You told me about being embezzled, and the 'dirty money' point of view your mother had when she made it, but that was a long time ago. And writing is *not* prostitution."

He punched the air with his forefinger. "Money is pure evil. If it weren't for money, I would be rich!"

With a sarcastic edge, she replied, "This I have to hear."

He washed the rest of the strawberries in a colander and told her how his publisher cleaned house and dropped all of its authors who hadn't made a sizable profit fast enough, or were known for not delivering manuscripts on time. He fell into both categories.

She shrugged. "I see their point."

Blood shot into his temples.

"Being a media buyer is all about numbers. If a client wants college-educated women with a median income of 50K, you buy the top three platforms that deliver them. Not numbers 4, 10, or 20. If you don't make your publisher money, why should they keep you?"

He fled to his office and slammed the door. I must remove her from my home this instant, he thought, or I will strangle her. And I must write. Though if it's all a numbers game, why bother?

From the base of the stairs she called out, "Treat your writing like a job! Start at the same time every day."

Which was worse? What she was saying or that goat-bleating voice? He bellowed back, "And how would you know that, oh paragon of literacy?"

"I read it in a magazine."

She was priceless. "How silly of me! If you read it in a magazine, it must be true."

"Go scratch your ass! And if you're not going to feed me, I'll feed myself."

He leapt out of his chair and to the top of the stairs where he could see her. "No! You are not allowed in my kitchen until I am sure you know what you are doing."

"Then get down here."

In a deadly serious tone, he said, "I can't."

She looked concerned. "Why? What's the matter?"

"I haven't finished scratching my ass yet."

She made her exaggerated eye-roll and walked away.

When he ambled into the kitchen, scratching his butt in an

exaggerated way and talking like a hillbilly, it set her off laughing. Even more when he tried to scratch hers and she fought him off.

He was beginning to love that laugh.

After their lunch of *salade Niçoise*, during which he taught her so much French both of their minds went numb, he said in English, "Amuse yourself, Al-*ees*. Clear your mind. Relax. Then meet me in the kitchen at precisely 2:00 for your next lesson."

She answered with a wink and a smile. "*D'accord, professeur.* But what I'd really like is to swim in your pool. Are you going to fix it up before putting it on the market?"

"No. The new owner will deal with it."

Though he wouldn't mind seeing her in a bathing suit.

TEARS, FEARS, AND BOUILLABAISSE

Alyce's next lesson began with a snack of goat cheese wrapped in oak leaves. Jean-Luc wasn't surprised she'd never heard of such a notion. He spread the tangy *banon* on rounds of crustless, toasted, herbed bread while speaking almost entirely in French. It was exhausting.

"Shall we speak in English for a bit, Al-*ees*?"

"Thank you."

He brought out a chilled bottle and flutes.

"Champagne now?" she said disapprovingly.

"It is not champagne." He showed her the label. "Only wine from the Champagne region can be called that. It is a Saumur sparkling wine."

He took the first sip. "It tastes like atonement. A moment of naughty damnation followed by a satisfying redemption. What do you think?"

She closed her eyes. Thank God she'd stopped wearing makeup. He hated how her mascara clumped her eyelashes together, her foundation covered her naturally pink cheeks, and the smell of powder buried her true scent.

"It tastes like kisses from a bashful child."

He was floored by her poetic description. "Perhaps there is a writer in you."

"After seeing how you struggle? I hope not."

Next on the agenda was *herbes de Provence:* dried rosemary, sage, oregano, marjoram, savory, thyme, and basil mixed together in their own grinder. It was to the French what salt and pepper was to everyone else. That got him going on how much he hated American restaurants, the way the waiters immediately accosted you with a giant pepper mill without giving you a chance to taste the food to see if you want more seasoning. And the grated cheese that was proffered with any pasta dish.

"That is never done in Italy."

"How many times have you been to America?"

"Once. That was enough. I was flown to Hollywood to be seduced into letting *The Horse* be made with a happy ending. I refused."

"Why am I not surprised?"

She wrote down the herbs he used and wanted to know precise measurements.

"There are no set amounts, Al-*ees.* You must feel them."

He excused himself, went upstairs, and came back with a black leather blindfold. Her face twisted in a most unattractive way.

"Listen, buster. Don't be getting any ideas."

"Sorry, mademoiselle. This is not your lucky day." He slipped it over her head. "It is to help heighten the sensitivity of your poor, plugged-up, unused, withering senses."

Once the blindfold was in place, he passed bunch after bunch of fresh herbs under her All-American petite nose. She was an exceptionally quick learner.

"Summer savory?"

"Excellent. Soon you will be able to tell wild thyme from garden thyme."

Jean-Luc took another moment to admire her innocent, plain beauty.

Until she opened her mouth and tried to speak French.

That lesson over, he asked her to cut the greens off the carrots and fennel. She did, then scooped them up to throw them out.

"That is the salad!"

"Huh?"

Once again her foreign ways made him laugh.

The phone rang. He let the answering machine in his office above them pick up the call. Through the open windows they could hear the caller leave a message. It was a woman he had recently met.

"Did I get the date or time of our lunch wrong?" she asked in a voice that was trying not to be angry.

He could see steam building in Alyce's face. When the call ended, she asked, "Don't you believe in honoring commitments?"

"Your French is improving. Now I will teach you how to make *pissaladière*. What your pizza wishes it could be."

"Don't change the subject. You stood up a woman without giving it a second thought?"

"I barely knew her. And she suggested the lunch, the place, the time. I do not remember giving her a firm yes. That is the truth. Should I have told her I was with you?"

He removed two aprons from a hook on the wall and handed her one covered with sunflowers. "You look like you were born down the road." That put a slight smile on her face.

His apron was classic white and covered his chest and upper thighs. Written across the front: Kiss Me, I'm French. They cheek-kissed three times. All ill will vanished.

"First we caramelize the onions." He took out a bag of pretzel rods and handed her one. "Put it in your mouth while you peel and slice them. Your eyes will not tear."

Alyce pretended it was a cigar, then dug into their task with it sticking out of her mouth.

After a minute she took it out. "You're right! No watery, stinging eyes."

The tart and sweet scent of freshly sliced onions filled the air as a thick layer filled a cast-iron skillet. Sprinkled on top were thyme, rosemary, and extra-virgin olive oil.

"We cook them on a low heat. No browning. Plenty of stirring."

Next was the making of the crust. Alyce watched intently as he added ingredients to a food processor and it worked its magic. As he slowly added flour when the dough was too sticky, she commented, "You look like a scientist in a lab."

"All cooking is science and art. Please stir the onions again."

He rolled out part of the dough and fit it into a rectangular rimmed baking sheet sprinkled with cornmeal. She did the other half. They added the onions, green and black olives, sprigs of thyme. She made a face when they reached the anchovies.

"These are not like the ones you are used to," he said.

She tried one. "Mmm. It tastes like a swim in the ocean, not pure salt and oil."

Another small victory for France.

When the *pissaladière* came out of the oven and cooled down, he allowed her one square. "The rest will be an appetizer for tonight."

After taking a tentative bite, she exclaimed, "It's zingy, crusty, gooey—and the onions give it a sweet finish!"

The delightful moment did not last. Her cell phone rang.

"Hi, honey, you just landed? Get my text? You won't believe what this kitchen smells like. I've been cooking all day." She winked at Jean-Luc. "After customs and renting a car, it should be about two hours to get here. Oh! There's an incredible open market in Nice anyone can direct you to. Jean-Luc said to look for a man with large copper pans set on an outdoor fireplace made of bricks. He makes *socca*—a nice snack that won't be too heavy… *socca*. It's made from chickpea flour and olive oil with salt, pepper, and fresh rosemary. I've had it here but his is supposed to be the best."

Jean-Luc said, "And get his fresh-squeezed grapefruit juice, too."

She repeated his suggestion and motioned she was going back to the cottage. "I can't wait to see you, sweetie. How was your flight…"

Honey. Sweetie.

Oh, this was going to be rich.

She soon returned, showered and in an understated light blue dress and sandals. Unfortunately she was back to wearing makeup. She twirled around to get his reaction before Nelson, Glorianna, and Luther arrived.

"Aside from the war paint, I approve. You look like a true lady."

"Nelson's never seen me without makeup. It's nothing compared to his mother. I think she applies it with a plaster knife."

"I can't wait to meet her." He rolled his eyes to imitate her. She playfully batted him on the arm.

Pushing up the sleeves of his white linen shirt, he said, "Now it is time for you to master bouillabaisse, a fish stew made from catches of the day."

"It better be good after what I spent on the ingredients."

"Your obsession with money is as unattractive as my lack of concern for it."

He asked her to go to the CD player in a hallway closet and put on Johnny Hallyday. It was essential she knew who he was. When she came back, he'd taken out a book on the "French Elvis." It was filled with photos.

Alyce gasped at one image. "She looks just like my sister."

He looked at Hallyday and wife number four (or five?) taken after they were wed. She was about 20 to his 50-something then;

a perfect pretty blonde who did nothing for Jean-Luc. Too much like a doll. And she could have been Hallyday's granddaughter.

Alyce launched into a monologue about her younger sister, Chantilly, and how ever since she was born strangers gushed over how beautiful she was. Alyce ceased to exist as her sister modeled, won beauty pageants, acted in commercials, and consumed all of her mother's attention. The moment she graduated high school she had a Ford modeling contract and was off to New York City to live in a big loft with other models while Alyce's home was a small, depressing basement apartment in Hoboken.

"That's why I hate when we're in public and people fawn over you. I know I shouldn't feel that way."

"With a name like Chantilly, how else could she be? I believe we grow into our names."

"Why couldn't they have called me Alyssa instead of *AL*-iss? Is that why I'm so practical and boring?"

"You are hardly boring. I imagine your sister is, though. She hasn't suffered enough."

He presented her with a bowl of striped baby clams and glossy purple-black mussels, and a brush. "Continue with your story. You scrub and de-beard, I'll rinse. It is important to remove all grit."

"De-what?"

He tried not to show his surprise. Truly, he did. "Remove the strings on the mussels."

"Oh! Yeah, right. Of course. Just pull them?"

She seemed to follow his instructions but was so engrossed in her story he had to watch her every move.

"So she married a rich guy and now she's pregnant. At 21."

"You do not like that she beat you to it, eh?"

"No!"

"I understand. It is your *issue*, as Americans say."

"Wanting to be a mother is not an *issue*. It's called natural. *Not* wanting to be a parent is an issue."

Is it possible she saw him as perceptively as he saw her?

He began to hum "La Vie en Rose" and soon they were lost in their own world as they prepped the *mirepoix* and worked on the seafood: *Rascasse rouge* (tiny rock fish not found anywhere but the Mediterranean), *cigale de mer* (the slipper lobster), slices of *Saint-Pierre* (John Dory), *baudroie* (monkfish), the head of a conger eel all would go into a big pot.

In the *mirepoix* pot he put carrots, celery, leeks, Spanish onions, garlic, seeded tomatoes, salt, and a *soupçon* of cayenne and saffron. He showed her how to make a bouquet garni of thyme, bay leaf, parsley stems, celery, fennel, and orange peel. That was tossed in as well, driving another intense aroma into their olfactory sensors.

"Now we wait a bit. Then add the clams and mussels."

"How do you know when it's ready?"

"You just do."

They tackled what he considered the key ingredient in bouillabaisse: the *rouille*. After Alyce tackled how to say it.

"*Rooehyeh*? It sounds like I'm throwing up."

"I will as well if you keep pronouncing it that way."

"I want to get it right!"

His head felt like it was being shrunk by a tight, large rubber band. "We will come back to it."

He explained that *rouille* was made in a blender with roasted red peppers, olive oil, garlic, and a bit of mashed potatoes to thicken it. "Or bread or bread crumbs, if that is all you have. Some add a little fish broth but that limits the use of any left over. I use *rouille* as a spread on sandwiches in place of mustard, on crackers as a snack, on baguettes as an appetizer."

"Mmm, that sounds great. No more mayo for me."

"There is nothing better than fresh-made mayonnaise," he

said. "And it is very simple. We will do that another time. We need to get to work on dessert now. It has to chill."

Crème au citron was a rich custard flavored with orange blossom water and thin strips of lemon zest. He used whole milk and plenty of egg yolks and sugar. Just like the scene in *Sabrina* where Audrey Hepburn learned how to crack an egg with one hand, he showed her that the trick was all in the grip, the wrist, the surface you cracked it on, and what you did with your thumb and fingers after. They were both amazed when she did it right the first time.

"Beginner's luck," he said. "Do it again."

She did and sweetly replied, "I have an excellent instructor, *monsieur.*"

"Don't you dare try to suck up to me. Oh, go ahead."

The sun fell lower in the sky, bathing the kitchen's yellow walls and honey-colored oak cabinets a deep gold. By 6:00, *Macédoine au Vin de Bandol*—a mixture of cherries, strawberries, raspberries, white peaches, pears, and peeled green almonds in red wine marinated in the refrigerator.

He noticed her brow was slightly furrowed. "What is on your mind, Al-*ees*?"

"How come you people eat such rich food and don't get fat? I haven't seen one overweight person here."

"You people? Whom do you mean? Men? Writers? Be precise."

"The French."

"Because we are perfect."

Alyce's eyes were getting a workout from the number of times she rolled them.

He asked her, "Why are the French like a rooster?"

"I have no clue."

"Because it is the only animal that will stand in shit and crow."

This time when her delightful laugh bounced around the

room, he felt a familiar heartache. He focused on the newly painted white room upstairs. He willed Colette away.

They started the final preparation: the dessert custard. He finished whisking and poured the creamy mixture into a heavy saucepan over low heat, gently instructing her to stir it in a large figure-eight pattern until the spoon was thickly coated.

"Do not let it get even close to boiling."

Alyce did so and after a minute seemed to be dreaming. A moment later she was turning off the burner and fleeing to her cottage.

How dare she run out like that! She could have ruined the custard. What could possibly have been so urgent? He poured the mixture into individual cups, tapped a touch of ground cinnamon on each one, and placed them in the refrigerator.

When she returned she was white as chalk.

Alarmed, he sat her in one of the kitchen chairs, rubbing between her shoulder blades. He knew she could feel the heat through her cotton shirt. He was born with abnormally warm hands.

"Stop it, Jean-Luc. I'm fine, I'm fine."

"You are having a panic attack. With the Mansfield Mafia about to arrive, it is understandable." He gave her back a final pat and grabbed her hand. "Come with me."

He led her to his living room sofa and pulled up an ornate leather stool from Morocco.

"Tell me what is upsetting you, Al-*ees*."

She made herself comfortable as she held his hand tightly.

"When I was stirring the custard it reminded me of how a baby smells. I suddenly wished I had one. Then I remembered I hadn't taken my birth control pills for *two* days. I've never screwed up. I ran to the cottage, popped them out of the dispenser, and froze. I heard my little *loirs* squeaking." Eyes tearing, she confessed, "I didn't take the pills... yet."

He felt a faint movement in his scrotum, dropped her hand, shifted on his stool.

Between sobs she managed to say, "I feel so unaccomplished." The back of her hand was wet from the tears it had wiped away. "I'm *scared*. About everything."

He grabbed a box of tissues from the bathroom in the hallway. She blew into one sheet so delicately it surprised him.

He nonchalantly said, "Life becomes most interesting when you are scared."

"To you. You're a writer who can turn it into a book. I can't do anything but be terrified. Aside from being nervous as hell over Nelson *and* his mother coming, let's see, I have no job, yet I can't stop spending money."

"A common reaction. But why would you need a job if you marry him?"

She hesitated before saying, "I've always worked. And I need to be able to take care of myself, especially if I get one whiff of him turning off like he did before. But a part of me doesn't want to work at all. A real job, that is."

She told him she'd gone to a mailbox a few weeks before to send out her résumés and almost couldn't do it. As soon as she dropped them in, she turned and stepped in dog shit.

Brilliant foreshadowing, he thought, and mentally filed it away for a book.

"Maybe I need to stay here longer," she said with a sparkle in her eye, "so I'll crow the next time."

He loved her sense of humor that was emerging now that she felt more at ease.

"How do you really feel about Nelson?"

"Like I won the love lottery. I knew the moment I saw him I wanted to marry him. I've never felt that way about anyone."

While he sorted out why her words bothered him, she lightly blew her nose again and pulled herself together. A most fascinating portrait emerged of her inamorato.

"I knew him through work. We were never that friendly. Then one day I ran into him, Carmelita, and their son. It was just one of those destiny things."

Destiny things.

"That's why his other relationships ended," she said. "Once they knew about her they couldn't deal with it."

"Does she have another man in her life?"

"Nelson says she dates, but I'm not aware of anyone." She wrinkled up her little nose and stared beyond him. "These are the times we live in. Blended families are hard to escape."

Brushing her hair off her troubled face, "You are very mature and kind to accept her."

He would bet his property that Nelson and Carmelita never ended their affair. He admired Alyce for putting on her blinders. Denial could be a wonderful survival mechanism. Eventually she would figure it out and either leave with a nice settlement and the kids, or take a lover of her own. Then again, he could be wrong. All wrong.

He hoped he was. She wanted marriage, children, stability. She should have them. He would hate to see anyone hurt her.

Especially Jean-Luc Broussard.

They both heard it at the same time: a car pulling up to the house.

"It's show time." Alyce sounded apprehensive.

"I will make myself scarce." He gave her a reassuring hug.

"At least meet them."

He turned to go up the stairs as they reached the front door. "Not now. We would seem too much like a couple." He waved her on. "I will come down later."

She gave him a penetrating look. "You really can be quite wonderful sometimes."

"Don't let anyone know that." He smiled. "It would hurt my reputation."

18

The Mansfield Mafia

Throwing open Jean-Luc's front door, Alyce sang out, "*Bonjour! Bienvenue!*"

She felt she should embrace Glorianna first out of respect but Nelson rushed toward her.

"You look fantastic! So French!"

They fell into a little smooch. Not too much with Mrs. Mansfield there.

Alyce whispered a line Julien had taught her; how great it was to kiss him. "*J'ai oublié comment c'est merveilleux de t'embrasser.*"

"Look at my darling Alyce," Glorianna interrupted. She scanned her up and down. "I *love* the new you."

They touched each other's shoulders and air-kissed, Glorianna's unmistakable Joy perfume that she used like a room spray descended on Alyce like a jungle mist.

The matron of Scarsdale society was wearing a carnation-pink pantsuit made from the finest silk money could buy and a creamy turtleneck (even though it was summer). Thrown over her shoulders was an Hermès scarf.

Luther, her latest assistant, flashed a mouth of big, fluorescent teeth, extended his hand, and over-enunciated, "You do look faaaaabulous. I'm Luther."

He, too, reeked of cologne and could have passed as the love child of Elton John and Mr. Clean. He was a big guy with a noticeable belly, shaved head, gold hoop earring in each ear, funky purple eyeglasses, and bling that was borderline too much. His linen suit was off-white, his shirt taupe with turquoise polka dots. Slung over one shoulder was a large brown Chanel tote.

"*Enchanté*," Alyce replied as she shook his hand. "It's a customary greeting here."

"I already told him that," quipped Glorianna. "I'm enchanted."

"I love the French!" he cried.

Glorianna pivoted her Charles Jourdan-clad feet to flaunt her scarf. Alyce now noticed its wine bottle motif. "Dressed for the part. What do you think, Alyce?"

She searched for a polite response but instead wickedly replied, "*M'as tu vu!*" It was an expression used to describe pretentious, vain people. Show offs.

Alyce cautiously eyed Luther. "Do you speak French?"

"I can kiss French. Does that count?"

Glorianna and Luther let out light ha-ha-ha-ha-has like two hyenas. Alyce attempted to join in. Nelson wore his I-have-to-be-nice-because-she's-my-mother look she knew well.

"Tell me that expression again and what it means," Glorianna demanded.

"Um, *m'as tu vu* means… something's beautiful. Yes, that's close enough."

Though Nelson was in his usual khaki pants and white T-shirt under a navy blue blazer, she viewed him differently than when they were together in New York. He might have Carmelita as baggage, a mother she couldn't stand, be from a social class way above hers, and still have the edginess of Manhattan reverberating inside him. Next to Jean-Luc, he was a safe harbor.

Luther poked his bald head into the living room next to them. "It's so artistic and *manly*."

Glorianna stepped in for a closer look and everyone followed. "What it needs is a good coat of paint." Admiring the African masks, she said, "It's so nice to be able to see without my glasses. What a wonderful invention Lasik is!"

She'd had cataracts removed, not Lasik. When she had a hip replacement last year she told everyone she had "a minor but pesky procedure on my foot."

Keeping the momentum going, Nelson said, "Something smells great, Ally. I'm so hungry I almost ate the steering wheel on the way here."

Glorianna added, "I could use a drink."

"An excellent idea," called out Jean-Luc as he descended the stairs. "My sister and her family will be joining us shortly."

Introductions were made. He graciously said, "It is a pleasure to have you here. Please make yourself at home. After all, it may be yours soon." He led them to the kitchen. "It is where most socializing occurs."

Glorianna asked, "What *is* that wonderful aroma? I'm picking up rosemary and seafood."

Jean-Luc said with deadpan sincerity, "I thought it was you, Madame."

Nelson coughed into his fist then whispered to Alyce, "Where's the *toilette*?"

"You just walked by it. I'll show you."

Grabbing the chance to be alone, they kissed. She pushed him away when he tried to pull her into the bathroom.

"We'll have plenty of time later!"

He put on an exaggerated pout. She retreated to the kitchen. Glorianna and Luther were commenting on the charm and "rusticity" of the kitchen.

Jean-Luc said, "I spent 40,000 Euros on *rusticity*?"

The hyena ha-has let loose again. Alyce avoided Jean-Luc's eyes.

Her guests spied the cottage through the kitchen windows facing the back. Luther deemed it "too cute for words." Glorianna added under her breath, "Look at the roof" and shook her blonde bun-head. Alyce noticed she'd added a bow to her chignon that matched her pastel suit.

While they were turned away, Jean-Luc made a sweeping arm gesture while holding his nose. Nelson returned and stifled a laugh.

"I can see why you love it here, Alyce." Glorianna said. "There's so much potential."

Luther's tongue was practically hanging out as he ogled a loaf of fresh-baked bread on the counter. "Does that taste as good as it smells?"

"Luther," Glorianna said sternly.

Soon the guests were gorging on the bread, two local cheeses, and olives. Fresh spinach crunched loudly as Alyce broke up each leaf and dropped them into the enormous pot holding the seafood.

"It's often added to bouillabaisse in the South of France," she explained.

The Girards appeared. Liliane gave Alyce an "is everything okay" glance after they cheek-kissed. The boys and Simon warmly kissed her as well.

Liliane was introduced to Nelson. "I have heard so much about you from Al-*ees*."

"Al-*ees*? I like hearing it said that way."

"So do I," Alyce remarked. "Now about that drink."

She reached for the *pastis*. Jean-Luc had something else in mind. The bottle was labeled Marc, pronounced *Mahr*. He said it was like grappa and made from the leftovers in winemaking, like the stems.

She caught Liliane's "stop it now" look. When everyone

took a sip she knew why. It tasted more like kerosene. Plenty of coughing and pleading for water followed.

The table was set for them to dine *al fresco*. Luther "just loooved" the tablecloth that was bursting with sunflowers against a blue background. "It's sooo Provence."

All but Jean-Luc and Simon walked off to tour the property. Alyce turned back in time to see him wet his finger and hold it in the air to see which way the wind was blowing.

They reached the edge of the woods and Glorianna stopped. "This is far enough. I don't have the proper shoes."

Liliane brought them to a clearing where they could see the overgrown vines rolling over the terrain. Alyce hoisted Benoit onto her hip so he could see.

Nelson excitedly remarked, "Doesn't it look beautiful? Imagine it fixed up, Mother."

In a loud whisper, she replied, "It looks like a lot of expensive work."

Liliane offered, "That has been reflected in the price."

Alyce added, "I'm more than willing to do whatever needs to be done."

She touched Alyce's arm, "My dear, you always get what you pay for."

As they headed back to the house, Alyce switched Benoit to Nelson while she and Liliane exchanged a stolen "what a bitch" glance. Alyce chose to focus on how wonderful Nelson looked holding a child.

Their inspection of the cottage began with Glorianna and Luther oohing and aahing over the Tree of Love flowers, sticking their faces in them just as she did the first time she saw them. Glorianna was smiling as she entered her little jewel of a home— until her hand jumped to her throat and her eyes bugged out.

"*What* are *those*?"

Alyce introduced them to her *loirs* (purposely not calling them dormice).

Luther chimed in with, "Yeeeee."

The boys wanted to play with them. Their mother issued a firm "*Non.*"

Nelson leaned in close. "Wouldn't you like your own babies?"

She blushed. If anyone heard him, they pretended they didn't.

Jean-Luc was on the telephone when they returned and motioned that they should go upstairs and look around. As they followed Alyce up the stairs, she remarked, "I've only seen his office to use his computer. This will be new for me, too."

They didn't say anything. She wondered if she was making too much of not being close to Jean-Luc. Liliane seamlessly told them how hard it was to get on the computers at school.

"We were going to buy more but as students began arriving with wireless notebooks and cell phones that can access the Internet, we decided not to."

Glorianna airily said, "Didn't Nelson send you an iPhone?"

"If I want to print things out, like real estate information, I need a computer."

"What a mess," was Glorianna's assessment of the office.

Liliane pointed out its high-speed connection and numerous outlets. "The electricity and plumbing were updated a few years ago."

They walked to the door that had been locked. Liliane opened it with no key. They stuck their heads in the room for two seconds. Alyce could have sworn the bare pale walls had something painted on them before. She remembered a large white oval. It had been too dark to see. Now it reeked of fresh paint. Where was the photo? Did he know she had been in there?

They briefly inspected the other guest room and then the master bedroom.

"Well, well, well," said Luther when he saw Jean-Luc's exotic bamboo bed. "If these walls could talk."

Glorianna went straight to the bathroom. "Not to mention this shower."

"Oh my gawd!" cried Luther.

"Do *you* like it, Alyce?"

She suddenly realized how weird it would feel to live here with Nelson. She would always be wondering what had gone on and with whom. Thank God she wasn't one of Jean-Luc's conquests.

"It's certainly different," Alyce replied.

Liliane's boys loved it. Apparently they'd never seen much of their uncle's home.

"I'll tell you this," Glorianna knocked on the stone wall, "tearing it out and renovating will be not be cheap or easy."

"The tile work is magnificent," Liliane interjected. Their eyes roamed over the floor, walls, and ceiling. All agreed it was gorgeous. "It was done by one of the best Italian masons, an admirer of my brother's work. Jean-Luc designed the tiles. You would spend a fortune to have it done today."

Glorianna headed out of the crowded room and haughtily decreed, "Unique or unusual is another way of saying *will hurt the resale value.*"

Alyce could see Liliane's temper beginning to flare. Was she cursing her eccentric brother or this monstrous American woman?

And who said anything about reselling?

"I looooove the French!" squealed Luther as he lingered in the bathroom.

Alyce feared she would hear him say that another hundred times before they left.

The warm summer evening fell comfortably upon them. Jean-Luc found it hard to concentrate on what these imbeciles were blathering on about as they enjoyed the cheese and rosé wine he served at the long outdoor table. He felt like he was center stage at a Greek theater and the cicadas were the chiding, opinionated chorus.

He threw clumps of wild rosemary, thyme, and white sage on the outdoor fireplace and watched Alyce make a mental note of the practice when he explained to her that it perfumed the air, stimulated the appetite, and calmed the spirit. Nelson had impressed him by picking up a dry New Zealand sauvignon blanc that was superb in its grassiness and the perfect complement to the grilled artichokes, which can wreak havoc with many wines because of a compound called *cynarin*, which tends to make wine taste sweeter. He did not voice any of this to his guests. He was tired of hearing himself pontificating like a bag of hot air.

He tried not to watch how sensuously Alyce ate her artichoke as she delicately dipped the leaf in lemon-butter sauce and slowly pulled her teeth over its spongy meat.

Glorianna had undoubtedly had a facelift under her several coats of makeup, and Botox injections. There was a shimmery quality to the upper half of her face, as though the nozzle of a pump had been inserted in the top of her head and had injected the air only so far.

Luther, he mused, was like a character who was used to walking out of a gay bar on a Saturday night without successfully picking up anyone.

And Nelson? He wasn't sure about him. He didn't want to like him, so it was clouding his judgment. He seemed nice enough. Jean-Luc just didn't see Alyce with him, or at least happy with him for long. Then again, she was so practical and hell bent on snaring the bourgeois dream.

Liliane effortlessly turned on the French charm, her years of dealing with Americans an asset. "Have you ever lived abroad?" she asked Glorianna.

The Grand Dame recalled living in London "when I was an unmarried filly."

Luther concurred. "I've seen photos. Va-va-voom!"

Glorianna lightly tapped his arm. "Oh, stop, Luther." She gave Jean-Luc a flirtatious eye-bat.

Jean-Luc held in a laugh by pinching the skin between his thumb and index finger. He could always spot a woman who hadn't been made love to properly in years. She was also probably trying to butter him up for the kill at the bargaining table.

He wished the cheese had been laced with cyanide instead of sage.

"Time for the bouillabaisse," he said, "Provence style."

Nelson, with his arm over the back of Alyce's chair, said, "Now this is what I call living." He gave her a light kiss on her neck that she relished.

Jean-Luc's appetite was rapidly decreasing.

After everyone was served, Jean-Luc recited his instructions on the ritual of eating this classic French fish stew. "Place two slices of toasted French bread rubbed with garlic on the bottom of a pure white soup bowl. White does not compete with the food. You may also keep the bread to the side if you like to... what is your word? *Dunk*. Then add a spoonful or two of *rouille* made with roasted red peppers, olive oil, garlic, and..." He looked to Alyce to finish.

"Potato, bread, or bread crumbs to thicken it."

It filled him with pride to hear her remember his words.

"Next we add the broth and then the seafood."

When that was done, Glorianna lifted her wine glass. In her best Julia Child voice she sang out, *"Bon appétit!"*

Aside from the sounds of spoons against bowls, lips smacking, and gentle moaning, a silence—finally—fell over the table. He looked over at Alyce and was momentarily transported by her loveliness.

Until he caught Nelson watching him, none too pleased.

Conversation danced among many topics. He was displeased to discover Nelson was not the dolt he thought he would be, especially about wine. Frequently, Jean-Luc would speak to Alyce in French out of habit. She would start to respond, then stop, sensitive to Nelson being left out. Jean-Luc could not believe how far she had come with her French since her arrival. And how careful she was not to bruise Nelson's ego. She certainly didn't care about bruising his!

He considered staying for the entertainment he was sure the Mansfield Mafia would bring. He also felt protective of Alyce. She had bottomless reserves of determination but lacked guile. He feared she was walking into a venomous snake pit. When he saw how happy she was with this man, something shifted.

He took a few more bites and made an announcement. "As much as I am enjoying your company, I must pack for my trip. I will be away for a few days on business." Liliane and Alyce eyed him curiously. "Al-*ees*, Nelson, enjoy your time here."

There were polite protests that he stay. He bid them "*bonne nuit*" and within 30 minutes was on the highway, Didon by his side. That is after Alyce confronted him as he was heading out the front door. "I thought you didn't drive."

"Of course I can. I just wanted to see how well you did."

Cue the eye roll.

If all went as he anticipated, letting Alyce and Nelson live there alone at the height of their passion would forever enamor them to his property.

If this was what she desired, even if it was a mistake, he wanted her to have it.

19

THE TALK

The instant Glorianna and Luther were dropped off at the *Hôtel Marlaison* that night, Alyce and Nelson couldn't wait to get back in the saddle at the cottage. He reached for her hand as he drove his rented BMW convertible over the speed limit.

"I'm going to love every inch of you," he said.

"I'm going to love every inch of *you*, but…" She had his full attention. "I screwed up on my birth control pills. I picked up condoms just to be safe. I'll be on track in a couple of weeks."

He let go of her hand. Her heart ker-flunked. Despite his remark about having her own babies, it was too soon to actually do it.

"I thought you wanted to be a mother," he said in a non-threatening way.

"Yes, when I'm married."

He glanced at her and smiled. "If you get pregnant, you will not be an unwed mother. You have my word."

Now her heart ker-flunked so much in the other direction that they drove right by the road they needed to take.

Once they turned around, she said, "There's something I've

been wondering about. Your mom and Luther are so chummy. Are you sure he's gay?"

"If it's an act, it's a damn good one."

"Your father doesn't mind?"

"Not at all. Luther does everything with her he won't."

"That's not a marriage I'd ever want to be in."

He reached for her hand again and gave her a reassuring, "Neither would I."

They entered the dirt road leading to Jean-Luc's and Nelson slowed to a stop. "Look at these fields of lavender and sunflowers in the moonlight, Ally. Pure magic."

As she watched him gawk in awe as though they were a fine work of art (as she had done many times), all that went through her mind was what a wonderful husband and father he would be; how perfect they were together.

At the cottage, they made love (*au naturel*) with an intensity she had never known with him. She made him laugh, and climax, when she said, "I'm sending your therapist a thank you card."

Just as she was on the verge of crashing through to that state of tension-free pure bliss, his phone rang.

It was Carmelita, enraged over a neighborhood kid knocking out one of Junior's teeth. Nelson did his best to calm her down, though he was upset, too. That wasn't a baby tooth.

This was hardly the first time Junior had been in a fight or caused trouble. Nelson went into the bathroom to pee and talk in hushed tones. Even though Alyce's eyelids suddenly felt like the steel doors of a vault about to shut, *Why is he whispering?* crept into her brain. She thought she'd made peace with those gremlins.

"I'm sorry," he said after the call. "Where were we?"

"It's okay, honey," she said, snuggling into her pillow. "It's been a *really* long day for both of us. Let's save it for the morning."

They started kissing again. The morning was too far away.

"Just do me a favor, sweetie," she said. "Turn off your phone."

The four Americans met Pauline at the *Hôtel Marlaison* the next morning. Alyce felt guilty about leaving her out of a commission on Jean-Luc's property, especially after he said, "She's going through a bitter divorce. She needs all the sales she can get."

Pauline, naturally, did everything she could to present the other properties in the best light. Alyce cringed every time Glorianna said *"M'as tu vu"* when she liked something and Pauline gave her a strange look.

Glorianna narrowed the choices to three. Jean-Luc's was, by far, the best value but would involve the most work and money to get it up to speed.

Alyce had a sick feeling when Glorianna and Nelson presented Jean-Luc with a lowball offer. It worsened as she realized what a pickle she was in. On the one hand, if she married Nelson, it would benefit them to get it for as little as possible. On the other, she wanted Jean-Luc to make as much as he could.

Jean-Luc and Liliane refused to drop the price one Euro.

When she and Nelson rejoined Glorianna and Luther on the Avenue Gambetta to shop and stroll, Alyce ramped up her sales pitch of why they should offer the asking price. She painted a mental picture of all that could be done to the house and grounds. She described a gift shop, wine tastings, and an outdoor café. She used her skills in media buying to do a cost analysis of the three properties.

"And it has one thing the other properties don't have and never will," Alyce said, businesslike. "Jean-Luc's celebrity. Great writers are revered here."

Glorianna tapped her bun-head. "You've never renovated a house, much less all that this will entail."

Alyce pulled herself up straight the way Jean-Luc did when he was offended, and almost punched the air with her finger the way he did. "If I can learn French, I can do anything!"

"Yes, I can see—oh, no! Ugh!"

Glorianna noticed a squashed date stuck to the sole of her expensive shoes. She stood looking helplessly at Nelson and Luther, who had no idea what to do. Alyce reached in her purse and pulled out a piece of paper from the small notepad she kept in it. Luther did the honors. Catastrophe averted.

There were frequent, highly unpleasant flare-ups between Nelson and his mother. Just as Alyce was thinking, *Can I stand this woman for the rest of my life?* Nelson privately patted her tummy and said with a grin, "Wonder if there's a croissant in the oven?"

Glorianna who?

At another point, when Glorianna was out of earshot, he said, "Now you know why mother-in-law jokes exist."

Yes, she thought, she had plenty of company.

At the end of another tiring day, Glorianna announced, "Luther and I are renting a car, taking a little road trip, spending a few days in *Paree*, and returning for the grand finale."

Alyce looked at Nelson.

He cleared his throat. "She means to finalize the paperwork on what we decide to buy."

His mother pulled him aside. They huddled in whispers. Luther walked over to a store window and pretended to browse as he whistled. Something was up.

Nelson came back, cleared his throat again. "Uh, she'd like to talk to you in private. Why don't you two have a drink before dinner? I'm still jetlagged, honey. I'll go up to her room and try to rest. Call me when you're done."

She did not have a good feeling.

The two of them spotted a place they'd been to before that Glorianna deemed perfect. When they went inside, the owner rushed up and said in fairly good English that they could only sit outside.

Glorianna surveyed the restaurant. "There are plenty of seats here."

He said, as if he were paying her the highest compliment, "Madame, only wild beasts mark their territory with an odor as strong as yours."

Alyce clamped her hand to her mouth in shock.

"I refuse to patronize this unimpressive establishment!" She pulled Alyce away.

"Thank you, Madame," replied the proprietor with a slight bow.

Alyce couldn't wait to report this exchange back to Nelson. And Jean-Luc. She could hear that blast of a laugh of his. She missed it, too.

They found another café and sat outside. "It's too beautiful a day to stay inside," Glorianna stated.

She ordered sparkling water with Angostura bitters and convinced Alyce to try it when she said, "It aids the digestion."

As soon as the waiter walked away, Glorianna said, "You certainly have transformed yourself, Alyce."

"I must thank you for encouraging it."

"Mr. Broussard is quite an attractive man, in that tortured artist way."

Alyce wondered if Glorianna was interested in him. "I suppose he is to some women, but you'll have a lot of competition."

"Me?" She patted her bun. "Are you sure he hasn't turned *your* head?"

She let out a yelp of surprise. "Not at all!"

The interrogation continued, slowly twisting into Alyce like a screwdriver. "You have quite a cozy arrangement, I would say."

She looked her right in the eye. "He's been very helpful to me as far as my French goes, but to him I'm a gauche American.

He only puts up with me for the money I bring in. Is there a reason why you're saying this? I'm only interested in Nelson."

"Speak from the heart, Alyce. No pretense, please. Why do you love him?"

Alyce confessed that the day she saw his name on Bernadette's appointment list, she had "a special feeling." When she saw him, it was even stronger. She repeated how he ignored her and how, she was certain, fate had put them together.

She felt like a beauty pageant contestant with 30 seconds to speak to prove she was worthy of the crown. From the look on Glorianna's face, she had passed that test.

Their drinks arrived and Glorianna was not happy to see there was no ice in her glass—the way drinks were usually served. Alyce had grown accustomed to it but sweetly asked the waiter, in French, to bring them some in another glass.

That taken care of, Glorianna smiled with approval. "Are you *sure* you want to marry Nelson?"

"Only if he wants to marry me."

"Of course he wants to."

The golden gong was struck. "He told you this?"

Glorianna answered with a smile. She sipped her drink and the sun glanced off several diamond rings. She felt Alyce out on what she wanted from life. How important was her career.

"I've had enough of the world of advertising," Alyce said. "Owning a vineyard and having children with the man I love would be a dream come true."

Would Alyce raise the children Episcopalian?

"I was brought up Methodist, but I don't belong to a church. Sure."

"How do you feel about private education and sending the children to prep school when they're of age?"

"Uh, haven't thought about that." She almost asked if she had their children's names picked out.

"Just think about it." She shook more ice into her glass.

"Now, let's talk about You-know-who. I don't understand how you put up with her and that surly boy, but I'm grateful you do. Unless you intend for that to change in the future."

Alyce took a moment to collect her thoughts. "Of course I'd prefer if she wasn't in the picture, but Nelson loves his son. I admire him for that."

She caught Glorianna's light lick of the rim of her glass before sipping her water. She had told Alyce once that was her secret for keeping lipstick from appearing on the glass and disappearing from her lips.

"Once you have children, won't the time he spends with them bother you?"

"If he's over here and they're over there, when will he even see them? Before you know it, Junior will be a teenager and in his own world. Or maybe he'll like having half-siblings and come visit in the summer."

"Kids today are so *progressive*."

"With all due respect, he *is* your grandson."

Her eyes flashed. "He was conceived with pure evil on the part of that woman. And believe me, he's cost us plenty. That's enough recognition."

She waited until Mrs. Mansfield did another lick-and-sip to say, "So I guess Carmelita won't be the maid of honor and Junior the ring bearer?"

She sputtered so much that Alyce had to say, "Just kidding!"

When she could speak again, "That wasn't funny. Now on to my next topic. Do you have any objections to a prenuptial agreement?"

That question she had thoroughly considered. It came up with her sister, who signed one before she married. At the time Alyce thought it unromantic and crass, but Chantilly said it protected her as much as him. "Better to negotiate when you're in love than when you're not."

"Not at all," Alyce answered Glorianna. "Of course, I'd have a lawyer look it over."

"Of course. Now is there anything you'd like to ask me?"

Without hesitation, she fired off, "Does Nelson truly love me?"

She slid her chair around, put an icy hand in Alyce's. She assumed it was cold from holding the glass with ice but couldn't be sure.

"I've never seen him happier. He so wants to be *respectably* married with children. With men, Alyce darling, timing is everything! He also wants to prove himself in a business venture of his own. And I'm sure getting away from me is a factor. I know I can be a tad overbearing."

Alyce needed to get away from her, too. That perfume!

Glorianna thankfully scooted back to where she had been. She also became even more businesslike.

"Nelson has talked about various entrepreneurial ideas for some time. His father and I have been encouraging, though we never thought he'd want to try something in another country. If this doesn't work out, I won't mind at all if you live close by and get involved in my charities." She added a hopeful smile.

It hit Alyce what was really happening. Nelson was asserting his independence and his mother was trying to accept it—or pretend to. Her style of delivery also made Alyce feel like she was watching a BOLD marketing presentation to snare a new client.

"It's a lot to think about, Glorianna."

"I understand. But really, how can you go back to that tiny apartment in Hoboken and another 9-to-5 job in the city?"

Was she ever right about that.

She patted Alyce's hand. "Have a lovely time in Paris with Nelson. Enjoy every minute."

"How can I not?"

As she paid the check, Glorianna said, "I'm going to skip

dinner tonight, dear. I'm exhausted and Luther wants to go out and play. By the way, the meal you made was superb." With a wink she added, "You can't go wrong making Nelson another one. Pretend as if you're already married while Jean-Luc is away. Let Nelson see how wonderful it will be. Be *sure* to wear sexy lingerie." Her sly grin faded. "I'm convinced that's how You-know-who enticed him in the first place."

And so, with a new slight fondness for her potential mother-in-law, Alyce and Nelson returned to the cottage.

Operation Put-A-Ring-On-It was underway.

20

Monsieur. The Reality Check, Please.

Raymond had been Jean-Luc's editor, dear friend, and father figure for more than 20 years; the only stable relationship in his life. He had discovered Jean-Luc in his teens through a chance encounter in a bookstore.

He was the only one who knew about Colette.

At their lunch in town, Jean-Luc noticed how much Raymond had aged in the 10 months since they last met. That was one of the curious aspects of life. One could look the same for years on end, then *hop*, a steep decline strikes.

Or your hair turns gray practically overnight at the age of 35.

Raymond was quite the ladies man when they'd first met: thick black wavy hair, raspy voice, tall frame, aristocratic heritage. Then he married and became a devoted husband and father. His home buzzed with love, activity, laughter, and occasional yelling. Jean-Luc's life, sadly, was not that different from when he met Raymond.

His editor livened up when he handed over a check. Jean-Luc

did not share his enthusiasm. "I was hoping for another zero on the end of it."

"Three thousand Euros to publish an out-of-print title in Japan is excellent in this market. Of course there will be more, *if* you make back the advance."

Their lunch orders were taken, including a side of pâté for the now-gorgeous Didon curled up under the outdoor table. Odalis, Raymond's Brazilian wife, insisted she be cleaned up before entering their villa. Having nowhere else to go on such short notice, he complied.

"Times have changed," Raymond said. "The young editors don't even want to hear stories of the old days. And ask my opinion on something current? Bah. It is time to retire, my friend. If you write your memoir soon it will be my swan song. Dark, brooding literary fiction is a hard sell now."

"You do not think my memoir will be dark and brooding, too?"

"There will be plenty of fun in it, too, I am sure."

Raymond gave him a look that said *please give it a try*. It was hard to refuse him.

"When I retire," Raymond said, "I will sell the Paris apartment and move to Avignon full time. I want to spend my final days with my wife and family. I wish I could tell you it will be easy for you to find another editor." His eyes were moist.

Jean-Luc felt a distinct change in the room. A heat. A reverberation. Which hurt more? The eventual loss of Raymond or hearing the words *spend my final days with my wife and family*? Was that damn American girl putting bourgeois ideas in his own head? He felt an unyielding jealousy toward Raymond.

"This is sad news, for you and me. Who can edit my work like you?"

"I have someone in mind. I'll involve him in the next one." He paused before asking, "Is there another one?"

Jean-Luc grunted. "I cannot think about writing at the

moment. As you know, I am going to be moving, perhaps very soon."

"How do you feel about selling your place?"

He gazed past him. "I will have no debts, less responsibility, and more time to write. What could be wrong with that?" His sigh that followed belied more.

Their lunch arrived, and before biting into his mozzarella, tomato, and basil sandwich, Raymond commented, "I think a change would be good for you, Jean-Luc."

He poked at his penne with roasted chicken and pine nuts in a creamy rosemary sauce. He barely touched his glass of white Bordeaux.

It prompted Raymond to say, "Let's change the subject. That is an excellent wine and I cannot bear to see you not drink it. How is it going with the student?" Life returned to his aging eyes. "I know something must be brewing there."

Jean-Luc became animated, unable to stop talking. He dug into his food, enjoying his wine, as he rattled off one funny Alyce story after another: being shuffled from host to host, the young men who were after her, being kicked out of a convent when she was found in the bushes with one of them, finding two naked men in the cottage.

"But she was wearing the most unattractive pajamas! And the ugliness that comes out of her mouth sometimes. She can match me any day. I call her my little sow and I am her big boar. I scared the daylights out of her pretending I was one in the woods. And then there are the baby *loirs*. She is keeping them as pets!"

"*This* is your next book! And it would be therapeutic to do a comedy after *The Horse*."

"I thought so too and started a notebook on her. But now…" He sat back in his chair. "I could not use her that way."

Raymond's food fell off his fork on the way to his mouth. In a hushed tone, he said, "*Sacre Dieu*. You are in love."

He could barely contain his anger. "Do not say such a thing! Me with an American?" He shook his finger. "No, no, no. I am too French. Besides, she is about to become engaged."

Raymond broke into a wry smile. "I am sure you could woo her away if you wanted to."

"And then what?" The remark prompted him to say in a very different tone, "Raymond, what is to become of me? I cannot believe I am saying this. I suddenly find myself, at times, longing to have my own family."

It was obvious Raymond could not believe it, either. He was about to take a sip of wine but was too shocked.

Jean-Luc clarified, "Not children of my own. I am afraid I will fall short as a father. An older woman whose children are grown would be ideal."

"Is the real Jean-Luc stuffed in a trunk somewhere and you are an imposter?" He returned to his wine. "Must be your age. I was approaching 40 when I decided to settle down."

Jean-Luc raised his glass in a toast "to change."

Raymond responded in kind. "And to Liliane for all of her help. How is she?"

"Her usual flinty self." He leaned in more and hissed so as not to be overheard. "I am not in love with Al-*ees*! I am ready to love, yes, but not her. It would never work. Let us change the subject this instant."

"I already changed the subject to your sister. You brought it back."

"I wanted to make that final statement. Now…" He told him about Julien Devreaux's novel-in-progress. It had a lot of promise and he couldn't help but make editorial notes. Raymond was almost as shocked by this news as he was to hear he wanted a family.

"*You* are editing?"

"Yes. I find it much easier to see the bad in someone else's writing than my own." "Is he paying you?"

"He offered, but I cannot take money from a writer, only from a publisher. Yet there is not one that would pay me to edit." He was sure the two women at the next table were trying to listen in on their conversation and lowered his voice again. "Raymond, I must make some kind of steady living beyond my books."

"Teach."

He groaned. "My knowledge has no relevance today."

"That is not true."

Raymond gently worked on him and by the end of the meal Jean-Luc agreed to attack his memoir while he was staying with him for the week.

"Only so you will stop your harangue about teaching."

At that moment he heard in his head Alyce mewling from the bottom of his stairs: "Just treat your writing like a job! Start at the same time every day. I read it in a magazine!"

"What are you laughing about?" asked Raymond.

"Nothing," he answered, "nothing at all."

MARLAISON

The Mansfield Mafia rendezvoused in the *Hôtel Marlaison* lobby one last time. They'd all had quite enough of acting like they adored each other. After lackluster air kiss-kiss-kisses were exchanged they went in search of a local café for their farewell breakfast. Glorianna refused to eat at the hotel due to their "ridiculous price gouging." She was carrying a pink parasol that matched her suit, sandals, and toenails.

Luther did not bother to hide his foul mood. He'd fallen head over heels for a young man who worked at a *pâtisserie*. Not only was he spurned, he'd gained more weight savoring delicious cakes and pastries as an excuse to see him.

They agreed on a café and sat outside. Alyce's inner thighs were so sore from lovemaking she had to sit down gently.

"Are you wearing sunscreen all the time, darling?" Glorianna asked as she perused the menu. "It's so important to preserve your youth."

"I thought a shot of Botox was all you needed these days."

She leaned into Alyce. "Don't ever go to one of those Botox parties. Only see a real doctor in a real office."

Alyce stroked Nelson's leg with her foot under the table. "I'd never put anything like that in my body, especially if I'm thinking about having children."

Speaking to everyone at the table, Glorianna said, "Oh, fiddle. They tell you not to take an aspirin when you're pregnant these days. When I was carrying Nelson, I'd get together with the other expectant mothers at the country club and we'd have a contest to see who could balance a martini on her stomach the longest."

Luther lightened up after that anecdote. When he looked over the menu, though, his glowering returned. "How do they stay so thin here?"

Alyce contributed, "My theory is they walk or bike a lot, only eat quality food when they're hungry, and consume just enough to fill themselves—which is about three bites."

Even more cranky, he said, "Give me one of those yummy mushroom crêpes. And what's taking so damn long for our mimosas?"

Despite the champagne in their drinks, breakfast was strained.

After their final *au revoirs* (and making sure Glorianna was out of sight), Nelson and Alyce ran to his convertible.

Revving the engine, he said, "Sweetie, let's throw a few things in an overnight bag and drive to Paris this instant."

She thrust her arms into the open air above her. "Wheeeee!"

"No," he corrected her, "*Oui.*"

His cell rang. Carmelita caught Junior smoking cigarettes in his bedroom.

"What! Of course he's acting out. He's just going to have to accept the situation. Take him to a new therapist... I'm having a great time, finally. Mother just left... Yes... Yes, of course. Bye."

He said to Alyce, "I didn't expect this kind of trouble from him until his teens."

Alyce was thinking the same thing. Junior was barely 10.

"Children have a hard time with change," he said. "His mother isn't taking it well, either. But I can't stay in this holding pattern forever."

Alyce had that hinky feeling again. Ah, screw it. They were heading to Paris. Nothing was going to bring her down.

PARIS, HYPOTHETICALLY

They hadn't yet spied the *Tour Eiffel* and Alyce could already feel the energy and congestion of a major city mounting around them. Then there it was. Looming above the city as though it had been placed in the wrong diorama.

"Paris, Ally!" He clutched her hand.

"Paris with *you*. I'm in heaven!"

They checked into an ultra-fancy *chambre supérieur* at *Le Royal Monceau* and lustily attacked each other. As always since arriving in France, he insisted she speak French when they made love. It turned him on so much she didn't mind, though she often recited grammar lessons.

Once they hit the streets, it was like the early days of their romance when they would stroll around Manhattan peering in shop windows; exploring new restaurants; seeing movies. All that mattered was passing the time together.

Her ability to understand a lot of what was being said to them, and even more of what was written, was a fantastic feeling.

When he suggested they visit the Eiffel Tower, she wondered what it would be like to see Paris with Jean-Luc. No doubt full of surprises in off-the-beaten-path places. If he owned a cell phone she would have called him for ideas. She wondered where he went. What was he doing? Who was he with, was more like it.

They walked by a large bookstore. Nelson said, "Let's see if Jean-Luc's books are here." He wasn't expecting to see an entire shelf devoted to him, nor was Alyce.

"See? He *is* a big name here."

He was suddenly deep in thought. "You're right."

Nelson's cell rang. Alyce braced herself for another Junior calamity. It was his dear mother. After a minute of him patiently listening to her, he interjected about Jean-Luc's popularity, then handed the phone to Alyce.

They had a perfectly superficial conversation. "There's a simply divine restaurant by the Louvre. Be sure to go to Hermès and buy a scarf. Don't forget to take photos. *Au revoir!*"

They strolled on. A pretty summer dress in a window caught her eye. Nelson bought it for her on the spot, along with a beautiful black straw hat that sloped down just below her right eye.

"I'll always cherish it, honey. It's my Paris dress."

He kissed her hand. "The first of many, my queen."

After a lifetime of feeling inferior, she finally felt the opposite.

When he spied a store that sold luggage, he pulled her inside, quickly picked out a very expensive set to replace hers and had it sent to the hotel.

She could get used to this. Already was.

They checked out a store filled with fun gadgets. She thought it was sweet when Nelson tried out every electronic sound machine that helps you sleep. He wanted to see if one mimicked cooing doves—their new signal to each other when they wanted to make love. None did. He couldn't find anything he wanted to buy. He already owned a personal groomer, portable pant press, automatic tie rack, electric shoe buffer, and turbo massage chair that cost over a grand.

She saw one like it and stretched out in the display model. When the hidden mechanical fists inside started rolling up and down her back, she said, "I bet Jean-Luc would love this. I mean, I think any writer would after sitting at a computer all day and night."

"We should get him something for being our host," he said. "What about this?"

Nelson brought over a shiatsu neck massager, about a foot wide. Two padded balls sprouted out of the middle and slowly gyrated. He turned off the chair Alyce was in and slid the massager behind her so the balls were on either side of her neck.

"Ohhh, that's amazing. How much?"

"About a hundred bucks. I'll get it."

"That's very generous, Nelson."

"Generous is my middle name, baby."

They walked out of the store holding hands. "Do you know how special you are?"

"No. But never stop telling me." They easily fell into an embrace on the street. He said, "I feel zo *Franch*. Now tell me about Jean-Luc's love life."

"*Non!* Ze French wom*en* are nev-*eh* indiscreet." She momentarily caught the last syllable of "indiscreet" on the roof of her mouth. It had taken a long time to get that nuance right.

He wasn't so playful when he said, "I see how he looks at you. He's in love with you, Al-*eeeees*."

She pulled back. "With me? Hardly. A woman broke his heart and he never got over it. He's in mourning." She gave him a peck on the lips. "Besides, I love *you*."

The moment they returned to their room she taught him the term *sieste crapuleuse*.

A few hours later, grumbling stomachs pulled them out of their lovemaking stupor. They went in search of a restaurant for dinner that the concierge assured them was elegant and romantic.

Their waiter was an older gentleman who didn't speak

English (or pretended he didn't) and had made this his life's calling. He had an air of effortless efficiency as he refilled a water glass or slipped in the proper knife without anyone realizing he had done it. He wouldn't dare rush his patrons.

She caught a look on Nelson's face that did not bode well. "What's the matter, sweetie?"

"If I'm buying a place here, I better start learning French, too. I'll check out the *Alliance Française* when I get back."

"That's a great idea."

"Not to mention a tax write-off."

"Let's start now." She picked up her fork. "*Fourchette.*"

He touched her hand. "How about we begin my first lesson in the *boudoir?*"

He returned to perusing the wine list that went on for pages. "Speaking of learning, did you know that restaurants typically jack up wine prices 300 to 500 percent? That's where they make their money. Whatever you pay for a glass is probably what the entire bottle cost them. You know how you can tell if they're gouging you? If the Beaujolais is more than 20 to 30 dollars."

The waiter was placing fresh slices of bread on their bread plates. She gave him an apologetic glance just in case, behind his poker face, he understood what Nelson had said. She inwardly viewed it as shop talk.

Lightly putting her hand on his forearm, she said, "Jean-Luc once told me it's best to try wines you're not familiar with in a restaurant. They're probably the best value and best tasting. Let's order the Meursault. That's one I don't know."

"An excellent choice, Madame," piped in the waiter, in French. Either he picked up on the word Meursault or he knew exactly what she was saying. "It will stand up to the flavors of the escargot."

She translated to Nelson. He snapped shut the wine list book and asked the waiter to bring them a Chablis.

"I'm sure it will be great," Nelson said to her. "French

Chablis is completely different from the American version. It's considered to be the purest expression of the chardonnay grape with little or no oak used in the process."

"I didn't know that, honey. See how much you're teaching me?"

When their server returned, Nelson tasted, gave his approval, and they went back to their goo-goo eyes state.

In a hushed voice, she said, "Wouldn't it be romantic to cook together?"

He caressed her hand. "I'm terrible in the kitchen, but I'd love to watch. Especially if you're wearing something sexy."

They moaned over the garlicky escargot. She could have eaten fifty of those slimy slugs that would have disgusted her before this trip.

Next came her *Crêpes de Haricots Verts* (crêpes stuffed with a green bean purée and dusted with freshly grated nutmeg) while he savored *Potage aux cèpes* (creamy mushroom soup bolstered with a healthy shot of cognac).

Her entrée was bouillabaisse. She had ordered it to compare it to the one she and Jean-Luc had made. The velvety *Chambolle-Musigny* Burgundy took the experience to another level—though she liked Jean-Luc's version of the stew with spinach better. It not only looked nicer with a little green floating in the bowl, it added a slight buffer to the pungent seafood. Nelson's rack of lamb with a pignoli nut and sage crust was melt-in-your-mouth divine.

She had no idea what the meal was costing. Her menu was *sans* prices.

Silence followed as the wonderful tastes transported them. Then Nelson put on his earnest gaze she'd seen when he'd called on Bernadette to buy magazine ads from him.

She stopped eating.

"Ally, I'm tired of dating. It hit me hard the other day." His department hired a guy seven years younger who was already married with a kid on the way. "I may have done it in reverse, kid first, but it doesn't feel right anymore to not have a wife."

Again she felt like the equivalent of a sofa being picked out to finish a living room.

Again she told herself to shut up.

He reached across the table for her hands. "Let's talk hypothetically."

She sat on the edge of her seat, spine straight as a broomstick, as he floated the idea that *if* they were to get married, how would she *really* feel about Carmelita and Junior? Was she pretending it didn't bother her? Nothing was going to change. He would still see them regularly, he would still have to budget them into his expenses.

Junior was one thing. Surely he wouldn't keep supporting *her* forever.

Think again.

He explained that, though his parents insisted early on that he put his financial obligations to Carmelita in writing, he didn't.

"I was young, obstinate, idealistic. I didn't want to be some rich asshole making it all about money. I thought if I treated her well, we'd be fine. I also thought she'd get a job."

The only thing she knew how to do was tend bar, which kept her away from Junior at night and wasn't the kind of thing he wanted the mother of his child doing. He sent her to cosmetology school. No salon that offered her a job was good enough for her and the good ones wouldn't hire her. Now a precedent had been set. The line of scrimmage was clear. She could sue him if he cut back financially. He'd end up paying out as much as he was now, maybe more, plus a ton of money to lawyers.

Alyce was ill-prepared to respond to this news. Thankfully, the waiter asked them for dessert orders. Nelson ordered *Reine de Saba*, the Queen of Sheba cake—the French version of what Americans would call Death by Chocolate. He ordered the most expensive German ice wine as well.

He said to Alyce, "It's made from grapes left on the vine to freeze. They not only have very little juice, they have to be hand-picked in the freezing cold. Very small amounts are made and good *half*-bottles start at 50 bucks. I'm ordering the one that's 300, figuring it's really worth a hundred."

"How about next time, honey? I've already had way more to drink than I should."

"Tonight is special, baby."

A familiar queasiness started to burble inside her.

The waiter approved of his choice of wine, but suggested a different dessert, something moderately sweet like *crème brûlée*, or non-sweet such as cheese and fruit.

Nelson ran his hand through his hair, something he did when he was ticked off or needed to prop up his confidence. "No, I still want what I ordered. Ally?"

She went with the *crème brûlée* and excused herself to go to the ladies' room. She imagined Carmelita sitting on her fat ass watching bad TV all day while Nelson footed the bill.

She made it there just in time to throw herself over the toilet. That expensive meal! This was turning into a replay of her birthday. How was she going to make it in the wine business if she couldn't hold her liquor?

She rinsed her mouth and saw a bowl filled with wrapped peppermints on a table with other toilette accessories. It offered everything but what she really needed: an antacid. She could still feel rumblings deep within.

She returned to their table and cautiously tried the *Eiswein*. It was too sweet but at what it cost, she acted like it was the best thing she'd ever sipped. He couldn't eat his chocolate cake fast enough. She slowly savored her dessert.

"Everything okay, Ally?"

"*Hypothetically?*" She tried to bring a playful spark back. "What more could I ask for?"

He wiped his mouth with a soft white linen napkin. "That's

what I love about you. You're a team player. Most women only think of themselves. As for what more could you ask for? How about this."

He reached inside his blue blazer and took out a small red velvet jewelry box. When he flipped it open, she practically fell into the table to get a closer look.

"It's *huge*."

Very pleased, he responded, "Tiffany D flawless, set in platinum, five carats."

"H-how many?" It was such an upscale restaurant she had to control herself—and the unpleasant feeling swirling in her gut.

"Only the best for my wife. C'mon, try it on." She sat back. "You do accept, don't you?"

She said nothing. She couldn't. She was praying to God not to throw up. She nodded yes.

He slid it on her left ring finger. It felt lighter than she expected and was too loose.

"Did you lose weight? Don't worry. That can easily be fixed."

"Nelson, I'm afraid to wear it. Someone might kill me for it."

"Honey, it's a copy. Mother's is, too. The real one's in a safe deposit box."

She blinked a few times. Huh?

"I wasn't going to travel with a $50,000 ring!"

Fifty-thousand dollars? That was more than she made in a year. Was she supposed to tell a mugger it wasn't real and expect him to believe her? She'd rather wear a smaller real diamond than a monstrous fake one. To say that would spoil the moment she'd been waiting for all these years.

Instead, she spoiled it by tossing her dessert into her half empty water glass.

"Too much alcohol and rich food, darling."

Nelson quickly took care of the tab.

They walked back to the hotel, not touching. She said

meekly, while trying not to cry, "Please don't take it personally. I just drank too much! And this is quite an emotional moment. Nelson, I've loved you since the moment we met."

He stared ahead.

Alyce was certain he was going to ask for the ring back. Since it was too big she had put it on the silver necklace she was wearing. She touched it one last time.

He looked at her and broke into a wide grin. "I can't keep a straight face any longer. What a proposal! Better stay away from the champagne at the wedding."

She ran into his waiting arms. "That's another thing I love about you, Nelson. Nothing bothers you for long."

"Don't worry, baby. We're a team. Right?"

"Right!"

22

Siren Song

I was reading O. Henry's **Gift of the Magi** when I came across a word I did not know. My frustratingly small five-year-old arms lifted my father's heavy brown dictionary from its place on the bookshelf. I did not want to disturb him while he read his newspaper.

I looked up "mendicancy."

Destitution.

I would soon know firsthand the word's meaning.

We lived in a modest third-floor apartment outside Paris, redolent with lemon polish from my mother's continuous dusting. Father, in a dark business suit, disappeared every weekday morning for work. I had no idea what he did other than "sales" and that it deeply upset my mother when he had to take business trips, which occurred often.

Today he was in casual pants and a sweater, signaling it was the weekend. If I was lucky, we would play pétanque in the courtyard. I waited for his cue while he sat in his favorite living room chair reading the newspaper. Birds flocked to the feeder he had attached to the kitchen window so Maman would have something to look at while she cooked.

He was tall, quiet, and so soft-spoken he sounded detached, as if he wasn't quite there. My mother was loud, as though she were trying to make him hear her in his distracted state.

Even at my age, I knew my father was good-looking by the way women responded to him.

The telephone rang. Maman wasn't there, having left to do some shopping. I assumed it was she who was calling because of the way my father spoke. His tone picked up ever so slightly. I ran to him.

"I would like to speak to Maman."

His face grew dark. He whispered into the telephone, "Can't speak. One hour."

He returned to his newspaper as if nothing was wrong. I went back to reading The Gift of the Magi. *Something did not feel right.*

After a few minutes he rattled his paper. "How would you like a bath, Jean-Luc?"

Maman usually did that.

He stood up and smiled. "Come. I haven't given you one in a long time. I need the practice."

I hesitated but his enthusiasm persuaded me to go along with it.

Soon I was in the bathtub, smacking my hands into a blanket of soft foam, watching white bubbles float away. My father soaped up my back and washed my hair as he gently hummed.

Just the two of us. So close.

"Will you be okay for a few minutes? You're a big boy, right?"

I nodded yes though I didn't want him to leave.

I heard him in the bedroom doing something for several minutes. Just as I was getting bored and chilly, the front door closed.

I crawled out of the tub, foam in patches over my small body, water dripping on the floor. I looked out the living room window. My father appeared below by his car. He put a suitcase in the trunk.

I had never seen him leave for a business trip wearing anything but a suit.

"Papa!"

I banged on the glass. He looked up, surprised, and smiled like a clown smiles, not real. He waved in an equally exaggerated fashion. I tried to open the living room window. I did not have the strength.

I stood there, cold and wet, crying "Don't leave! Don't leave!" as he drove away.

I remember wiping the water off the floor so Maman would not be upset with me.

I never took a bath again. Only showers.

My mother put on a good front to the world. The tears came when I pretended to be asleep, when the strange men began showing up. She would put me in my room, close the door, tell me to stay there. I heard their voices. Some were polite, others made sounds like animals when they went in her bedroom. I thought it was a game they were playing. Once I went in to join them.

"Maman! I want to play, too!"

They were undressed.

She began beating the man, telling him to leave her and her child alone. He quickly fled, after shaking his fist at me. His angry face haunted me in nightmares for years.

I never saw the men again. I didn't see much of Maman, either. She worked two jobs now: a waitress during the day and somewhere at night she wouldn't talk about.

In the evening, when I was confined to the depressing cabbage-scented apartment of an elderly woman in our building, I drew pictures of bulls being stabbed, men being decapitated, buildings toppling. I wanted to

Jean-Luc ripped the yellow-lined pages off the pad and threw them in the trash can in Raymond's office. He did not want to relive this. He did not want people to feel sorry for him.

Marlaison

She had called her parents right away and was pleased to find that Nelson had asked her father for her hand before he proposed.

"I raised the subject of his child and his relationship with the child's mother," her father said. "I thought it was commendable of him to be there for his son emotionally and financially—especially in this age of deadbeat dads. But I thought his financial responsibility to Carmelita should end when the child became an adult. He said that was a long way off and his situation was complicated. He would think about it."

Her mother's joyful reaction was, "Mrs. Nelson Mansfield sounds like a name right out of 1940s Hollywood! I'm so happy for you, Alyce. You've been dreaming of this for a long time." Her tone changed. *"Don't rush into getting pregnant.* With your sister expecting, I can imagine how you feel. You can be quite competitive with her. I still believe you should be married a year before becoming a parent. Especially given Nelson's circumstances."

Alyce did not tell her she had stopped using birth control.

"Have you set a date?"

"When I brought it up, he was evasive. Should I be upset?"

Her frosty response was, "From what you've told me about Glorianna, it may be entirely up to her. I do hope I have a say in this. I *am* your mother."

"I'll be sure you do."

"And what about the other woman in Nelson's life? Does she know?"

"Yes. Their son's been a real handful. I think it's bothering him the most."

"As long as Nelson makes you feel like you come first, this might work."

"No might, Mom. It *will* work."

Alyce ladled Aurora sauce over fresh steamed mussels and handed Nelson the white bowl. "It's like a Normandy white sauce with a little tomato paste added to turn it a coral pink."

He gave her a dazed look.

She still could not believe they were engaged. She thought about sending a photo of her gigantic ring to her sister, but that would have been too *m'as tu vu*.

After their delicious lunch of mussels, Alyce parked herself by Jean-Luc's still-covered pool to study while Nelson hooked up a Wi-Fi router in the office.

It didn't take long before she heard him cursing.

She found him at Jean-Luc's messy desk, trying to decipher the router instructions.

"I *have* to get online and I can't get this thing going."

"Aren't you on vacation?"

"I'd rather spend an hour a day staying on top of emails than 20 when I get back."

She handed him a cold glass of Kronenbourg, a French beer.

His gulp was followed with "That hits the spot." He eyed her in her two-piece bathing suit. "So do you."

"Let me at that thing."

"You were just at it an hour ago."

"I mean the router! Maybe it's a translation issue."

"Be my guest."

As she grappled with the instructions, Nelson looked around Jean-Luc's office. He peeked behind the office door. "Interesting." He'd found a black cape, black pants, and a black leather mask dangling from the top of the hanger they were on. Black tape covered the eyeholes.

It was the mask Jean-Luc had used while giving her the herb lessons. What she'd thought was a sign of kinkiness was part of a costume. Or was it a costume he used in the bedroom?

"I think it's a Zorro outfit," he said. "That Jean-Luc is one weird dude." He took a beat before saying, "But if it turns you on, I'll wear it."

He proceeded to don the cape and break into a flamenco/bullfighting dance, swooshing it around, clapping and stomping his feet, ending with "*Olé!*"

No doubt Jean-Luc actually knew how to flamenco dance *and* slay a bull. She did not share that with Nelson.

She enthusiastically applauded. "Bravo!"

"Hey, maybe your next challenge should be learning Spanish."

"I'm still trying to learn French."

Nelson turned his head. "What's that noise?"

"The mailman," she said. "He delivers it on his moped."

He went downstairs after he left, still wearing the cape, and brought back a stack of letters.

"Look at this, Ally." It was an envelope from a bank in Zurich. "He has a Swiss bank account. Could he have a fortune stashed away?"

She watched out of the corner of her eye to make sure he didn't look too closely at Jean-Luc's mail.

"With him, who knows? Hey, I got it!" With a click of the mouse she was online. "Yes!"

Nelson now seemed more interested in the filing cabinets lining the far wall. He walked closer to inspect them. Starting with the top-left one, he slid open the drawer.

"Are you snooping, Nelson?"

"I'm just scanning the folder tabs. I'm not taking anything out."

"And?"

"Pretty wide range of topics. Spanish-American War, Mako Sharks, Oedipal Complex, Punishment Ancient Rome, Napoleon, Nondormant Volcanoes, Geospheric Strata Theorem, Pavlov, 5th Century Egyptians, Raising Chickens, Coal Mining, Brazilian Beetles, Psychedelic Bands, Poisonous Tropical Plants."

"Doesn't sound like they're in any kind of order."

"Each one has a number. Somewhere he must have a ledger that tells him where everything is." He counted 24 drawers. "There have to be thousands of documents."

"No wonder he can't function in the real world. He has the brain of a Martian."

"Well, well, what's this?" he said, as he studied a drawer on the far right. "It says *B-a-n-q-u-e Declarations*. That's bank, right?"

"Stop."

"There's no lock. How private could it be? You said he doesn't care about money, so—"

The moment he pulled out the drawer an alarm began to wail.

"What the hell did you do!"

"SHIT!"

They looked everywhere for a way to stop it. Under the desk, in the closet, inside a lampshade. No matter how much they cursed and banged into each other and cursed some more, they couldn't get it to turn off.

"I told you not to snoop!"

"I just opened the filing cabinet. I didn't look at anything!"

"You were going to!"

Within a few minutes, the piercing sound of the alarm was joined by a police siren.

"Great, Ally! Just great!"

"You still have the cape on!"

He ripped it off and threw it at her. "You're practically naked."

"Why would I be wearing—"

"Wait," he said, "I have an idea."

She and Nelson opened the front door with a smile.

"*Bonjour!*" she sang out. "*Excusez-moi de vous déranger, madame, mais j'ai un problème.* We accidentally tripped the alarm and cannot turn it off."

Call them Jacques and Gilles. Jacques was the taller, tough one. Gilles the shorter, nice one. They regarded Alyce in the cape and Nelson in the black leather pants and mask (without the tape over the eyeholes). An amused look was traded.

Gilles asked for identification while the other went upstairs to turn off the alarm.

"I'm a student at *Marlaison Ecole Française*. This is my fiancé. We were just having a little, uh, fun. You know, a *sieste crapuleuse*." That caused him to smile broadly.

They escorted her to the cottage. She showed them her school I.D. and their passports. A mute Nelson followed. They were more interested in her body. Good! Anything to make them forget what had happened.

Gilles asked in a friendlier tone. "Where is Jean-Luc?"

"He left a couple of days ago. I have no idea where he went. He knows we're here."

The two officers walked away and spoke in hushed tones. At one point they laughed. She took that as a good sign. Nelson kept giving her the strangest look.

"We will not tell him this happened, but do not touch anything that is not yours."

Jacques added, "And next time, take your Bad Boy Nap in your bedroom."

After they left, Nelson said, "So what the hell did they say?"

"That they won't tell Jean-Luc and to stay in our bedroom."

"What did you say?"

Then it hit her. "Holy shit! I spoke French the entire time!"

They calmed themselves with a round of beers by the pool and were soon laughing about the incident. She wondered, "Do you think he has hidden cameras, too?"

"Maybe that's why he wanted to leave us alone."

She waved to the house. "Hi, Jean-Luc! Come on, Nelson. Smile."

He looked far from happy. "I bet he's going to write about us."

She thought about that as she took a sip of her beer. "I never would have learned French if it hadn't been for him, which makes him look good. How unflattering could he be?"

He reclined in his lounger. "I love how positive you are, but you can also be very naïve."

Her faced burned with embarrassment. "I'll take naïve over negative any day."

She walked into the cottage and slammed the door. He was only able to put her in a good mood when he talked about a wedding date.

"How does next spring sound?" he asked. "Unless, of course," he eyed her stomach, "we've made a lasting souvenir. Then we'll move it up."

That suited her just fine. All of it.

AVIGNON

Raymond had a good laugh seeing Jean-Luc in orange spandex shorts that a previous guest had left behind. Then he turned uneasy.

"You are going to run? Not in those shoes. Try mine."

They were a bit big and almost as garish as the shorts but would work.

"Do not overdo it, Jean-Luc. I know how you are. Let me give you some bottled water. Take it easy. Do plenty of warm-up exercise."

He dismissed him with a "Yes, yes."

"Go to the park down the road about a mile. There is a track there."

"Is it flat?"

"Yes."

"I want a challenge. I'll find a hilly area."

Raymond shook his head. "You do not listen to anyone, do you?" As Jean-Luc walked to his car, he called out, "Did you make a decision about the job yet?"

"No!"

"Wait! The water."

Ten minutes later, Jean-Luc was pulled off to the side of a remote road. He stretched for 15 seconds before slapping his thigh and saying, "Come on, girl."

Didon, still looking dainty as lace, came bounding toward her master. When he started to run she stopped and whined.

"I'm in my prime! Come, Didon. Come."

She obeyed. They began running up a long slope.

Jean-Luc had had enough of regurgitating the past. He concluded what he really needed was fresh air. He was impressed with Alyce's discipline with her daily jog; how she eyed the trim, toned Nelson. Only five years separated him and his preppy opponent, yet his gray hair made him look like he could be Nelson's father. Alyce's "metrosexual" suggestion that he dye it didn't seem so ridiculous all of a sudden.

He also had to clear his head of something else. Raymond uncovered that a professor in the Department of Modern Letters at the nearby *Université de Provence* had left unexpectedly. They were frantic to find someone for the fall semester, two months away. He mentioned Jean-Luc *might* be interested in filling in. Within 24 hours, Jean-Luc had received five separate ego-stroking calls from people he knew there, including the dean.

He stopped, panted, cursed, kept going. Didon again whined and did not want to go on.

"It's called exercise," he wheezed to her. "The way I eat and drink, it's—" He gasped. "It's only a matter of time before—"

He had to stop talking out loud to his dog. Not only because he looked foolish, but because he could barely breathe.

As the road grew steeper, the pain increased in his chest, along with the feeling that he was going to throw up or pass out.

He slowed down.

Raymond's words that he was in love with Alyce returned to him.

Nelson was sure to propose to her in Paris. Would he write it in the sky as they were milling among the throngs at the Eiffel Tower?

She soon would be out of his life forever.

Thank God. Yes. Thank God.

Jean-Luc looked at Didon, his companion for the last 10 years. Her eyes had become milkier. How much longer would she be with him?

Another wave of indigestion. A sharp jab in the middle of his back.

As he ran, barely, he entertained once more the possibility of teaching. *That's* why he felt sick. Being a guest lecturer was one thing. Teaching full time?

More shooting pain. Was he that out of shape?

He must exert control over his mental state. He had been reading Herrigel's *The Method of Zen* that morning and was stopped by the sentence: *He must get beyond the opposites in which he is still caught, as a prelude to a transformation that is no longer of his own doing, but is something that "happens" to him.*

Damn. Was an elephant sitting on him? He sank to his knees, clutching his chest, trying to catch his breath. Didon barked in his left ear, sounding far away.

He crumpled to the ground like an aluminum can being stepped on.

Oh, the indignity of dying this way. He had envisioned something more grand and romantic. A lightning bolt through the top of his head. Flames engulfing him while trying to rescue someone. A spray of bullets from a jealous lover.

A heart attack. How *American.*

At least he was dying in France.

In damn bright orange spandex shorts!

Hog Heaven

MARLAISON

The first class of the day usually began informally, with everyone talking about what they had done the night before or over the weekend. Alyce's Monday news of becoming engaged was met with applause.

"But Al-*ees*," commented Ulrike, "I do not see a ring."

When she pulled it out on its chain, more than one hand clapped onto a mouth.

"That is the biggest diamond I have ever seen!" Jutta cried.

Alyce quickly slipped it back out of sight. She thought about telling them it wasn't real, but before she could, the trim, chic instructor Claire in fashionable red glasses had found the hook she was looking for. They were soon off and running on the subject of marriage in France.

"We are more pragmatic about it," Claire said, in French, of course. "Often couples do not become formally engaged. They live together first. The wedding itself is often low-key."

Trousseau came from the French word *trousse*, or bundle. A bride wearing white originated with the French. *Chiverie*, the banging of pots and pans outside the newlyweds' room, was also Gallic. That led to everyone talking about customs in their various countries. Interestingly, India and Japan, where many marriages were arranged, had some of the most lavish weddings.

Not many of the MEF students stayed as long as Alyce. As a result, she hadn't formed any lasting friendships. That changed with Ulrike and Jutta from Germany. They were about Alyce's age and there for six weeks. They spoke English well. During a class break, Ulrike, the more forthright one, said, "It's a good thing you didn't fall for Jean-Luc. I read about him online. He would have messed up your head."

Jutta added, "But he can mess up mine any day! I'm kidding. I am off French men after—"

Ulrike nudged her with her elbow.

"What? Is there something I should know?"

"Ulrike, Al-*ees* is engaged now. She should know." Turning to Al-*ees*, "Your previous hosts, Julian Devreaux and his father…"

"They tried to seduce us."

"At different times. Not together."

"We found out they are famous for doing that."

Yves was no surprise. But I'm-not-a-dog-like-my-father Julien? That adorable prick.

Back at Jean-Luc's, Nelson convinced Alyce to road test Jean-Luc's wild carved granite shower. It was easily agreed it would not be touched should they buy the place. Alyce still had no idea whether the sale was going to happen. Nelson said "I need time to think about it" and she was effortlessly giving him that space. Pre-France she would have been nagging him.

As they dried off, he asked, "What delicious meal are you going to whip up tonight?"

"Something simple. A chicken daube."

"What's that?"

"A braised dish marinated in wine, deglazed and then slowly stewed."

"I can't believe what a good cook you've become." He sheepishly added, "Remember when I told you not to cook at my apartment because the ventilation wasn't working? It was really so you wouldn't burn anything again."

"What?"

Instead of being upset, she laughed.

"I've become very picky about freshness," she said. "I need to clip some herbs in the woods out back. Want to come?"

"Have to check my email."

She changed into a long shirt and sweatpants for added protection against the scratches and bites she received the last time. Before she headed into the woods, she remembered Jean-Luc's warning about dangerous boars and found the suede bag he kept his gun in. She made sure the weapon was locked.

Holding it with both hands, arms straight in front of her, she aimed it at nothing in particular as she revisited what it felt like to shoot one. She was a pretty good marksman in her Camp Wumpamockasee days.

She slung the bag over her shoulder, picked up a wicker basket, and was off.

She passed the rabbit hutch, the *pigeonnier.* Then which way did they go? She headed to the left. After walking for a bit, she glimpsed something. Pulling back branches, she stared at a headstone: blank, gray, about two feet tall and not old.

She walked around it, lifting off more foliage to make sure nothing was written on it.

As she was assuring herself it wasn't a headstone at all, just some kind of art Jean-Luc had made or put there, the brush about 20 feet away moved, followed by a loud, ugly snort.

A rush of heat circled her neck and shot into her face. Her heart felt like it was going to pole vault out of her chest. It couldn't be Jean-Luc. She'd conjured up a ghost from this grave!

A huge head appeared with black devil eyes and long, thick, yellowish, pointy tusks jutting from its mouth. It regarded Alyce as though she were its next meal. Oh God, what it could do with those tusks.

She screamed as loud as she could. Only problem, it was in her head. Nothing came out of her mouth.

The next thing she knew, she was up a small, shaky tree, trying to get the gun out of the bag. She succeeded, dropping the bag in the process.

He was right below. Baring his teeth. Making an awful noise that was somewhere between a snort, a bark, and a pig's oinky shriek.

She didn't want to kill him.

The tree began to bend. And bend.

Something rustled in the thick brush behind her. More snorting. There were two! They darted off into the brush. More squeals and snorts. Were they mating or fighting?

Right then, getting mauled to pieces didn't seem a whole lot worse than the pain of trying to keep from peeing. She struggled to get her pants down using one hand. As relief swept over her, panic was right behind. What if her pee attracted the boars?

The moment she finished, KERRRRRRACK!

The branch gave out.

So did her knees when she hit the ground. She willed herself to stand, pull up her dirty sweatpants over her dirtier ass, and grab the gun that had fallen out of her hand.

GRRRUUUNNKK! One was running toward her.

She flipped the lock off.

Aimed.

POW!

She'd forgotten how loud a gun was.

The boar squealed, wobbled, and limped into the brush. The other ran off.

The one she'd shot was still alive, shaking and shrieking. Its back leg was bleeding. Without thinking, she shot it again. Right in the head.

She heard in the distance, "ALLY! ALLY! WHERE ARE YOU!"

She was gasping for air and barely got out "Over here!"

When Nelson found her, he was thunderstruck. "What the hell?!"

She proudly blew on the pistol. "Guess we're having a boar daube tonight."

Disgusted, he said, "You're kidding."

"Hell, no! Boar meat is delicious, I'm told. There's no way I'm not cooking this sucker. He almost killed me! There's a wheelbarrow in the garage. Let's take him to Eduard, the butcher."

She gathered up the suede bag and walked with Nelson, higher than high from the adrenaline coursing through her. She didn't notice Jean-Luc's notebook tossed into the brush.

For now.

Eduard was not as pleased to see her boar as she had anticipated. Clasping his hands to his face and spewing a few "merdes," he dashed to his front door, quickly lowered its shade, and locked the old brass doorknob, double-checking it.

"*Mon Dieu*, mademoiselle, you cannot kill a boar outside hunting season and without a permit!"

Her face flushed. Nelson's turned ashen.

"Could she get arrested? Fined?"

"It was in self-defense, Eduard! Self-defense! There were two coming right at me!"

"Oh!" He threw his arms in the air and casually re-opened his store. "That is another story."

Very excitedly, in a rush she could barely understand, he told her all the dishes she could make with its various parts.

"How about a daube?" she asked, then turned to Nelson. "Let's have a big feast with students from the school."

He slipped his arms around her waist. "Sure, honey. It'll be good practice for all the parties we'll soon be throwing."

Eduard was beaming. "You are an enchanting couple!"

As he went about cutting the shoulder into cubes like stew meat, he said, "Invite them in two or three days. It is not the usual, but marinate the meat in *white* wine, since it is summer, overnight. A viognier would be ideal. No stock! Only wine. Add onion, a little orange peel, bouquet garni…I will write it down for you. Just remember, marinate day one, cook day two. It is even better day three." He put his fingers to his lips and kissed them. "The perfect marriage of the flavors."

Alyce thanked him profusely. Nelson insisted he take some.

"Maybe a little for myself. I cannot sell it at this time of year."

Alyce and Nelson were in awe as he masterfully attacked his work while whistling.

"It's like watching an artist," Nelson said. "It's not so bad anymore." Then he joked as he snapped more photos for the Alyce Slays A Wild Boar album, "Think I should tell Mother to use one of these pictures on the wedding invitation?"

He kissed her on the lips. The butcher smiled from ear to ear.

"I think I'm in heaven," she said.

"Hog heaven," added Nelson.

She laughed too hard.

"Tell me how you did this, Al-*ees*. You are very lucky you were not hurt. *Sangliers* are dangerous when angry."

She delighted him with her story (leaving out the part about peeing in the tree.)

As they were leaving, Eduard insisted they take a cut-up chicken. "Not everyone likes boar."

Once home, she called Liliane's house, but there was no answer. She had email addresses for her and the students she wanted to invite and put the word out that way.

Alyce and Nelson spent another quiet evening together: Nelson on his computer doing vineyard research while Alyce made a wonderful meal she called *réchauffé*.

"It's French for heated leftovers," she said.

"The French can make anything sound elegant."

The cicadas hummed and all was good. Nelson tickled Alyce when he mimicked Eduard. "We are such ze enchanting cup-*el*!"

When it was time to clear the table, Nelson said, "It already feels like home here."

They were soon in a loving embrace. While slowly stroking his back, she said, "You're going to buy it?"

He hesitated. "Let me see how I feel when I get back to New York."

Her reply was a long kiss. While it grew in intensity, she concentrated on one wish: *The put-an-ocean-between-them trick will work in this case, as well.*

AVIGNON

Liliane, her two sons, Raymond, and his wife Odalis dolefully watched Jean-Luc curled into a fetal position in the guest bed at Raymond's home. His nephews, each holding one of their mother's hands, stared at him as if he were a grotesque animal caged at a zoo.

Raymond looked the worst. He was at that age where friends and relatives were vanishing from the face of the earth at an ever-increasing rate. Odalis stood behind them, hand under her chin, contemplating how to handle this situation.

"I know what you're thinking," Jean-Luc said from his bed. "Why didn't he die?"

Liliane replied, "No, I am thinking, why did he live? There must be more for you to do on this earth."

"Yes, Jean-Luc," said Stéphane. "Much more." Benoit nodded and said in his small voice, "Marry Al-*ees*. I want her to be my aunt."

Jean-Luc's eyebrows formed perfect arches.

"I cannot do that, Benoit. She is spoken for."

Stéphane said, "We met him. We like you better."

It warmed his heart that he had hardly been the perfect uncle and they still thought that. "I am afraid there is nothing I can do about it."

"But there is something you *can* take on," offered Liliane.

"The *Université* almost withdrew their offer," Raymond said. "I had to do quite a tap dance to convince them you just needed a little more time to think it over. I never mentioned your incident."

His sister and nephews moved closer. She said, "There are many applicants and those from within lobbying for the position."

"Everyone agrees you are brilliant." Raymond eased his frame onto the edge of his bed. "But can you teach? Are you reliable? Are you sensitive enough?"

"Yes, you are," said Stéphane. Even Benoit nodded in agreement.

Liliane said, "I love you, Jean-Luc, but I am having another child and cannot take care of your life anymore." With a rougher edge, she added, "I also run a school filled with foreigners in need of constant attention, in case you forgot."

"I do not need anyone to take care of me!"

Odalis politely extracted herself from this argument with a soft, "Excuse me."

He was so tired. "Why did that car have to drive by and save me?"

"You are being your usual dramatic self," Liliane said. "You would not have died."

He had been diagnosed with stress cardiomyopathy, a reaction to extreme emotional upheaval that pumps large doses of hormones and other chemicals into the bloodstream. They can be temporarily toxic to the heart and mimic a heart attack but cause no permanent damage. He would be fully recovered in two weeks. A complete overhaul of his lifestyle was ordered that included drinking much less, not smoking at all, easing into exercising regularly, and his favorite: reducing stress. The doctor told Jean-Luc to lower it as though it were a dial he could turn up or down.

Had the boys not been standing there he would have told them he was now obsessed with morbid thoughts of how he would die. Would it be while he was doing something ordinary, like tapping the shell of a soft-boiled egg he was about to eat, or in the white heat of an argument? Every man dreams of dying after making love to a beautiful woman, but even if he were that lucky it would be a contemptible cliché. The worst would be during his sleep. He wanted to know death was descending upon him, observe its every nuance. Nor did he want a tawdry scene with loved ones gathered around his bedside.

Liliane intruded with, "You can move into a nice apartment at the *Université* for visiting professors. If the Mansfields don't buy your property it can be auctioned off. Or wait for a buyer. But the sooner you have real money in the bank the better."

"Have you heard anything from them?"

"Not yet, but Al-*ees* and Nelson rarely leave the premises. They're behaving like smitten newlyweds."

His plan was working. If only his heart didn't wish otherwise. He eyed Benoit. Why did he have to make that comment about marrying her? Children are so intuitive.

"I must go now," Liliane said as she picked up her purse. "We have a two hour drive back to Marlaison."

Raymond added in his eternally optimistic way, "You may even like teaching." No wonder he was able to stay gainfully employed in the cutthroat world of publishing for so long. "Look at how well you did with the American girl."

That brought a smile to his sister's face. "She was hopeless until you became her tutor. My spectacular challenge is now a spectacular student! She has been moved ahead two levels."

Stéphane turned to her. "What about us? We have been teaching her, too."

Jean-Luc knew they had kept it on the most rudimentary

levels. Nevertheless, Liliane kindly indulged them. "Yes, you and Benoit have been a big help, my darlings."

What made him think he might actually be cut out for teaching was his experience with Alyce. But everything about her, their situation, and the style in which he taught was different. The restrictions of a classroom and teaching schedule would make him insane.

He sat up. "Not a word to Al-*ees* about any of this! I am healthy as an Angus steer!"

"Not until you say yes or no about the position," Liliane demanded.

He plucked a white tissue from the box on his nightstand and waved it at her. "I surrender. Happy?"

Odalis appeared at the doorway. He saw immediately what she was holding and snapped, "Damn you!"

Raymond reached out and touched his shoulder. "I asked her to see if you had been writing anything."

She handed her husband his crumpled pieces of yellow legal paper, now flattened out.

"Oh, go ahead and read it. I don't care anymore. I don't care about anything."

"I read it," Odalis said. "You must write more, Jean-Luc. You must."

He turned over, pulled the pillow over his head, and screamed. Then he jumped up, grabbed the box of tissues, and yanked several of them out, filling the room with floating white squares.

"Okay! Okay! Okay! I surrender. I'll write my memoir."

By the time he was done with his ridiculous tantrum, everyone was laughing and applauding.

If only his books were as funny.

24

A Summer Feast

MARLAISON

In class the next day, Alyce told the wild boar story. In French. It was a huge hit.

Claire exclaimed, "Al-*ees*, you are a *raconteur.*"

More people from various countries were invited to the boar feast she and Nelson were throwing the following night. The guest list grew to Ulrike and Jutta, two Danish men, one Japanese woman, two Brits, a South African and an Eastern Indian woman. Plus Liliane and her family.

As Alyce and Nelson set the long teak table that had turned gray from being outside, she was sorry Jean-Luc wasn't there, though she was glad she was rising to this challenge on her own. Well, pretty much on her own. Nelson helped some, but mostly sat at his laptop staying in touch with clients and reading about winemaking.

She stopped to watch how the sun at that hour bathed the kitchen in golden light, turning it more yellow, and pointed it out to Nelson.

He looked up for a second. "Yeah, honey. It's beautiful."

The Girards arrived first. Stéphane and Benoit loved the photos of the wild boar in the wheelbarrow. Nelson offered to take them to the scene of the crime. Simon joined with the suede gun bag over his shoulder.

Walking away, Liliane turned to Alyce. "Nelson is good with children and easy to be with in general. And he comes from money. I can see why you are attracted to him." She paused. "Have you made any decisions about the future?"

"In terms of the property? I expect an answer soon. I'm as anxious as you are to move forward. I just have to let him make the final decision."

"You know your man best. I'll alert you if anyone else is interested." She added with a smile, "You killed a wild boar and cooked it! I cannot believe it."

As other guests arrived, Alyce put them to work grating cheese and turning the slices of *aubergine* (eggplant) roasting on the open fire in the back. Nelson was a wonderful host, too. Being in sales, he knew how to turn on the charm.

They finally sat down to dinner while singing along to the universally appealing Frank Sinatra. They weren't far into the meal when Alyce heard a familiar bark. A powder puff of pure ivory came prancing toward her.

"Didon?"

Her long feminine face was shaved. Above it was a crown of white, accented with a pink bow. Her paws and the tops of her legs were shorn, too, with a big alabaster puff in between. Her tail was bare with a big pom-pom at the end. Finally, she looked like a poodle. And she smelled wonderful.

Jean-Luc, however, didn't look so good as he gazed at everyone from the kitchen. She excused herself and went inside. "Are you mad that I'm throwing a party?"

"Not at all. It is nice to see the place enjoyed."

"You don't look very happy."

"I came down with the flu when I was in Avignon."

"What made you go there?"

"My editor."

"Ah. How is she?"

"*He* is fine." He noticed the ring dangling from her neck. "Are you betrothed?"

"Yes." It came out with a defiant edge.

His pale blue eyes burned into her. "He did not know your ring size?"

She archly responded, "That's not unusual. I can get it fixed."

He took it in his hand, inspected it. "But of course it would be vulgar."

She snatched it from him. "But of course you would say that."

"What are you serving?"

She lit up. "A wild boar I shot in the woods while gathering herbs."

He didn't believe it. She showed him the photos.

"I would not miss this meal for anything. How did you make it?"

When she told him she used white wine, he made a face of disapproval.

"Eduard told me to do that!"

"Hmpf. He was, how do you say, messing with your mind?"

"Wait until you try it, Mister Never Wrong."

He took out a silver spoon and tried a bite, savoring it as though it were an $800 bottle of wine. "Hmmm."

"Well?"

"Not bad. Too much brandy. Did you flambé? Light it?"

"I just poured it in."

"You need to flambé. It makes it smoother." He took another bite. "Not enough deglazing. A daube is all about deglazing. But for a first try, I am impressed."

Coming from Jean-Luc, that was indeed a compliment.

He came outside and warmly said, "Salutations, friends. Welcome." There was no need to say who he was.

She moved from the end, opposite Nelson, so that Jean-Luc and Nelson could face each other. It didn't seem right for either one to step down from their positions of power. She squeezed in a chair to Nelson's left, cater-cornered.

Soon she was regaling Jean-Luc with the boar story after apologizing to everyone for repeating it.

Ulrike called out, "It is too good not to repeat!"

This time Alyce left in the part about peeing while in the tree. She knew Jean-Luc and the little boys would love it, and with all the drinking, everyone roared with laughter.

All but Nelson. When she was done with the story he cleared his throat, leaned into her and said, "You can edit out the peeing part in the future, dear."

It stung her to hear him say that. Okay, they were eating. With strangers. Maybe it was inappropriate. Still she hissed back, "It's not like your mother is here. Lighten up."

Throughout the meal, Alyce watched Jean-Luc expertly draw out of everyone what he wanted to know, like a surgeon in the operating room. He started with the Indian woman, Gitali, whose marriage had been arranged. He explained to his nephews what that meant.

A crestfallen Stéphane said, "Your parents tell you what to do *forever*?"

Gitali seemed genuinely happy about it.

"I can't imagine marrying someone I didn't know well," Alyce commented.

Jean-Luc pointed out that 50% of all American marriages end in divorce and the rest are of questionable quality.

Nelson said, "That's your dismal view."

"Yes, Jean-Luc," Alyce concurred. "Must you look at

everything through a cracked window? *La Vie en Rose!* Put on some rose-colored glasses."

"Some of the best unions I've ever seen were arranged," he argued.

He took a poll around the table and Alyce was surprised that half of the guests agreed arranged marriages were perfectly acceptable, including Nelson.

She shook her head. "Not for me."

"But you are so practical, Al-*ees*. You are driven by logic and numbers. Why wouldn't it appeal to you?"

"It just doesn't."

"Knock it off, Frenchie," Nelson nearly yelled at him.

Everyone momentarily stopped talking. Oh no, Alyce thought. Nelson's had too much to drink. Jean-Luc seemed almost pleased that he had succeeded in getting him to blow his cool.

Jean-Luc shifted his focus to the Japanese woman and her religious beliefs. He startled her when he said, "I sense you do not practice Shinto, Buddhism, or Confucianism."

"Yes, you are right. But how did you know?"

"Intuition."

She was a Catholic, unusual for someone born and raised in Japan. An intense discussion about religion followed until Alyce said, "Jean-Luc, in America we say there are two things you should never discuss at dinner. Politics and religion."

"You would like me to keep the conversation nice and dull? Perhaps you will like this joke instead." He eyed his nephews. "On second thought, never mind."

Liliane rose. "It is time for us to be going anyway."

The boys protested but Simon agreed it was past their bedtime. When he and Jean-Luc cheek-kissed goodbye, he whispered, "Tell me the joke later."

Once tender ears were gone, Jean-Luc resumed.

"An American woman had a facelift. She went to a McDo's.

That's McDonald's to some of you. She asked the boy behind the counter, 'How old do you think I am?' He said, 'Uhhh. Thirty?' She exclaimed, 'I'm 47!' She asked a shopkeeper the same question. The woman said, 'Oh… 35?' She was thrilled. Then she sat on a park bench and a man sat down next to her. She turned to him. 'How old do you think I am?' He replied, 'I can tell your exact age if I feel under your blouse.' She was taken aback but agreed. He reached under her shirt, then under her bra and felt around for some time. Finally he said, 'Forty-seven.' She gasped. 'How did you know?' He said, 'I was standing behind you at McDo's.'"

It brought the house down (except for Nelson) and set off a round of silly jokes poking fun at every culture.

Despite Nelson's edginess, Alyce didn't want the night to end. Neither did the female guests who acted in Jean-Luc's presence like sun-starved house plants that had been moved outdoors.

Around 11:00, he pulled her aside. "Serve the orange juice."

"What orange juice?"

"It is how you let guests know it is time to leave."

He kept frozen concentrate on hand for emergency situations, though it pained him to serve anything of such mediocre quality.

Ulrike and Jutta stayed to clean up, though Alyce sensed they really wanted to hang with Jean-Luc. When he said good-night and went upstairs, they quickly finished the dishes and left.

Didon would not lie down in her old place. She moved to the other side of the kitchen and watched Alyce, chest out, front paws delicately crossed.

Alyce was jolted from her good mood when, back in the cottage, Nelson said, "I don't want you staying here after I leave. I'm putting you in a hotel until school is over."

"Don't be ridiculous." She held up the ring. "We're engaged, remember?"

"I don't trust Jean-Luc."

Her mother always told her: "Pick your battles."

"I'll do it to make you happy, but I don't think you have anything to worry about."

"We'll see about that."

Triangles

"Are you sure you're okay?" Alyce asked Jean-Luc the next morning as she made café crèmes for everyone.

"No, I am not okay, Al-*ees*. I am dying for a cigarette but have vowed to quit."

"Good. I know you can do it."

That only made him feel worse.

Nelson nodded at the bag with the shiatsu neck massager they had given him, much to his delight. "Try it out. Maybe you'll forget about smoking."

"Maybe after I have a cigarette."

Nelson impatiently checked the time on his cell.

"The croissants will be ready in 10 minutes," she said stiffly.

"I'm going to miss that smell."

She poured his coffee. A distinct tartness flavored, "All the more reason to come back right away."

He matched her with, "How did you know that's exactly what I was thinking?"

There was a new tension between the lovebirds. She would not look directly at Jean-Luc.

"The coffee is perfect, Al-*ees*."

"Beginner's luck again?" she asked.

"You are not a beginner anymore."

She told Nelson how she was able to crack an egg with one hand on her first attempt.

"How nice."

He could feel his devilish side ready to erupt. It vanished when Nelson said, "Alyce will be moving into a hotel today."

She pounded coffee grounds from the espresso maker into the garbage, her back to them.

"You did not like it here?"

Alyce turned. "Oh, no. We love it here."

"I see." He took another sip of his coffee. "Now that you are engaged..."

"Exactly," said Nelson. "See, Ally? It's the appropriate thing to do."

"Fine!" she cried as though it wasn't at all, giving Jean-Luc a shred of hope.

"Tell me, Nelson. What does your son and his mother think of you buying property here?"

Alyce looked intensely curious as she settled on her stool.

He cleared his throat, shifted in his seat. "That's a good question, Jean-Luc. Since I need to use all the vacation time I've accrued or lose it, I was thinking of bringing them over in a couple of weeks so Junior doesn't feel left out."

He could feel Alyce's temper rise when she said, "Why not just bring *him* over."

He shifted again, took another sip of coffee to buy time. "We better see how this is going to work with all of us, Ally. Plus, she wouldn't want to be away from him that long."

"Maybe it would do them both good to be apart for *once*."

"Let's discuss this while I finish packing." He stood up with his coffee.

She forced a smile. "I need to keep an eye on the croissants."

After he left for the cottage, Jean-Luc hummed "La Vie en Rose."

"Not one word out of you!"

"Now, now, Al-*ees*. Are you not glad I brought it up?"

How he had come to love her glare.

He pulled the massage device out of the bag. "Shall we give it a test run in my bedroom?"

"Go right ahead."

"I want you to help me."

"All you do is plug it in and turn on the power button." She pointed at the device. "If you want the balls to roll this way, push this. If you want—"

"I want you to show me. Set the timer so you don't burn the croissants."

As Alyce found an electrical socket near his bed, he pulled apart the red panels hanging from its frame and climbed on the spacious king-size mattress. She positioned the machine behind his head so he could nestle his neck into the space between the two balls.

"Shit! This hurts!" Alyce jumped to turn the switch off. Immediately he grabbed her arm and did not let go. "Don't touch it! I love it! Ohhhhhhhh. Now make the balls turn the other way. Yeeeeeees. It's like a big Swede pummeling my neck. Brunhilda! That's what I will call it. Aaaahhh."

She was giggling with delight and within moments he could feel the tension releasing, not just from his neck. Though he hated that it came from Nelson, he absolutely adored it.

He couldn't help himself. He pulled her to him but the grinding balls made the effort quite comical as she resisted. He rolled off Brunhilda, turned her off, and tried to kiss Alyce again.

"No!"

"How can you slay a wild boar *and* cook it to perfection and not expect me to fall madly in love with you?"

She did not jerk away. She looked sad.

He said softly, "When you said you had to have your engagement ring re-sized, were you talking about the diamond as well as the band? That jewel is just not you. It's more his mother."

She confessed it wasn't real and why. "I can understand his reasoning."

He thought it was the most insane thing he'd ever heard. "What else is troubling you—other than Carmelita and Junior?"

She reached for his hand. He was sure his heart was going to act up on him again. He held it tightly to convey *I am here for you in whatever way you need me to be.*

She did not confess what he wanted to hear: that she was hopelessly in love with him. Instead she said that she felt as though a flashing neon light went off in Nelson's brain that said GET MARRIED NOW and she happened to be there and would do.

"It is a question that has confounded mankind for millennia," he said. "Can you fall in love if you do not believe wholeheartedly that you want to do so? Or do you meet someone and then you want it?" He let go of her hand. "Either way, I would not lose sleep over it. He wants you to marry him. I pray to God he feels *something*."

He turned his massager back on, rested his neck between the grinding balls. "Al-*ees*, I am the last person you should consult on this matter."

He felt his throat closing up on him. He rested a hand over his heart, a feeble form of protection.

As she rose to leave, she said, "We only experience through contrast, right?"

"Very good. Who said it?"

She smiled. "Montaigne."

He smiled even more. He waited a moment before saying, "There is one comment I would like to make. Because of your lifelong rivalry with your sister, I think you are drawn to competitive triangles. Nelson's baggage, as you call it, may iron-ically give you a certain comfort. It is familiar."

Her eyes widened as she took that thought in.

"Every relationship has a third force at play somewhere. It is what creates the glue to keep it together. Too much, though, can create unbearable friction. You must decide what you can live with. Now tell me, how did he propose?"

It wasn't as trite as he had imagined, nor was it that special. What made it unusual was her throwing up! The combination of her now being engaged coupled with the hilarity of the story caused a new sharp ache in his chest.

Gasping for air, he begged, "You must leave before I have another attack."

"Attack?"

"*Merde.*"

"What?"

"I damn near died because of my feelings for you."

He filled her in on the details of his cardiomyopathy as she gaped in horror. Her voice cracked. "I don't understand. I thought you wanted me to marry Nelson."

"I do not want another man to even look at you! But I cannot give you what you need, Al-*ees*. I cannot be the perfect reliable husband and father. When I am creating, I am not a responsible person."

"But I'm responsible! You write and I'll take care—" She abruptly stopped.

Aha! He was filled with euphoric delight until reality hit him.

He sat up, cupped her face in his hands. "There is nothing I would love more than to watch you blossom over the decades."

Her arms slid slowly, limply to her sides.

"You are the most fragrant flower I have ever inhaled, and in the next moment you are a tetanus-infested rusty nail that has impaled my foot, and in the next you are teaching *me* what I need to learn! Al-*ees*, you *fascinate* me." He tenderly grabbed her hair, certain it would be the last time he touched it. "But I would not be good for you."

"I can't believe you're saying this."

He changed his tone as he whispered into her ear. "This is for your benefit, not mine. I do not think you are in love with Nelson, my Al-*ees*. You are in desperate *fear*. You know it is all a charade. Honey, sweetie, honey. You think you are being sensible *and* living every girl's dream to win the heart of the man who won hers first. You will be nothing but a pawn to him and his evil mother. Is that what you want?"

She pulled away, so shocked by what he'd said that her hands flew to her chest.

A familiar smarmy voice said, "Excuse me for interrupting."

Alyce jumped up. Jean-Luc tried to save the situation by saying to Nelson, "I was just telling her about the heart problem I had when I was away."

"Really? You had to whisper it in her ear?"

"We are just friends, I assure you. An old girlfriend is coming to take care of me." A lie.

"I'm glad to hear that." Alyce said with a shade of jealousy. Or was it anger? Her face and chest were flushed.

The oven timer sounded its alarm.

Back in the cottage, it didn't take long for harsh words to fly.

"I'm staying here until whatever crazy woman he's using shows up. He's not well."

"No, you're not."

"You're bringing Carmelita here and have the nerve to say that?"

"Why are you upset all of a sudden? You told me you were okay with her."

Alyce negotiated with Nelson that she would move into a hotel as soon as she let the *loirs* go.

"They need a little more time," she said. "I have to make them a nest, ideally in a hollowed-out tree."

Nelson had become attached to the baby dormice as well. Calmer now (oh how she loved that he didn't stay angry for long) he said, "Okay, honey." With a warm hug, "It's a good sign your mothering instincts are so strong." He let go. "But why can't Jean-Luc or his lady friend take care of them?"

"He has responsibility issues. I wouldn't trust him to follow through. And no other woman will see to them the way I do. The last one killed the mother!"

Right there she knew Jean-Luc could not give her what she wanted, if she was capable of thinking that. And did he really love her, or did he just want to get her in the sack? His line about her being in fear, not love, had to have been a selfish ploy. She kicked herself for falling for him. It had happened in such a sly, come-from-behind way, she hadn't even realized it until she stupidly blurted out that line about her taking care of everything.

She gazed at Nelson adoringly and thought of how lucky she was to have him.

They agreed she'd drive him to the airport and keep the car he'd rented. She wondered to herself how much longer she'd be (secretly) paying for the car Jean-Luc was using. She hoped this new woman had her own wheels.

As they were loading Nelson's luggage in the BMW, she noticed a funny-looking red car in the driveway that wasn't the one she had rented.

"It's a Renault Kangoo," Nelson said. "A minivan used for people with wheelchairs but its high interior and boxy look caught on with the public. I think it's kind of fun. Jean-Luc's?"

"Just a minute, honey. I'll be right back."

The word *honey* jumped out at her in a way it hadn't before, like a big rock on a smooth road. Damn that Jean-Luc.

She found him at his computer. "Where's my car?"

"I returned it and put a down payment on a car with a check Raymond had for me. Do you like it? I'm waiting for another one to pay you back. I didn't want to cost you another dime."

It was time to get to the bottom of Jean-Luc's finances. "There was something in the mail from a Swiss bank. Have a secret account there?"

He stopped clicking his mouse, turned around and said as nicely as he could, "What else did you go through when I was away?"

She straightened up. "I brought in your mail. It was on top."

"A wealthy woman who was madly in love with me—the affection not returned—left me 10,000 Euros a year in her will. I refuse to spend it on myself. Now that I know it has arrived, I will reimburse you, plus interest."

Like the woman sporting an engagement ring who came back to get her Lexus, Alyce was astounded to have a sudden change of heart. "What you taught me was worth every penny."

He gave her an assessing look. "Are you sure your wonderful Nelson is that worthy of the new you?"

"Oh, shut your pie hole."

He threw his head back and laughed, causing Alyce to light up inside.

Grabbing a pen and paper, he asked, "Is pie hole one word or two?"

With that she was out the door.

Too soon she and Nelson were having their last lingering good-bye kiss at the Nice airport. Hugging her as though she were the last woman alive, he said, "If you want to stay in the cottage, that's fine. I have to trust you, too."

What an amazing guy he was. So what if she had to share him once in awhile. If she was with Jean-Luc, she'd be competing against Colette all the time. It was fine.

Really, it was fine.

26

Drenched in Failure

Alyce was summoned to Liliane's office.

"Two things. First, my brother." She explained that Jean-Luc had to stay focused on writing his memoir and stay healthy. "He told me you know about his medical scare. He must take better care of himself or the next time it will be worse."

"That's up to him."

"True, but you are a good influence in getting him to exercise." She leaned in and lowered her voice. "Second, he has an opportunity to teach at the local university. If he does not have the book proposal done in a week he must take the job. All he needs is an outline and one or two chapters. I know he will be miserable in the world of academia, and make everyone miserable around him. Please, if there is anything you can do to get him to write that proposal, do it."

Alyce sat back. "Me?"

"You have a special way with him."

"No, I don't. Besides, he said an old girlfriend was coming to be with him."

"That is news to me."

Liliane called him. At one point in their conversation her

mouth twisted ever so slightly. Alyce heard her say, "You and your *harmless* white lies." She hung up. "He said that to appease Nelson, who walked in on you two and thought something was going on."

She could feel her face grow warm. "Nothing was going on, I swear!"

Liliane clasped her hands and said as though there would be no further discussion, "I have even more faith that you can do this."

Liliane eyed Alyce's ring still on a chain necklace. "You can take that to André to have it fitted properly. That is, if you stay engaged. His mother is not someone I could put up with."

"She's the least of my worries. Wait until you meet the mother of Nelson's son."

She prodded Alyce about the other topic she wanted to discuss: the Mansfield's interest in the property.

"A decision will be made soon," Alyce said, "The Mansfield Mafia, I mean, Express, is about to arrive. Nelson, Glorianna, Luther, plus Nelson's son and his mother Carmelita."

Liliane visibly paled as her mouth dropped.

"I know, I know," said Alyce. "A real cluster fuck, as they say in America."

Liliane poked the air the way Jean-Luc did when he was upset. "You must keep Jean-Luc focused on his writing! You must! Now what was that charming term you used?"

"Cluster fuck?"

She threw her head back and laughed, reminding Alyce of Jean-Luc. "I love it!"

"Glorianna's pronunciation would be different, though." She mimicked her future mother-in-law's head toss and bun-pat perfectly, and said in an uppity tone, "*Clustier fouquoi.*"

Liliane clutched her pregnant tummy as she repeated "Cloo-stee-*ay* foo-*kwa.*"

Alyce took advantage of the light moment. "Uh, Liliane. On

a more serious note. Right before I encountered the boar the other day, I saw a headstone. It was blank. It also looked fairly new. Any idea whose it is?"

"A headstone? No."

"Could it be Colette?"

"Who?"

"The love of his life, I thought."

She looked surprised. "He told you this? He must have been joking."

He was drunk at the time so maybe he was. "Then whose grave is it?"

Now looking perplexed, Liliane thought for a bit before saying, "He may have buried his other dog there that died last year and did not want me to know. A headstone is expensive."

"Please don't ever ask him about it!"

A confused Liliane tossed her auburn hair. "I will try to remember not to mention it."

"If you hear anything about her, you'll tell me?"

"Colette. You have my word."

Jean-Luc was sitting up in bed with boxes of photos around him, studying one picture. He felt strangely detached from the young man with dark hair blowing in the wind while on a Greek tycoon's enormous yacht, a raven-haired beauty at his side.

Thekla. That was her name. They spent a month twisted in the sheets in her family's estate on Crete while her parents were away. No matter what she did to amuse him, no matter what gifts she gave him (especially that), he lost interest.

What was his age then? Nineteen. Half his age now.

He squinted and tried to see himself at double his current years: 76.

He gazed at Didon under the window, basking in the sun

shining through it. What would it be like if humans only lived as long as dogs?

He heard Alyce's car pull up. Didon's head lifted. She didn't bark. She knew its sound as well. Jean-Luc also knew Alyce was mad from the way she stomped up the stairs to his office.

"I'm in here."

She angrily appeared by his bed.

He greeted her calmly. "Hello, Al-*ees*. How was school today?"

"No way would I have stayed here if I thought you were going to be here alone."

"I was merely stating a mistruth so Nelson wouldn't erupt. But I heard you arguing anyway. By the way, this is for you." He handed her an envelope.

She counted €3,500 inside, more than he owed her. She hesitated. "Thank you."

"You are welcome. I have appreciated all that you have done for me."

She scanned the boxes of photos next to him. "Liliane has assigned me the task of making sure you write your memoir and stick to your lifestyle changes. The first thing I'm doing is throwing out all of your cigarettes."

He made a face as though he'd just sipped vinegar. "I already did."

"How can I believe you?"

"You simply will not find them anywhere." His eyes went from her feet, up her calves and stopped at the hem of her dress.

The voice of a fishmonger's wife jarred him. "Stop looking at me like that! Now, what are you going to do with your life? Why are you so *stuck*? What is it?"

He brought his gaze to her perturbed face. "I do not feel I deserve success."

"Why?"

A familiar pain walloped him in the ribcage. He desperately wanted to feel worthy, to be "un-stuck."

"I do not know any other way to feel. As for the book, I don't know where to start, where to end, what to say, what not to say." He looked at her sadly. "And it makes me feel like I'm the biggest asshole I've ever met."

"That's your start! I'd read a book that opened like that."

The light finally went on in his foggy brain. Alyce was the person he should write it for. How much more mainstream could he get?

She moved to the edge of the bed. What followed was better than any session he'd had with a psychiatrist.

"You *need* to do this, not only for the money. You have to come to terms with the past in order to move on. See yourself as though you're a character you've created."

"I can't."

"Yes, you can." She picked up the photo he had been holding. "Is that you?"

"Of course it's me!"

She looked at it closer. "Wow, you were pretty hot." She eyed his current unruly hair. "I bet if you cut that mess you'd feel better, more focused."

"You would not be able to resist me."

"Yeah, right." She picked up another photo. It was from 10 years ago, his hair a rich brown.

"Would you really be responsible and take care of me if I lured you away from Nelson?"

"No!" She threw the photo down. "I had a moment of temporary insanity."

She told him not to think about the words yet. Visualize the book itself, what the jacket will say, how it will be marketed, how someone interviewing him will introduce him and the book, what they'll ask.

"Then fill in the rest."

Snapping his fingers, he said, "Like pouring batter into a cake pan!" His tone completely changed. "You have no idea what is involved in writing."

"But I do know a lot about an area you don't know about, or don't care to know. Marketing."

He knew exactly what he needed to write about, but the shame would leave him a marked man to the world for the rest of his life.

"Al-*ees*, I thank you for what you are trying to do, but I am out of time. The property will be sold, as it should be. It is time to live somewhere that does not have sad memories."

"What do you mean?"

He covered his eyes with his hand. "Failure. This place is drenched in failure."

She did not respond. When he looked up, she was biting her lip.

He continued. "What about the happy ending you love so much? How does it end now? An *American* who was my *tenant* takes my home from me."

She waved the thought away. "You don't have to write your entire life story. I saw that movie *Angela's Ashes*. That was based on a memoir about a guy's awful childhood. I won't mention it again, but if Colette is what's stopping you, end the book before she comes along. It will still be riveting, I'm sure."

His Muse kicked him in the shins.

"Stay here." She turned and walked away, allowing him to admire her. "I'll be at your computer writing."

He pulled shut the long red panels around his bed. From his dark crimson cave he heard her occasional mutterings as she typed. He drifted off to sleep until the phone woke him up.

"Am I disturbing you, darling?"

It was Isabella. She was visiting friends in Rome and hoped he had changed his mind about having her there. No matter how many times she insisted she had nowhere to go, he would not relent. She had lived by her wits all her life. She would be fine.

Alyce was also on her mind. "You have not slept with her?"

"I am incapable of conquering anyone now. I have the vigor of a flat tire."

He brought her up to date on the sale of the property. When she asked where he would live once it was sold, he said, "I'm thinking about a hotel. I would not have to give one thought to housekeeping or repairs. But I could never find one with a big enough kitchen."

He thought of the pleasure he took in creating his yellow one and the sadness over letting it go.

"Enough about that. Anything new with you?"

With bitterness she said, "Robbie offered to help set me up in an apartment, then I'm on my own." She wanted that apartment to be in Marlaison. "The light is exceptional and the weather allows for painting outdoors most of the year."

He still could not say what she wanted to hear, that they should live together. His thoughts had already moved on to another woman—the one who was spurring him to write while she was kicking him out of his house.

Alyce came running into the room, pulled back two panels, and poked her head in while waving a piece of paper at him. He eased himself out of the conversation with Isabella, but not before agreeing he would see her should she return.

"She's coming back?" Alyce said with alarm.

"I thought you didn't feel comfortable being here with just me."

"That was before I wrote this! You have work to do."

He sat up in his bed and read out loud her words in a theatrical tone. "Mysterious. Mercurial. Mesmerizing. Al-*ees*, you know these words?"

"I'm not illiterate, dammit. And I did know Dickens wrote *A Tale of Two Cities*. I was half asleep when you asked me. Go on."

"*One of France's most treasured authors, Jean-Luc Broussard, has remained an enigma to his loyal fans.*" He grabbed a pen off his nightstand and crossed out something. "Loyal fans is redundant. Just fans. No. Cut everything after enigma... *for more than two decades. Can it be that long? Now he takes you inside a world even he could never imagine: his own.*" He looked up. "*Très bien.*" He continued, pen poised like a weapon. "*Abandoned by his father as a child, he grew up an outcast, his mother warding off desperate poverty by selling her body.*"

He put a line through "desperate" and handed the pen to her. "I will edit later." He kept reading. "*His groundbreaking novel* Taming the Black Sun *debuted when he was 16, thrusting him into a life of fame, femme fatales, and fleeting fortune.* No, much too much alliteration, especially after mysterious, mercur—"

"Just keep reading!"

"*Both adored and detested for his eccentric behavior, he has lived in a mental institution, been arrested for public nudity, and can count presidents and princesses among his friends and lovers. Though many women have tried to capture him, he has never married. He now reveals what is truth and what is fiction as he confronts his most haunting demons.*"

He put the paper down. "What demons?"

"You know better than I."

His hands trembled slightly. "I cannot believe you wrote this."

"I just thought about TV shows. They're always *revealing* and *confronting* something."

Revitalized, he sat up and hugged her tightly. The scent of her hair made it hard to control himself. He kissed her neck. She did not resist at first, then stiffened, moving her hand between them and pushing him away.

"I'd love to keep you in my life as a *friend*, Jean-Luc. I'll do whatever I can to help you through this. You've done so much for me."

"Ah, this is my fate. For you to be married with children and me to be a lonely, bitter writer." In as bright a tone as he could muster, he said, "I hope you will be very happy, Al-*ees*."

Her "Me, too" lacked just enough assurance.

The Horse

At the *supermarché,* the friendly Marie-Laure tempted her to try a few of her samples. While enjoying her third briny black olive seasoned with thyme, she heard "Al-*ees?*"

She turned and saw a familiar angelic face. "Sister Therese!"

Alyce was delighted to see her. The feeling seemed mutual until she recalled why she'd been kicked out of the convent. That damn little devil Julien. She blushed.

Sister Therese said in a most circumspect way in front of the Olive Lady, "You are welcome to return anytime. God's heart is always open."

"What about Mother Superior's?"

She flashed her blissful Nun Smile. "Hers, too."

Alyce doubted she would ever walk through those thick cold walls again, but it was nice to not have that weighing on her conscience.

Then again, if it didn't work out with Nelson, she might reconsider.

When she returned to Jean-Luc's with her arms full of groceries, the house phone was ringing. She could hear him typing. He let the answering machine in his office pick up. It was someone named Claudia calling to see how Jean-Luc was… it had been so long… she thought of him so much. There was a mix of concern, insecurity, and heartache in her voice.

Alyce shook her head.

She made a simple dish of sautéed chicken and *herbes de Provence*, roasted asparagus and a salad, wondering if the activity might get Jean-Luc downstairs. It didn't.

She brought him a plate.

He barely looked up. "*Merci, merci.*" He kept on typing, lost in another world. She was thrilled to see him working and tiptoed out.

From her cottage she called Liliane and gave her an update.

"That is not the only good news, Al-*ees*. Nelson made a better offer. Not great but good enough. We have to get a signed contract and a deposit—that is, if Jean-Luc accepts it."

Alyce's heart was racing after they hung up. This was really happening. She looked out from her cottage to Jean-Luc's office window. She heard his phone ring. Liliane calling.

Though the birds tweeted cheerfully and the sun shone brightly, she felt sad.

She settled by the pool and started on the English translation of *The Horse*. It was dedicated "To unforgivable sins."

I prayed I would soon die.

In my small room was a foam mattress thinner than a phone book, a faded brown blanket that smelled of mildew, and a tiny window near the ceiling with bars that taunted me with a sliver of blue sky. Beneath my skin, diseased cells surrendered to the vagaries of my atrophied soul; a soul that had winged through life like a fearless falcon and was now inspissated with the toxicity of drugs, rotten food, and guilt…

Inspissated?

Nevertheless, before she knew it, she'd read 50 pages. It was as though she was inside Jean-Luc; unlocking a door that led to his soul. The narrator was a writer who had checked himself into a sanitarium to get away from his debtors and to dislodge his writer's block. What block? His description of the horse went on for four pages. She knew every square inch of this animal. What a gift to be able to do that.

She could see why this was a success and why his readers, especially women, adored him. He was achingly vulnerable.

Oh, no, she thought. Oh, no.

She checked on Jean-Luc. He was at his computer working on the proposal.

"I'm reading *The Horse*."

He frowned. "What took you so long?"

"You're a great writer, Jean-Luc. I probably gave you terrible advice."

"On the contrary, you made me realize that as much as I would like to think my work deserves special treatment, it does not. A book is merely a commodity to be consumed, like food or gasoline. The more I look at it that way, the easier it is to write."

She was skeptical as to how long this attitude would last.

She returned to the pool. Another 50 pages later, she put down the book and tried to imagine a happy ending.

Look at her, Jean-Luc thought. Put to sleep by my writing.

He studied her firm body, modest breasts, and revolting pierced bellybutton poking out beneath his book that was splayed, face down, across her midsection.

He gently lifted the book off her.

She woke up. "Oh!"

"What was it about this page that put you to sleep?"

"It wasn't the book."

"Yes, it was."

"No it wasn't. I love your book. It's, well, it's not exactly a page turner. It's a page *wallower*. So much detail!" She added a harder edge to, "Which doesn't add up to an easy read."

She swung her legs around to stand. "I'm going to the beach. I have to cool off."

"Don't move."

He returned carrying a stack of old leather-bound books. Tapping the top one, he said, "You want to see *wallowing?* Read this! All seven volumes of Marcel Proust's *À la Recherche du Temps Perdu.*" He slowly repeated the title.

"Looking for the time that is missed?"

Brightening, he said, "Close. *In Search of Lost Time.* Or as you say in America, *Remembrance of Things Past.*"

"I know that title." Eyeing the stack, "It's *that* long?"

"When you finish my book, take a look."

"Don't count on it."

Now in a better mood, he said, "I'll take you to *L'ile de Porquerolles.*"

Heading to her cottage, she said, "I can go by myself, thank you."

"I'll make us a picnic. You did an excellent job getting me started on my memoir."

"We can't stay long. You have work to do."

"I'll be editing what I've written. That's work. What a good team we make."

She paused before heading to her cottage. "That's what Nelson says."

He stopped himself from saying "A team would be deciding to buy this property together." It wasn't her money. And what did he know about being part of one?

28

TRUTH

As the ferry left Marlaison for the popular island getaway, Didon stood on her hind legs against the side and let the wind whip around her face and ears. Jean-Luc pulled his long gray hair that was blowing in every direction into a ponytail on top of his head. He fancied he looked like a samurai. Attired in white linen pants and a matching shirt with the sleeves rolled up, it was an elegantly offbeat look that always proved a winning combination with the ladies.

Until Alyce giggled and wouldn't tell him what was so funny. Finally he got it out of her.

"With your hair like that, when the wind hits you look like a giant smokestack."

There was just enough of a breeze to make it easy to stay on the island for a long time, though he wasn't sure if he could take it for long. He walked in the opposite direction from where he and Colette once parked themselves, but it was useless. He looked out at the sea and saw himself hanging onto the side of her bright yellow float as she lay on her back, bobbing up and down in the surf, a tiny pool of water filling her bellybutton.

"Look at the color of the water!" Alyce cried, as she settled on the beach towel he'd brought along. "It's almost the same as the sky."

Her comment startled Jean-Luc. Colette had offered a similar observation.

The beach was neither crowded nor deserted. Many of the women had discarded their tops. Alyce did not. A pungent combination of sea, suntan oil, and sweat mingled in the air. After making herself comfortable on a large towel, she took a big sniff.

"It's a little funky."

"Funky," he repeated with her American accent. "A splendid word I should use more often."

He made a mental note to jot it down in his notebook. Wait. It was in the suede bag that held the gun she used to shoot the boar. Did she find it?

She interrupted his thought with, "Oh, no. I think you should use words like pissiated more often."

"Like what?"

"Whatever that word was in the first paragraph of *The Horse*."

"*Inspissated.* It means dense."

He grabbed the old green beach umbrella he'd dug out of his garage and managed to refrain from ramming it through her head.

Very sweetly she said, "Why not just say dense?"

"It is my duty to elevate the reader."

She blithely slathered on tanning lotion. "Sure you're not just showing off?"

With great force, he lodged the wooden umbrella pole in the sand right next to her left arm, making her jump. "You are giving me horripilation."

"And what is that?"

"Making my skin crawl. Goose flesh."

"You know, that's actually a cool word. I take it all back."

He settled on his towel a few feet from her. Didon curled up on a special cushion he'd put down for her so she wouldn't get too hot on the sand. He took a deep breath to dislodge the mistake he now thought it was to come back here. Then Alyce had the audacity to open his book to the last page and start reading.

"Hey!" She rubbed her head where he had just thwonked her with his foam sandal.

"At least do not do such a thing in front of the author!"

While she read, Jean-Luc went over what he had written the last two days. After awhile, he glanced at Alyce. She was utterly entranced by his words. There is no greater high for a writer than to witness that. Anytime he heard her chuckle he had to know why. He found it interesting what made people laugh. Often it wasn't anything he intended to be funny.

Looking over at her again later, she was in such a rapturous state that a dewdrop of drool had formed at the left corner of her mouth. He felt a sharp spasm in his stomach as he forced himself not to laugh.

She wiped her mouth and checked the time on her phone. "Okay, I need to take a break."

"An excellent idea."

He pulled out pâté, baguette slices, radishes, tomatoes, anise-flavored butter cookies, and the apricot-rosemary iced tea that she loved. They didn't say much as they ate. It was the kind of day to be savored by just being.

Refreshed, she tackled the rest of the book.

He prayed to his Muse to guide him. His thoughts kept returning to Colette under the same umbrella Alyce was now beneath, Colette running her fingers through his chest hair, his inability to cry. Really cry. It was as though his tear ducts had been severed.

Alyce cried for him.

"The horse died!" she sobbed.

As she delicately blew her nose into a napkin, he said, "It is *fiction.*"

"You're such a good writer. It feels real. How could anyone want to put a happy ending on it?"

There was hope for her yet. "Do that again."

"What? Read it?"

"No, blow your nose. You are not a little sow at all. You are an embarrassed geisha. A fragile orchid of beguiling femininity."

She gave him a look like he had two heads. So much for the geisha.

He coached her on how to do a Japanese titter with one hand lightly over her mouth. "Look at me for a split second... more intensity... more!... that's it! Now look down quickly. Again... Perfect! Next you should go to Japan for three months."

She seemed to be mulling it over and he was surprised to find himself wishing he hadn't put the notion in her head. "I should warn you, it is an extremely difficult language. Much harder than French." Not true.

"Oh," she seemed dismayed. "Never mind, then." She stood up. "I'm going for a swim. Ow!" She began to limp. "I have a cramp in my foot."

"I can take care of that. Sit back down." He had never failed to seduce a woman with his world-class foot massage. "Lavender scented lotion is best. Our sunscreen will have to do."

As he began to work it into her feet, he admired her pink toenails.

"Are you kidding?" she said. "I need a pedicure desperately. I went into a nail salon and they said they didn't do them. At first I thought they didn't want me as a customer because I wasn't chic enough, but there were no big chairs you sit in with the tub at the bottom for your feet. Then I saw women stretched out in elevated lounge chairs, like they were at the dentist's but they were being manicured. Now, *that's* the way it should be. Anyway, I must have gone to four places and they were all manicures only. I couldn't believe it. Finally, a woman I thought was being nice opened a phone book and wrote down the address of where I could get a pedicure. I took an expensive cab ride there only to discover it was a *podiatrist.*"

Jean-Luc roared. "You did not ask for a *pedicure esthéticienne.* What a funny story, Al-*ees.* Why did you not share it?"

She pulled her face into a cruel smirk. "Gee, maybe because I felt like a complete idiot? Why didn't they just tell me—ooooooh! That feels great."

He stayed there until he felt the tight rubber band of tension in her release, then slowly moved up her muscular calf. He had her now. Her sleepy eyes opened. All he needed was the right verbal key and the door of resistance would swing wide open.

She pushed his hand away. "Even if I weren't engaged, that hair of yours."

"Perhaps you are afraid of me?"

She ignored him. "I'm going for a swim now." As she got up, she said, "Maybe you *should* get Isabella back here."

She seemed unusually preoccupied when she returned from her swim. She then went for a long walk. When it was time to pack up, Jean-Luc said, "You seem subdued, Al-*ees.* I would think Nelson buying the property would have you deliriously happy."

"I've been feeling weird lately, Jean-Luc. I think it's because I have to let the *loirs* go. And the reality that my life is about to radically change." She looked at him straight on. "And I'm worried about you, how your life is going to go."

He handed her the picnic basket, much lighter now, as he grabbed the umbrella and their tote bags. "Are you sure you might not be pregnant?"

He couldn't see her eyes through her sunglasses but noticed her jaw tighten. "That, too. I never went back on my birth control pills after my panic attack. Nelson was all for it."

It was as though an ax lodged in his chest.

He tried to sound upbeat. "You will be a great mother."

Her smile was not as trouble-free as it should have been. He was sorry for declaring his love to her now. Sorry for saying she was in desperate fear. He should never have intruded on her Cinderella dream.

They were silent on the ferry to the mainland. He often saw her biting her lip.

They hadn't driven far in the car heading home before she said, "I have a confession to make. When you and Pauline went out to dinner, I was looking for something to write on when I was at your computer. I found a large metal key and wondered what it opened. At that point I knew Nelson was interested in your place and thought I'd just look around to see how many rooms there were. Really, I didn't snoop. But I should have asked you."

He never suspected she went in there. "And what did you see?"

"The key opened the door that was locked upstairs. Before I could turn the light on, you came back. It looked like something was painted on the walls but I couldn't see much except a big white oval. I did see a photo, though. Half of one, that is."

He said nothing.

"The room was repainted and the photo gone when all of us looked later. Then, when I was walking in the woods one day, I saw a headstone. A new one. Jean-Luc, if I'm going to live there, I'd like to know if something, well, out of the ordinary happened. I need to stop wondering. I'm sure my imagination has made it worse than it is."

He pulled on to the shoulder of the road they were on and turned off the engine. He did not look at her as he took off his sunglasses and set them on the dash.

"Al-*ees*, I am sure your imagination has not let you down."

Seeing how distressed he was, she fished out a bottle of water from her bag.

He took a sip, handed it back, and reclined his seat so he could stare out at the topaz sky. He placed his elbows on the armrests, crossed his hands in his lap. He easily organized the story in his head. He had retold it mentally a thousand times.

"The royalty checks were growing smaller each year. I tried to give up writing and make a go of the vineyard. There was a jazz singer named Margot who played the South of France in the summer. She'd flirted with me for years. There was something about her that told me to stay away. When she approached her late 30s, I was living with Nicole, a travel writer.

"Margot possessed an incomparable radar, for she would call every night Nicole was away to see if I wanted company. Finally I said yes. The affair with Nicole was on the wane. She no longer checked in with me every day when on the road. More than once I called her in the early morning and she did not answer.

"Margot's intense focus on me naturally appealed to my ego. I was very careful about using protection. A condom is more than a barrier to pregnancy and diseases. They create an emotional wall as well. I could not take care of a family so I willed away the desire.

"When Margot and I finally made love, I reached for my protection. She stopped me. She said, *It would be too painful to have you inside me. Could we leave that out?* Did she mean physically or emotionally painful? Had she been raped? In love? I was too drunk and aroused to question her. I released on her stomach, went for a tissue. She said, "I'll do that in the bathroom." I rolled over and fell asleep. Little did I know she scooped up my sperm and placed it inside a device that was like a miniature turkey baster.

"We made love the next night. I should have known when she again insisted on cleaning up in the bathroom while carrying her purse that something was up. I was intrigued by her odd behavior, and she implied she had a dark secret. She was a cunning woman. She knew exactly how to string me along.

"She was determined to have my child. She claimed it was something she had never felt toward anyone else. That's why I was turned off—and on—by her. I saw something in her eyes."

He looked over at Alyce, who had reclined her seat as well and was curled on her side, eyes wide. "Was she the woman in the photograph?"

"Yes." He turned back to the blue sky. "There was nothing wrong with her. She knew how careful I was from a friend of hers. It was a long shot, but she took it."

He pushed himself back into the seat, tried to relax.

"When she told me she was pregnant I refused to believe it. Then she told me what she had done. I was furious. I was sure it would bring nothing but sorrow to our lives and especially the child's. I lived in fear she would force me to take a paternity test and publicly acknowledge the child as mine. I wanted my child to have a father, but I did not want the father to be me. I would feel an even greater failure."

He sipped more water from the bottle Alyce had given him.

"She quickly gave in to a wealthy Norwegian who lived in Paris and had been chasing her. He thought the child was his. They married. I knew Nils would be the better father. Yes, it hurt me deeply—ah! That is an understatement. I felt like my insides had been dug out with a burning hot shovel. But I felt it was the right thing to do for the child."

Alyce's hand flew to her mouth. "All of my talk about having children. I'm so sorry. And the baby *loirs*…"

He picked up his sunglasses, cleaned the lenses with his shirt. "Please do not repeat any of this. No one knows."

"Not even your sister?"

He shook his head. "Only Raymond, my editor. Liliane became more involved in my life after this happened, when I truly couldn't function."

"Oh, Jean-Luc," she said quietly.

His hands stopped moving. "Margot died of a drug overdose. Though classified as accidental, I doubt it was."

"Wait. Your child. Colette?"

A long pause passed while he swallowed more water to open his throat again.

"Margot managed to arrange visits when Nils was away on business. We were not lovers, but it was impossible to erase Colette from my mind and heart once I saw her. Her big blue eyes looked right into my soul and her curly brown hair was just like mine as a child." He took a deep breath. "I have never known a child to have such a sweet scent.

"You only had to tell her something once and she would remember it. She would point to something, pull me to it, and say in English, 'John look!' Understanding at such a young age that she was making a pun on my name. She loved to watch me make lavender honey and wasn't at all afraid of the bees. Of course not. She was a child. She didn't know they could sting."

He reached for the key in the ignition. "I cannot talk about it anymore."

She stopped him. "Wait, where is she? How old..." She gasped.

"The headstone you found is hers. She would be almost six today."

He slammed his hand on the dash. "It was an accident that would not have happened had I been paying attention instead of lost in another world! If I had been more responsible!"

"What do you mean?"

"I had cleared out the library upstairs to turn it into her room. I was ready to fight Nils for her, even though he had the money to hire the best lawyers and would win. I was even willing to marry Margot. I wanted to be Colette's father more than anything I have ever wanted!"

Alyce's image blurred from the tears rushing into his eyes.

"She fell asleep on the living room sofa while her mother went to buy a snack Colette loved: graham crackers and peanut butter. I said I was going to get them. Promised Margot I would. A simple thing like that. And I didn't. See? I would be a terrible father.

"I was painting a mural of characters from the books I read to her. It covered every wall of her room. I was completely caught up in paints and shadows and brushes and seeing her beautiful face light up when it was done and how I was going to make her mine when—"

He looked out the side window. "I was about to paint Humpty-Dumpty. Humpty Dumpty sat on a wall, Humpty Dumpty had a great fall...

"Margot appeared at the door. *Where's Colette? She's not on the couch.* I flew down the stairs screaming her name, feeling a dread only a parent can feel.

"I knew. I knew.

"I went out the front door, she the back." He whispered, "I have never heard screams like hers before and pray to God I never will again. The pool had been emptied for a repair." He pinched the bridge of his nose to stop the tears. "Why did I not cover the pool? Why?"

Alyce's voice broke when she touched his upper arm. "And I kept bothering you to fix it. Oh, darling, I am so sorry."

He refrained from clutching her hand. Her calling him darling would register later.

"Nils, that bastard, knew I had little money, but had to make me pay. He tried to take the vineyard and I wish he had. I could no more run a vineyard than I could fly to the moon. I gave him my art collection worth $1,000,000. Only some toys, the other half of that photo with her in it, are buried here. She rests for all eternity near Oslo."

He shook his head. "Margot went straight into a sanitarium and was dead a year later. As for me, the only way I knew to anesthetize myself from the pain was to write. I stopped making wine, honey. Stopped seeing friends, women, and wrote my last novel. My sorrowful career was briefly revived, but at what price?"

Alyce dabbed her eyes with a tissue.

Though not the most comfortable place for a hug, she managed to put her arms around his neck and hold him while they both cried. There was no one else in the world he wanted to make happy more than Alyce. But there was nothing he could do about it, absolutely nothing. And now she knew why.

He started the engine. "I will understand if you wish to pull out of buying my property. Though I would not be surprised if your admirable American pluck gets you beyond the tragedy that happened there."

She was picking at her tissue now, shaking her head. "What a sad story. I'm only thinking about your loss. Your terrible loss."

They said nothing the rest of the ride that was often punctuated with sniffles.

29

The Loirs and the Notebook

Between Jean-Luc's confession and the summer heat, Alyce had no energy. While she had clarity about him and, she had to admit, relief that Colette was not a woman, she was confused over something else.

How *did* she feel about living there now? One of the names she had suggested to Nelson for their new property, and their wine, was La Vie. The life.

It was too overwhelming to comprehend. She wanted to talk it over with Nelson. Isn't that what you do with someone you're going to spend your life with? Shouldn't he know what occurred here? Something stopped her. She would be invading Jean-Luc's privacy. He had shared something deeply personal with her. She would respect that.

But she had to tell someone. It was like a dam ready to burst inside her. There was only one person she could trust not to blab.

Her father.

After a deep sorrowful sigh followed by "That's very sad," he said, "You could have a priest come out and bless the property if it makes you feel strange living there."

Alyce thought for a moment. "Doesn't every place have some kind of catastrophe in its past? Who knows what Indians were killed on the land where your house is. I'm sure someone died making the Holland Tunnel I commuted through every day. They died making the bridges around New York."

"That's true. Death is part of life."

"I shouldn't let this get to me."

"I will say this. I think Jean-Luc is wise to move away. But I still can't believe you might be living in France. It was hard enough having my girls move to New York."

She heard the gloom in her father's delivery and was instantly inside him, connected to a child in a way that only a parent can be. Alyce was appalled by her own self-centeredness to leave Minnesota. Yet, she had to, or feel trapped and unfulfilled the rest of her life.

The agony of letting go of a child never hit her before like it did today.

She looked lovingly and sadly at her baby dormice. She had to release them immediately, an act of solidarity.

Tomorrow.

Tonight, she had to brace herself for the return of Isabella. That confused her as well. Why should it bother her?

The next day her scream brought Jean-Luc and Isabella running.

She rushed out to meet them. "Sorry! I didn't mean to scare you."

"What is it?" Isabella asked with annoyance. "The *loirs*?"

"Are you okay?" asked a concerned Jean-Luc. "Is the male stripper back?"

Isabella whipped her head and long hair around. "Who?"

She didn't want to tell them. She knew how it might make them feel. But they'd find out soon enough.

"I'm pregnant."

It seemed to hit Isabella the hardest. At first she suspected

Jean-Luc was the father. They cleared her up on that point. "Lucky you," was her final statement on the subject.

Jean-Luc's reaction was hard to read. "I am happy for you, Alyce." He repeated what he'd said before. "You will make a great mother."

Isabella said on a nicer note, "If you would like to commemorate where your child was conceived, I do commissions."

"I'll bring it up when Nelson gets here and can see your work." The moment felt awkward.

She texted Nelson: *Let's video chat.* She wanted to see his face when he heard the Baby On Board news.

He wrote back: *Slammed before coming over. And with the time change…I'll be there before you know it. BTW, Jr was in the ER last night. Thought he broke his arm in a fight but it's just a sprain.*

She phoned her parents. There was no answer. She called Liliane. Her reaction was, "Why do you not sound so excited?"

"I don't?"

"No."

Alyce searched for an answer. Liliane gave it to her. "Perhaps you feel it is too soon. You want to be married first. And it is your first. I was terrified when I found out I was carrying Stéphane."

"I won't disagree."

"And with all you are marrying into, well, it is easier to terminate these matters in France than in America. I can send you to my doctor who will give you a pill."

"Liliane," she said sternly. "I couldn't even kill baby rodents."

"I cannot be the judge of how you view this. Some would say it is not a child yet." Alyce heard someone come into Liliane's office. Speaking in code, she said, "I must go, but let me add not to get too excited about this until it is a certainty. Trust me, I know."

Yes, Alyce thought, a lot can go wrong in the first trimester. She would be very careful who she told right now.

She fed milk to her furry babies that had grown considerably since she found them. They now drank from a bowl instead of an eyedropper.

It was time to say goodbye.

Better to do it before Nelson and company arrived. They were probably safer in the woods than in the clutches of that bratty kid.

She headed into the kitchen in the main house to get the suede bag that held Jean-Luc's gun. If she met wild boars once, she could meet them again. He was starting to make espresso. She told him what she was doing as she pulled out the gun to make sure it was locked.

"Where is my notebook?" he asked. "It was in there before."

"I don't know. It must have fallen out when I went up that tree. I'll look for it while I'm out there."

"I'll go with you. I need a break. But first, have some coffee."

"I shouldn't drink that if I'm pregnant."

"That is nonsense. But as you wish." He stopped what he was doing.

"Are you sure you want to be part of my letting them go? Won't it…"

"I encounter reminders every day. I have learned to cope."

He offered to carry the ventilated box containing the dormice.

"No, I'll do it," she said. "I want to stay close to them as long as possible."

"I understand."

They passed Isabella, who was painting while viewing the vista of overgrown, unkempt grapevines in the distance. What was on her canvas didn't look anything like the view. Instead it was cleared with rows of vines, green rolling hills, the *maison* clean and in the open. Alyce noticed a photograph taped to the bottom of the easel.

"I'm inspired by this photo of the way it was when it was a working vineyard, while observing the natural light now," she said. "See what you have to look forward to?"

"It's beautiful, Isabella. If Nelson doesn't want to buy it, I will."

She smiled then looked at the box in her hands. "What is that?"

"I'm releasing the *loirs*."

"Ah," she turned back to her painting, "at last."

Alyce had never thought about what it must be like to make a living as a painter until she met Isabella. It certainly wasn't easy. As she glanced down at the box she was carrying, she reminded herself why she had forgiven Isabella for murdering the *loirs'* mother.

The babies had given her comfort when she needed it most.

As they walked on, he said, "They're big enough now to live on the ground. I'll find just the right spot." He stopped at the rabbit hutch that was missing a door. "Wait, this is perfect. It's low enough so they can get in and out, and they will have some protection."

"Some? I want complete protection. Can't a wild animal or bird get in here?"

She realized what she'd said when she saw Jean-Luc's sad face.

"You cannot give them complete protection, Al-*ees*. Ever."

Together they made a nest of twigs and leaves inside the hutch. She'd brought a bag with pieces of apple, shelled hazelnuts and sunflower seeds, and laid them out inside, as well. She also brought a small plastic tub and filled it with water from a bottle. In another she put milk.

Her heart was heavy as a concrete brick as she placed each

one inside. They darted around, unsure how to react to so much space. Two went for the food, another for the nest.

The last one sat on its haunches and stared at her as if to say "You're deserting us?"

Jean-Luc put a reassuring hand on her shoulder. She blew kisses to them, walked away, and blubbered.

Jean-Luc rubbed her back with his warm hands as they embraced. In a small voice she said, "I have nothing to cry about. They're back in nature where they belong."

"And you can check on them every day until you have your own baby."

She stopped hugging him and grabbed his arm. "Please don't make any mention to Nelson that I'm pregnant. And ask Isabella to do the same." His searching look caused her to say, "I'm waiting for the right time to tell him in person."

"I would consider waiting until the troublemaking boy has gone."

That wasn't a bad idea, thought Alyce, though she couldn't wait to see Carmelita's face when she heard about it.

They walked on, looking for Jean-Luc's notebook. She said it was near the headstone. He knew exactly where that was.

"We're getting close," he said.

She looked for the tree she'd climbed. Jean-Luc was about 10 feet in front of her when she thought she saw it. She had been more focused that day on being mauled by a wild pig than where she was. She looked around the trunk. There it was. Some water damage had seeped into the notebook's pages but they were still readable.

She was about to call out to him but saw that he was standing still, head bowed, hand over his heart, chest heaving as he silently sobbed.

Her chest tightened. How do you ever get over losing a child?

She didn't mean to read his notebook, but as she tried to carefully un-stick the pages she couldn't help seeing: *Yeesh.*

She flipped through it, glancing up to see if Jean-Luc was watching her.

Solde/sold

Twat

Birds bouncing off the screens. Boing.

Bring it on!

Pygmalion. Is that a disease?

Kisses from a bashful child

Destiny thing

She felt like an insect that had been pinned to a board at a science museum, an amoeba under a microscope.

She looked again in his direction. He was staring her down.

She clasped the notebook to her chest as he walked toward her.

"I know what you must be feeling," he said calmly. "That I have been using you for material this whole time."

She felt her face flush with embarrassment. "Nelson said you would write about us and it wouldn't be pretty."

"Al-*ees.*" He held out his hand for the notebook.

She began ripping out pages.

"Stop!" He tried to wrest it from her. She crouched down so he couldn't get it. "Those notes go back years! Very few are about you and I quit writing when I realized—"

She scattered the torn pieces to the wind.

He held up his hands. "I don't have it in me to fight about this."

In her fit of anger and raging hormones she'd forgotten that he'd just been standing at Colette's grave. Her actions seemed as juvenile as anything he had ever done. She handed him the notebook.

"Sorry. I overreacted."

"I quit making notes about you and I wasn't sure why. It was Raymond who deduced I was in love with you."

She felt terrible now. Also flattered.

Even more so, confused.

She gathered up as many pieces of paper as she could and shoved them into the suede bag. "I'll put them back together." She had to add, "Even the pages about me."

He half-smiled. "There is nothing about you I will ever forget."

30

THE DEVIL AND HIS PAYCHECK

When she told Nelson about releasing the babies she did not mention Jean-Luc's notebook. She was starting to understand the way an artist views life, starting to appreciate it, too. What would the world be like without them? Jean-Luc should be free to write whatever he wanted, just as Isabella was free to paint whatever she wanted. She remembered what he'd said the night Julien came to dinner, about how writers are scavengers and how hard it was to take from people he loved.

She needed something to calm her nerves—a drink at least—to brace her for the impending *clustier fouquoi*, but she wouldn't indulge in her condition, even though Liliane said it was fine to have a glass of wine with dinner.

Jean-Luc said, "You are a beautiful fecund wreck."

"Remember, you and Isabella aren't supposed to know about the fecund part."

Glorianna and Luther were ensconced at the *Hôtel Marlaison*, Nelson was in the cottage with her, and Jean-Luc and Isabella were barely speaking to each other. Not because they were mad. They were lost in their creative worlds.

Carmelita and Junior were to arrive in two days. At first

Nelson was coming with them. Glorianna said in an email: *Nelson traveling on his own, now that you're engaged, is the proper way to handle this.*

It seemed pretty Old School thinking to Alyce, but showed that her future mother-in-law was on her side. She needed all the reinforcements she could get.

Then the pre-nup arrived at her lawyer's.

Diandra Solomon, who Alyce's sister had recommended, called from New York as Alyce was pulling into the parking lot of the *supermarché*. She took out a pen and notepad.

Her lawyer's first words were, "It's not bad, but there are some strong strings attached."

The good news was the quarter million dollar "signing bonus" Alyce would get after their honeymoon that made every hair follicle on her head stand at attention.

"You must be joking."

"Wait until you hear the rest."

If they stayed married until the kids were out of the house and then decided to divorce, she would receive $2,000,000. "That's approximately $100,000 a year if it lasts 20, with no adjustment for inflation. All your expenses will be paid during the marriage, but unless you stash money away and invest wisely, that won't give you jack toward a similar lifestyle. There's also a morals clause that has to go."

Did the car just tilt sideways?

"As for the property in France, your name is not going on the deed now because it's being bought by a family LLC."

"What's that?"

"Limited liability company. Once you're married, you'll be family, so then you'll be a co-owner. I've looked that contract over carefully and you will always be entitled to 25% no matter how big the defined family gets. If it decreases, your share grows. For example, if Mr. and Mrs. Mansfield die, you and Nelson own it 50/50. I think that's fair."

"You're dealing with a family who views marriage as a business partnership. The less romantic you are about it, the better. Look at this as an employment contract a high-level executive signs when joining a corporation. The payout, if you part ways, is the golden parachute."

She strongly urged Alyce not to sign it without requesting certain changes. "They'll respect you," she said. "But you can't be too demanding either. It's delicate."

Diandra shifted her all-business tone to a friendlier one when she asked, "Alyce, do you love Nelson?"

She'd carried a torch for him for so long, she answered without thinking, "Yes, but…"

"But?"

Alyce tried to put what she was thinking into words. "I'm no wheeler-dealer. It's hard for me to relate to this."

"Keep reminding yourself it's nothing personal. And don't think this is written in stone. I do post-nups all the time. Once you pop out a baby or two, you can renegotiate—especially if they're male."

"Actually, I'm pregnant now."

"Congratulations! Do you know the gender?"

"No. I'm not that far along. Nelson doesn't know. I'm waiting for the right moment to tell him."

"Don't wait too long. That's quite a bargaining chip if we get stuck on something."

"Use a baby as a *bargaining chip?*"

"Like I said, don't take it personally."

How much more personal could you get than to have someone's child?

With only $2,071.58 in her savings account, Alyce was staggered by the wealth she would acquire once they married.

She called her parents. They were thrilled about another grandchild coming, even her "hold off" mom. She shared the news about the pre-nup.

Her father said, "Be careful, Ally. The devil often comes with the biggest paycheck. Don't ever tell Chantilly this. Yours is more generous than hers."

That made her feel good until she wondered why.

Her mother, on an extension line, cut in. "Okay you two, stop looking for the black lining in the clouds, not the silver. I think it shows that the family knows what you've agreed to put up with regarding You-know-who and their child. And that you mean more. That's what matters."

Alyce walked into the market, dazed. She forgot half the things she was supposed to buy.

When she returned home, Nelson was waiting for her. He instantly sensed a shift.

"What's wrong, honey? "

"I just talked to my lawyer about the pre-nup, that's all."

He nervously ran his hand through his hair. "I can't talk about this, Ally. My parents are the ones with the money, not me. After what happened with Carmelita, they're insisting on this. Let's keep it between our lawyers, otherwise it'll kill the romance. Everything will be fine. I just want to be with you and our children forever."

She couldn't keep it from him any longer after he said that. "Guess what, honey? You're going to be a father again a lot sooner than you thought."

She expected him to be thrilled.

"You're pregnant already?" He moved away.

Hurt by his reaction, not to mention feeling like she'd made some stupid tactical error, she moved back too. "I thought that's what you wanted."

He came over to her, trying to stroke her hair. She stopped his hand.

"I was in shock. This is wonderful news." He seemed to be forcing himself to ramp up his excitement. "Wonderful! But we shouldn't let the cat out of the bag yet."

"Why not? I'd think Glorianna would break into a tap dance."

"Let's wait until Junior and his mother leave. He's been behaving badly lately, as you know. Let's give him time to adjust to the idea of a stepmother first."

Even though Jean-Luc had made the same suggestion, that burning rage she felt whenever they entered the picture surged forth. She barely managed to bite her tongue.

"Okay. But what about your mother? Why wouldn't you want her to know?"

"Of course I'll tell her. I just need to time it right."

He rested his hands on her shoulders. "I know my mother when she's had a few drinks. She'll blurt out something to Carmelita and it'll get vicious. Junior is trouble enough these days. We'll tell Mother after they're gone." He smiled. "Then we'll start talking about the wedding. Is four months from now too soon?"

Alyce agreed to his plan.

On the morning of the closing on Jean-Luc's property, Nelson watched Alyce from the bed as she raced around to get ready for class. She bent at the waist and flipped her head over to brush her hair out nice and full.

In a tone that was pleasant, but left no room for discussion, he said, "I'd like to move into the *Hôtel Marlaison* when you finish school today."

She flipped back up, her hair standing out in all directions. "Why?"

"It's time to sever ties with this guy, Ally. It's business now."

"I'd rather not pack up everything if I'm going to be moving back in."

"Take what you need for a month," he said. "He has to be out by then."

She stood another moment before realizing how ridiculous she looked. She patted her hair down and started packing. She thought about Jean-Luc's health. A move was a lot of work. He would need help. Her voice of reason said: *He'll have plenty of money from the sale to hire it. And he has Isabella.*

When she was set to go, Nelson stood up and wrapped his arms around her waist. "I know you and Jean-Luc are close, but some friendships aren't meant to last."

"I can't even be friends with him?"

His grip tightened. "You'll be so busy fixing this place up and making new friends, it's best if he's not around to distract you."

"Aren't *we* going to be fixing the place up?"

He did his nervous hair brushing with his hand again. "I can't quit my job the moment I take ownership. I have to hire the right people, make it a viable concern. I figured you'd be the intermediary during that time." He looked at her tummy. "So much for schedules, right? But don't worry. I'll be here in nine months. You have my word."

The idea of being a pregnant newlywed and not with Nelson full time hadn't entered her mind. Before she could say "Let's talk about this," his phone rang. She could hear every word Carmelita was screaming.

"He lost his passport! What if he gets his identity stolen? How are we going to fly?"

Nelson closed his eyes and was probably counting to 10. When he opened them, he said to Alyce, "Have fun at class today. You can see what I'll be dealing with."

How much she would be dealing with was going through her own mind.

Property and Promises

Liliane closed the door when Alyce entered and invited her to sit in the same chair where she had been told she was getting the boot from her previous hosts.

"What a summer," Alyce said as she rubbed the wooden arms of the chair and reflected for a moment. "I can't believe my time here is almost over."

"If we ever do an advertising campaign we should use you as our spokesperson. What a transformation." Liliane offered her a chocolate from a box a student probably gave her. She often received tokens of appreciation from her clients.

Alyce waved it away. "There's caffeine in chocolate. You still eat it when you're pregnant?"

Liliane looked momentarily alarmed. "But of course. And thank you for getting Jean-Luc to work on his memoir. I just heard from Raymond. There's a bidding war for it!"

"That's fantastic!"

"Al-*ees*, you succeeded where all others have failed."

She took a chocolate after all. "I don't feel like I did anything special."

"It may be more what you did *not* do. He said to me last

night on the phone, 'She will not even make love to me. After nearly dying, it is the least she could do!'" She tried to control her amusement. "He finally meets the perfect woman and cannot have her."

The sweet now felt like a rock in Alyce's stomach. "I'm sure it's not the first time he's wanted something he couldn't have."

"Just keep doing whatever you are not doing."

Alyce crossed her legs and glanced down. "Nelson doesn't want me to stay friends with Jean-Luc after today. We're moving into the *Hôtel Marlaison* this afternoon."

Liliane pecked her forefinger at her. "He does not own you!"

Alyce felt herself move back in her chair as if she'd been physically poked.

"Trust is essential in a marriage, but it does not mean you need to tell him everything or obey his every word."

She gave Alyce an imperious look, as if she had to uphold the dignity of all women.

"Of course not. Of course he doesn't own me."

"It is of the utmost importance that Jean-Luc not lose his focus on his memoir. Between moving, Isabella, and health issues, it is certain to slip through the cracks. Please, *I beg you*, keep him on track. Make sure he doesn't waste time fussing about in the kitchen to avoid the blank page, either! Al-*ees*, his entire future depends on it."

Alyce couldn't tell if Liliane was contemplating what she had said or which chocolate to devour next.

"Like chess, Nelson is protecting his queen."

"That's silly," Alyce replied. "Jean-Luc has Isabella now."

Holding up a delectable truffle, "Then why did she not get him to write his memoir, eh? And remember, the queen is the most powerful piece. She can move any number of squares, any direction." She nodded to Alyce's belly. "Especially when she is eating for two. Does Nelson know?"

"Yes, but he doesn't want to tell anyone else yet."

"I understand. I always wait until I am past three months to share it. I have had my disappointments." She popped another chocolate. "Though everyone knows when I start eating these it is certain that I am pregnant again."

If only that were the reason why Nelson wanted to be secretive. Thankfully the bell rang that signaled the next class was starting. Alyce headed toward the door.

"You are not going to the closing, Al-*ees*? I was going to offer you a ride."

"No. I become part owner after we're married."

Liliane did not hide her alarm. "I hope you have a very good lawyer handling your affairs." An even worse thought struck her. "That awful woman's perfume! I am sure to be ill."

Charles Latrou's assistant was hurriedly opening all of the windows at the law office as Liliane chatted pleasantly with Nelson and Glorianna, charming them as best she could. Charles, the *notaire*, stood just over five feet tall. What he lacked in height he made up for in attitude.

Jean-Luc willed away a scream. At least Luther wasn't along as well to stink up the place.

Mrs. Mansfield said in a voice that reminded him of the screeching brakes of a train, "Before we sign the papers concerning the sale of the property, there's one thing we'd like Jean-Luc to sign."

Charles poked his nose into the air. "What is this?"

"I wanted to give you a chance to see it beforehand," she said in a way Jean-Luc knew was a lie, "but it just arrived this morning from my lawyer. If you need more time, then we'll have to hold off on the closing."

"I have to be at a very important meeting in 40 minutes," Charles barked. "This is very—what is the word? Unappropriate."

"*In*appropriate," Nelson said, trying to exert some authority.

His mother said, "And don't forget we're doing your client a big favor by letting him stay rent-free another month."

Liliane did not look pleased and moved closer to the window for fresh air, unconsciously rubbing her belly. Jean-Luc knew she had timed several payments around this closing.

"What is it now?" Jean-Luc asked. "You want another break on the price? We can end this meeting this instant if that is the case."

"No, that's not it." Glorianna lightly cleared her throat. "The family is, understandably, concerned that you will write about us and will not grant permission unless we are allowed to read what you've written in advance and given our full approval in writing."

Even Liliane was taken aback. "Madame Mansfield," she said as kindly as she could, "you should have mentioned this earlier."

Charles shook his head and straightened up as much as his frame would allow. "This is absurd!"

Jean-Luc and Charles would be talking about this one for a long time. And was Alyce in agreement or were they doing this without her knowledge? She must have told Nelson about the notebook.

He calmly said, "Let me have a look at your document."

Without reading a word of it, Jean-Luc held it front of her face and tore it in two.

"Kiss your *steal of a deal* goodbye."

Glorianna's eyes bulged out of her Botoxed head. Nelson's response was smooth and every bit the salesman that he was. "Come on, Jean-Luc, can't you see our point of view on this?"

"We are upholding *your* reputation," she said haughtily. "You can uphold ours."

"Is that what you call exploiting my name?" He leaned in toward the Royal Assholes. "You obviously have no idea how creativity works. You also have no idea what a cliché you are. And your ego is so big, you would think any character bearing the faintest resemblance was you. Are you saying I cannot create someone who lives in New York? Who sells advertising? Who is a socialite? Who wears enough goddam perfume for the entire city of Marlaison? I would not sell my property to you if my life depended on it!"

Nelson squirmed in his seat. "Gee, how do you *really* feel? Heh, heh, heh."

Glorianna's voice went up an octave. "Has there been a miscommunication? We heard you were writing a *memoir* and don't want to be in it without seeing what you've written. We're not public figures. We're entitled to our privacy!"

"And so am I! It is bad enough I have to answer to publishers."

Liliane moaned. "I don't feel well" and stuck her head out the window. They were still able to hear her say, "I do not think a memoir by my brother, as adored as he is here, will ever be read by many people in America."

She would apologize profusely for that comment later.

Liliane continued. "What could he possibly write that would be offensive? You finessed a good deal on his property? I would think your friends would be impressed. And you're saving him from financial ruin. You are an *angel* to him."

In French, Jean-Luc said, "Don't push it."

His sister smiled politely as she brought her head back in. "Don't you push it."

In English, Liliane stated, "It has been my observation that those who are immortalized in this way are flattered."

"Indeed," Jean-Luc said. "Most people are upset when I do *not* write about them."

Their words seemed to soften the Americans. Nelson and his mother stepped outside to discuss it.

A few minutes later, they returned. She announced, "We've

reconsidered, Monsieur Broussard. You will not have to sign the agreement."

Nelson said, "If you write anything libelous, we'll just sue you for all you're worth."

Charles ranted in French that they would kill the deal on principle. That they did not deserve to own property in Marlaison! Jean-Luc pointed out to him, in French, that it was nothing to worry about. If what he wrote was fact, they could not win. If he made them into fictitious characters, it would be hard for them to win their case. Furthermore, any legal proceedings would only boost book sales. His lawyer calmed down.

"Fine," Jean-Luc said, "I am not concerned in the least that I will write anything worthy of a lawsuit."

With a flourish, Nelson whipped out a Mont Blanc pen and sat down to complete the paperwork. Jean-Luc was stone-faced as one paper after another was passed before him. He glanced at each title to make sure Glorianna hadn't slipped a gag order in with them.

When all was said and done, Jean-Luc was handed a check for €969,000. He had to admit, it felt damn good to see it.

To Nelson and Glorianna's surprise, he joyfully kissed them on their cheeks—right, left, right—before they left.

"The end of an era," Jean-Luc said to Charles and Liliane when the Americans were gone. "Who would have thought it would have turned out like this? And how fantastic it would feel to get rid of that place." Hugging his sister, he said, "I feel liberated!"

"If I did not have morning sickness, I would feel the same."

He kissed her on her cheeks as well. "I am lucky to have you as my sister. I promise not to burden you again. Of course, I will give you a nice chunk of this money."

She conveyed a look of pure love he rarely saw. "If you would like to start a trust fund for the new child, like you did for the others, I will not say no. But you do not have to give me anything. Relieving me of my accounting duties is payment enough."

Charles stifled a laugh.

Liliane, picking up her purse, appeared to be deep in thought. "I hope Al-*ees* is not making a big mistake."

"What do you mean?" asked Jean-Luc.

"Three months ago, I would have said she and Nelson were perfect for each other." She eyed Jean-Luc.

Charles broke into a smile. "Ah, you devil, Jean-Luc. What have you been up to?"

"Nothing!"

His legal counsel pulled up his short frame again. "Let me share a popular American expression. It ain't over until the fat lady sings."

Jean-Luc looked out the window that afforded a view of the parking lot. He saw the Mansfields standing outside their car having what looked like an argument they were trying to keep from escalating. An idea struck him. After his outburst it might not be easy to pull off.

"Liliane, wait a moment before you go."

Nelson saw him coming first and signaled to his mother to stop talking. She turned and put on a fake smile. So did Jean-Luc.

"I would like to apologize for my behavior, madame, monsieur. I am, like any artist, sensitive when it comes to my work."

Glorianna adjusted her Hermès scarf around her shoulders. "Apology accepted." He gave them the opportunity to apologize as well. When they didn't, he almost scrapped his plan. It was Liliane's comment about Alyce making a mistake that spurred him on.

"I would like to invite all of you," he looked at Nelson, "including your son and his mother, to dinner in your new home. Isabella and I will make a meal that will outshine any restaurant. Consider it a goodwill gesture, a celebration of a new beginning for all of us." He bowed to Glorianna when he said, "I am grateful you bought my property." To Nelson he said, "I am grateful to Al-*ees* for saving me 50,000 Euros on the commission. It is the least I can do." He playfully wagged his finger at Mrs. Mansfield. "And I will not be writing about this."

Glorianna was thrown by his generosity. So was Nelson. She said, "I'm not sure about inviting…"

"Mother," he said sternly, "this doesn't mean she'll be coming to Thanksgiving dinner and all of your parties. If you acted like you didn't think my son was a *leper* for a change, we'd probably see a big change in him. It would certainly make my life easier, especially with *my getting married*."

"Well…"

He drew his mother into him and whispered what sounded like *I'm making you happy, now make me happy.*

She patted her bun-head. "I suppose if Alyce doesn't mind, why not? Maybe we'll all get along just fine."

They set a time and Jean-Luc watched them drive off.

What did *I'm making you happy* mean? Was that what he said? Alyce had mentioned Glorianna was hell-bent on "extending the Mansfield brand" and that she'd felt as though Nelson had woken up one day, decided to get married, and she would do.

Jean-Luc's assessment was that he truly adored her. Or he was a very good actor.

There was more to this. He could feel it.

He thought of one of his Golden Rules for storytelling: Look for the woman and follow the money. If his instincts were correct, the trail was about to take a new turn.

THE NELLY AND CARMELITA SHOW

Alyce and Nelson's suite at the elegant 18th-century *Hôtel Marlaison* had a sensational view of the Mediterranean Sea. Dotted with small fishing boats and luxurious yachts, it was a scene she had seen on postcards around town. She didn't even mind that Glorianna and Luther were staying there as well. When Nelson's mother insisted that Carmelita and Junior stay at a lesser hotel a few blocks away, Alyce again found herself liking her future mother-in-law.

As for Luther, ever since Alyce introduced him to *Le Gentil Gendarme*, who hooked him into the gay scene in Marlaison, she could do no wrong.

Before she took off for school, she and Nelson stood on their balcony, arms around each other, glowing with love. Alyce said to Nelson, "I can't believe your mother is going to be breathing the same air as Carmelita and Junior tonight."

"She wants to manage any damage control. You know how Carmelita can get. If Junior acts up, at least it won't be in public. And she doesn't trust Jean-Luc."

Alyce didn't trust him either. Regardless of his denial that he wouldn't write about the Mansfields (it appalled Alyce to no end when she heard what had gone down at the closing), she still suspected he was either trawling for material or going to play a cruel joke of some kind. Either way, tonight could turn out to be more unpredictable than her 27th birthday.

What she did offer was, "That's quite a lot of people to entertain."

"It was his idea, honey. We'll bring some excellent wine and it'll be fine. Besides, this is our new home. Much more interesting than eating out."

She could hear his mother saying, "Not to mention cheaper."

She turned to go. A thought stopped her. "Your mother floored me when she asked me if I'd like to get breast implants for the wedding! As if I'd do that after nixing the Botox. It was all I could do to not blurt out that I was pregnant. I really wish you'd tell her already."

"Sounds good to me."

"When?"

"I meant about getting implants."

"What!"

He covered his face as if she was going to smack him. "I'm kidding. I love you just the way they are."

"You better."

"I just wouldn't object if you wanted to have implants at some point."

That comment gnawed at her. After she gathered everything for school, she asked, "Are Carmelita's real?" They had to be at least DDs.

He kissed her goodbye. "I have no idea. Have a great day, honey."

During her midmorning break at school, she texted Nelson to see how things were going. He'd driven to the Nice airport to pick up Carmelita and Junior, the final members of the CF. Their flight was due in at 10 a.m. The airport was two hours away.

That left plenty of time to get back to Marlaison and be rested for the evening soiree at Jean-Luc's.

He answered: *STILL IN NICE. SO FAR SO GOOD*

She went to the toilette and noticed small red stains in her panties.

No! They seemed different from a period. She searched out Liliane. She wasn't in her office.

Alyce's breasts were still tender. That must be a good sign, though they also grew tender before her period.

Every hour she checked. There was a tiny bit more blood. Maybe her period was slow getting started because she'd just gone off the pill? She felt a bit relieved. It was too early to get pregnant with Nelson anyway.

A crushing grief came over her at the thought of losing a child.

Around 4:00, Nelson called. "We're just leaving. Time flies when Nelly's mom has a credit card and there are new stores to conquer. Can you pick up some wine?"

"Nelly?"

"Yeah, can the Junior. He's on a Nelly kick now."

"I hope you don't hit traffic."

"Can we get out of this dinner? Make it tomorrow night?"

"He's cooking for eight people. I'm sure it will be exceptional."

He let out a long exasperated sigh. "Okay, we'll make it."

She managed to say through her teeth, "Drive safely."

Her outfit for the evening was a snug black skirt that tapered to her knees and a simple pink top that gathered between her breasts, accentuating them. So what if Carmelita's were bigger? A lot bigger. She had to show she didn't care. The neck opening of the blouse was so wide it almost fell off her shoulders.

At the last moment she switched to a strapless push-up bra. Her breasts were quite tender. The glorious feeling of being pregnant surged through her again.

It was past 7:00 when Nelson showed up at their hotel room—the time they were to be at Jean-Luc's. He ripped off his shirt.

"You want to have sex *now?*"

"No, I have to jump in the shower."

She was about to tell him about her spotting but it was obvious he couldn't focus on her as he ran around like a cartoon character. She also didn't want to introduce the possibility she might not be pregnant until she knew for sure. Her period, if that's what it was, was still extremely light.

He was ready in under 10 minutes. Carmelita and Junior, however, did not possess his speed. Alyce and Nelson waited outside their hotel for five minutes. Another five.

Alyce called Jean-Luc. "We're running late."

His light-hearted "We are having a fascinating time entertaining the other guests" was followed by him lowering his voice. "At least they're not giving me a migraine from their cologne. They are scent-free tonight, thank God. Rain is in the forecast and we will be dining inside. Hurry up!"

Finally 10-year-old Nelly appeared. He was slouched over and walking in that thug-like way of putting one shoulder forward then the other. It was 75 degrees and he was wearing a black leather jacket. His dark hair was slicked back.

Alyce put on her best smile and tried to open her heart to this boy, who must feel terribly marginalized. She got a stand-offish arms-at-his-sides response as she kissed him three times on his cheeks.

"That's the way they greet each other here."

"Yeah."

"Did you get taller since I last saw you?"

"Yeah."

And gained a few pounds. She noticed one of his hands covered with an Ace bandage.

Nelson said, "I better see what's taking her so long."

After several strained minutes in the car where Alyce tried to talk to Nelly and he ignored her while playing a video game, he said, "Put on the radio."

"Put on the radio, *please*."

"Yeah."

"Let me call our host *again* and tell him we're on our way."

Jean-Luc reported, "They're playing *pétanque* while we hide out in the kitchen and drink. If that woman sings out '*Bon appétit*' when we sit down to eat I win 10 Euros from Isabella."

"I have no doubt you'll win."

When she hung up she reached for the radio.

"Nah, I don't wanna hear it now."

She crossed her arms and thought about how much she wanted to teach this kid the words "thank you."

The clock kept ticking. She was surprised—and thankful— Nelly was being well behaved until he said, "They should be done about now."

She turned around. "Done with what?"

He looked at her with the maturity of an adult. "Their *quality* time."

A searing sensation shot up through her toes and into her eyeballs. No, he couldn't be saying...

He smirked and went back to his video game.

With all pretense of politeness gone, she fired back, "You're just like your mother, trying to screw with my head. Well, I'm not going anywhere, Junior, so get used to it."

"It's Nelly, dammit!"

"Nasty is more like it and don't swear!"

He muttered, "I'll say whatever the fuck I want."

"*Not to me.*"

She turned more to look at him straight on. "Can we get through this evening without giving our hosts even more reasons to despise Americans?"

He let out a mocking laugh.

The door next to him opened. Carmelita got in, glaring at Alyce. She had toned down her tarted-up look so much Alyce barely recognized her: a creamy loose-fitting summer pantsuit, low-heeled sandals instead of her usual spikes, tight top, and bling on top of bling. Her jewelry was a dainty diamond bracelet, one diamond channel ring on her right hand, and a simple gold chain necklace. Her wild mane of dark ringlets with golden highlights was restrained in an updo.

Reading Alyce's mind, she said, "I been gettin' *French Vogue*."

"You look great, Carmelita. Welcome." Alyce turned to her fiancé, who wouldn't look at her as he put on his seat belt and started driving.

A voice screamed inside of her: *He's fucking her.*

Followed by: *Don't even go there. You're being paranoid.*

"Shit, my battery is about to die!" the kid whined. "I can't play my video games!"

Nelson angrily turned the car around. Father and son dashed into a convenience store by the hotel while Alyce's blood pressure went up another five notches. Carmelita scrutinized the gleaming rock that now sat on Alyce's left ring finger, re-sized by André.

"Now, who could say no to that?"

Alyce glanced at her rummaging through her Kate Spade purse, hurt and trying to hide it. In that moment, Alyce felt sorry for her. Carmelita loved Nelson and could never marry him because Glorianna wouldn't allow it. No wonder she and her son were obnoxious.

She thought of Sister Therese's advice to be compassionate, took a deep breath and stayed silent. What could she possibly say to make things better?

"As long as nothin's changin' for me, I don't care what Nelson does." Carmelita took out a mirror and admired herself. "'Cause I deserve it."

So long sympathy. He paid $5,000-a-month rent for her two-bedroom apartment in Soho. That was just the tip of the iceberg. What had she done for him? Raised a high-maintenance brat.

"I'm missing something," Alyce said acidly. "You don't work. You live in the lap of luxury. We're never going to be soul sisters, but let's at least act civil."

"Sure, Annie."

"Thanks, Caramel Latte."

She snorted and patted her hair the same way Glorianna did. "What-evah."

Alyce thought of the glass of wine Liliane had said was okay to have with dinner. Hell yeah, she was having one tonight.

33

CLUSTIER FOUQUOI

As they neared Jean-Luc's, Carmelita said loudly, "A *dirt* road?"

"I think it's charming," Alyce said, overly nice.

Under her breath, she replied, "You never grew up on one."

Nelson remained expressionless and silent.

"Whoa, Dad! Look at that old Mercedes!"

Nelly shot out his door when the car stopped. Within two seconds he was inside the wheel-less two-door convertible up on blocks in the open garage. He was just like his father when it came to cool cars, Alyce thought. Nelson's smile indicated he had the same idea.

Jean-Luc appeared at the door wearing jeans and a yellow cashmere sweater. He was clean-shaven, gray hair pulled back in a ponytail, and looking indisputably handsome.

He gave them all, even Nelson, the one-two-three kiss and started toward Nelly in the Mercedes. "Please join the others while I get to know this interesting young man."

Isabella was slicing fresh bread when they walked in the kitchen. "*Hola!*" she sang out. Alyce could tell she'd been drinking. One eyelid drooped more than the other.

After introductions, Alyce said to Carmelita, "Try the goat cheese from a farm nearby. It's amazing."

"I don't do goat."

She and Isabella started speaking in Spanish. Alyce couldn't make out what they were saying literally, but knew it was the usual introductory banter. She heard Carmelita say she was from Cuba, Isabella asked where Junior was, and she said with Jean-Luc and to call him Nelly.

Through the kitchen sliding-glass doors she could see Glorianna and Luther in the backyard examining the cottage, wine glasses in hand. She was making wide gestures as if to indicate the lovely morning glory vines covering almost every square inch should be taken down.

Over my dead body, Alyce thought.

She called to them from the door. "Sorry we're late."

Glorianna gave her a look of sympathy.

When she came inside and acknowledged You-know-who with a fake smile and three cheek kisses, Carmelita's eyes registered shock.

Sounding moderately phony, Glorianna asked, "How was your flight?"

"Just fine, ma'am, just fine."

"Oh, don't call me that." Her cheery tone changed. "Mrs. Mansfield will do."

Luther was introduced. "I loooove your hair." Carmelita approved of his admiration. Glorianna did not.

In addition to wine, Alyce had picked up an assortment of exotic fruits: pear-shaped *wax jambu* with thin pink skin and white insides, *rollinia* the flavor of lemon sorbet that looked like a golden artichoke with leaves that never grew, and *sapodilla,* which were small, brown and furry with orange flesh and a caramel flavor.

"The *grumichamas* are the sweetest cherries you'll ever eat," she said as she started washing the various fruits.

"I just loooove being in another country," trilled Luther.

"And *mamey* is kind of like an avocado that tastes like a peach and an apricot."

Glorianna commented, "You're so continental now, Al-*eees.*"

"Where's the bathroom?" asked Carmelita. She did not come out for awhile.

Isabella wasted no time pitching her paintings to Nelson and Glorianna. Alyce watched her body language. Was she trying to get him to buy her work or her?

Jean-Luc and Junior returned, giving the clear impression that they had become best buddies. He did have a way with kids. Again she saw him with Colette and felt his unbearable heartbreak.

Carmelita reappeared when she heard her son's voice.

Isabella presented Nelly with fresh, warm rosemary bread topped with goat cheese and chopped basil. He made a face that was worse than the one he gave Glorianna when she lightly hugged him and tentatively patted him on the head.

"Don't ya have any candy bars or cookies?"

Jean-Luc nearly barked, "*I* baked that bread! You will love it."

"Nelson," Glorianna said archly, "Maybe it's time to send this child to boarding school?"

Carmelita pursed her lips, grabbed Nelly's shoulders, and drew him to her.

What a great idea Alyce telepathically relayed to Glorianna.

Nelson cleared his throat. "Sure, I'll look into schools around here. With his mother living nearby, of course."

Carmelita broke into a smug grin. A new thought zapped into Alyce's brain. Could this have been Nelson's plan all along? Live far away from his mother in the enchanting South of France with his new family and have his other one close, too?

Nelly wrested himself away from his mother's grip and examined the appetizer. "You made this?"

"A real man knows how to cook, Nelly."

He cracked up. "Ne-*lee* sounds funny." He reluctantly took a slice, smelled it, and tried a small bite. With his mouth full, he mumbled, "This is great!"

In no time Jean-Luc had him learning the French word for everything he was eating: *pain, romarin, fromage de chèvre.* From there it went to table, chair, plate, glass, knife, fork, spoon. To encourage him to learn more French (which Alyce now wished he wouldn't do), Jean-Luc handed Nelly the electronic translator Alyce rarely used anymore. He showed him how to look up a word in English or French. He was enthralled.

"You have a good ear for other languages," Jean-Luc exclaimed. "It is because you are young and used to hearing Spanish at home."

"I don't hear Spanish."

Carmelita said, "I'm an American now. Why would I speak it?"

"What a pity," said Glorianna. "It's such an asset." She nudged Luther.

"Yes!" he piped in, "I'd give anything to speak Spanish."

Carmelita's face was as expressionless as stone.

Jean-Luc lectured Nelly on how important it was to learn as many other tongues as possible, as young as possible. "You will be able to seduce any woman, trust me."

Nelly glanced at Isabella's ass as she bent over and checked on something in the lower oven. "Really?"

Ten years old and he was already a dirty old man.

After finishing his snack, Nelly pulled out a device from his leather jacket and started playing a game.

Jean-Luc said with alarm, "What is that in your hair, Nelly? A spider?"

He jumped up, swatting furiously. "What? Where? Where?"

Jean-Luc reached behind him and produced a one Euro coin and gave it to him.

"Wow!" He studied the currency. "That's cool. Teach me."

He held out his hand. The boy high-fived. "That is not what I want."

"Yeck. You want me to hold your hand?"

"I want that wretched thing you are playing with."

He slowly gave it to him. Jean-Luc slipped it into a drawer.

He showed him the magic trick as Isabella lubricated everyone else with a nice sparkling *Prosecco.* They allowed Nelly a small glass, as most French children were accustomed to having.

"Moving to France sounds good to me," the boy said.

Glorianna quickly interrupted. "I'm thinking Switzerland. Much better schools."

Alcohol has a way of smoothing rough edges. By the time everyone settled at the large dining table next to the living room and a local *rosé* was dispensed to go with the main course, the mood was more jovial.

Especially when Glorianna raised her glass. "*Bon appétit!*"

Alyce didn't dare look at Jean-Luc or Isabella.

"Damn, this chicken stew is *good,*" exclaimed Carmelita. "It's got somethin' different in it. I can't figure out what it is."

Again, Alyce couldn't look at them. She knew what they had done.

Jean-Luc first described the marinade he used: red wine, cognac, sliced onions and carrots, garlic, thyme, bay leaf, fresh rosemary, and black pepper. Then he browned the *lapin,* added onions, *lardon* (similar to bacon), flour to thicken, and mushrooms.

Nelly was furiously entering letters in Alyce's electronic translator. "How do you spell that word for chicken? L-a-p-a-n?"

"No, chicken is poo-*lay,*" he said. "P-o-u-l-e-t."

"That's close to *pollo*, Spanish for chicken," said Carmelita, now liking her son learning another language.

"Then what's the other?"

"L-a-p-i-n."

He punched it in. "Rabbit? Gross!"

Carmelita spit a mouthful of food onto her hand.

Everyone else was tipsy enough to find the humor in it, even Glorianna, who discreetly put her fork down and never used it again.

Luther caught his breath. "Now I get it. This whole French thing is peasant chic."

Alyce thought Jean-Luc would be deeply insulted. Instead he found his comment so outrageous he laughed along with everyone else.

He turned to Carmelita and asked, overly politely, "Tell us about your childhood. Where were you born, what was your family like?"

She coolly replied, "I don't remember."

Jean-Luc, soothing and warm, said, "My father left when I was five. We became quite poor and my mother," he eyed Nelly, "she couldn't find a real job and had to make money illegally." He was riveted. "They are both dead. Now I am writing a memoir."

His fist landed on the counter with a loud *thunk,* startling them all.

"I would give every possession to my name to have one more conversation with them! To ask them the very questions I am asking you! What if you died tomorrow? What would your son know about you?"

Nelson, who was sitting next to Alyce on the other side of the table from Carmelita and his son, said, "He has a point, Lee-lee."

Lee-lee, Alyce thought.

"Do *you* wanna know, Nelly?" his mother asked.

His "yeah" showed more enthusiasm than usual.

Glorianna and Luther sat stiffly as Carmelita told a wrenching tale of being born in Cuba after Castro's guerilla troops overthrew Batista. The family farm was confiscated in the name of socialism. Her father was thrown into prison for stealing right after she was conceived.

"He was tryin' to feed his eight children. I was the last one. I lived in poverty until I escaped on a boat to Miami, a little kid and skinny as my pinkie. I understand why your mama became a, you know, did what she did. I was lucky I had a religious *tia* in Miami who took me in and was super strict. I had a hard time in school not knowin' the language. I ended up droppin' out. I was a barmaid at a hotel on Miami Beach, in my 30s, when I met Nelson."

She studied him with what sure looked liked more than friendship in her eyes. "He looked so sweet. Like he would never hit me or hurt me."

Nelson looked down and cleared his throat.

To hell with being pregnant. Alyce poured herself another glass of wine. Jean-Luc, sitting to her left at the end of the table, pushed a pitcher of water in her direction.

Glorianna interjected, "I'm beginning to understand you better, Carmelita."

A silence fell over the table but for the sound of Alyce brushing breadcrumbs into a neat pile by her plate.

"Nelly," Jean-Luc said brightly, "Let me show you another magic trick."

Within moments the mood shifted as he demonstrated how to do the classic Handkerchief and Vanishing Coin Trick. The look of wonder and concentration on the boy's face would melt anyone.

"First, you place a flesh-colored rubber band around your fingers and thumb," Jean-Luc instructed. "Place the scarf in that hand. With your other hand, put the coin into the handkerchief.

Let the rubber band slide off of your fingers onto the silky cloth so it now surrounds the coin. Slide your hand up to the end and shake the handkerchief. It looks like the coin has disappeared but it's really stuck in the scarf held tight by the rubber band."

"Cool!"

A thunderclap rumbled close by. The wind kicked up. Jean-Luc closed the sliding door to the patio and suggested Nelly go upstairs to practice the trick.

Alyce knew there had to be a reason he did that. With all the alcohol being consumed mixed with Jean-Luc's expert interrogation skills, more confessions were sure to come.

Droopy-eyed Isabella swayed as she talked. She seemed sad. Alyce supposed it was because she had no children and how much she'd like to have one with Jean-Luc. He should tell her about Colette. She wouldn't take it so hard. But that was between them. She had her own problems to deal with.

Lee-lee.

And what was going on inside her own body? She'd had a bit more staining but it wasn't like any period she'd ever had.

Jean-Luc put out a beautiful spread of local cheeses and the fruit she'd brought, complimenting her choices. He also filled the empty wine glasses with a Muscat. No way was Alyce touching that.

Carmelita's vanished faster than the coin in the handkerchief.

Glorianna and Luther were shitfaced. Some of her hair had fought its way out of its tight little bun. When they laughed at the same time it reminded her of sounds from a haunted house. "Hoo-hoo-hoo-hoo! Hah-hah-hah-hah!"

Nelson was a drinker who knew his limits. Another attractive quality about him. But he looked troubled, distracted. Maybe he hadn't had *enough* to drink. He took a rather big gulp of the Muscat.

Alyce could tell by the way Carmelita studied the bottle of dessert wine that her eyesight was going. She put it down and struggled to remove her jacket until Jean-Luc, the closest male to her, assisted. Her low-cut top captured every heaving of her massive bosom.

Moments later, "Oops!" Carmelita spilled a good portion of her drink down her front. Alyce glanced at Nelson, expecting to exchange a humorous boy-is-she-drunk look. Instead he was transfixed as she dipped a white cloth napkin in a glass of water and dabbed at her chest.

Just as Alyce was about to give him a good hard pinch under the table, Isabella leaned in and asked Carmelita, "Are your sensational breasts real?"

"I really think that's none of your business," Nelson said nervously as he popped a *grumichama* in his mouth. His mother agreed.

Isabella didn't care. "So many American women have them. It is the status symbol, no?"

"They was all saggy after Junior was born so Nelson gave 'em to me as a birthday present."

A numbness started around Alyce's ears and rapidly spread.

"I thought you had no idea."

Nelson spit out a seed. "It was a tactless question, Ally. She's entitled to her privacy."

Glorianna raised her glass. "A toast to my expanded family!"

Alyce fired off, "You're not answering my question."

"You was talkin' about my boobies to her?"

"Why don't you just fix her damn gold tooth, too?"

"That's enough!"

Claws popped as she and Carmelita, sitting directly across from each other, stood up at the same time.

"He don't fix my tooth because he *likes* it. And he likes my boobies and my big fat ass. And the way I talk. Right, Boo?"

Nelson stood up and tried to pull Alyce from the table.

"Let's *go.*"

"Let's *not.*"

"He don't marry me 'cause his world don't approve." She glared at Glorianna. "Specially her. She was gonna cut him out of her will if he didn't marry soon. But it ain't gonna stop him from lovin' me and it ain't gonna stop me from lovin' him! Don't look at me like that. You *gotta* know the score by now."

"It was an idle threat!" Glorianna yelled, as she jumped up and leaned toward You-know-who. "I would never do such a thing! He loves *Alyce.* Very much so. Accept it!"

With a sudden hard yank, Alyce shook off Nelson's hand from her arm. "The score?"

Luther let out an "Oh, shit."

Glorianna's hair completely fell out of its bun when she screamed "Dammit to hell, Nelson! Why do you have to be like your father! You told me not to say anything because you were going to handle it! I should have known you couldn't do it."

Nelson exploded right back. "You've made my life as miserable as you've made his! I want to be far away from you and be a success on my own so I don't have to be manipulated by you for the rest of my goddam life!"

Alyce was stunned to hear him say that but it didn't stop her from grabbing his shirtsleeve and saying, "What about manipulating *me*? What the hell is *the score*, Nelson? Say it! Say you're still fucking her!"

Glorianna sounded like she was choking.

Luther muttered, "Oh, shit shit."

Nelson brushed his hair off his forehead twice. "Not in a long time."

"What's a long time?"

Carmelita answered. "Depends on what you call *it*. All the way? Right after you got engaged."

He gave Alyce a pleading look. "I swore it would be the last time. And I've been true to you ever since."

Carmelita smirked. "Kind of."

Alyce covered her hot face with her hands. She had never been so humiliated in her life. She looked at Jean-Luc and Isabella. Their eyes were wide with expectation.

Nelson tried to take Alyce's hand. She wouldn't let him touch her.

"My therapist said I should have done this a long time ago. I didn't want to lose you, Ally. I love you. But I love Carmelita, too. I thought we could work this out."

Through tears, she said, "Let me guess. You haven't been playing squash with your friend Ken twice a week, have you?"

Glorianna screeched, "We'll give you whatever you want! Just marry my son and give me grandchildren!" She zinged Carmelita with eyes so intense Alyce was surprised she didn't melt. "That child is not going to be the sole heir." She shifted her evil gaze to Alyce. "Ronald has had a mistress for years. It's called a marriage of convenience. You're not going to do better than the Mansfield name!"

Alyce nearly laughed when she said, "I couldn't do worse!"

Jean-Luc jumped to his feet. "Bravo, Al-*ees*!"

All at once an intense pain from the vicinity of her right ovary shot around her back, up to her right shoulder blade, doubling her over.

"Al-*ees?*" Jean-Luc asked. "What is wrong?"

Carmelita drummed her long nails on the table. "I knew you was dreamin', Boo."

The pain faded. Through tears, Alyce yelled, "Boo this, bitch!"

Alyce grabbed her wine glass and threw it at Carmelita's head. Her curls were so thick it bounced off. She threw her glass at Alyce, who managed to dodge it. The mayhem worsened as Alyce took a swing at Nelson, Isabella tried to intervene, and Carmelita socked her in the eye, sparking a catfight between them. Jean-Luc grabbed Alyce from behind and pulled her away as she tried to kick Glorianna. Luther was holding *her* back from scratching Alyce's eyes out.

Another jolt, even worse than the first one, caused Alyce to let out a bloodcurdling scream that stopped everyone.

"Something's wrong with the baby! Something's wrong!"

Glorianna, Carmelita, and Luther all shouted: "BABY?"

Alyce yanked off her ring and threw it at Carmelita. "You can have him and this! It's *fake.*" She eyed her chest. "I'm sure you won't have a problem with that."

Alyce lifted the bottom of her blouse a couple of inches, removed the diamond stud from her bellybutton, and threw that at Nelson.

"Give that to your next victim. OW!" She grabbed Jean-Luc's shoulder. Through gritted teeth, "Take me to a hospital."

Nelson ran to her. "I'll do that. I'm the father."

"I don't want you anywhere near me! If this baby lives, it's mine. All mine!"

"No!" cried Glorianna.

At that moment Nelly barged into the room, full of excitement over the magic trick he had mastered. "I got it! Watch!" He immediately sensed something was wrong.

Alyce delivered her final words to Nelson with just the right touch of condescension the French do so well.

"*Faute de grives, on mange des merles.* For want of thrushes, one eats blackbirds."

34

Loose Ends

"It could be a burst appendix," the doctor examining her said, "but I suspect an ectopic pregnancy."

An ultrasound revealed he was right.

She sat on the examining table, still in mind-numbing pain, clutching Jean-Luc's hand, Glorianna and Nelson banished to the waiting room.

The doctor, an older man who exuded the aura that he had seen and heard everything, coolly explained, "There is nothing we can do to save it. We can wait until the morning to see if nature takes its course. If not, we will have to operate."

It? Alyce thought. My child is not an "it."

What he said next wasn't good, either.

"Your fallopian tube on that side will still be intact, but there will be scar tissue. Any time a woman has an ectopic, the chance of having another typically doubles. You may never have this problem again and you may have it over and over. There is simply no way to tell."

The doctor excused himself. She burst into tears. Jean-Luc rubbed her back and squeezed her hand. "Al-*ees*, you will live a full life whether you have your own children or not."

"I'm going to lose my baby."

"It's not your fault. Life never goes the way we planned."

"Don't you dare say this is for the best."

"Please. Your indestructible optimism has not rubbed off on me that much."

That at least made her smile.

Yet, as the anesthesiologist instructed her the next morning to start counting backward from 100, she was convinced this *was* a blessing.

Quatre-vingt-dix-neuf. Quatre-vingt-dix-huit. Quatre-vingt-dix-sept.

When the surgery was over and she was fully coherent, Jean-Luc was still there for her.

"I know this doesn't compare in any way with your loss," she said as she tried to get comfortable to no avail, "but I have a better idea of what you've been through."

"Do not minimize it, Al-*ees*. You have lost a child you wanted very much, even if you did not want the father. You had a connection only a mother can have."

"Where is he?"

"Outside if you want to see him."

"His mother, too?"

"Yes. Are you sure you are up to it?"

She nodded. "If you see a nurse, ask if I can have some more pain medication." Her stomach felt like a mule had kicked her.

He stepped out as they stepped in.

Glorianna rushed to her. "Dear Alyce. I'm *so* sorry."

Nelson tried to act like everything was fine. He bent over to kiss her on the lips. She turned her head.

"Ally, can't we get beyond this?"

Scrutinizing him and his mother, she said, "Why would you want to? I'm defective merchandize. I may never be able to give you the heirs you want so much. And I never want to hear the names Junior, Nelly, Carmelita, Lee-lee, or Boo again as long as I live."

Nelson solemnly asked, "Sure you don't want to think about it?"

"No! I can't believe you'd even want to patch things up. You should just marry her already. You love her! And I can't imagine *any* woman putting up with—"

Glorianna cut her off. "As long as you have your eggs and a uterus, you can still have a child. In-vitro isn't cheap, but that wouldn't be a problem."

Alyce stared at her. "Did you not hear the part where Nelson admitted he still sleeps with You-know-who?"

She stiffened. "And did you not hear the part where I said my husband has had a mistress—"

"Stop!" She clutched at her aching tummy. "Get out of my life forever. You're *both* fucking nuts." Pointing at Nelson, "You sleep with that trashy Carmelita and I can't tell a story about peeing my pants when a boar is about to attack me? I feel sorry for you, Nelson. Trying to be two different people must be exhausting. Just pick one and stick to it. The property you bought is your problem. I'm moving on with my life."

"What are you going to do?" asked an incredulous Nelson, as though nothing could be better than being with him.

At that moment a nurse came in and shooed them away to give her a painkiller. Her last image of Nelson was him blowing her a kiss.

"Kiss my ass!" was her response.

Soon a warm feeling coated her insides and she was blissfully floating back to unconsciousness. She saw the face of Sister Therese before her.

"Everything will be fine," she said. "Your guardian angel is with you."

Alyce was discharged the next day. Jean-Luc was waiting for her. She thought back to the day she first saw him at Andre's store and couldn't stand him. The feeling had been mutual. Now she was thrilled to see him. What a funny, unpredictable friendship they had formed. She was already missing it.

"I've been very busy since your operation," he said as they cheek-kissed. "You look much better than you did yesterday."

"I feel much better," she said, as he snapped the seatbelt in the Kangoo for her. "But I hope I never go back to being that gullible, shallow girl again."

Once behind the wheel, he said, "What you cannot do is go back to America. I will find another place with a cottage."

"Not so fast."

He angrily revved the gas and poked the air in front of her. "I may have made you mad at times, but I never once saw you laugh with Nelson the way you do with me. Not once!"

"And don't make me laugh now. It hurts."

Once they were on the way, he moved to the subject she desperately needed to talk about.

Jean-Luc theorized that Nelson fell in love with Carmelita the moment she flashed her gold tooth. She was the perfect match for him. Very much like his social climbing, demanding mother, right down to the same cadence in their names. She was also the complete opposite.

"The ultimate forbidden fruit," he said. "I'm sure you suspected what was going on. You wanted to believe him. That is love, Al-*ees*. You may still love him, though you feel a fool. I do not think it was a charade on his part. He was being honest when he said he loved you both, according to his definition of it." He waved his hand. "La, that is life."

She made a pitiful face. "Yeah, la la la."

"We always hold a certain respect for those who betray us.

There is selfishness at the heart of their actions. How can you not think highly of someone who will stop at nothing to get what they want? I despised Margot for what she did, and I admired her for having the nerve to do it, especially as I fell in love with Colette. You would never have had the experience here had it not been for Nelson. You are a completely different person because of him. A much better person."

That lifted her spirits. As they pulled up to his former home, she was glad to have one last visit. She commented, "I'm surprised they're letting you stay here."

"A contract is a contract."

"Then what?"

"I'm looking at places tomorrow with Pauline. Either I will find something I like or I'll move into a hotel."

"With Isabella?"

"Come to the kitchen and I will bring you up to date on what has happened."

He poured her a glass of her favorite apricot-rosemary iced tea. She glanced around the big yellow kitchen she would always remember.

"Isabella is gone. I did not make love to her once after her return. For a moment she considered making a play for Nelson, but she could never put up with all that came with him. She is on her way back to Spain."

He raised his glass in a toast. "To Isabella. May she find the right man for her, and soon."

Alyce was slow to raise her tea in return. It hurt her stomach.

"As for Nelson, I almost ripped his head off for what he did to you—and his wicked mother." He picked up an envelope that was on the kitchen counter. "Here is a check for $10,000 to help you through this transition. I am sorry I could not get more."

She stared at the envelope. "You did that for me?"

"I am not finished." His face glowed. "Just like the happy ending of a Hollywood movie, Nelson finally stood up for the mother of his son. He is going to send her to school in another city to speak French and become sophisticated, and then marry her! Of course, she is not you and she will never find a teacher like me. Good luck."

It took a moment to absorb this news. She still felt a pang of defeat. Carmelita had won. Something else hit her as well.

"Jean-Luc, I get it now. Carmelita is my sister Chantilly! You were right about my being drawn to competitive triangles. If I remove myself from that, I'm actually happy! They belong together. Totally. Nelson finally did the right thing. I'm…I can't believe I'm saying this…*proud* of him."

Jean-Luc was beaming, an expression she rarely saw on him. They burst into laughter. How crazy was life?

"Ow! I have to stop! It really does hurt."

What made her calm down was looking into her own future and seeing nothing. Not even a job.

"Do you feel well enough to make it to school tomorrow?"

"Claire promised a champagne toast at the end. I have to show up." She focused on him. "I'd like to stay in a hotel tonight. Can you recommend some place besides the *Hôtel Marlaison*?"

"Why not the cottage?"

"I want to be where there are no memories of Nelson. And don't suggest your bedroom."

He looked miffed. "Al-*ees*, you just ended an engagement, lost a baby, and had surgery." He took another sip of his tea. "I know the perfect hotel. *The Bonne Santé*."

"Good health. Sounds like the right place for me right now." She stood up, "But first I want to check on my *loirs*. What do you have in the refrigerator to feed them?"

Alone, she carried chopped apples, milk, and water in the same picnic basket they used at the beach. As she approached the old rabbit hutch, her heart pounded. Would they be okay?

The nest was empty. She looked around, called like always

by mimicking the sound they made. Had something killed them? Had they moved away? Were they off looking for food?

She placed the apples inside, filled the plastic tub with milk, the other with fresh water.

The birds chirped madly.

Something told her the dormice were in heaven along with the tiny life that had been growing inside her. As she was about to cry, she felt something on her foot. A gray face with big black eyes stared back at her.

"You're okay!"

She gently lowered herself to the ground and the critter, bigger now, climbed up her chest to be coddled. Another appeared. No more.

She still didn't name her furry loves. More than ever she didn't want to become attached.

An Offer She *Can* Refuse

Alyce's low mood sank again when she entered her last class and saw a stack of beautifully wrapped presents on the table. She had to let them know the wedding was off. In French, of course.

When everyone was seated, she stood up. "Before we begin, I have some news. I am no longer engaged." After the murmurs subsided, she motioned to the table, "I am very happy I'm not marrying him, but I appreciate your thoughtfulness and hope you can return what you bought."

Claire stepped forward. "Since you say you are happy about this, Al-*ees*, would you object to opening the champagne?"

You have to love the French.

In no time, Alyce the raconteur was standing in front of the room revealing the broad strokes of what happened (minus the swearing, and her ectopic pregnancy that she wasn't ready to talk about).

Claire said, "We are always weak when we are in love."

When she reached the fight that followed the Moment of Truth, the class laughed and laughed. She laughed as well. At last.

Liliane poked her head in the classroom door. "I cannot say that I was upset when I heard the news." She invited the class to come to the cafeteria for a surprise.

When they walked into the large room, thunderous applause erupted. Alyce didn't know why until she saw in big letters on a banner: *FÉLICITATIONS ALYCE!*

She spotted her first hosts, the elderly farm couple Fabien and Fabienne, followed by Solange the widow and Philippe the dancer, and the Devreauxs, all smiling and clapping with the highest regard for her.

With a microphone in hand, Liliane said, "Thank you for coming today to honor Al-*ees* Donovan, who arrived three months ago and came close to leaving us rather quickly." Everyone chuckled until Liliane said with an approving smile, "But she did not leave. She did not give up. She was determined to master French like no student before her. Al-*ees*, you are a role model now." Alyce hung her head in a mixture of embarrassment and pride. "And I think you would be a spectacular *teacher* to beginning English-speaking students. When can you start?"

More applause rose around her.

"*Me* teach *here?*" Tears of joy were unstoppable. It was the biggest compliment anyone could ever pay her.

Someone whispered in her ear, "Even I think you would be an excellent teacher."

In a beige suit and white shirt, the clean-shaven, closely cropped Jean-Luc was *très* debonair.

"You cut your hair! It looks great, Jean-Luc."

"Will you accept the position, Al-*ees?*" asked Liliane.

She took the microphone and said with a French accent, "But, of course!"

After mingling with admirers she didn't know she had, and apologizing profusely to her former hosts for behavior they now found amusing, Jean-Luc held out his hand.

"Let us go for a drive and discuss your future."

She bid *adieu* to all with lots of cheek-kisses, even Julien.

"You are a bad boy," she whispered.

He shrugged. "Not all the time. I am a good bad boy."

"Then you'll be a great writer one day."

Her last stop was Liliane. "I know I said yes to your offer, but I was in a state of shock. I need to think about it."

She smiled with complete assurance that she would not change her mind.

As they drove off, Jean-Luc said, "Look in the glove compartment for an envelope. I am giving you what I would have paid Pauline for finding a buyer—"

"Stop!"

"—I am also paying you back for your expenditures as promised and throwing in extra for helping with my memoir proposal."

"You already did that."

"Raymond has sold it for a staggering amount of money. Between that and the sale of the house, I am in very good shape right now."

"That's great about the memoir, but there you go again being too generous. You have to think of yourself, Jean-Luc."

His voice was soft when he said, "I am going to write about Colette. I must do it. You deserve a million Euros for lessening that pain."

"It wasn't me. You were ready to let it go."

"You're being too self-deprecating, Al-*ees*. You need to think more about yourself, too."

She opened the envelope. There was a check from Jean-Luc for €100,000.

"Jean-Luc!"

"Liliane thinks that is fair. I do not wish to hear another word of protest."

She was still stunned by his gesture when they pulled up

to the storefront of a real estate agency, its window filled with pictures of properties. Alyce had walked by it many times and studied the photos, longing to buy one. With all that money in her hand, a wave of temptation to buy her own place rushed in.

No, no, no. That was crazy.

"The Mansfields do not want the property and offered to sell it back to me," Jean-Luc said. "I am not interested. I have moved on in my head and my heart. Pauline is their broker so she will make her commission after all."

Alyce liked that he was concerned she got something out of the deal.

"If you are up to it, will you look at properties with me? I value your sensible opinion." He held her hand with both of his. They were as warm as ever. "You need to put your mind off recent events."

"No kidding. Let me pop a painkiller and I'm ready."

Pauline's first words were, "You look handsome with your new look, Jean-Luc."

"You can thank Al-*ees* for that."

She curtailed her flattery.

He had narrowed his property search to the following criteria: view of the Mediterranean, enough land to give him total privacy, at least four bedrooms, *no* swimming pool, a large kitchen and a price tag not one penny over €500,000.

Alyce knew this wasn't going well when he said, "Let's see the rest of it" and Pauline said, "There is no rest."

"Don't even bother showing me the others. I'll go to 700."

Alyce didn't hide her groan of disapproval. He was going to be broke again. He really needed someone he could trust to manage his money.

Pauline hopped on her phone to line up more viewings as Alyce and Jean-Luc waited in her car.

"Pauline is looking happy these days," he said. "A most

seductive quality." He ran his hands through his new short hair-cut. "I cannot get used to this."

"Neither can I. If you'd like me to leave you two alone, that's fine."

"She is not nearly as seductive as you, Al-*ees*. There is not a trace of stress on your face."

"Wait until the painkiller wears off."

As Pauline came toward them, Alyce noticed that she walked like a woman sprouting wings that had been previously clipped. From knowing Jean-Luc, Alyce was starting to see life through the eyes of a writer. It was richer, more interesting. Certainly never dull.

Two hours and five houses later, nothing was close to promising. The last one was 20 minutes outside of town.

Alyce awoke from a nap to hear Jean-Luc warily ask, "What is the story on this one?"

"I saved it for last since it is in the opposite direction of the other houses. With four hectares, it is too much land for most private owners and not enough for commercial purposes."

"Tell me its story," asked Jean-Luc.

"A British couple used it as their vacation home. The husband died in the U.K. after a long illness. The wife is highly motivated to sell. She hasn't been here in a year. She said it was meant to be enjoyed by lovers. It would not be the same without him. They had been high school sweethearts."

"Ahhhh," was all Jean-Luc replied.

"The price has just dropped."

As the houses became sparser and farms became more frequent, he approved. "I am looking for serenity the moment I am close to where I live. I can feel it here. It has good emotional karma, too. My former property was bought from a couple who were divorcing. I should have known better."

Pastures surrounded the property except by the main house, which had been beautifully landscaped. It was a classic two-story

Mediterranean villa: roof of curved orange tiles, countless palm trees, rough stucco exterior.

When they walked through the front door, Alyce began to tingle. It was beautifully decorated in a down-to-earth way. Definitely Jean-Luc.

The foyer's floor was made of yellow, blue, and white tiles. A large Moroccan archway led to the living room that looked out on a vista of the sea. There were just a few fishing boats here and there. The sun-dappled water sparkled as though a net of diamonds was strewn across it.

"Oh, Jean-Luc," Alyce said softly, "the sunsets must be incredible here."

Pauline was smiling. Yes, the real-estate cupid had pulled back his bow and struck deep into his target.

"I love the kitchen!" he cried. It was spacious and a soft yellow. "It is even better than mine. I always wished there had been room for a dining table. Now there is."

They walked through glass sliding doors to the large backyard. There was a *pétanque* court and a small cottage overlooking the water. They immediately inspected it. The wall facing the sea was floor to ceiling glass. Alyce couldn't imagine a more peaceful place on earth.

"*Merveilleux!*" he said almost to himself. "This will be where I write."

"There is another guest cottage down the road that is part of the property," Pauline added.

As they walked to the house, Alyce was jolted by the sight of another Tree of Love just like the one at her former cottage.

"It is perfection," he said. "How much?"

"It started at 950. It is now down to your magic number, 700."

"What about the furnishings?"

"Everything is negotiable. I will look into it."

"Jean-Luc. Your budget."

He ignored Alyce's comment as they walked through the

rooms upstairs. "I wonder what the master bedroom looks like." Upon seeing it, "Fit for a king, Al-*ees*!"

The large bed had an ornate carved wooden headboard and a mattress that looked two feet thick. "Yep," Alyce said, patting it. "You'll be having fun with someone on this in no time."

"I will be too busy to have fun."

Pauline cocked her head. "You are not looking together? I thought—*Pardon.*"

For the drive back, Pauline talked nonstop to Jean-Luc about being single at her age. Alyce's mind went to visions of herself as a cat-loving spinster who spoiled other people's children.

And never had her heart broken again.

When they returned to Pauline's office, she wrote her home number on her business card before they parted. "In case you lost it, Jean-Luc."

"I will be in touch," he said.

Once on the road, he suggested, "Let us dine and discuss what I should do."

"Sure you don't want to do that with Pauline?"

"Not tonight."

Alyce pushed him playfully on his upper arm. "You go, Jean Ho."

"Do not call me that. I have outgrown that phase."

She turned her head away from him and let out a "Hmm."

They found an outdoor café and ordered *suppa d'erbiglie* and *fricassée d'agneau à la niçoise*. He took a sniff of his cabernet after they had their respective tastes.

"It is like you, Al-*ees*. Its complexity did not strike me immediately."

"I disagree. It's more like you. Very set in its ways."

"We will see about that."

Alyce accidentally put the cork in her mouth thinking it was a piece of bread.

"You are so funny, Al-*ees!*"

"Ha, ha, ha. It's the painkiller. And no more wine for me. Let's get down to business."

They hashed out the property he wanted to buy from every angle. Was there any way to make it income-producing? He could rent out the cottage. He could possibly rent out some of the land to a vineyard or farmer. Or turn it into a lavender field.

"I should not deal with any side businesses," he said. "Writing is what I do, Al-*ees.*"

Working off the calculator in the phone she had the use of until the end of that month's billing cycle, she came up with a budget for him. Any income from writing or teaching would go into a separate savings account.

"It's the sacred nest egg you never touch," she advised.

"Yes, yes. I will stick to it, I promise."

"Don't rush into this decision, Jean-Luc. At least sleep on it."

"Did you say you want to sleep with me?"

She pretended she didn't hear him. "I need to get back to the hotel. I'm fading fast. That anesthesia must still be in my system."

He was a perfect gentleman when they parted. He gave her three cheek-kisses and bid her *"Bonne nuit."*

Once inside her lovely hotel room, she walked onto the terrace and took in the picturesque harbor. She loved the idea of teaching at MEF, but live in France year round? She was surprised to find herself missing her parents, and even her sister. She did *not* miss living in Hoboken or a tiny apartment.

She stood in a Zen-like state trying to see into the future. Suddenly something Jean-Luc had said came to the surface. Then she saw it: a crystal-clear plan for her future.

He had suggested that day at the beach that she go to Japan to learn Japanese. Wouldn't it be nice to spend the summer in a different country each year and learn a new language? What could she do that would allow her to take summers off?

Be a teacher.

But not at MEF. Summer was their busiest time.

She would move back to St. Paul and get a teaching degree. Maybe she would marry another teacher so they could travel together. If not, that was okay. She wanted to live life to the fullest, with or without children, with or without a husband.

She gazed at the Mediterranean Sea that night, committed its image to memory, and said her final *au revoir*.

36

ADIEU?

The next morning, Alyce had just stepped out of the shower when there was a knock on the door, followed by a man saying, "Room service."

She pulled on a robe and said through the door, "I didn't order anything."

"A complimentary breakfast from the management, mademoiselle."

She opened the door and motioned to the gentleman to put the tray on the terrace. He did not hand her a bill to sign and waved away her offer to tip him.

The moment she approached the table, something seemed odd. She sat down, trying to put her finger on it. Wait a minute. It looked exactly like the breakfast Jean-Luc had made for her the morning they went walking in the woods for herbs and he pretended to be a wild boar. Two eggs sunny-side up sprinkled with herbs and nestled on brioche. Fanned across the top of the plate were paper-thin slices of green apple and pear decorated with swirls of cinnamon. Bite-size pieces of *melon de Cavaillon* were just as they had been before.

There was an envelope with her name on it. Inside, on Jean-Luc's stationery, was written:

There once was a girl from St. Paul
Who had one mean caterwaul
To have it plucked out
She had to duck out
In one hour to the café Mistral

When Jean-Luc spied Alyce, he crouched behind a car parked in front of the café. As she walked by on her way inside he popped out.

"HAH!"

She jumped back in fright. "Damn you! Why do you do that? It's very immature."

"Because you know you love it. And I love it when you scold me."

They got in his Kangoo with Didon in the back and drove to the last house they'd seen the day before. Pauline had given him the key. As they entered, Didon set off to inspect every nook and cranny.

"They agreed to sell it, *with the contents*, for 650,000 Euros if I paid cash. That is not over my budget, is it?"

"It's an incredible deal. Grab it."

He waited for a lecture to follow but it didn't come. Alyce seemed different today. Detached, yet self-assured.

They walked out to the terrace of his future home. On a teak table was a large vase he had filled with the flowers that she loved: jasmine, roses, sunflowers, bougainvillea and *Brugmansia x candida.* Angel's Trumpet to him; the Tree of Love to Alyce.

He asked her to take a seat on the side with a view of the sea. "Wait here."

He returned with the bottle of Dom Perignon he had been

chilling in the refrigerator, along with three elegant flutes. Edith Piaf began singing "La Vie en Rose."

"What's this?" she said. "You bought the property?"

"Not yet. It is nice that the sound system plays out here, yes?" Didon positioned herself at the table, panting happily at Alyce.

"Is that flute for her? I've seen everything," she said. "Oh, sorry, I'm not supposed to talk when that song is on."

"It's okay now. In fact, I feel the best I have ever felt in my life."

She was wearing an achingly feminine floral dress, no jewelry, no makeup; the most beautiful woman in the world. He could not live one minute more without her.

A light breeze came up. She ran her hands up and down her bronzed arms.

"Are you cold?"

"No, it feels nice to have the sea air on me." She perked up. "It's like being caressed by nature."

"Another poetic observation of yours." And each one a precious gift to him.

He removed the foil wrapping on the bottle faster. As he worked out the cork he suavely commented, "You look terribly French today."

"You're not looking too bad yourself. I really love the new haircut." She hummed along with the song.

Ah, she wanted him as desperately now as he wanted her.

"Too bad I've sworn off men and I'll be leaving soon."

Bop! The cork sailed across the table and landed in the *pétanque* court. Didon chased it.

Paying no mind to her joke, he said, "From now on, that will be our *cochonet* when we play."

"When *you* play."

He poured champagne into the three flutes. "Do you think this place is me?"

"Absolutely."

He looked in her brown eyes. "Is it you, Al-*ees?*"

"If I had the money and wanted to live here, sure."

"Why would you not want to live here?"

"I have other plans. Besides, you'll have plenty of company to keep you entertained. I'd rather not be in the way."

"I did not mean live in the cottage. I meant live here in the main house with *me*, as my partner in life."

Her delicious laugh flew out into the summery breeze. "You can't be serious."

"Do you think I would ask such a thing after what you have been through?"

"Jean-Luc, I'm… but…" She looked around dumbstruck. "*You* with an American?!"

"Al-*ees*, I cannot believe that I am saying this. I *love* that you are American."

He set the champagne bottle in a silver ice bucket.

"That's very sweet, Jean-Luc, but…"

"*But?*"

"I've decided what I want to do with my life. It was something you said that day on the island that got me thinking."

Oh no, he thought. What did my big mouth do now? As she told him of her plan to move back to Minnesota and become a teacher with summers off to learn new languages, his stomach flopped like a freshly caught fish in a bucket.

He finally asks a woman to make a life with him and she says no!

She happily threw her arms in the air. "I'm so, so, soooo glad I didn't marry Nelson."

"La Vie en Rose" ended right as she held up her flute. "Let's toast to—AHH!"

She finally noticed what he had slipped into it and now deeply regretted: the perfect ring for her. It had an intricately woven, delicate silver band with a nice-sized emerald. It said to all who gazed upon it that a woman of quality, worth, and good taste was wearing it.

He opened his jacket and pulled from his vest pocket a rectangular box. "It goes with this."

It was the beautiful necklace she had admired in the antique store when she thought *solde* meant sold, not on sale.

Her hands covered her open mouth.

He came behind her and clasped it for her. She admired her reflection in the metal ice bucket.

"It's perfect, Jean-Luc." She was beaming. "And the story that goes with it."

He dipped the ring into bucket to rinse it off, dried it with his shirt, and handed it to her. She held it up so that the sunlight reflected on it.

"It's absolutely beautiful."

She slid it on her right ring finger. It fit perfectly.

He looked at her as if to say: *Never having made love to you, I still know you better than Nelson ever did*.

"I intended to put both of our names on the deed. No prenuptial nonsense."

She took a sip of the delicious bubbly as she searched for her answer.

"Not too much," he said, "or you will ruin this proposal, too."

He moved a chair next to hers as he presented his case. "I love your idea, Al-*ees*. But, number one, it is late July. How could you be accepted to a school in September that quickly? Number two, I will have plenty of free time between books, and you know the only reason you can speak French as well as you do is because of me. To get the most out of your ambitious plan, you would have to have me as your tutor to complement your classes. Now where would you like to spend next summer?"

She pulled back and gave him a look of pure indecision.

Trying to read her mind, he rushed in with, "You will be the accountant, but you will give me a small allowance that I can throw away as I please."

"What about children?"

He took a breath before saying, "If that is our *destiny thing*, we will hire a governess who will live in the cottage and watch our children like a hawk. If it will make you more comfortable, it can be a gay man so neither of us becomes suspicious."

Alyce cautiously answered, "A child needs a structured environment, Jean-Luc. That's not going to be easy if Daddy stays up all hours."

"That is what the governess is for."

"You can't accomplish anything if you aren't disciplined. I refuse to governess you."

He made an exaggerated sour face. "If you have a routine, *I* will have a routine."

Alyce mentally tried to change gears and calm her heart as he took her hands in his. As always, they were warm and comforting.

The more he showed a willingness to change, the more he acted like a man ready to grow up and make a commitment, the more he talked about children, the more reasonable and normal he acted, the more nervous she became!

"Eternal happiness is an illusion," he said, "but that is no excuse to sink into the indulgence of unhappiness. I am tired of playing musical chairs with women. You are the only one I want, the only one I wish to make a new home with—one with no memories from our past. We will look out at the sea every day and feel renewed. I will do whatever I have to do for this to work. I love you, Al-*ees*. More than any other man ever will."

Alyce's mind raced for the right words as her skin flushed and heart pounded.

"I must hear you say it," he said, "that you will live here with me and we see how it goes. If it is an official proposal you want and a big diamond—"

"No! I can't begin to think about marriage right now."

Enticingly he said, "I have one more surprise for you. What is your answer? Yes or no?"

"My answer is *whoa*. I'll commit to being with you for one year. I need proof that you've really changed, not a bunch of talk." She looked at the ring on her right hand. "Until then, I'll apply to schools in St. Paul for next September and we'll say this is a friendship ring, *d'accord*?"

"You are a sorceress, Al-*ees*. Every day with you is exquisite torture."

"Now what's the surprise?"

"First, a toast."

She raised her glass and took a moment to put into words what she was feeling.

"To a decision we will never regret."

"Not romantic enough."

"Okay. And at least a year full of love, laughter, and great food. Oh! I know." She recalled an expression she'd learned on her last day of class. "*Qui ne risque rien n'a rien.*"

He who risks nothing, has nothing.

Jean-Luc's toast? "To my one and only thrush. And no more blackbirds."

"Awwww. Wait, one more. A toast to your haircut."

After clinking and sipping, they fell into a long overdue first kiss that only a real man could have given her. So different from all that preceded it.

The air was wonderful; fresh and light. She felt reborn. Maybe it would work with Jean-Luc. It was worth a try, especially when she couldn't imagine not having him in her life.

Dreamily she replied, "You can grow your hair to your ass and I wouldn't care."

Smiling, he said, "Now for your next surprise."

He walked into the house and came back with a black shiny shopping bag with pink tissue paper peeking out of it. A slinky dance beat began to play.

"This is Grace Jones's version of 'La Vie en Rose'," he said. "Do you know it?"

She shook her head no as she moved to its sensuous rhythm and investigated the bag. She took out a small box and opened it, not knowing what to expect.

"Pink sunglasses?"

"The lenses are rose-colored, my darling."

She tried them on. Everything she looked at—the sea, the house, the Tree of Love, Didon, and Jean-Luc—had a nice, reddish warm glow.

Especially when he pulled out a matching pair from the bag and put them on.

He held her close as they moved to the music. "Al-*ees*, I cannot take another step forward into our life together unless I know how it feels to dance with you."

She was delighted to discover he was a great dancer.

As the sun rose higher in the topaz sky and bathed their future home in gold, and the music of approving birds swelled around them, they moved effortlessly around the terrace as though they had been doing it for years.

He said softly, "You do know that you changed me more than I changed you."

"You're right. I deserve a medal."

He brought her even closer. "If you keep up your insults, *I* will be the one calling off this trial arrangement."

"*Au contraire*," she whispered back. "You'll call it off if I stop."

With a naughty laugh, they danced on.

LAGNIAPPES

"Tree of love"

Recipes Provençal

I trust you enjoyed your stay in Marlaison, a fictitious town based on Hyères, France. Please see my website for "The Story Behind the Story." When I was writing *Opposites Attack*, I studied many French cookbooks and made many of the recipes in my head. Now, I've actually made them and will give them to you with Alyce and Jean-Luc in my head. First, Alyce imparts the recipe in her fast, practical way with "creative license" suggestions. Jean-Luc, a fussy purist with no regard for how long it takes, chimes in. To him, the more time spent in the kitchen the better. It keeps him from having to write. You decide which muse you will follow or whether to merge the two.

Check my blog for more recipes and let me know how your versions turn out. http://jomaeder.com/read/blog/

My deepest gratitude extends to Mary-James Lawrence, Francophile/chef/Provence custom tour guide/hostess extraordinaire, for her stellar feedback, especially with the wild boar daube. www.maryjamesprovence.blogspot.com. Also to wine connoisseur/author/bon vivant Mark Oldman for his oenophilic input. www.markoldman.com.

I chose to start with the wild boar daube in Chapter 24 for two reasons. First, it was a turning point for Alyce that boosted her confidence as a chef, hostess, and raconteur. Not to mention sharpshooter. (Slaying and cooking her *sanglier* was nothing compared to learning French.) Second, I'm on a mission to convince more people to eat this meat. Wild boars, warthogs, *sangliers*, feral swine, whatever you want to call them, are a menace that needs to be controlled! They destroy property, crops, and can be dangerous, even lethal, in America as well as abroad. Have fun YouTubing that.

Boar is a lot like beef and isn't at all gamey. It's on the dry side because it has little fat, which makes it good for you. Lots of deglazing is important. Because Alyce made her daube in the summer, she used white wine to make it "lighter," though traditionally in France it's made with red wine in cooler weather when a hearty hot stew tastes best and the bitter oranges are available. Also, it's *sanglier* hunting season then.

Never use stock, only wine. Jean-Luc subscribes to the notion that you should only cook with wine you would drink. Alyce agrees, but the only wine she wouldn't drink is wine that's turned to vinegar. She feels wine you would drink but not serve company is ideal to cook with.

A warning about eating game you've hunted yourself. You could be exposing yourself to salmonella, hepatitis-E, and more. It's better to buy it over the Internet from a reputable company or have an experienced butcher cut up your bounty. I used Dartagnan.com to buy my wild boar. The company is owned by a Frenchwoman. How can you go wrong? Their boars are wild and "humanely trapped" (whatever that means) in Texas then processed at USDA-inspected facilities.

If you must have the boar fresh, spend the extra money and have it delivered the next morning, not afternoon. The frozen boar I ordered was great. It arrived in a Styrofoam box that could be repurposed as an ice chest. Inside were reusable freezer bags. Very nice presentation.

Allow one day to marinate, one to cook. It's even better the third day. And now, ladies and gentleman, I turn you over to Alyce and Jean-Luc.

Santé!

A daubière in action

WILD BOAR DAUBE FOR 10–12

YOU WILL NEED:

A big pot or bowl for marinating
13 qt Dutch oven ideal (or two smaller ones), or a *daubière*
If you cook this in the oven (versus on the stove) the Dutch oven will be very heavy and hot. Make sure you have the strength or help on hand, especially if your oven is in a high location.
2 big pots for browning and sautéing
1 large bowl, 1 medium bowl
2 wooden spatulas

A *daubière*, a pot designed especially for daube, has a recessed lid for wine or water to act as insulation. When the steam rises off the top of the daube inside, it doesn't evaporate as quickly because the lid is cooler. This leads to a basting effect. Cool, huh? You can do part of the cooking on the stove or in an oven and then move it to the *daubière*, or do it all in it. I like to rest it in a corner of a burning fireplace. It makes a lovely burbling sound and is quite romantic.

Ingredients

7–8 lbs wild boar stew meat, thawed, rinsed, dried, and cut into 2–3" pieces, fat removed (This amount will yield elegant French portions. For heartier appetites, use more meat)

3–4 bottles of red wine

3 oz. brandy, cognac, or whiskey (optional)

2 lbs of peeled carrots, 1–2" pieces

1 head of garlic, cloves peeled

3 stalks of celery, sliced (optional)

Bouquet garni: 1 sprig each of rosemary and thyme, 1 bay leaf, the stems of a parsley bunch. Tie them together.

Strips of peel from 1 orange (not the whole rind, bitter orange is best)

3 T butter

1/3 c flour

1/2 c extra virgin olive oil (French EVOO imparts a rich but subtle flavor. Find it on the Internet. A l'Olivier is from Nice, and divine.)

1/2 lb slab of unsmoked bacon cut into lardons (1/4" wide by about 1" long). If you can find *couenne*, pork skin, even better. Tie it up in a nice bundle and slice it after it's cooked. It's a treat to get a little bit of fat when eating the daube. (Or you can pick it out, but that's only allowed on doctor's orders.)

Sea salt and fresh ground pepper to taste

1 bunch of parsley leaves, chopped

Marinate

Place boar in a large pot or bowl and mix with vegetables, bouquet garni, and orange peel. Pour two bottles of wine over it and marinate in refrigerator for 24 hours, stirring a few times.

Preparation

Blanche and rinse lardons of bacon. Separate vegetables from meat. Keep the marinade with herbs and orange peel. Brown vegetables in olive oil and a little butter. Add a *little* salt and pepper. Salt, especially, is like T.M.I. Once you've hit Too Much you can't go back.

In your Dutch oven, on the stove, brown the meat in batches in small amounts of olive oil. Don't crowd them. Deglaze three times. (That means add red wine until the meat is about half covered and burn the liquid off quickly. Don't let anything blacken). Add the lardons at the end. If you want to add brandy or cognac, here's where you do it. But flambé it (light it) to take the edge off. (That's according to JL. After singeing my eyebrows when I stood too close, I just pour it in.)

Add the vegetable mixture to the boar meat. Sprinkle with flour. Add marinade. Add wine until it's almost covered. Rinse pans with a little water and add to the pot. Simmer gently for 1–2 hours. If you don't have a *daubière,* keep simmering another 2 hours. You can also skip the stove and put it in the oven at 325 degrees for 2-1/2 to 3 hours, depending on size of your pot. If you do have a *daubière,* after you've simmered 1–2 hours, transfer everything to the *daubière* and place it in a corner of the fireplace (with a fire going). Simmer gently for 1–2 hours and enjoy its special sounds.

I have to say this because it's so Jean-Luc. He does not use the term "preheat," as in "preheat the oven to 325 degrees." He says there's no "pre" heating it. You heat the oven until it reaches the desired temperature. He hates the term "prerecorded" as well. He can really drive me nuts. But not nearly as nuts as he drives himself.

Serve in bowls with rosemary mashed potatoes first (see next recipe), daube on top of the potatoes, then garnish with chopped parsley. JL hates when I do this, but I throw some currants on top, too. He says Americans have repulsive sweet tooths. Or is it teeth? Well, he can go fly a kite in the rain. That's how I like *my* daube. Savor every bite! (Honestly, if you told everyone they were eating fancy beef stew they'd probably believe you. Don't tell JL I said that.)

Jean-Luc: *I always use a nice French wine for cooking. Alyce? Any old wine will do. But of course…when you are someone who would drink any old wine. If you must make this in the summer, use a Viognier to cook with and to drink. I would never consider doing it then but if you have fresh boar, "go for it," as my little sow would say. For a red wine, I recommend anything from the Rhone Valley, especially Châteauneuf du Pape or Côte Rotie. Or Côtes du Rhône for the best value.*

If you are tempted to use bacon for the fat, do not. It becomes stringy and adds too much of a smoky flavor. Refrain from using alcohol in this dish (other than wine) unless it is flambéed. Flambé exists for a reason: to infuse a subtle aroma and flavor of the alcohol. Adding it directly is not the same. However, we already know about Alyce's "plugged-up, unused, withering senses." She is making progress, though. Baby steps.

I add cèpe mushrooms on occasion. If you can't find them, any fresh ones will do. Celery is not optional! The aromatics of carrot, onion, and celery—the foundation of mirepoix—are at the heart of many French dishes. I would place the flour in a bowl and then coat each piece of boar evenly before browning, not add the flour later. Ideally, slow cook the daube in a daubière pot in a fireplace over 2 days and add the mushrooms (sautéed) the second day. Sometimes, in small villages, it is prepared before church on Sunday and dropped at the boulangerie to finish in the baker's oven.

Baked apples are a nice dessert with a daube. That is where I would add a splash of cognac.

ROSEMARY MASHED POTATOES

(spooned into each bowl before ladling the daube over them)

You can also make this with potatoes (peeled) in big chunks that have been steamed or baked. Just *don't* cook them with the daube. Sweet potatoes are nice, too. They're fairly new to France and considered a specialty item. In Nice, a daube is sometimes served over a matching meat ravioli. For example, a lamb daube would use lamb ravioli.

   2 lbs potatoes, any variety

   2 T extra virgin olive oil

   1 T kosher salt

   2–3 sprigs of fresh rosemary, 1-1/2 Tsp dried rosemary

   2 T butter

   1/2 to 1 cup cream or milk

   1/2 to 1 cup yogurt

   Salt and pepper to taste

   Heat oven to 400. (204 Celsius). Or steam or boil the potatoes.

Wash the potatoes in cold water and peel. Cut into quarters. Place in a shallow roasting pan. Drizzle olive oil over the potatoes. Toss the kosher salt over them, erring on the side of too little than too much. I pour some into my palm and sprinkle with my other hand like pixie dust until it looks like enough. You can add more when you mash.

Rinse the rosemary. Snip the leaves from the stems and sprinkle over the potatoes. Stir so it's well mixed. Roast potatoes in the oven, uncovered, for 30 minutes. Test to see if a fork pierces a potato easily. If so, they're done. If not, roast longer.

Transfer the potatoes into a large bowl and mash a bit. Add butter then slowly add the dairy ingredients, a little of each, until it's the right consistency. You may not need all of it; you may need more. Mash away. Add a little salt and pepper if you think it needs it.

Jean-Luc: *Always use fresh herbs when you cook, with the exception of oregano. It can be dried and rubbed between your palms for optimum flavor.*

PAN-SEARED SEA SCALLOPS

This dish with braised fennel was introduced toward the end of Chapter 7. I had just arrived at Jean-Luc's and he and Isabella thought it would be *so* funny to pretend they didn't speak English. I wanted to stay as far away from them as possible, but the aromas pulled me right out of my cottage like a little hummingbird to a red honeysuckle. Later, when I found out how easy it was to make, it became one of my favorites to whip up. My mind always goes back to those early dinners with the two of them, which leads to the infamous "twat" moment, and then I can't stop laughing.

INGREDIENTS FOR PART 1

12 sea scallops (the large ones, aka U/10 or under 10 in a pound)

Zest of 1/2 an orange

2 T fresh orange juice

1 T olive oil

1/4 t cinnamon

Flour

Fresh-ground salt and pepper

1 gallon Zip-loc bag or bowl

Ingredients for Part 2

Olive oil

Juice of 1 orange

Fresh-ground salt and pepper

Rinse scallops and pat dry. (If smaller scallops are used, they'll cook faster.) Combine orange zest, orange juice, olive oil, and cinnamon in Ziploc bag or bowl. Add scallops and marinate 15–20 minutes. Drain. Dredge in small amount of flour seasoned with salt and pepper.

Heat empty sauté pan until hot. Add olive oil to just cover the bottom of the pan. Add scallops. Be sure not to crowd them. Sear on first side until brown, about 1–2 minutes. Turn and continue to cook for 1–2 more minutes. Add orange juice. Juice should evaporate quickly. Season with salt and pepper. Remove and serve.

BRAISED FENNEL

3 fennel bulbs

2 T olive oil

1/2 T butter

Fresh-ground salt and pepper

chicken stock

Fresh Parmesan, Comté or Cantal cheese, grated

Cut off the leafy fennel stalks and a thin slice from the bottom. Remove any tough or scarred outer pieces. Cut each bulb lengthwise in half. Quarter if the bulbs are large.

In a heavy sauté pan, heat olive oil and butter. Place fennel, cut side down, in pan. Season with salt and pepper. Sear until golden. Turn to sear each side. Once browned, add chicken stock to come halfway up sides of fennel. Cover and simmer until tender, about 15 minutes. While you're doing that, turn on broiler or heat oven to 375 F/190 C.

Check for tenderness with the tip of a knife. Remove cover, increase heat to high, and reduce stock to a glaze. Remove from heat. Continue in sauté pan or transfer to ovenproof gratin dish. Top with cheese of choice. Place in oven or under broiler to melt the cheese.

PISSALADIÈRE (A TYPE OF ONION TART)

I chained Jean-Luc to his computer to write. Also so he can't see me make my E-Z *pissaladière* (or the spelling of "easy").

Pissala is a fish paste made from anchovies. I've left it out of this recipe. Trust me, this is plenty pungent without it. Anchovies alone are enough to cross it off a lot of people's list, especially with shallots, garlic, and olives as well. But it's one of the first things Jean-Luc taught me how to make (Chapter 17). I'll always have a soft spot for it. What I love about the anchovies is the lattice-like appearance they make. You can always use them and then pick them off. You'll get a hint of the sea. JL hates when I add tomatoes, but in the summer, when they're at their peak, I can practically bathe in them, they're so good. I'll put them on anything. They do need to be seeded and strained or they'll be gritty and goopy. If you use onions instead of shallots, remember to put a pretzel in your mouth when slicing them so your eyes won't tear. Rest it between your lips. If you want to do it JL's way and make the dough yourself, be my guest. As always, use fresh, local, organic produce if you can. That's all that really matters.

INGREDIENTS

1 pizza dough already made but not frozen. It will look like a big beige blob wrapped in plastic at your supermarket deli or refrigerated baked goods section. You can also use phyllo dough or a pie crust you roll out.

1-1/2 to 2 lbs shallots or onions

3 T olive oil, preferably French like Puget or A l'Olivier

1–3 cloves of garlic, diced

2 T butter

Fresh-ground salt and pepper

2 bay leaves

Fresh thyme or 1 T dried

Fresh rosemary (leaves only)

A dash of cornmeal

20–25 anchovies. The best are from an international market or specialty store, like an Italian market. Look for white ones. The closer their origin to the Mediterranean, the better.

1–2 tomatoes (optional)

20–25 oil-cured black olives that you'll slice in half. I buy them already pitted. You can guess which ones JL uses.

Rolling pin

Slice the shallots/onions. Heat the olive oil in a large skillet on a medium flame and add them and the garlic. Plop the butter in. Add salt and pepper to taste, and the thyme, rosemary, and bay leaves. Stir together. Stop to take a deep inhalation. Orgasmic, isn't it? Your kitchen will have this aroma the next day, so you better like it.

Lower flame and heat oven to 450°F/232°C. Continue to caramelize the onions/shallots with lots of stirring. Don't let them brown. What the heck, squirt half of a lemon in there if you have one. Meyers lemons are the best.

Gently rinse the anchovies so they're not super salty. Dry them on a paper towel. They're very delicate. Who gets the skin off these tiny things anyway? It can't be a machine, can it? I'm afraid to ask JL or he'll spend 20 minutes explaining it.

Sprinkle cornmeal on either a pizza stone or baking sheet. Roll the dough in it as you knead. Use a rolling pin to flatten it out.

DISCARD BAY LEAVES. Spoon shallot/onion mixture with a slotted spoon to drain excess liquid over the dough until it comes close to the edge. Now crisscross the anchovies and add the olives in between the crosses. Place the tomatoes by the olives if you're using them.

Bake until the crust is golden brown, about 12–15 minutes. Let it cool a bit before digging in. Darn. You know what I forgot to add? Lavender! The culinary kind. Always have some around. Just a *soupçon* when you're caramelizing the onions.

If you have leftovers, try it in the morning with eggs on it. *Pissaladière* has real spunk, I'll say that. Not for dainty eaters. Gotta run. Jean-Luc just heard the timer go off and will be down in moments to inspect/avoid writing. When he sees the tomatoes, he won't touch it. Fine. Leaves more for me.

Jean-Luc: *With tomatoes and without pissala, this is unequivocally*

American-style pizza trying to be pissaladière. The fish paste can be anchovy paste out of a tube, though fresh pissala is divine. It's made of anchovies seasoned with cloves, thyme, bay leaf, and black pepper and left in an earthenware jar for a month. Spread some over the dough, then add the onion mixture (I prefer onions). Make your own dough. Use a food processor if you must. Only use fresh herbs. As for adding lavender, please! Do not listen to her. It is mainly used in sweets. She acts as though she just discovered cinnamon.

For a wine accompaniment I would recommend a nice, crisp rosé or a light red, like Beaujolais (say a Morgon or Moulin-a-Vent). For the more adventurous, try a light red wine from the Jura region.

Alyce: And when you've had enough wine or don't want it at all…

APRICOT-ROSEMARY TEA

4 cups of boiled water

2 bags black tea (English Breakfast is my favorite)

1 small sprig of rosemary (a little goes a long way)

2 cups of apricot nectar

Sparkling water or club soda

Let the tea bags and rosemary steep in the boiled water for 10 minutes. Remove rosemary and tea bags. Add apricot nectar. Stir. Chill. Fill a glass halfway with this mixture and the other half with sparkling water. I didn't like it at first but it grew on me. It's kind of smoky with a sweetness that has texture and feels like it must be detoxifying you. Adjust the amounts of the ingredients to your taste. If apricots are in season, add a few peeled slices. Delicious!

I make two batches, one with caffeine and one without so I can drink it at night, too, otherwise it'll keep me up. It's my drink of choice to wash down my daily vitamins after my morning coffee. Jean-Luc refuses to take vitamins. He says "Americans have the most expensive urine on the planet." We'll just see who's right in the long run. Which reminds me, it's time for me to jog. Without Jean-Luc, of course. I sure wish Raymond had taken a picture of him in those orange spandex shorts.

Jean-Luc: *No Comment.*

DISCUSSION QUESTIONS

1. Do you think Alyce enjoyed herself too much or too little while on her adventure?
2. How do food and cooking assist in the transformation of Alyce?
3. How did each character's childhood affect them as adults?
4. What are your thoughts on a "marriage of convenience" or an arranged marriage?
5. Jean-Luc eventually states that writing is "a commodity." Do you see this a sign of positive growth or as an abandonment of artistic ideals?
6. For most of the story, the author uses various means to conceal Colette's true identity. How does knowing the truth change your perception of Jean-Luc?
7. French is "the language of love." How would Alyce's experience have been different had she gone to a different country and learned another language?
8. Who (or what) do you think is the true antagonist of this story?
9. With which character do you most identify, and why?
10. *Opposites Attack* has a number of themes: nontraditional family, culture shock, odd-couple romance, and more. What do you think is the most important one?

NAKED DJ

a novel from Jo Maeder

EXCERPT

THE DANGLING CARROT SOCIETY

I approached the gnarled wooden door of Boba 47 and remembered my ex's formula for seduction: flash your target a look that says *I want to rip your clothes off this instant and throw you across that table.* Then split because you're so busy.

In the case of Rick Rivers, though, seducing him to offer me a job without giving him the wrong idea would be tricky.

On my first try at this technique I wound up with Krazy Karl, my number one Loony Tune fan. I wondered how long it would take him to track me down in Manhattan. He'd succeeded in the ten other markets I'd worked in. But this was the end of the line. I was done changing my name, hair color, and address—and if WBRR didn't work out, I was done with radio.

The restaurant's slinky music, subdued lighting, and earthy textures easily put me in the right mood for the Hire Me Hustle. The last time I saw Rick was at an industry event in L.A. He had long, straggly hair and was wearing a stained Staind tee. I did a double take now when I saw him wave to me from the bar. He sported a buzz cut, gray suit, yellow tie. His last vestige of hipness was a goatee the size of a postage stamp.

Even in this dim light I couldn't miss his tiny gray teeth when he checked out my miniskirt and tank top.

"Lookin' like a rock star, Jeri!"

"Thanks, Rick. It's Jazmyn now. You look *great!*"

He had only been at 'BRR a few months after turning around another heritage rocker in Phoenix. Like me, he hadn't been born when most of the music was made. Rick had his ass on the biggest line of all: New York. A half a rating point can mean millions in lost or gained revenue.

"Nice tattoo," he said as we settled in at our cozy table and he eyed my upper left arm. "Never seen anyone do half. Didya chicken out?" He snickered.

I'd only heard that line a thousand times but kept smiling. "I vowed to finish it when I made it to New York." I didn't mention Ree's left arm sported the other half.

"A beautiful segue, Janice."

"*Jazmyn.*" I spelled it for him.

"Right. You're from Richmond, Virginia, aren't you?"

"A long time ago."

He'd been on a rock station there after I'd left. We talked about the city that marked where the South began. Everything to the north had Washington, D.C. flavoring it.

"I couldn't believe how stuck in the past *some* people were," he said. "They still referred to the Civil War as the War of Northern Aggression, and they called me a Yankee. I'm from Baltimore." He paused before saying, "I bet you ran into some problems with Mr. Ree."

"A few."

A twinge of anger went through me, thinking about the racism Ree and I faced when we were together. It wasn't *that* bad, but when you feel it from your father, you don't forget.

"Still in touch with him?"

"Ree? No!" I leaned back from the table, waving my hands. "Absolutely not."

"Yeah, I've known a few recording artists. What a crazy life. What egos."

"Yeah, DJs are bad enough."

"Too bad my days as Rad Rick are over. So, any significant other back in Dallas?"

"No one will be moving here with me, if that's what you're asking."

His eyes shifted to my boobs. I focused on his wedding band.

"How's your wife?" She looked about 18 when I met her. That got his eyes off my chest.

"She's fixing up the place we bought on Long Island and couldn't be happier." In the next second he slipped into a perfect thug rapper imitation of Ree, arms moving in downward motions. *"The strip-ah, the strip-ah, the strip-ah. I tip-ah, I tip-ah, I tip-ah."*

He obviously thought it was funny so I smiled back.

"Man, I loved that song. I love rock, too. But that was a fucking *smash*."

"Yep." I rubbed my tattoo. "It certainly was."

"Still is. It tests really well. What, ten years later?"

I was glad to hear that Ree was making money off that song. The down side was that I'd have to hear it for the rest of my life.

Rick said, "I hear Starz is giving a huge push to his new single."

"You can't do better than having Nigel Hamilton-Jones in your corner."

"I'll say."

I couldn't believe my buddy Nigel was in charge of Ree's big comeback. He wouldn't let me hear the new song until he took me out to dinner tomorrow night. I couldn't wait to see him again. Hear the song? I'd hear it eventually. May as well get it over with.

"You've never worked at a rock station before," Rick said, "but I think you'd be great. You've got that smoky voice, a sense of humor, and a youthful edge."

"Any station that doesn't play Mr. Ree, is a-okay by me."

"Um, how young are you?"

"The lower end of the 25 to 35 demographic."

"Perfect."

Rick ordered the $20-an-ounce Kobe-style Washugyu beef. I asked for one of the least caloric entrées. Sashimi. As soon as our had-to-be-gay waiter walked away, Rick got down to business.

"What do you think of the station?"

I had my line ready.

"It's like an old pair of faded, comfortable jeans you can't part with." I left out *but never wear.*

"In other words, it sucks."

We both grinned. WBRR wasn't just any old Classic Rocker. It was the mother of them all. It debuted over four decades before on the same day the Beatles released *Sgt. Pepper* in America (June 2, 1967). It broadcast live from the original Woodstock in 1969. It was the station everyone tuned in when the news broke that John Lennon had been shot — and mourned with when he died. Its DJs were once as famous as the rock stars they interviewed. Now its ratings were in the toilet.

"The average age of the DJs is what, 60?" I said.

Rick had a nervous habit of picking at his postage stamp. "Don't let Cat Cruz know you think she's that old."

He was talking about the beautiful Latina woman who had been holding down middays for about 15 years. Cat was short for Catalina. She used to call herself the Cat Woman until the Batman people served her with a cease and desist. She'd just turned 40; the baby on the staff.

"So what's up?" I said. "Changing formats?"

"Nope. Research shows WBRR has unbelievably strong loyalty and recognition as being *the* spot on the dial for rock. The jocks are like family members to the listeners. That doesn't mean we can't renovate. *Slowly*."

His cell rang. He gave the caller I.D. a glance. "It's the little woman." He lowered his voice as he talked to her and kept his eyes on my chest.

While I discreetly gazed around the low-lit room trying to spy someone famous, I thought about Cat Cruz. She was stunning. Why did she go the radio route and not TV? Usually radio chicks were like me, fairly attractive but not super skinny model material. Cat's claim to fame was having posed naked for a major men's magazine when she was in college. According to Nigel, she made more mistakes on the air than all the other DJs combined, but she was gorgeous and a minority (excuse me, "woman of color") who sounded white. She'd have to kill the general manager's dog to get fired.

Every time I'd lost out on a job because I wasn't the right race, I thought of all the guys who'd been passed over because they didn't have a uterus. Or men *and* women who weren't the right age anymore. That's life. The radio life.

"Excuse me," Rick said as he stood up. "I'll be right back. I have to tell my son a bedtime story or he won't go to sleep."

I strongly suspected he was telling the "little woman" a bedtime story.

What did renovate slowly mean? Was he going to offer me overnights? The radio equivalent of Siberia. And could Isis, the woman doing it now, the one whose every word I analyzed as a kid and wanted to emulate, be in her *70s*, as Nigel guessed? Maybe she was retiring.

I took out my phone and did some social to pass the time. With my new name, I had to start fresh in every way. I grabbed @JazmynBrownNYC on Twitter.

Rick returned with a satisfied look on his face. Definitely phone sex.

"So where was I?"

He told me the latest consultant hired to turn around WBRR had renamed it.

"The jocks are to call the station '99 the Bear' and nothing else," he said.

"The *Bear?*"

"What's wrong?"

"Well…" How could I put this tactfully? "Sounds great for a station in the Rocky Mountains." Seeing his crestfallen face, I added, "Wall Street hates bears. If they were going to name it after an animal, call it the Bull."

"Too much like bullshit."

That would have been perfect.

He unleashed his pitch like a windup toy. "I want this station to play the best rock of yesterday *and* today. I want talent that brings *energy* to the airwaves. Who'll get it out of its time warp. The expensive oldsters will start to go as their contracts end. Do *not* repeat that." As if they and everyone in the business wouldn't know. "You'll be a star in the new regime. Hell, you may end up in mornings or afternoons. I know a woman in drive time is rare in this format, but if you rack up better numbers…"

I pegged Rick as a card-carrying member of the Dangling Carrot Society. But he had me.

Bear schmear. Bring it on.

"The Dick and Dork morning show are going to have 'Bare it on the Bear Thursdays' where girls come in and take off their tops for major prizes."

"Wow…real theater of the mind."

He ignored my sarcasm as he slowly twirled his glass around as though he were grinding it into the table. "Chopper's giving away a tricked-out Harley with a big angry grizzly on it, we're going to have people dressed as bears handing out station stuff all over the place, and Maxx is going to have the Barenaked Ladies do an acoustical concert on his show."

I admired Rick's do-or-die outlook. Nigel was the same way

with the records he promoted, forging on with a winning attitude whether he loved or hated the product or artist.

"That brings us to the lovely Cat Cruz and you."

I sat up straighter.

"I'm going to leverage the Barenaked Ladies connection
by calling the midday show...The Barenaked *Radio* Ladies and
have *two* hot women on instead of one. Would you have a problem pretending you were doing the show nude?"

"Right." He assured me he wasn't joking.

"Cat might actually take her clothes off," he said. "She's an
exhibitionist, you know, but you wouldn't *have* to." He pulled
at his chin some more. All he needed were horns to complete
his devil look. "Unless you wanted to. I'm sure a nude pictorial
could be arranged."

I clutched my folded arms, rubbed my unfinished tattoo.

When I was starting out in radio, I was asked to slather myself with honey and have hundred-dollar bills stuck all over me.
Selected listeners would have five seconds to grab as much money as they could. Ree intervened. The station had no problem
talking the traffic-reports girl into doing it. In the madness that
ensued, one of her breast implants ruptured.

Our cheerful server appeared with our food.

"Excuse me," I asked the waiter with a charming smile,
"would you do your job naked?"

"Only if you left me a *really* big tip, honey." He flitted off.

In the dead silence that followed, Rick laughed nervously.
"It's pretend, Jazmyn."

"A pictorial isn't."

"Just a suggestion. Not a deal-breaker."

The more I turned over the Barenaked Radio Ladies idea in
my mind, the more I hated it. What I hated more was not being
on New York radio.

"Rick, you could pair me with the Wicked Witch of the West.
I have to be on New York radio at least once in my life."

He chuckled. "Yeah, wicked witch..."

"What's that mean?"

He didn't answer. As for the show itself, he wanted me to run the soundboard.

"That means Cat is still the star," I said.

"No, it doesn't. Howard Stern runs his own board. It puts you in *control*."

Rick's offer was 90K, union scale.

"The magic number is 100. And you're asking me to pretend I'm naked? Please."

It was almost triple my last salary, but New York was three times as expensive. On the other hand, I had no income at the moment. I had lingering doubts about Cat, but we shook hands on it.

In no time flat my sashimi was nearly gone.

"Miss lunch?" Rick asked.

I pushed the plate away.

"Uh, Jazmyn, we'll put you up in a hotel for two weeks, but would you mind moving to a less-expensive place?" It wasn't really a question. "Parker Meridien's too rich for our blood."

The seduction was over. I was now in that new gainfully employed state of mind; a mix of relief, terror, challenge, and enslavement. I also felt like a space capsule finally landing on another planet after 11 years. Instead of a loud, rocky *thunk* it was soft, measured, exciting.

ALSO FROM JO MAEDER

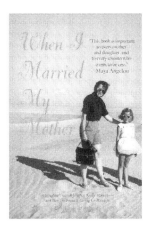

WHEN I MARRIED MY MOTHER

*"This book is important to every mother and daughter,
and to every woman who wants to be one."*

— *Maya Angelou*

In this memoir, who would think a diehard New Yorker caring for a declining, doll-collecting, estranged, hoarder mother in the Bible Belt would turn into the adventure of a lifetime? Throw in bingo-playing drag queens, longstanding family feuds and unresolved guilt in every direction, and Jo finds that love blooms and laughter erupts in the most unlikely places. She found that rather than dreading her new role, she embraced it. Surprisingly, these were some of the best years of her life— and her mother's.

Not only a helpful guide to those navigating their own story of a loved one in decline or now gone, *When I Married My Mother* is a you'll-laugh-you'll-cry story for all. The eBook and paperback editions include bonus material of an author interview, Mama Jo's favorite cookie recipe, caregiving tips, and discussion questions.

About the Author

Jo Maeder was a radio DJ in South Florida and New York City who once went by the air name "The Rock and Roll Madame" and followed The Howard Stern Show. She now lives in North Carolina and is a writer/bird nut. She travels, cooks, and bakes decadent cookies whenever possible. Ditto dancing. Read "The Story Behind the Story" that inspired *Opposite's Attack* on Jo's website. Connect with Jo there or through:

www.jomaeder.com
Photo by Meg Busch and Jo's droid

A Message from Vivant Press

If you love a book, word-of-mouth (and mouse) keeps it afloat in the vast sea of reading choices. Tell your local bookstore. Leave online reviews. It makes a difference. The number of stars and how recent the review impacts Internet searches. One sentence is enough to count (though the longer it is, the more weight it's given). Sharing links where a book can be bought helps, too.

See a typo or inaccuracy? Please bring it to our attention. Use the address listed at the front of this book or write to ContactVivantPress@ gmail.com. Merci beaucoup!

27495862R00194

Made in the USA
Charleston, SC
13 March 2014